Clouds & Daydreams

Elizabeth Knight

Creative Wonder Publishing

Knight, Elizabeth
Clouds & Daydreams
Editing: Swish Editing
Cover artist: Chaotic Creatives
Formatting: Creative Wonder Publishing
ISBN: 979-8-88958-051-5 (ebook) / 979-8-88958-052-2 (paperback)

❀ Created with Vellum

Dedication

When I started out as an author I quickly developed some close connections to some readers. We became good friends and still are to this day, which I value more than anything. One of these reader friends announced she was having twins, two little precious girls and one of them she decided to name Elizabeth. From that point on we referred to her as Baby E, my name twin. Baby E finally entered this world along with her sister, but this is when her battle began. This little warrior princess was born with a heart defect and spent her first few weeks in the hospital. Feedings were a challenge but her mother was there with her every step of the way fighting alongside her. The doctors didn't want to do surgery just yet since she was so small and wanted her to gain some weight before making any big steps. So began the feedings every couple hours all day and night.

This was one lucky girl to have two older brothers who doted on her and helped wherever they could, even taking turns for feedings. Baby E earned her title as warrior princess, always full of smiles, laughter, a love of wearing tutus, and listening to rap music. Her favorite stuffed octopus Pearl, was with her wherever she went, always keeping her company. Unfortunately just before Christmas 2022 Baby E passed away having shared her special light with this world for only a year and a half.

My heart broke when my friend shared the news of losing this precious life. Her family had done everything for their child even to the point of my friend renewing her CNA so she could be Baby E's care giver at home and avoid being in the hospital longer than they needed. My friend is a beautiful selfless soul devoted to her friends and family who would take time out of her day to help beta read for me. Later she shared it was what she'd do with Baby E in her lap during her feeding times. They would read and snuggle together making every moment count.

This little life never got the chance to see where her story would take her, so I decided to write her one. On paper I could give Baby E so many experiences and adventures al- lowing for the impossible to be possible. I couldn't think of a better way to do this than choosing to make it an omegaverse where she'd be doted on and given ten lifetimes of love.

Yes this book is fiction but it has so many elements of Baby E in it's pages. I got to listen to her mom share memories and all her favorite things giving me the chance to ensure this life is never forgotten. So when I say that this book is full of all the best moments I really mean that and this is only half of the story, the beginning of their love story and I can't wait for you all to read it! I have been given permission from the family to share this information

Author's Note

This book is fiction although it's inspired by the life and struggles of a real person. I am not a medical professional and none of the medical situations in this book are meant to be taken as truth or fact. Any inaccuracies depicting this real disease are meant to be creative license to fit the story and not to spread misinformation.

Please be aware that this book might have some triggering content due to medical conversations, injections, and talks of surgery.

For a more detailed list of content warnings please check out my website: https://www.elizabethknightbooks.com/omegaverse

BAILEY-ROSE

R ap music beats filled the room as I sat in front of a wide full-length mirror. An easel with a blank sheet of paper pinned to it was before me. I stared into my eyes, one a crystal blue color and the other an almost seafoam green. Both were full of the heartache I felt as I sketched out a self-portrait. My hair, a color melt of violet into sky blue normally styled with a bouncy wave, hung disheveled and unwashed. Just like my room, usually a bright and cheerful pastel explosion, was cast in shadows. I felt dark, dull, and hopeless.

The only light I allowed was the soft fairy lights around the mirror which were enough to see my sheet of paper. It also created the shadows I needed to portray my despair in this moment that I couldn't achieve any other way. Nothing says heartbroken like a woman wrapped up in a fluffy pink, cloud-patterned robe wearing bunny slippers. I'd only given myself white, gray, and black on my palette to draw and paint with because there was no more color in my life. The only man I thought would love me—see past my broken-ness—had betrayed me.

What was the point of color in the world?

"LouLou," Crew, my older brother, shouted from the other side of the door to be heard over the music. "Open this door right now."

I was lucky enough to have two older brothers who doted on me. Eli, the oldest, was an Alpha and Crew a Beta.

They still lived at home to make sure their fragile baby sister was looked after. Our parents weren't really home, traveling the world, conducting business and saving all the orphaned children along the way. Their mission was to build schools in poor countries so every child had a chance to better their situation. It was a dream my late father had of one day achieving, but he never got to see it happen.

Jet-setting didn't leave much time for my parents to spend looking after their only daughter, who happened to have a genetic defect that caused me to have congenital heart failure, among other things. It was the same genetic defect that stole away my papa, and one of my mother's bonded-pair, twelve years ago. His death was what pushed my mother and Daddy Rawr to stop wasting time and put Papa Addy's dream into motion.

To be clear, I don't, nor have I ever resented my parents for not being around. Everyone deals with a tragic loss in their own way, and doing this for Papa was what made them happy. When we had the chance to all be together, they were completely invested and present, never letting anything else get in the way. It was how they showed us they cared by providing their full attention to my brothers and me, no exceptions.

Truthfully, any other parent who had an Omega daughter with a life-threatening issue would be hovering over every aspect of my life. Especially after losing Papa Addy, most moms would keep their child in a protective bubble to ensure that fate didn't happen to them. However, I was blessed with parents who trusted me to know what I could handle. After all, it's my body, and I was well aware of the signs that told me I was in trouble. Besides, if I really needed to talk, there was no doubt in my mind that I could easily get a hold of them. They were amazing at keeping us in the loop as to where they were and for how long. They always said they didn't like to stay in one place for long—too much life to live. The money we have from our family being on the ground floor in the oil refining business allowed them to do as they pleased.

"LouLou, you have two seconds before I use my key," Crew hollered. "You know I try to give you all the privacy in the world, but this is going too far."

I promptly ignored him, grabbed another pink Peep, and bit off its head. The gooey, sickly-sweet marshmallow was a balm to my soul and the only comfort I needed in this life. Okay, maybe I needed Zebra Cakes too, but I ran out of those last night. Soon I would have to resort to Oatmeal Cream Pies as my source of nourishment.

Blinding light filled my room, making me slam my eyes closed as they burned from being in the dark for so long. Groaning, I dropped my paintbrush and covered my eyes with my hands to lessen the burn.

"Holy hell, LouLou," my brother muttered as he entered my room. "This place looks like a bomb went off. Wait. Fuck, are you still in the same clothes from four days ago?"

His voice sounded closer, but I just kept ignoring him, hoping he'd go away. When the burning finally subsided, I picked up my paintbrush and resumed my portrait.

"The hell, LouLou, is that a *Peep*? Those haven't been sold for months. Were you hoarding them?" Crew asked as I saw him cleaning up the remnants of my dwindling supply of nourishment.

It was strange to see him so ruffled since Crew was the free spirit in our family. He owned a well-respected recording company and even had a studio built on our property so someone was home *all* the time. I didn't mind, though, since Crew was my best friend out of my two brothers. There was a five-year age gap between us, but you could hardly tell with him being a big kid. He taught me tons of card games during the times I was admitted to the hospital for one medical reason or another. When I was twelve, he taught me poker against our parents' wishes. Crew was always there to distract me from the fear of being in the hospital. He often brought his best friend Ulysses, or Lysse as I called him, to make the game more interesting. I don't think I would have made it through all those days without Crew by my side.

"LouLou, are you even listening to me?" Crew demanded as a pair of hands scooped me up off the floor and set me on the edge of my fluffy bed.

Finally, I admitted defeat, knowing Crew wouldn't leave me alone until I talked. "What do you want me to say, Crew? What's out there that I can't just do right here in the safety of my own home?"

My brother rolled his green eyes that matched his father's. "LouLou, do you know how stupid that sounds? You just graduated from college, and now is the time to explore the world around you. What about the art studio Mom and Dad gave you as your graduation present? Have you even gone to see it since you got home?"

"You know I haven't," I grumbled. "As soon as I returned home full of hopes and dreams for the future, it all blew up in my face."

"Lou..." Crew started with a sigh. "Randall isn't worth all this. Don't let that shitstain steal your joy. He's not good enough for that."

"Easy for you to say... you never liked him," I pointed out.

Crew shrugged. "True, but that doesn't mean my advice is wrong."

"Yes, it does," I argued, chucking a cloud-shaped pillow at him. "There's no way for you to know how I feel. You've never had your heart broken before."

"Hey," Crew snapped. "How do you know I've never had my heart broken?"

I cocked my head and gave him an unimpressed look. "When the hell could you possibly have had time? You and Eli made taking care of me your whole personality... there was no time for anything else."

Crew pouted at me before taking a seat beside me on the bed. "That's just mean, LouLou."

Puffing up my cheeks, I let out a dramatic breath. "Yeah, that was a low blow," I admitted, flopping back on the bed. "How could so much change when I was only gone for three months? I had to be on campus to finish my final project, which, mind you, was sixty percent of my grade."

"This has nothing to do with you being gone and everything to do with some punk ass bitch who couldn't keep it in his pants for that long. If he knew he couldn't manage not getting his dick wet for that long, he should've just been honest," Crew muttered.

Turning my head, I looked over at him smirking at the expression on his face. Randall was a lucky man that I didn't want retribution for cheating on me, or Crew would have put that asshole in the hospital.

"I love you, bro," I told him, patting his leg.

He looked down with a grin. "Now I know you've lost your mind saying shit like that."

"Oh fuck off. I tell you that all the time," I shot back, laughing as I shoved him as hard as I could, but he barely even shifted to the side.

With my genetic disorder, in combination with my heart issues, it stunted my growth, so I was on the small size. Yup, this twenty-five-year-old was a whopping four foot eleven, meant I stood no chance against my two six-foot brothers when they wanted to throw their weight around, which Crew did more than Eli, being the playful one of the two.

"Yeah, you do, LouLou," Crew agreed as he tugged me on his lap and wrapped me up in a hug, a hug I hadn't realized I desperately needed. "I love you too, even if you smell like stale gym socks."

"That's it... get the fuck out if you're gonna talk like that," I said, wiggling out of his arms to stand before him, arms crossed. "Go on, you've now seen I'm not wasting away in the corner sobbing to the point of dehydration, so I'd like you to leave me to my wallowing."

"Ah-ha... and how long should I leave you to wallow? Do you plan to ever reenter the world at large? Something tells me you're just planning on hiding out forever," Crew challenged, showing no signs of moving.

I tossed up my hands. "You really want to do this to me?"

"Do what? You haven't told me anything about what's really going on in that head of yours. LouLou, we talk about everything, so why can't you talk to me about this?" Crew pleaded, worry filling his expression.

I attempted to run my fingers through my hair, only for them to get stuck on the snarls since I couldn't remember when I last brushed it. Ugh, I was a mess, but I just didn't give a shit. It's not like anyone outside of Crew and Eli would know or could see me.

"It's not that I can't talk to you about this... we have, many times," I reasoned. "If I tell you how I'm feeling right now, you have to promise me you won't try to fix it. Don't run to grab your super-brother cape and swoop in to fix my problems. Right now, I just want to say how I'm feeling and not feel guilty, stupid, or that my feelings are invalid because I'm not seeing the so-called 'big picture.' "

Crew scratched at his jaw while taking the time to consider if he could do this for me. "Fine, I promise to sit here and listen to what you have without trying to fix it the moment you finish telling me how you feel. You need me to be an empathetic sounding board right now, and that's what I'll be."

Unsure if I believed him, I crossed my arms and gave him my best glare. "Do I need to make you pinky promise?"

"Oh, we're pulling out the big guns." Crew gasped in mock horror shielding himself from me as I threatened him with another pillow before bursting into laughter. "No, you little grumpy kitten, you don't need to make me pinky promise."

With a sharp nod, I climbed onto my pastel pillow explosion of a bed. I made it so it felt like I was sleeping on clouds and flicked on the switch that illuminated the rainbow fairy lights woven in the canopy above my bed. This conversation needed a little more cheerfulness, and I was definitely going to need Pearl for this. She was the giant stuffed octopus Eli got me for my tenth birthday, which I had to spend in the hospital. He told me that if I got lonely, Pearl had eight arms to hug me with so I wouldn't ever feel lonely.

"The harsh reality is that I'm going to end up alone," I stated as I rested my cheek on Pearl's big, round, squishy head. "No Scent Matcher will take me. I don't meet the qualifications since I'm an Omega with a genetic defect. Why in the world would they want to risk more people having this issue? Did you know there's a sixty percent chance of passing this on to my children?"

I could feel Crew holding himself back from speaking.

The effort was so great it was almost as if it took on a physical presence. Yet he held to his promise and kept his mouth shut.

"You understand part of this since you can't hire the Scent Matchers to help find your pack, being a Beta and all. Which, I think that rule is shit," I said with an irritated harumph. "Betas have the ability to be scent-bonded, but it's just not as common as it is with Alphas and Omegas. Even so, you should have the chance to be partnered with others to create your own pack and work with them to match with an Omega," I ranted, waving my right arm around, adding emphasis to my words.

Doing that got me so worked up my heart monitor started beeping. Crew's hand snatched my left hand and pulled it to him so he could see the reading on my tracker. When he didn't comment, I knew it was in a safe range, just tipping over into the danger zone.

"Lou, we aren't talking about me right now," Crew commented as he sprawled out on his back, arms under his head. "I'm well aware of my struggles, but that hasn't been my priority. I'm not worried... it'll happen when it happens. Now, let's bring this back to you and your feelings without getting worked up about it."

Blowing out a breath, I returned to the point I was trying to make. "Ninety percent of our society uses Scent Matchers to find their scent-bonded Omega. Since I can't be entered into their system, no one knows I exist, leaving me to hope and pray I might find an Alpha or a pack that will want me. It's a proven fact that if you don't go through a service that can access the whole goddamn country... soon the world, if the news is telling us the truth, you won't find your scent-bonds. This leaves you with the only option of someone liking you enough to date you and possibly one day bond based on their attraction to you as a person."

Crew rolled his head to the side to look at me instead of the twinkling lights of the canopy. "Why do you make that sound like a bad thing?"

"It's not for most people, but I'm not most people," I countered. "Crew, a minute ago, I got upset for you and set off my monitor. Having children is beyond high risk for me, but that would only be if I could ever manage to have sex."

"No one has ever said you can't have sex," Crew argued. "Not that I want to think about that because... ew. My point is, no doctor has told you that's off-limits."

"That is true, but do me a favor... the next time you have a sexy time with one of your Beta friends, borrow my spare monitor and see if you can keep your heart rate under eighty-five beats per minute. The. Whole. Time," I challenged. "I bet you a hundred bucks that thing will go off like crazy."

"Of course it would. My resting rate is in the mid seventies. You've learned over the years to keep yours in the high sixties so you don't set that damn thing off," he countered. "I get your point, and I wasn't trying to fix the situation. I just didn't want you stating facts that weren't true."

"Whatever," I grumbled. "Then I'll say it's challenging to have sex and find a partner who is willing to navigate the terms. Randall only managed to figure it out a few times, and it absolutely wasn't worth the effort with him."

Crew stuck his fingers in his ears and started yelling. "La la la, I hear nothing. My baby sister is pure as the driven snow, untouched by mere mortals, and certainly no man named fucking Randall."

I snickered at that, knowing it would make him uncomfortable. "I thought you said we could talk about anything?"

He chucked a pillow at me. "Anything but that. We can talk about whatever you want that involves everyone's clothes staying on."

"You're safe. That was all I was going to say about the matter anyway before you made a big deal about it," I shared, then sighed and flopped against my pillows. "I thought Randall was the one. We met in the hospital when I had pneumonia from that stupid cold anyone could handle while his brother was also getting treatment. There were no surprises when it came to the fact that I'm a broken, defective Omega who will be needy and high maintenance all her life. He liked me for me... or so I thought."

The image of that woman's face as Randall railed her from behind played on repeat in my head.

"Why bother going out with me in the first place?" I asked, not really expecting an answer. "Bottom line is I'm not the Omega anyone wants. Knowing this, why would I put myself out there to be rejected, insulted, laughed at, or cheated on? All I want to do is give what's left of my broken heart to someone for the rest of the life I have to live. My fairy tale doesn't exist out there in the real world. It's too jaded and pragmatic to take a chance on the factory reject."

My bed jostled as Crew crawled up to lay beside me and slid his arm under my head so it rested against his shoulder. He's always smelled like carrot cake to me—full of spice and life but earthy at the same time. It fit who he was as a person full of life, jokes, and fun, but when you needed him, he was there for you like now.

"I'm not saying this to try and fix anything, but I just can't hold back from saying it," Crew said, then paused a second. "Randall is fucking lucky to be alive for making you feel this way. If I ever cross paths with that shitstain, I will give him a black eye as a warning to the world that they should stay the fuck away."

"Did you want me to invite him over?" I asked. "I'm pretty sure I could guilt-trip him into talking to me face-to-face."

"LouLou, are you trying to put me in jail?" Crew demanded.

I let out a sigh. "No. I just really wanted to see you lay his ass out flat, and if it happens randomly, I might not be there to see it."

"Damn, that's cold." Crew chuckled. "I like it."

"Thank you for listening," I shared, nuzzling into his comforting presence. "I'm still not leaving my room, though."

Ulysses

It was good to be back.

Finally, after almost eight years of traveling all over the country, I was once more in Windermere. I'd gone right from college to work for a company that my family bought into fifty years ago, Infinery Petroleum Industries. My family operates the downriver portion of the refinery process or, as most people understand it, finding and drilling for oil. My job was to establish new drilling sites by installing the oil pumps, train the new team, and ensure they followed state guidelines for operation. Once complete, I would move on to the next site or revisit a location that might be struggling. This didn't lead to a life with a permanent home, a budding social life, or regular hours.

After graduation, all I wanted was to be on my own and start my career. So I got right down to business making things happen while traveling the world. However, something changed two years ago when I turned twenty-eight. I suddenly realized the time for a family was running out, and the glamor of travel was all but gone. Working hard to have the life I wanted was important, but here I was with a well-stocked bank account and nothing else. This realization led me to sign up for the Scent Matching service to help me find a pack, a family unit, if you will, of men I would be compatible sharing a life with.

For me personally, I was looking for a group of brothers. Men who I could count on, experience life alongside each other, and one day have a family with our Omega. After my new pack was formed through the Matchers and we got to know each other, we decided it was time to find our Omega. Building a pack was step one in becoming a family, and now we needed that last piece of the puzzle to complete the picture.

As a whole, we chose to only accept scent options from female Omegas, but as we approached a year and a half with no luck, we started to doubt our choice. So far in my life, I've never been drawn to men in an intimate way, which was the same as my packmates. However, now we all started to question if excluding the option of a male Omega was the right choice.

When you're scent-bonded with an Omega, that's it. You're done. That Omega is the one you were meant to be with, and no one else will do. Some people compare it to soulmates, like the ones you read about in books. If that were true, then it wouldn't matter what gender your Omega turned out to be. They would be our scent-bond and perfect for our pack, end of story. Coming to that conclusion as a group, we decided the next check-in we had with our Matcher, we would inform them of the change.

Breaking down the last box of things I'd just unpacked, I looked around my room now that it was properly set up. The guys bought the house while I finished my last project, which took six months longer than it should have. They'd been living here full time while I came back every chance I could to spend time with them. We'd tried out other areas since my packmates were from different places, but as a family, we agreed this was the right city for us. It offered everything we needed, and I was glad to be done with all the moving.

"Hey," Warrick said as he knocked on the open door to my room. "You need any help?"

I looked over my shoulder at him and grinned. "Your timing is perfect as usual... I just finished."

Warrick was the guy who liked everyone, and everyone liked in return. He could get along with the worst people who would drive anyone else insane and have them eating out of the palm of his hand. My logic was since he had such a baby face, everyone treated him like a kid, not almost thirty and a successful business owner. His bar, The Fat Mule, was one of the coolest spots in town. The place was packed during happy hour and had a two-month waitlist for table service on the weekends.

Warrick flashed me a shit-eating grin, his brown eyes telling me he knew I was done before he asked. "What can I say?" He shrugged. "I just know the best time to make an appearance. It's a talent, you know."

Rolling my eyes, I grabbed the five other flattened boxes and dropped them in his arms. "You're absolutely right about that. It's uncanny how you knew there was no way I could carry all the garbage out in one trip. Now we can do it together, and my unpacking will be complete."

"That's me, the ever-helpful pack brother always looking for ways to be of service," Warrick answered cheerfully as he backed out of the room with his armload.

"Be careful on the stairs," I warned.

Warrick groaned. "Look, I keep telling you it's because Vili used the wrong cleaner on the wooden steps that I slipped. Seriously, I'm not that clumsy."

"If that's the story you're sticking to," I teased as I gathered the garbage bags I'd filled with packing paper, listening as he walked down the stairs. When there was no sound of crashing or swearing, I knew he had safely made it down.

Having moved from place to place meant I didn't have much stuff. For most jobs, I stayed on location for roughly four to six months. There was something cathartic about knowing this was the last time I had to unpack for a good long while. I finally had a place to call home and a room I could make my own. An odd thing to get excited over at this point in my life, but as they say, your priorities change.

Just as I was about to head down, my phone started to vibrate. Glancing at the screen, I saw it was Crew, my best friend since I was ten years old. His family was the founder and controlling members of the company my grandad bought into. I hadn't had a chance to catch up with him this week, so I grabbed the phone. "Hey, man," I answered. "It's official, I'm back for good this time."

There was a whoop of joy on the other end and clapping of hands. "That's what I'm talking about. I needed some good news today."

Immediately, I was frowning. The only thing that could bring Crew down was something going on with Bailey-Rose. "Happy I could help, but is everything okay?"

A growl of frustration echoed through the phone. "LouLou hasn't left her room in almost a week. Right after she got back from college, Lou found out the dipshit she was seeing cheated on her. She made me promise not to beat his ass, but with how hurt she is, I'm not sure I can hold back."

Anger flared through me at the thought of someone daring to do that to my Rosie. Growing up, Crew and I had been instant best friends, but it was easy to see that his baby sister was the most important person ever to Crew. So if I wanted to hang out with him, I hung out with her, which I quickly learned was no hardship. Bailey-Rose was, hands down, the most pure, kind, loving woman I've ever known. As we got older, the three of us became a tight-knit group until I left for college. Being five years older than her made it challenging to stay connected, especially when I felt like I was in a whole different part of life than her.

When I came back for the summers during my first and second year, we all hung out, but then Rose drifted away and spent less time with us my third summer back. Crew and I stayed best friends, allowing me to hear what she was up to. While I didn't get to spend time with her, I still felt like I'd been kept in the loop about her life.

Or so I thought because I knew nothing about her dating someone. Last Crew told me she'd gone to finish her degree at Golden Oaks University of Fine Arts for the last three months. How long had she been dating this guy? Where did they meet? How dare he fucking think it was okay to cheat on her while she was gone. Now I was kicking myself for not reaching out to her. In hopes of rebuilding our friendship, I wanted my moving back to be a surprise, so I made Crew promise not to tell her.

"How can I help?" I asked. "Do we need to roll up on this fucker and explain what he did was unforgivable?"

"No, she made me promise if I did anything to him, she had to be there to see it. LouLou is out for blood when it comes to Randall. Which is a new side of her," Crew explained. "As for what you can do, I think it might be good for her to know you're back. I've kept her in the loop about you just like you asked me to for her, so I know you're still friends even after all this time. Honestly, I think she needs a little tough love, and I can't do it when it comes to her."

I had to laugh, knowing he wasn't kidding when he said that. Rosie was his kryptonite, and Crew couldn't say no to anything that wouldn't cause her harm.

"Seriously, man," he continued with desperation in his tone. "She looks like a sad, wet, abandoned kitten left in a box on the side of the road. I don't know what to do. I need your help."

I glanced at my watch and saw it was late afternoon. I was supposed to have dinner with my parents tonight, but I had plenty of time to swing by the Thatcher house first. "Give me a half hour, and I'll be over."

"Thanks, man, I really appreciate it," Crew said, his relief clear. "Eli just tells me to let her be, and she'll come out when she's ready, but I don't think he understands just how bad her state of mind is. Between you and me, I'm seriously fucking afraid this is the final straw, and she won't be able to snap out of her depression. The last time it got this bad, you took her for the day, and whatever happened, she was back to her normal self."

"Wait, she never told you what we did?" I questioned.

I knew exactly what day he was talking about, and I'd never expected her to keep it a secret. That made me curious as to why Rosie chose not to tell him when they talked about everything.

"Nope, not a word. Said it was between you and her, and nobody else needed to know," Crew explained. "Don't even think about telling me now, either. If she's kept it to herself this long, it meant a lot to her."

"All right, I'll keep it to myself," I assured him. "See you in thirty."

Setting my phone down, I yanked off my shirt and headed for the bathroom. I needed to shower before going to my parents' place, so better to be ready for dinner if I ended up needing to stay longer than expected to help Rosie. That woman had been through enough in this life to last three others. There's no way I would let some shithead mess with her self-confidence and self-worth.

Pulling up the driveway, I entered the gate code Crew sent me since they updated it after I last used it. That didn't surprise me one bit. Eli was the type of man to stay on top of keeping his family safe, and changing the gate code from time to time was one way to do that. I'd forgotten how far back the house sat on the property they'd owned and lived on for generations. The house itself was fairly conservative for someone of their net worth.

It was a sprawling two-story home with a cobblestone circle driveway. I'd always liked the feel of this house because even though it was large for five people, it didn't feel that way. The biggest change since I'd been gone was Crew had a recording studio built on the side so he could work from home. I parked off to the side in the area meant for Crew's clients, not wanting to be in the way.

I tossed the car into park and sat there for a moment. Crew and I met up all the time when I came back into town. On the other hand, Bailey-Rose and I hadn't seen each other since I graduated college. Even then, I didn't get a chance to do more than wave at her before her mother whisked her off for a girls' weekend. I'd felt special, though. Rose made sure to come and support me, but the fact she didn't even try to talk to me hurt more than I'd like to admit.

Taking a deep breath, I shoved open the door and got out. This was Bailey-Rose, the girl who cried when she found out caterpillars turned into butterflies. She couldn't understand why the caterpillar wasn't good enough as it was created, hating that it needed to change. Rose asked me once why caterpillars had to evolve for people to like them. I didn't have an answer for her, and honestly, I'd never thought about it that way before. Never in my life have I met another human with such a pure heart who saw the world in technicolor instead of black and white.

When I reached the front door, it flew open, and there was Crew with a big grin on his face. "Look what the cat dragged back home."

We both laughed as we gave each other a bro hug with some sound thumps on the back. Crew was a solid dude who took care of himself, so I grunted a little at the force of his love.

He pulled back, shaking his head. "Damn, you've gotten soft. Good thing you're back so I can toughen you back up again. I'm seriously in need of a gym buddy who can keep up."

I followed him into the house, through the grand foyer, and into the sunken living room with plush suede couches. This home was meant to be lived in, so while all the furniture was high-end, it was still practical. Crew flopped onto the loveseat and propped his feet on the coffee table. After slipping off my shoes, I followed suit and sat across from him on the chaise end of the sectional couch.

"So how does it feel to know you won't be packing up and leaving in a few months?" Crew asked.

"Fucking amazing," I answered. "If I'm being honest, I don't think I realized just how much I was beginning to resent having to do that. At first, it was great. I got to see all kinds of places and visit almost every state in Preidon. Then the shininess of it all wore off once I met the guys, and our pack formed."

My best friend dropped his feet and locked eyes with me. "Was it worth it? Going through all the hoops to find a pack?"

"Yeah, one hundred percent," I answered without hesitation. "I get your reluctance, though, allowing someone to decide your fate. All they have is your information along with a scent card for the Scent Matchers to work with. For me, it only took a month before they called the five of us together for a meeting. Some people can wait years, but I was lucky. The strangest part of the meeting was walking into that restaurant and knowing four other people were there to see if they wanted to create a pack with you."

Pausing, I thought back to that day when the hostess walked me back to the private room they'd reserved for us. Warrick and Yun-Sun were already there chatting when I strolled in. Gareth arrived shortly after, and then Vili burst in ten minutes later, looking like he'd rolled out of bed.

"It took us about a half hour to realize how comfortable and easy the whole thing was. It was almost as if I'd known them for years, even though we didn't know each other's last names." I shrugged and grinned at Crew. "Don't worry, though. No one is going to take your best friend status. These guys are friends for sure, but you and I... well, we've got history they'll never be able to beat."

The set of Crew's shoulders relaxed slightly at this, but I don't think even he realized how worried he was until I said something. Growing up and caring for Bailey-Rose didn't leave Crew many opportunities to make friends. I know he'd never change a thing, but even if he never said it, I knew how important our friendship was to him.

"LouLou got all pissed off about the whole Scent Matcher subject, and I didn't even know how to respond. I get that Betas don't react to scent the same way you Alphas do. However, it doesn't mean we don't notice them or aren't influenced by it when we build connections. We just have more choices and freedom in the matter," he commented, dropping his head to stare at his tattooed hands. "I really don't understand why Betas are only allowed to participate if an Omega selects them or have an Alpha who brings them along."

Society as a whole has always taken Betas for granted. Yes, we Alphas are seen as superior because our genetics make us a prime specimen of our species. Alphas are highly intelligent, driven, instinctual protectors, and are able to bond with Omegas creating a soul-level connection for life. I have no idea where these enhanced qualities appeared in our history or if they were introduced medically. What I do know is Betas got the short end of the stick.

"I'm sorry, man. If I had an answer for you that made sense, I would give it," I offered. "What I can say is that, for the most part, we normal people don't view Betas as lower-class citizens. If those idiots in our government stepped out of their bubble, they'd know nothing in this world would be done without all of you."

Crew nodded absently as he wrung his hands. "Yeah, I know, but it doesn't make it easier when you watch everyone else find their pack and fall for their Omega. LouLou doesn't think I know what it's like to have my heart broken or feel rejected, but in reality, I know far better than most. She and I are alike in the world, viewing us as people to be passed over."

"Wait! What?" I snapped. "She thinks that about herself?"

He lifted his head and looked at me. "Why do you think I called you here? I'm really, really, fucking worried, Lys. I've never seen her this down before."

"Do you think there's something else going on besides the breakup?" I questioned.

"Fuck if I know," Crew said, tossing up his arms in defeat. "It was like pulling teeth to get her to talk to me the last time. Lou knows I won't force her to pull her shit together, which is why you're the perfect person for the job. You've always had a way of handling her firmly but not being a dick."

I frowned at that. "I'm not sure if that was a compliment or not."

"It was, I assure you. As a man who is weak to the whims of his baby sister, I am amazed by your skills in LouLou wrangling," he explained as he stood. "Speaking of which, we should probably make that happen so you can get to dinner with your parents."

"How did you know I was going to dinner with my parents?" I asked, following him down the hall to the back set of stairs, which were closer to Rose's room.

"Oh, that... I was on the phone with Eli when I mentioned you were going to stop by. He commented that your father told him about dinner and not to make you late," Crew answered.

I chuckled, knowing how thrilled my parents were that I was home. Being their only child, they were happy for me to spread my wings but were still happier to have me back. "This shouldn't take that long, and if it doesn't go well, I think they'll understand if I explain."

Crew stopped at the end of the hall where the double doors to her room stood. "I'll warn you... this place is a war zone."

"Seriously, you're one to talk," I teased, remembering the state of disaster his room was in growing up. "Stop stalling. If she gets mad, it will be at me, not her precious big brother."

Without knocking, he twisted the handle and pushed in the door, waving for me to go ahead. After stepping into the room, it was hard to see much in the soft glow from the strings of what appeared to be Christmas lights. The main lights flicked on, and I was standing in the middle of a pastel explosion. I couldn't help but smile as I saw morose self-portraits and other various representations of Rose's mood littering any flat surface. Food and candy wrappers littered the floor, mostly centered around the full-length mirror where her paints were set up.

Looking past the clutter and pain she was clearly in, I noticed the feel of the room. Everything was soft—in color, touch, and appearance. This was the most Bailey-Rose atmosphere I could have ever imagined. It was all female but had a gentle elegance to it so as not to make it feel child-ish. Rosie had always had an artistic eye, which was clear in her chosen color scheme and how the furniture flowed in the space. The room's main focus was the large bed covered in pillows and various stuffed animals of all shapes and sizes.

I almost couldn't make out the lump that was our mopey little Omega until she shifted under the covers. Rose let out a disgruntled sound followed by muffled irritation. "Go away, Crew."

Now that I knew where she was hiding, I strolled over to the bed, grabbed a fistful of the lilac comforter, and yanked it back. She was all tangled up in her favorite giant octopus that I swore never to tell anyone she slept with every night. Looking up at me sleepily with her dual-colored eyes and colorful hair all mussed was my Bailey-Rose.

The next thing I knew, there was a squeak of surprise, and I was purring loudly with my face tucked against her neck as I balled her up on my lap. My senses were flooded with the heady sweet scent of rose when it first opened after a day of rain. The tart, bright notes of black cherry followed, balancing out the sweetness of the rose but not overpowering it. Both scents blended effortlessly into the perfect combination that had me nuzzling against her, wanting to bathe in her scent.

"Lysse?" I heard her say, her voice just as I remembered it—musical and soft like a fairy. It matched the blue and purple hues she'd dyed her hair, only adding to the logic that she was, in fact, magical.

Not even bothering to lift my head, I answered her, "Yeah, little Rosie, it's me..." using all the willpower I possessed, I lifted my head and looked into her wide, shocked eyes, "... and you're my scent matched Omega."

At that statement, her jaw dropped. Seconds later, the sound of her heart rate monitor snapped me out of my scent-induced haze. I fumbled for her wrist, panic spiking through my chest.

No, please, God. I just found her.

BAILEY-ROSE

ooolllyyy shit.

H Ulysses Ford was a scent match.

My mind whirled as I tried to process that information as he stared into my eyes with his green gaze that had a ring of copper around the iris, making them mesmerizing to look at. Growing up, I'd looked at them a thousand times, but it wasn't until I'd turned sixteen and he'd come home for the summer that I realized I had a major crush on him. In retrospect, it made sense now, but with my condition, I was kept on medication to keep me from going into heat, so it took longer for my scent to come in strong enough for an Alpha to notice it.

Now here I was sitting on Lysse's lap, rolled up like an armadillo, mouth hanging open, and realizing I hadn't showered in a *week*. The poor man just shoved his nose into my nasty, dirty hair, huffing it like it was the best drug he'd ever taken. I'm pretty sure a chunk of Peep was lost in there somewhere, if not honey from the various cups of tea I'd made over the past few days.

This was my worst nightmare come to life.

The man I'd secretly been pining over for *years* was tenderly cradling me in his arms, and I was cosplaying as a trash panda. Panic took over my mind as all these thoughts slammed into my head at once while being assaulted with the most divine combination of rich, decadent milk chocolate with cheerful notes of orange to cut the sweetness for the perfect taste. Part of me wanted to lean in and lick him to see if he tasted as good as he smelled. Before that could happen, everything came to a screeching halt as my monitor registered the riot of emotions happening in my body.

"Shit," I swore, trying to look at my wrist, but Lysse was already gripping it and checking at the number.

"What's your limit? It used to be ninety... has it changed?" he asked, his tone all business even as he held me tenderly and pulled me closer to his chest.

"I shouldn't go above eighty, but eight-five is the I-need-to-go-to-the-hospital-now number," I answered, unsure if that was the answer he was looking for.

"Thank fuck, it only hit seventy-seven." He sighed, resting his head on mine.

Not having seen Ulysses in years, I'd forgotten how big he was. I felt like a child all bundled up on his lap with his arms easily wrapping around me. His light golden brown hair was long enough to pull back into a ponytail. A short beard covered his jaw, giving him a slightly rugged appearance that I found incredibly sexy. Lysse had always been a fan of the outdoors, going hiking, camping, biking—all the things I couldn't. However, I'd been glad that he'd managed to be one of the few people who could talk Crew into leaving for a day or two for them to go camping. The man had a silver tongue and knew how to use it to get his way, no matter how set in our ways my brother and I were.

Then a realization hit me, and I was wriggling out of Lysse's arms, to which I got a disapproving noise, but he let me go.

Grabbing the closest pillow, I hurled it at Crew. "You promised," I yelled, snatching up my next weapon.

Crew dodged the first but didn't see the second one coming right after, and it biffed him in the face. "Lou—"

"Don't you LouLou me, you liar," I shot back. "You said you'd let me be, and I could wallow without you trying to fix things."

One after another, I chucked whatever I could grab until a hand wrapped around my wrist and another my waist causing me to freeze.

"Rosie, you need to calm down. You're setting off your monitor again, and it's taking everything in my willpower not to wrap you up like a burrito and make you settle down," Ulysses whispered in my ear, his beard brushing against my neck as I felt the heat of his breath being so close.

My whole body locked up. Honestly, I'm not sure if I was even breathing as I registered how his entire body was pressed against my back. The stuffed, fluffy, smiling cloud fell from my hand, and I melted against the Alpha behind me like I no longer had bones.

"Good girl," he said with a purr.

And this is how I die the happiest woman of all time.

"How did you do that?" Crew asked, the awe in his voice snapping me out of my daze.

I glared at my brother. "Don't you even think about changing the subject, mister. How could you break your promise to me?" I demanded.

"How dare you accuse me because I one thousand percent did not," Crew countered. "If you remember correctly, I said I wouldn't try to fix things the moment you told me what was going on. It's been two whole days, LouLou. Tell me, what part of that is breaking my promise?"

"Damn you and your contract skills," I muttered. "Technicalities aside, why in the world would you drag poor Lysse into this while he's just visiting? I'm sure he has far better things to do than deal with someone impersonating a cave troll." Taking a breath, I looked up at the man in question. "You really should keep your distance. I haven't showered in a few days."

"She means a week," Crew interjected, which earned him a scathing look and a middle finger from me. "What, you think that's what's going to gross him out? LouLou, the man is an avid backpacker, trail biker, and camper. He's gone a week without showering many, many times."

"Crew," Lysse cut in as he turned me to face him. "I got this, man."

Dropping to one knee, he cupped my face with a tenderness that I'd only gotten from my family. He took a moment to tuck some hair behind my ear so it wasn't falling in my face anymore, making me blush. "Rosie, I smell nothing but a sweet, pure scent that tells me that you're mine. As for what Crew did, I don't blame him for being worried about you. Seriously, though, I've never seen a man with a bigger little sister complex than him."

That got me to smile, which he returned readily.

"I think it's safe to say that neither one of us expected me to stop by and find myself uncovering the Omega my pack and I have been looking for over the past year and a half," Ulysses explained. "Setting that aside for just a moment, I want to clear up a few things first. The most important of them being that I'm not just here visiting... I've moved here permanently. My pack has already been here for six months. I was the last to join them, but I'm back for good."

My brain started to short-circuit at this. *How could no one tell me he was back?* I glanced at Crew, who remained a safe distance away but grinned like a fool from where he sat on the stool in front of my vanity.

"No, don't look at him like that," Lysse chided, turning

me around to face him. "I asked him not to tell you, to keep it a surprise."

His hands slid from my face to glide down my arms and take my hands. "My hope had been to find a way to rebuild our friendship because I missed having you in my life. Although it looks like that's not going to be much trouble now, is it?" He winked.

I fidgeted in his hold, painstakingly aware of how much of a hot-mess express I was right now. Everything in me just wanted to curl up against him and breathe in his scrumptious scent, but I just couldn't let myself relax, knowing I'd been living in these clothes for a week.

"Lysse, I'm beyond thrilled that you're back, and trust me when I say I would love to discuss what just happened between us. But I *really* need a shower," I explained. "Give me fifteen minutes to clean up and make myself more presentable. Then you have my undivided attention for as long as you want."

Crew snorted but wisely didn't speak about the underestimation of showering time needed on my part.

"Okay, maybe I'll need thirty minutes, but I promise to hurry. I'm guessing with how you're dressed, you have dinner plans with your family, and I don't want you to be late," I amended.

"Bailey-Rose, if you think I'm still going to my parents' house for dinner, you're delusional. I'm not going anywhere you're not," Ulysses stated, making my fluttering heart melt.

Chewing on my lip as I tried to hide my grin, I lost the battle against my blush, feeling my cheeks heat. "Still..."

"Shower," he finished. "I hear you, Rosie. Shower it is."

Rising to his feet, Lysse stepped out of my way, and I hurried to the giant walk-in closet. I grabbed a simple T-shirt dress, undergarments, and spandex shorts to wear under the dress. I was never one to risk flashing people because I always forget I'm wearing a dress. When I got in the zone while painting, I sat in odd ways and didn't always remember what I was wearing in those moments. Turning to head to the bathroom, I crashed into Ulysses, who'd followed me into the closet.

"Oh shit," I swore as I bounced off him, but he instantly caught me. "Sorry, I didn't realize you'd joined me."

"Don't be sorry. I didn't make myself known. It's not your fault," he assured me, tucking me against his side as we exited the closet.

Having no clue what to do with this situation, I let him guide me over to the shower and turn on the water for me. To my shock, he searched the bathroom until he found the closet with extra towels and sheets. I watched as he pulled out a fresh set of towels in a soft mint color and set them on the stool next to the shower door.

Ulysses noticed me watching him, and he raised a brow. "What?"

"Um..." I started, confused at his confusion. "I'm waiting for you to leave."

He frowned. "Leave?"

"Yeah, so I can take my shower. I kind of need to get undressed, and the shower is all glass," I pointed out.

"I'll turn around, but I'm not leaving. Your monitor went off twice really close together, and I remember that time you passed out from the heat of a hot shower. I'm not taking the chance that something happens and you split your head open or worse," Ulysses answered.

Letting out a sigh, I walked over to the sink and set my clothes off to the side before facing him. "Look, I get you're fully aware of my condition and all that goes with it, but you only remember what it was like for me as a kid. Yes, my heart-rate threshold is lower, but I'm really good at managing my illness. I've been doing it for twenty-five years now. I promise I'm going to be fine. If I get lightheaded, there's a bench in the shower for me to sit on."

His fingers brushed along my jaw as he stared intently into my eyes. "I can't bear the thought of anything happening to you when I just found you, Rosie."

"It'll be fine, I promise," I assured him. "Now get out so I can once more become human and shed this trash-panda look I've been rocking."

"Trash what?" Lysse questioned.

"You know, a raccoon... because they like to dig through the trash yet are still cute and cuddly-looking," I shared, trying to stifle my laughter. "Guess an old man like you wouldn't know the cool kids' lingo."

He gave me an unimpressed look. "Five years doesn't make me old, Rosie."

"We'll see about that," I countered as I started to shove him. "Out you go. Go on, git."

Reluctantly, Ulysses complained, and I shut the door, twisting the lock just to be sure. Seconds later, it was unlocked and opened just enough so it wasn't latched.

"I'll stay out here, but I'm going to sit just outside the door so I can hear if you need me," Ulysses informed me.

Blinking at the door, I didn't quite know what to make of the situation, but I decided it was rather adorable for him to be that worried. After a moment, I snapped myself out of the daydream and got to the matter at hand. I needed to redeem myself for that terrible first meeting with a man I'd yearned for and somehow magically ended up being and would spend the rest of my life with.

In a flurry, I stripped out of my clothes and hopped into the shower, letting the scalding hot water burn away the last remnants of my wallowing. Crew was right—Randall wasn't a great catch. Yet when the world, outside of your family, tells you you're not good enough to love—part of you starts to believe it. It was beyond rare to find your scent match by chance since they could be anywhere in the world. In come the Scent Matchers, who built a central database to find each person the perfect Alpha or Omega.

Giddiness bubbled up inside me as the reality of what just happened registered. A little squeal of joy burst out of me as I danced under the water. The dream I'd been wishing and hoping for just became a reality, and with a man I'd always pictured kissing me good morning and goodnight.

What would the other members of his pack be like? How many were there? Were they all the same age? All I really knew was they'd been matched up and together for a little over two years and only because Crew told me.

Then a thought hit me, *What if they didn't feel the same way Lysse did and decided they didn't want a broken Omega?*

Some of the excitement dwindled, but I decided to give love and the chance of having a pack one more chance. If this didn't work, then I knew it was a fruitless effort, and I could find a peaceful life on my own.

Ulysses

All my instincts were screaming at me for not having Bailey-Rose in my sights. I'd never truly understood why Crew acted the way he did around her when it seemed like she could live a fairly normal life. Now my eyes were opened to the dread of not being around if something happened you could've prevented.

In all the things I've heard and read about the changes that happen after finding your Omega, none of them ever talked about the intense protectiveness that overtakes you. Yes, Alphas innately are wired that way, but I felt like everything was on overdrive. I strained my hearing when I heard a little squeak from inside, but when nothing else followed, I relaxed slightly.

"Wow... you got it bad, bro." Crew snickered as he squatted in front of me. "Just a suggestion, but you might want to call your pack brothers and give them a heads-up. I can call your parents if you want to avoid that conversation for a bit."

I rubbed my forehead, trying to decide what the best plan was. If I told my parents right now, they'd want me to bring her over immediately, which would be beyond overwhelming for Rosie. Better to give her a few days to adjust to this new realization before my family added their two cents. They would mean well, but since Mr. and Mrs. Thatcher were always gone, they'd taken to looking after Crew and Bailey-Rose like their own.

"God, my mother is going to be over the moon," I muttered. "She loves Rosie like a daughter already. This will just make all her dreams come true."

"Just think, you've now secured the favorite-child spot for life," Crew pointed out as he raised his phone to his ear.

"I'm an only child, asshole," I shot back, tuning out whatever he was telling my mother as I pulled out my phone.

Now the question was, do I call or text? We had a group chat, so maybe it might be better to get their attention first, then call them. Warrick wasn't working at the bar tonight, and the others should be finishing up their day at this point, so it was a solid chance we could all talk.

ULYSSES:

Guys, I have major news. This is not a joke. I need you to answer me right away.

WARRICK:

Are you okay?

GARETH:

Do I have a minute to finish this meeting or do I need to step out right now?

ULYSSES:

I'm fine Warrick, better than fine.

ULYSSES:

Gareth, if you're serious about it being a minute, otherwise you're gonna want to tell them to come back another day.

VILI:

This sounds like it's a good news! I free if call is needed.

The second I finished reading his message, I hit the dial button, and an electronic ringing sounded.

"Dude, didn't you say you were going to your best friend's house?" Warrick asked when he answered. "What could possibly have happened in the forty-five minutes since you left the house?"

"I'll tell you when the others get on," I said, listening for the beeps that meant another person answered the call.

Taking a second to pull the phone away from my ear, I heard the water still running, which I was thankful for. It wasn't that I was trying to hide I was talking to my pack, but I knew I wasn't going to be able to keep my cool as I told them. This had been a tough journey for us as we started to feel hopeless with one failed scent card after another.

"Yo, Ulysses, you still there?" Gareth called, snapping my attention back to the call.

I cleared my throat, suddenly overwhelmed with what I had to tell them. "Guys..." I started, unsure how to even describe what just transpired. "I-I found her. She's here with me. Well, not right beside me. I got kicked out of the bathroom so she could take a shower, but I'm just outside the door."

"Ah... one, that sounds a tiny bit creepy, if I'm being

honest. Two, who the hell is she, and why was this an emergency?" Warrick questioned.

A growl of frustration slipped out at how terribly I was explaining this. "I found our Omega," I blurted.

"Hold on, what did you just say?" Yun-Sun pressed. "I feel like I'm missing part of the story. Where are you right now that you'd be sitting outside some woman's bathroom while she showers?"

"Yah, sounds little bit creepy," Vili added, his heavily accented voice making him distinct on the call.

"I'm at my friend Crew's place. We've been best friends for years. Earlier, he called me to help him with a situation that had to do with his little sister, Bailey-Rose. I've known this girl for just as long as Crew, and we'd been close before I left for college. Now, I see her for the first time in several years only to discover she's my scent matched Omega," I explained. "Look, the bottom line is all of you need to get over here now. There's more to this whole situation, but I'm not doing this over the phone. Just get your asses over here."

"Holy shit! This is for real, isn't it?" Gareth asked in disbelief. "Why wasn't she in the Matching system?"

"All of that will be explained, Gareth. There's a legitimate reason, but I'm not saying anything until you've all had the chance to meet her," I assured him. "I'll send you guys the address, but I've got to go... the water just turned off."

"So mysterious, this is exciting," Vili said, and I could picture the giant smile on his face.

Finding our Omega was important to all of us but even more so to Vili. He'd come to Preidon from Numoland three years ago to run the international portion of his family's jewelry business. He knew no one and didn't speak our language well—even now, there are times we have to explain the meaning of phrases or slang that's not commonly used. When he joined the pack, it was like we'd given him the greatest gift in the world. There was nothing more important to Vili than this new family, and it certainly made the transition of combining five existing lives into one smoother with his help.

"You have no idea, Vili, so I suggest you all hurry the fuck up," I urged before hanging up and immediately texting them the address and gate code.

The sound of someone clearing their throat had my head snapping up and halfway standing to protect this doorway by any means necessary. When I saw it was Eli, I relaxed slightly, but only slightly, as I registered the look on his face wasn't all that pleased. Then again, this man was never one to express clear emotion to anyone but Bailey-Rose.

"Eli," I greeted with a respectful nod.

While his second father might own the majority of the company in name, Eli is the one who ran the damn thing. That wasn't the reason I tended to be wary around him, though. When it came to Rosie, Eli was ruthless in his efforts to keep her safe behind the scenes so as not to tip her off. That Alpha's Achilles heel was in the form of a tiny loving Omega—also known as his baby sister. In some ways, Crew got to stay being Rosie's brother because Eli took on more of the father role after their father, Adrian, passed away.

"Why are you sitting in front of the bathroom door?" Eli questioned, his frown deepening as he crossed his arms. "I'm telling you right now it better be a good answer because scent match or not, I won't allow you to pressure her into *anything.*"

His icy tone was cold enough to give me the chills. I had zero doubt he would uphold that threat if he felt I was stepping out of line when it came to his precious sister.

"Eli, I know we don't know each other all that well, even after all these years. That being said, I will say this once," I bit out through clenched teeth, trying to keep calm at his unspoken accusation. "I would *never* pressure or manipulate Bailey-Rose into anything she didn't want to do. Only the lowest of the low would dare to do that to a person, regardless of their connection. Now that we've cleared that up, I don't want *ever* to hear you question my intentions when it comes to Bailey-Rose. Her safety, happiness, and well-being have been important to me since the day I met her."

Eli's jaw flexed, probably not used to people speaking to him in such a manner, but I didn't give a flying fuck. How dare he question my motives when I'd never given him a reason to think less of me. I'd known Crew and Rosie for almost twenty years. This kind of treatment was reserved for strangers, not family friends, and I wouldn't let it stand.

Taking a deep breath, Eli closed his eyes and let out the breath slowly as if trying to calm himself down. I knew his protectiveness over Rosie was intense, but I'd never seen this side of him before. Typically, the Eli I knew was calm and even-tempered about everything, to the point I sometimes questioned if he might be a robot. Even as I looked at him now with his perfectly cut hair, close-cut beard, and pressed navy suit giving him an air of detail and control, I also knew that man worked out like a beast, which had me considering a new motivation other than keeping himself in peak condition.

When he met my gaze again with blue eyes the same color as Rosie's right eye, I saw the barest flicker of fear that I questioned if I was right. "I apologize, Ulysses, that was beyond rude of me to attack you in such a manner. I think it's just been a shock to return home, learn of the events that transpired, and then find you in her room while she's showering has set off my protective nature. Bailey is still so fragile from what occurred with Randall, I overreacted."

Hearing him apologize and seeing the true regret on his face, I relaxed, stepping away from the door to close the gap between us. I offered my hand to him, and he gave me a quizzical look but took the offered hand.

"It's nice to see you, Eli," I greeted, hoping to start this interaction over. "In case you haven't heard, in a surprising turn of events, your sister is my scent match. I truly hope we can build a good friendship since I know how important you are to Rosie."

He gave me a wry smile. "Sucking up has never been your strongest skill, you know that, right?"

"Figured it couldn't hurt," I answered with a shrug and a grin. "It did get you to stop glaring at me, though."

A huff of laughter was Eli's response as he ran a hand through his perfectly styled hair. "I'll be honest, I knew this could happen one day, but clearly, I wasn't prepared for it."

"Is anyone? I came over intending to cheer her up enough to leave her room," I pointed out. "Just so you're aware, I called the rest of my pack, and they are heading over. I thought having her meet them here would be less stressful for her. She set off her monitor twice fairly back-to-back, which is why I was sitting outside the door while she showered," I explained, feeling it couldn't hurt for him to have the reasoning.

"Ah, yes, it would make sense for you to think she needed that," Eli commented with a nod. "Just to set your mind at ease, she truly has been able to manage her condition with little involvement from us. I suppose being an adult helps since now she understands the details of what her body goes through and how best to prevent dangerous situations."

I raised a brow, not believing the calm he was portraying. "Right, and that knowledge has set your mind at ease enough to delete her heart monitor alerts from your phone?"

Eli started to answer then stopped, giving me the answer I already knew. "You rushed home from the office because you already knew she had two alerts back to back, making you worry. You knew I was coming over, but I can't figure out why you thought I was causing the problem?"

"Honestly, I don't think it had anything to do with you. If Crew had been standing in this room, I would have chewed his ass out for upsetting her," Eli answered honestly. "I should have known that Crew would be hiding, though. He texted me what happened and didn't even bother to speak to me when I tried to call. That brother of mine could make a nun pull out her hair with how he handles certain situations."

He didn't have to tell me that. I was well aware of that trait in my best friend. My phone buzzed, and I glanced down to see it was Warrick letting me know he and Vili were pulling up to the gate. *Shit, they'd made it here in record time.* Then again, Warrick wasn't known for following the rules when it came to speed.

"Well, I'm about to flush him out from his hiding spot since two of my pack brothers are here," I shared as I texted Crew to greet them because I wasn't leaving this room until Rosie was ready to meet them.

"Indulge me as I make this request because I know you can't do anything about it, but please don't let them hurt her. Bailey has been rejected time and time again by people who make snap judgments about her condition. You are one of the few people who saw past the disease and limitations to find the amazing woman underneath. Those men have no idea how lucky they are to be matched with her," Eli said, his voice so full of emotion and vulnerability it had me looking at the man in a new light.

Eli, just like Crew, put his lives on hold to be by Bailey-Rose's side without a second thought. Now here I was, appearing out of thin air and changing the life they'd created for the three of them. Traditionally, once the pack finds their match, the courting begins, allowing the Omega time to get to know their new pack. It also provides the chance to establish residency if they need to move states or out of the country. Now I see it also gives the family time to adjust as well to the idea their loved one is going to start their own family.

"I couldn't agree with you more, Eli. These men are good men, and I have no doubt they will see the diamond that she is, even if there might be a few minor flaws. At the end of the day, she's going to be the most precious thing to us," I assured him.

BAILEY-ROSE

There I stood in front of the mirror, my hair fresh and clean with a bouncy curl making it look like cotton candy. Wanting to erase my first impression after five years of not seeing each other, I swiped on some mascara and applied a sheer lip gloss to give me a little polish. I did a quick twirl to ensure I hadn't missed anything, also needing to double-check that my soft pink T-shirt dress, splattered with white stars, wasn't caught in the back of my white shorts. Going out in public like that once was more than enough for me.

Feeling there wasn't any reason to keep stalling, I took a deep breath and blew a few strands of hair out of my face. "Here goes nothing," I told myself.

I switched out my bunny slippers for another, cleaner, pair that were covered in strawberries, then headed for the bedroom. Pulling open the door, I found Lysse leaning against the wall beside the bathroom entrance reading something on his phone as it buzzed.

"Popular fella," I commented.

A smile tugged at his lips. "If only that were true, but it seems you're the popular one here."

"What?"

Tucking his phone into his back pocket, he pushed off the wall and faced me. "I told the rest of my pack about what happened. The last of them just pulled up and should be joining the other three in the living room. Crew is babysitting them to avoid getting in trouble with Eli."

My mouth went dry as the meaning of his words connected to my brain. "They're *here*? Now?" I whispered.

Ulysses reached out and took my hand, tugging me forward until he could wrap me up in a hug. Bending, he rested his head on mine and began purring, instantly turning me into boneless goo. Fisting my hands in his shirt was the only thing that kept me from becoming a puddle at his feet.

"Rosie, it's going to be all right," Lysse murmured. "These are good men. I wouldn't have told them about you if they weren't. You've recently been hurt, and I understand why you'd be wary of jumping into anything too fast. All I expect from this is for you to meet them, that's it. Eli and Crew are both home, so you're not alone with just the five of us. You're safe in your home where you call the shots."

Tilting my head back, I looked up into his expressive eyes and read the honesty there. "You thought of everything, didn't you?"

"All that matters right now is you, so yeah, I did all I could think of to make this easier for you," Lysse admitted.

"Okay, we can go meet them." I relented, taking a deep breath of his chocolaty-orange scent.

In a move that almost had my heart truly skipping a beat, he kissed my forehead tenderly as he gave me another reassuring squeeze. "I'll be right next to you the entire time. Do you remember the code word Eli made you come up with to tell Crew and me if you were in trouble?"

With that childhood memory unlocked, I recalled that day Eli sat us down, furious that I'd been having trouble breathing, and neither of them noticed.

. . .

"Bailey, why didn't you tell them you were in trouble?" Eli demanded.

Pushing my bottom lip out in a dramatic pout, I gave a sniff. "Because I don't want people to know my heart doesn't work right. They make fun of me when they find out."

Eli considered this a moment then an idea struck. "What if you come up with a special word or phrase that you use when something's wrong, and you need them to check on you."

"Like what?" I asked, not understanding.

"Well, it needs to be something you wouldn't say normally but not so odd people notice," Eli explained.

Closing my eyes, I thought long and hard about something I wouldn't say often yet being totally expected. Then I thought of it...

"Holy flying Purple People Eater," I answered.

Ulysses chuckled, a bright smile on his lips. "God, that's still funny as ever."

"You know Mom didn't like us to curse, so I came up with alternatives," I said in my defense.

"Personally, son of a biscuit was my favorite. I've even used it a few times which always made me think of you," he shared as he caressed my cheek with the back of his fingers. "No matter how much time has passed, you're always in my thoughts, Rosie. Now it makes sense, and I feel like I should apologize for making you wait so long for us to find you."

Heat flamed in my cheeks as he looked at me with such an intense gaze it was almost a little too overwhelming. "All that matters is that we did find each other. If my life has taught me anything, it's not to keep looking back... there's too much to look forward to. More so now that you did find me."

"God, I don't think we deserve you," Lysse muttered as he intertwined our fingers and led me out of my room.

I walked slightly slower as we descended the stairs, trying to concentrate on keeping my breathing calm as we got closer and closer to the living room. Then something caught my attention.

Was someone making blueberry muffins?

The soft, sweet aroma of crystalized sugar called to me as the tart berry cut the sweetness, giving you a refreshing note to balance. I was caught in the aroma, which connected to moments baking with my mother, slathering the muffin in butter, and the delight of eating something I helped to make. It was a scent that held such a tender memory, and it only became stronger the closer I got to the source. Warmth enveloped me, tucking me close like I was still that version of myself in the memory.

"Hello, Bailey-Rose," a voice rumbled under my ear.

I started to panic as I realized I hadn't been smelling a real muffin at all. It had been an Alpha, an Alpha whose lap I'd climbed right up on so I could nuzzle my face in his neck. Feeling me tense, my blueberry Alpha started to purr as he ran a hand gently up and down my back. As if to prove I wasn't the only one affected, he buried his nose in my hair, taking deep breaths of my scent.

"You're fine to stay right where you are, sweetheart," he assured me.

I cracked open an eye to see what was going on and found another man watching me with a dopey smile on his face. "Hi," he greeted with a little wave when he noticed me looking at him.

Uncurling my fingers from Blueberry's suit jacket, I gave him a wave in return. "Hey."

"Holy shit, you're adorable," he blurted, then winced,

waving his hands as if to erase what he'd just said. "Shit, sorry that came out weird and a little creepy, which I didn't mean at all."

"Are you seeing this right now?" another strange voice asked. "The master of small talk is totally off his game. I didn't think that was possible."

Sitting up, I looked into the face of the man whose lap I'd commandeered. He had stunning spice-brown eyes full of color variants, giving them a unique quality that had me wanting to see if I could even create a color with paints to match. His heritage was of Asian descent which created the perfect bone structure for such an intense pair of eyes, making them even more intriguing. His black hair was cut close to his head in a buzz cut that suited him and gave me the urge to see if it was as soft as it looked. I refrained, feeling that I'd invaded his space far more than was appropriate when I didn't even know his name.

"I'm Bailey-Rose," I managed to squeak out. "Sorry about making myself at home on your lap and now lingering when I should move. This is very unlike me... I never do things like this. Please don't think I'm the type of woman who just climbs onto anyone's lap," I rambled, shifting to get off this nice blueberry-smelling man's lap.

Just as I was about to push off his legs to stand, he pulled me back to his chest. "You're right. It wouldn't be a wise choice to just climb onto anyone's lap. However, when it comes to me as one of your Alphas, it's my job to ensure your needs as our Omega are met. So if you have need of me or my lap, there is no reason for you to hold back."

Who was this man? First, he smells edible. Second, he took zero issue with me acting odd, and now gave me an open invitation to cuddle whenever I want. *Have I died and gone to heaven?*

"Maybe you want to tell her your name so she knows who just agreed to give her unlimited affection," Ulysses suggested with a chuckle.

"Oh... I guess I did neglect to share that, didn't I?" he said, looking a little sheepish. Picking me up, he got to his feet, only then to place me in his spot as he stood before me. "It's so incredibly lovely to meet you, Bailey-Rose. I'm Yun-Sun Lee, a member of Ulysses' pack. It would appear we are scent matched as well."

"What gave you that impression?" the same snarky man asked from behind Yun-Sun.

Peering around the Alpha standing in front of me, I spotted the man in question. He had a head of curly ash-brown hair with a close-shaven beard covering his rugged face. I started to get up when Yun-Sun offered me a hand and pulled me to my feet. Giving him a grateful smile, I walked over to meet this sassy man. He wore jeans, boots, and a polo that had a business logo with a bull's head on it and *Watson Ranch Beef* written under it.

When I got a few steps away from him, the scent of fresh lemons reached me first, but the cool, smooth flavor of iced tea followed, making me desperate for a drink. "Why do you all smell like my favorite things?" I asked no one in particular but continued to stare down the man before me.

This time, I held myself back from climbing into another man's lap. However, I couldn't keep my body from leaning in to get a better whiff of the scent. It made me want to grab a book and lay out in the sun on a hammock.

"Screw holding back," the man muttered seconds before he surged to his feet and picked me up. This move instinctively had me wrap my legs around his waist as he smothered his face in the crook of my neck. "God, I fucking love cherries, and you, little miss, smell like a whole-ass cherry pie."

I giggled as his beard tickled my skin, making me relax instead of being so rigid in his arms.

"Even her laugh is adorable," Alpha Hi mumbled. "She's going to kill us with how cute she is."

"Warrick, she's not a puppy," Ulysses commented. "Dig deep in that brain of yours and find a different word."

"Why is her being like a puppy bad? I think adorable is the right word for her. Everything about her is cute, like a puppy," another man interjected. His voice had a fascinating timbre with his accent.

Twisting, I tried to see where he was in the room, but Alpha Sweet-tea was having none of it and nipped at my neck. That single move set off every nerve ending in my entire body. It was as if someone set off fireworks that all started to shoot off at the same time. My breathing became rapid, and for the first time, I felt my pussy throb with need.

I'd been on medication since I was fifteen to prevent me from ever having a heat. My body couldn't handle the physical response to the hormone shift that we Omegas dealt with every three months. It was a time we became the most fertile and perfumed like mad. This is what called to whatever Alphas were near, letting them know it was the best time to breed. During this time, it could send the Alphas into rut, which was an almost mindless need to mate with the Omega. All in all, a heat meant a group of supercharged horny people who wouldn't heed any warning regarding keeping my heart rate or blood pressure in mind. As if to prove everyone right, my monitor started buzzing, telling me I needed to calm down *right now.*

"What the hell is that?" Alpha Sweet-tea asked.

"Purple People," I rasped, trying to concentrate but feeling this man's panic wasn't helping. "Flying—"

"I got you, Rosie. I hear you loud and clear," Lysse said as he pulled me from the other Alpha.

The pounding of feet told me Crew and Eli were almost there with what I really needed.

"Lay her on the couch, now," Eli barked.

I let out a whine as I flinched at the Alpha command in Eli's order as Ulysses laid me down, stroking my hair out of my face. "Shh, it's gonna be fine. Crew has your meds... he's just prepping the injection."

The sting of the needle on my upper arm told me relief was coming, and I needed to keep breathing. While the medication was fast-acting, it worked better if I could convince my body to stop panicking as the medication did its job. I pictured sitting in a meadow with my paints, watching the butterflies drinking from the wildflowers as they swayed in the gentle breeze. Focusing on the movement, I tried to match my breathing to the gentle wave of flowers, which would expedite the slowing of my heart back down.

"Do you need the oxygen?" Crew asked.

I shook my head since my mind was clear, and I didn't feel lightheaded. A cool cloth was placed on my head, giving me something to focus on other than the panic my anxiety wanted to dwell on. It was a trick Eli found in his many hours of research into holistic alternatives for my condition. Most didn't work or help, but this simple trick of the mind was fantastic.

"Wh-what just happened," Alpha Sweet-tea demanded. "Please tell me I didn't do something wrong to cause this. Did I hurt her? Is she going to be okay? Fuck, why didn't I listen when you told us to take it easy with her?"

"Gareth, you need to take a deep breath, or you're going to hyperventilate," Yun-Sun warned.

"Please, I need to know she's okay... *please*," Gareth begged, his voice choked with emotion.

My breathing was almost back to normal. However, the pulse in my ears told me I wasn't out of the woods yet, but I couldn't let him think this was his fault. Turning my head, I found Gareth standing there hugging himself tightly, his expression almost tormented. It broke my tattered heart to see him so broken up over this.

"It's not your fault. I was born like this," I said, holding his gaze. "I'll be okay. The medicine is working, and once my heart rate is back to normal, it will be like this never happened."

Gareth scoffed. "Yeah, I don't think I'm going to forget that right after I nipped at your neck... you almost died."

I smiled at him, knowing this wasn't going to be easy for any of my Alphas to adjust to. "When you're worried about almost dying every day, it doesn't become quite as scary as you think."

"What do you mean?" Yun-Sun asked as he stepped up beside Gareth, followed by the other two Alphas whose names I hadn't gotten yet.

My gaze shifted to Lysse, and he gave my hand a reassuring squeeze, knowing I didn't want to tell these men the truth, especially after the dramatics that just happened, displaying the ugly truth of having someone with a chronic illness in your life. The one thing we never want to be is a burden to our loved ones, but that's exactly what we are, even if they don't see it that way.

"I have a genetic disorder and because of that, when I was born, I had a hole in my heart as well as a valve that doesn't work properly. When I was strong enough as a baby, they did repair the hole, but it took longer than they would have liked because I struggled with gaining weight so they could safely do the surgery. This led to some complications that I still deal with to this day," I explained.

Lifting my left arm, I showed them the heart rate monitor. "One of the most important things is to keep my heart rate under a certain number so it won't overwork my heart. I take medication to help stabilize the rhythm, make my blood thinner so it's easier to pump, and another to ensure I never go into heat."

The one Alpha I hadn't gotten a good look at gingerly took my hand in his, twisting it this way and that to look at the monitor on my wrist. I couldn't help but lean in to get more of his scent I could only describe as s'mores. He wore round gold-rimmed glasses that slid down his nose, but he didn't bother pushing them up, intent on examining the monitor. His hair was a coppery strawberry blond that was mussed and haphazard as if he runs his hands through it a lot. When he looked up from my wrist and met my gaze, I was greeted with the softest caramel-colored eyes I'd ever encountered. They oozed warmth and some worry as he searched my face as if to ensure I was truly okay. What I didn't see was pity in them, and that's what I'd been most worried about.

I had to smile at his mustache that slightly curled up at the ends, adding to his effervescent smile. It also looked like he was trying to grow the rest of his beard with the stubble coming in, but I think I actually liked it as just the mustache. It suited him in an eccentric kind of way.

"Tell me, *herlig*, do they force you to wear dis?" he asked in a rather serious tone that didn't match the question.

"Ah... yes?" I answered as more of a question. "Well, I

have to wear the monitor, but I've had different kinds over the years."

"Why they make you wear something so ugly? No, no, I make you something better, more pretty, delicate, like you," he decided with a nod.

"You'll have to forgive Vili. His family has been in the fashion business for generations," Alpha Hi explained. "Oh, I'm Warrick, by the way."

Having them all there distracting me from the hysterics my body had just put me through had me much calmer. So much so I started to sit up. All of them surged forward to help, crashing into each other which then caused them to swear under their breath as they glared at one another. This made me giggle and caught all of their attention.

Hands slid under my shoulders and hooked around my armpits to hoist me into a sitting position. I looked up to see Eli's blue eyes and worried furrows on his brow. My big overprotective brother, Eli, was the pinnacle representation of the Alpha designation—dutiful to a fault. He'd always taken on the responsibility of keeping me safe from everything and everyone—even Crew. We would play together all the time as kids while Eli would observe. He'd make sure Crew didn't take it too far or talk me into doing something stupid, which had happened a time or two when big bro wasn't looking.

Eli was ten years older than me, and I suppose it was hard for him to feel like anything other than a fourth parent. How else do you explain why he's decided to still live at the house as a thirty-five-year-old man? He had no pack, no love interest, and took over our father's role in the company the moment he could, running the day-to-day operations. He always told me he didn't feel it was right to build a life for himself until he knew his baby sister was taken care of.

The man had the biggest big-brother complex I'd *ever* seen. Even though we fought over stupid things on a daily basis, I loved him dearly. Plus, he was the one to nurture my love of art. The moment he figured out I had a knack for it, he put me in any art class he could find. Without my art, I wouldn't be the woman I am today. It allowed me to express myself in a way that had nothing to do with how physically fit I was. The people I painted doing all the things I wanted to experience gave me the chance to live out those dreams in my imagination. There could be no greater gift than Eli seeing my potential and showing me all it could provide.

"Hey, B," he murmured. "You need anything?"

"Nah, I'm good," I assured him. "I think today was just full of a lot of surprises."

Eli nodded, his gaze flicking over to the men around me and then back to me. "I'll be in my study just down the hall."

"Roger that," I answered, giving him a thumbs-up.

He dropped a kiss on my head before he left with Crew following. I was really proud of them for leaving me after an episode like that. Normally, I would have one of them glued to my side for another few hours just to be sure.

When I returned my gaze to the men who appeared to be my Alphas, I sheepishly smiled. "Welcome to life with Bailey-Rose."

GARETH

It was amazing to me how she could just sit there so relaxed with her legs crossed, hugging a pillow as she watched us take our seats once again. The sheer terror that hit me at the thought I'd done something to cause her harm nearly sent me into a tailspin of dark, intrusive thoughts. Taking precautions, I sat directly across the room from her so I could stay in her line of sight, but there would be no chance of causing another problem.

"Why don't we try this again," Bailey-Rose suggested. "Let's start with you..." she decided, pointing her finger at me, "... tell me your name, what you do for work, and one thing that's your favorite. It can be anything... food, music, movie, literally anything you would tell someone is your favorite something. Then let's round it off with something you dislike."

Shit, I hated these kinds of icebreaker questions. You always find yourself struggling to figure out the best way to give the person what they're looking for in the answers you give.

"I'm Gareth Watson. As for work, my family owns Watson Ranch, the largest beef cattle ranch and meat distributor. My role is to ensure we keep our cattle happy, healthy, and slaughtered in the most humane manner possible. We need meat to eat, but the experience for the cattle going through the process doesn't need to be minimized because they're animals," I shared.

Her mesmerizing dual-colored eyes grew wide with awe

at my words. It would seem she was a person who agreed with me on this matter, which was genuinely nice to know.

"As for my favorite..." I started then paused and pulled up my pant leg, "... would have to be these boots. I'd be lost if they stopped making them since this has to be my tenth pair."

Shooting off the couch, Bailey-Rose hurried over and grabbed my ankle, pulling it up so she could get a better look. While the woman might be tiny, she was sure stronger than she looked.

"Doc Martens makes work boots?" she gasped. "How cool is that?"

"Not what you would expect from a cattle rancher, is it?" I teased.

It was fun to see how people expected you to be a country bumpkin just because you worked in agriculture. I hated country music. I was more of a heavy metal, hard rock kind of guy. I didn't wear a baseball cap or a cowboy hat either, although I'll admit I was partial to Wrangler jeans, but that's because they were hands down the best.

"The unexpected is always more fascinating," Bailey-Rose answered as she perched on the sofa next to me. "Now, what I want to know is if your dislike is as equally unexpected?"

That had me frowning as I thought about what I disliked. Telling her something like I hated raw onion or the way people sniffle incessantly was stupid. She was asking this question to get to know who I was. If I answered her with the most truthful fact, I wasn't sure how she would react.

"I don't think this will be unexpected, but it is the one thing I can't stand. My dislike, as you called it, would have to be when you give a warning or rule for the person's safety, and it's disregarded. Everything about my job is to ensure humans and animals have the safest environment to work and live in. When I create a rule or post a warning which is ignored, causing someone to end up hurt has to be my biggest dislike," I shared.

Bailey-Rose cocked her head to the side, causing some hair to fall into her face. Without a second thought, I reached out and tucked it behind her ear, letting my finger trail along her neck's soft, smooth skin. A hum of pleasure emanated from her, making me smile to see my touch was welcome.

"Gareth, that was definitely an unexpected answer," Bailey-Rose commented. "I assumed you'd go for the easy choice and pick a food. Yet you chose to give me a rather personal response which I greatly respect and value. Were you underestimated a lot as a kid?"

Startled by the question, I blinked at her a few times. "Why would you ask that?"

"I don't mean this to sound creepy, but I tend to study people. Each person has a different way they move, act, or express themselves. Learning to see these nuances is what gives life to my paintings," she explained. "I feel like you're used to people assuming one thing about you when you're rather the opposite. You were so shocked that I enjoyed your innate contradictions to the labels people would put on you, so I took a guess."

Part of me didn't know how to feel about this woman seeing me so clearly after having just met her. While another side found it liberating not to be forced into a box I didn't want to be in.

"I have two older brothers who run our family business who match the label of rancher to a T. When it came to me..." I shrugged, "... I don't know if it's because I'm the youngest, but I wanted to forge my own path. I have a master's degree in ethics and sustainability, which is the opposite of what people would think of someone in the cattle business. However, my whole goal has been to ensure our company does the best it can for the product we produce and, on the same hand, the people who consume it."

To have Bailey-Rose's full attention focused on me as I spoke with an authentic interest in what I was saying made it hard to concentrate. All I wanted to do was wrap my arms around her and snuggle her close as I breathed in her sweet scent. It was like my Alpha brain hadn't learned anything from what happened moments earlier. I needed to take this slow and learn what she could handle safely before just throwing caution to the wind.

"I think that's rather inspiring," Bailey-Rose shared, reaching out to take my hand. "You have pride in what you do, and it's a noble cause people don't think about but should. Thank you for sharing that with me. I feel like I can see the type of man you are."

"Is it a man you think you'll be fine having in your life forever?" I asked before I could stop the words from coming out of my mouth.

Why the fuck would I ask her that? God, put the damn woman on the spot, asshole.

"Gareth, we're scent-bonded, meaning we were made for each other," Bailey-Rose stated like that should be all the response I needed.

Once more, my body betrayed me as I wrapped her up in a hug. My family had never thought less of me or given me any reason to feel like I didn't measure up to my brothers. Yet I sometimes struggled with being the odd man out and accepting that's okay. Now here I was with my scent-bonded Omega, wondering if she'd think I was enough, only for Bailey-Rose to cut through the bullshit and say it like it is.

"I'll be honest, I didn't really believe it when people said shit like that," I murmured into her hair, not really wanting the others to hear me. "But it turns out they might be right."

Bailey-Rose let out a soft giggle as she hugged me back. "I didn't believe it either... seems like we were proven wrong."

Not willing to let her go just yet, I tugged her over to sit on my lap, side saddle, so she could still see the others. "So who gets to go next? I set the bar pretty high with my answers, so let's see what these pack brothers of mine have."

"I pick you," she announced, pointing at Vili.

The man practically bounced in his seat, so excited to be chosen next. "Oh yah, I so happy to be picked next by our pretty lady. My name is Vili Rantala, and I from Numoland. Three years ago, my family decided to expand business to Preidon and put me in charge."

Out of all my packmates, Vili was the one who was perfect for Bailey-Rose. He was like a living teddy bear full of joy, boundless energy, and could always make you smile. Vili was also the only one of us who didn't have any siblings. Which made it even more impressive that his family sent him to another country to run this branch of their business, knowing he would be looking for a pack. I've heard him talk to his parents on the phone or through video calls, but for one reason or another, we were never introduced to them.

"What kind of business?" Bailey-Rose asked as she adjusted herself in my lap to rest her head on my shoulder.

Was she tired? Were all of us being here too much for her? Should I make her rest? I had to snap myself out of the spiral I was clearly going down as my Alpha nature demanded I ensure our Omega was taken care of. I had to remind myself that Bailey-Rose has been living with this condition her whole life, so if she needed a break or to rest, she would tell us, right?

"We are in business of jewelry," Vili answered. "My family owns Silveda, a high-end jewelry company that specializes in one-of-a-kind pieces. You see, we make all things by hand, no automated machines do work which means no two pieces are same. It is one thing I love about my job, gifting people with something that make them feel special."

"Ooh... so that's why you asked about my monitor," Bailey-Rose commented, connecting the dots.

"Yes, I make you something special," Vili assured her. "No pretty lady of mine can wear something so hideous. It would make me cry to see it on you."

I was a little worried she might take offense to that, but Bailey-Rose just smiled. "I would love to wear something you've made for me."

Vili's smile was blinding at her answer as he adjusted his glasses. "It be perfect, just like you."

"Well, that covers the things he likes and doesn't like, wouldn't you say?" Warrick pointed out, making me roll my eyes, knowing he was hoping she would ask him next.

If Vili was a teddy bear, then Warrick was a damn puppy. He loved making everyone laugh and liked to be around people all the time, soaking up the energy they gave off. Warrick was the life of the party, unlike me who enjoyed a quiet night with the guys. Anytime something new and interesting popped up in the city, he'd try to drag us along to experience it with him. I'll hand it to the man, though, he knew how to run a business and made a damn fine cocktail.

"Let me guess, you have your answers all thought out and want to go next," I teased, my voice dry with sarcasm.

I snorted as Warrick shot dual finger guns at me with a wink. "You guessed it. So what do you think, little cherub, can I go next?"

I cringed at the pet name, but it made Bailey-Rose laugh, so I didn't make fun of him for it. However, if he thought that was going to stick, I was going to have to nip that in the bud.

"Cherub?" Ulysses commented with a raised brow.

Warrick scowled. "I was testing it out, okay. Sometimes you don't know how something is going to sound until you say it out loud. Clearly, that wasn't the right choice, but we didn't know until I tried."

"Whatever you say," Ulysses mumbled.

I knew Ulysses was a good guy and a perfect fit to our pack, but there was something to be said for the fact the rest of us have spent way more time together. The man had no idea the strange rabbit holes that Warrick would take us down. Some of them had us laughing so hard we nearly pissed ourselves, while others made me wonder how hard it would be to smother Warrick in his sleep.

"Guys, enough," Yun-Sun said in his soft, commanding voice. "Sweetheart, who would you like to hear from next? This is your moment to get to know us how you feel most comfortable."

In our world, there are Alphas and then there are *Alphas*. In our pack, we had two of the latter—Ulysses and Yun-Sun. While Ulysses had a commanding presence that made you stand at attention, Yun-Sun was one of those Alphas who didn't need to do or say a thing to let you know they were in charge. Yet when he opened his mouth to speak his mind about something, *everyone* shut up and listened.

Bailey-Rose tilted her head back and looked at me. "Who should I pick? I don't want either of them to be offended that they were last."

Why in the hell she was asking me, I had no fucking clue. Sure, I could be a blunt glass-half-empty kind of guy who always had the snappy comeback, but I wasn't the person you went to for people advice.

"No matter what you do, someone will always go last. It's just the nature of taking turns doing something," I reasoned. "None of us will think badly of you no matter which of them you pick to share next."

She frowned at my answer, making a little wrinkle appear on her forehead. I worried that my answer upset her, so my solution was to press a kiss to that damn adorable wrinkle in hopes it would distract her. When I looked at her face pulling back from the kiss, her eyes were wide, and her cheeks were redder than they had been a moment ago. My gaze fell to her lips as she nibbled on the lower one, making me wonder what it would be like to kiss those glossy lips.

One of the guys cleared their throat loudly, snapping me out of that thought process. I had to shift how I was sitting slightly to hide the boner that sprung to life at the mere notion of kissing her. I sheepishly grinned at the others, knowing they guessed where my thoughts had been heading. *Fuck, Warrick was right—she was so goddamn cute.*

"Um, right," Bailey-Rose stammered. "Warrick, why don't you go next since you're so excited."

"Yesss," Warrick cheered, nearly jumping out of his seat. "Ah, sorry, sorry, didn't mean to get that excited. I promise I'm not so volatile, but when something monumental comes along, I have a hard time keeping my shit together." Warrick flinched at the swear word, quickly looking between Bailey-

Rose and Ulysses. "Oh fuck, I didn't mean to swear. Goddammit, I did it again."

Warrick had gone from manic, playful puppy to sad, dejected puppy in all of five seconds. Bailey-Rose pulled out of my arms and sat next to Warrick, who looked like he wanted to crawl into a hole and forget he existed.

"Hey, it's no big deal," Bailey-Rose soothed, grasping a hand and pulling it away from his face. "I don't give a shit if you swear as long as it's never at me. Trust me, I look all cute and harmless, but just ask Ulysses what it's like when I'm mad. No one wants to deal with that, believe me."

The look of horror on Warrick's face was priceless, but it expressed how all of us were feeling at her comment. "Why the hell would I ever swear at you? God, I think I would sooner kick a puppy than speak to you like that."

"Then it looks like we won't have any problems. So cuss away, my friend... it won't bother me one bit," she assured him.

Warrick looked less panicked about the situation, but I still don't think he believed her that it wasn't a big deal. Can't say I blame him. None of us have cussed or used vulgar language since she walked into the room. Well, scratch that. I might have when I thought she was dying from something I did, but still, it fit the situation. Whether we realized it or not, it seems our little Omega was bringing out the gentlemen in us.

BAILEY-ROSE

id these guys seriously think I would be offended by a little swearing? Had they forgotten I grew up with two brothers who fought daily? I get that I'm perceived as some Hello Kitty character, but I've also lived in the real world just like them. It was rather adorable when Warrick got so flustered, though. It made me realize I wasn't the only nervous one here.

Warrick shifted in his seat and cleared his throat as he ran a hand through his stylish dark-brown hair. "If you say so, little dumpling."

Gareth snorted this time at the pet name while Lysse rolled his eyes. I didn't mind that one, but the others were right. Little cherub wasn't something I wanted to be called. For now, I was more intrigued to see how many different nicknames he'd come up with. They all seemed rather uncommon or hilariously cliché.

"As I mentioned earlier, I'm Warrick, Warrick Shaw, and it's a delight to discover I'm one of your scent-mates," he said, placing his hand over his heart and bowing to me. "I'm the proud owner of the bar called The Fat Mule. It's only been open for roughly half a year, but my family has been in the hospitality and restaurant industry forever. If you've ever heard of the Shaw Group, that's my parents."

I could feel my eyes widen at that bit of information. The Shaw Group was a name everyone in the upper crust of society has heard of. They own some of the most exclusive hotels, resorts, and restaurants in all of Preidon.

"Holy shit," I blurted as I gawked at him.

Warrick snickered, shaking his head. "Ah hell, even when you swear, it's the cutest thing ever."

My cheeks burned as I blushed, ducking my head so he didn't see how much his words affected me. Other than my family, I wasn't used to other people showering me with so many compliments and sweet words, and it was a little overwhelming. Most of the time, I was too shy for people to notice me unless they knew who my family was. Then they wanted to be my friend just to use it as clout, not actually having any actual interest in me.

A hand cupped my chin, and I was swept up in the scent of cinnamon-candied pecans that made me think of the fall festival we have in town. Gently, the hand urged me to look up so I met Warrick's citrine gaze. It was the first time I'd seen them so serious as he studied my face, but once he deemed nothing was wrong, he gave me a playful grin. "Seems our Care Bear doesn't know what to do with compliments, hmm?"

I just shrugged and bit my lower lip, having no idea what to even say to that because it was one hundred percent true.

"Allow me to warn you that you'll have to adjust because I can guarantee all of us will be showering those on you," Warrick informed me. "Seriously, though, is it that uncommon for people not to notice how perfect you are?"

I know he meant it as a compliment, but the sting of my reality and experiences were quite the opposite. Pulling out of his grip, I turned away as I clenched my hands. "I'm far from perfect," I whispered. "There are many things I can't do or experience because of my condition. No one wants to invite the girl who can't even drink or dance to go party with them."

"Well, that's short-sighted of them," Warrick scoffed.

"Not really," I countered. "All I'd do is hold them back from having fun or make them feel guilty for leaving me behind at the table so they can go dance."

A low growl emanated from Warrick as he grabbed my hips and pulled me onto his lap so I straddled his legs. My hand shot out to keep from falling forward into his chest with the abrupt movement, but as his scent hit my nose, all I wanted was to be wrapped up in his arms like Yun-Sun had done when I climbed into his lap. Instead, Warrick cupped my face in a firm grip, forcing me to stare directly into his face.

"Bailey-Rose, I know we just met, but this is the one warning you get from me. If I hear you ever speaking down about yourself again, I'll spank you hard enough that the sting of it is imprinted on your brain forever," Warrick warned. "Fuck everyone who made you believe that bullshit so completely that you just argue with me to prove them right."

Stunned, I just sat there. *Was he right? Did I defend them?* I started to argue but stopped, replayed what I said to him, and realized he was right.

"So what that you can't drink? There is more to life than getting shitfaced and forgetting how you made an ass out of yourself while you were drunk. Trust me when I say those people aren't having as much fun as you think they are," Warrick continued. "As for the dancing, there are hundreds of different styles we can try until we find one your heart can handle. Plus, now that you're a matched Omega, the only people whose opinions should matter are ours and your family's. And, because I can't hold back after looking at your perfect face, I'm going to kiss you if you'll let me."

I gave an approving squeak, unable to actually form words at how he'd gone from a fun-loving goofball to possessive Alpha at the flip of a switch. Warrick slowly closed the gap between us, giving me time to change my mind. Clearly, he couldn't see the cheering and waving pom poms going on at the prospect of this sexy Alpha kissing me.

The moment his lips touched mine, it felt like fireworks were going off in my brain. How many movies and books have I read where they describe this very moment? Too many, but fuck, if this wasn't everything I ever imagined and craved in my life. My hands fisted his shirt as I sank against him, wanting to feel as much of him as I could pressed against me. A need I'd never felt before unfurled in the pit of my stomach, making me whine at the strange and wonderful sensation.

Warrick kept the kiss rather tame, too tame for my liking if I'm being honest. He held me tight as he pressed his lips to mine again and again before moving to cover every inch of my face in a flurry of kisses. It took a moment for my brain to register that he was speaking as he peppered my skin with affection.

"You are perfect. You are mine. Your skin smells like summer and sunshine. I'm the luckiest Alpha in the world to have you," Warrick murmured into my ear before kissing just below it and pulling back to meet my gaze. "I don't even have to question it. The thing I know I'll love more than anything in the world has to be you. Equally, the thing that I hate is anyone who dares to make you ever doubt how exceptional you are. So to combat that, I'm going to make it my life's mission to remind you each and every day how I see you."

Tears pooled in my eyes. There was nothing I could do to stop it, not when it felt like he was stitching back together my broken heart one word and kiss at a time. *Could it be that I've been blind to how I've allowed others to put me in a box and make me believe I wasn't worthy of this kind of love?* Warrick didn't try to stop me from crying. He merely cuddled me close and began to purr, rocking slightly from side to side, allowing me to feel the emotions I was going through.

I don't know how long I stayed there or when the tears stopped falling, but I had no interest in moving from where I was. Like when the others held me, I felt safe, warm, and cherished. In an odd way, I felt like a battery had been left empty and was now starting to recharge, showing me how drained I'd been this whole time.

Another hand ran down my back. "Hey, Rosie, can you drink this for me?"

With Warrick's help, I sat up and found Lysse with a glass. I knew by the pink hue that it had my electrolyte powder in it. Being locked away in my room eating junk food and drinking primarily tea and hot chocolate, this was probably a smart call. I struggled to keep my electrolytes in balance on a good day, but with all the crying, bad food, and excitement going on, I was probably horribly dehydrated.

Taking the glass, I spotted Eli leaning casually in the doorway, watching. I was proud of him for leaving me alone with the guys after my spell when normally he wouldn't have let me out of his sight. There was no doubt in my mind he was the one who made the drink and brought it over but was kind enough to let my newly-matched Alphas take care of me.

My oldest brother was one of the most amazing people I knew, and I wanted nothing more than for him to find his own happiness. Maybe now that I'd soon be out of the house and with my pack, he could focus on himself. I mouthed my thanks, and he nodded but didn't budge. Letting out a sigh, I rolled my eyes and lifted the glass to my lips, knowing he wouldn't leave until I drank the whole damn thing.

Finished, Lysse took it from me and sat on the coffee table watching me carefully. "I think it might be best if we let you rest."

"What? Why?" I asked even as I sank back against Warrick. "I'm good. Besides, Yun-Sun hasn't had a chance to share."

"Sweetheart, we don't need to accomplish everything in one day when we have the rest of our lives together," Yun-Sun pointed out. "It's clear you're tired, a lot has happened, and none of us want you to overdo it."

I scowled at the man, feeling like a little kid who's being told to go to bed when there's a party going on. "I think I know what I can handle."

He gave me a patient look, but a smirk was tugging at his lips. "Of that, I have no doubt, sweetheart. Would you humor me and take a moment, close your eyes, and *really* listen to your body? If you're absolutely confident you don't need to take a break, then I won't say another word."

It was hard to argue with someone when they made an infuriatingly reasonable request. Letting out a heavy sigh, I closed my eyes and took a few deep breaths.

"Good, now I want you to start at the very top of your head and work your way down, taking stock of how your body is feeling," Yun-Sun directed, his voice soothing.

With my eyes closed, I realized my ear was resting over Warrick's heart, and I got lost in its steady, solid sound. Moments later, it felt like I was being carried somewhere, but that didn't make sense. I hadn't figured out how my body was feeling yet.

"Good thing I had the staff come in straight away to clean in here." I heard Eli say, his deep voice distracting me from what I was doing. "The sheets have been changed as well, so you can settle her in there."

"How did she not realize how tired she was?" Gareth asked. "Should we be worried?"

"No, I'm amazed she lasted as long as she did after her episode. Normally, that would have worn her out to the point she'd be in bed until the next day," Eli commented. "I think she was so worried about you guys freaking out, it gave her the determination to ensure you were all right."

"Our pretty lady has big heart," Vili added. "This we need to keep eyes on."

A sigh escaped me as I was placed in my bed, sinking into the puffy mattress topper that made it feel like a cloud. Immediately, I reached out, randomly searching for Pearl. I couldn't ever relax if I didn't have her close. Knowing she was with me told me I was safe, where I should be, and everything would be all right.

Instead of finding Pearl, I grasped someone's arm. When I dragged it close, I was once more transported to that summer morning baking muffins with my mother. Wrapping my arms around the limb, I nuzzled my cheek against it and started to purr—something I never knew I could do.

"Do you hear that?" Yun-Sun asked, his voice soft as if worried he would wake me. "Did you know Omegas could do that?"

"No."

"So goddamn fucking cute."

"Not puppy, our pretty lady kitten."

"How is that possible?"

They all said, talking over one another in excited voices, making me grumpy enough to stop purring and exchange it for disgruntled grunts.

"Shh, sweetheart," Yun-Sun soothed, stroking a hand over my head. "Just sleep. Ignore everything else and be at peace."

His voice was like melting butter on chocolate chip pancakes easing my irritation until I resumed purring. While I was comfortable, I still felt like I was missing something, so I rolled over and curled myself in the crook of Yun-Sun's body. This was better but not quite right.

"What do you need, Rosie?" Lysse asked as his finger stroked my cheek.

I cracked open an eye and found we were in my bedroom. Somewhere in my brain, I already knew this but hadn't accepted the fact I'd fallen asleep and lost to Yun-Sun's challenge. Ulysses sat on the edge of my bed with Pearl in his lap, ready to hand her over since he knew she was essential to my life. Yet when I looked at my beloved octopus, all I could think of was how pissed I was she was on his lap and not mine. That took me by surprise. Never had anyone or anything in my life replaced my need for Pearl.

Feeling confused, tired, and unable to answer his simple fucking question, I let out a loud, frustrated whine. It was natural for Omegas to whine when they were overwhelmed, sad, or upset. It was akin to babies crying as a means of communication. Omegas were highly sensitive to emotions —theirs and others. So when we became, for all intents and purposes, paralyzed by the emotional overstimulation, we whined, triggering any Alpha nearby to instantly tend to the distressed Omega. From what I've heard, when the Omega is scent matched, their whines demand attention from their

Alphas. Betas still feel the urge to be of help, but for Alphas, it's an undeniable instinct.

I got to witness this as all five of my Alphas were instantly on my bed, forming a circle around me. Warrick was stretched out along the headboard, nuzzling his face into my hair, Lysse held my hand, Vili had my feet in his lap using his thumbs to massage one, and Gareth's hand rested on my hip. Yun-Sun wrapped his other arm around my waist and tucked me tight against him like a perfect big spoon. Finally, the feeling that something wasn't right vanished, and I let out a contented sigh, twining my fingers with Lysse's so he couldn't leave.

"This is what I need," I mumbled, wriggling so my mattress formed around this current position.

Yun-Sun

Never in my life did I believe such a precious gift as Bailey-Rose would appear. Her angelic face, which was so expressive when she was awake, looked so peaceful as she drooled on my arm. It didn't matter that it went numb an hour ago or that I was still fully dressed, only having removed my shoes at the door when I came in. Thankfully, I'd taken off my suit jacket earlier as we talked, or I would have been sweltering. Our little Omega was a furnace, but I would let her burn me alive just to hold her for a moment longer.

A wave of possessiveness washed over me when the bedroom door opened, and I curled around her. When I saw it was the others who had gone to get us food, I relaxed, taking a moment to indulge myself and bury my nose in the crook of her neck. Bailey-Rose was aptly named for her sweet floral scent that reminded me of summers at our beach house. The whole back porch was surrounded by rose bushes, my mother's favorite flower. It had been ages since I last thought about that place, but only happy memories existed in that home.

"Do you think if one of us slides in to replace you, she'll let go?" Gareth asked, looking between Ulysses and me.

"Rosie's always been a cuddle monster, but this is a little extreme." Ulysses chuckled. "Normally, it was getting her to let go of Pearl, which, even dead to the world, was a struggle. Our girl has learned to sleep through pretty much anything, having spent most of her childhood in and out of the hospital."

It broke my heart even to imagine what that must have been like for her growing up. While I envied Ulysses for knowing her as a childhood friend, I was eternally grateful that one of us knew what she'd gone through.

"I'm fine to stay here," I shared, kissing the back of Bailey-Rose's neck.

The others just gave me a knowing look but didn't argue. Ulysses managed to switch her hold from him to her stuffed octopus which I was told she always slept with. Warrick had gone back to the house and gotten clothes for us since it looked like we wouldn't be leaving here tonight. While I would like to get into relaxed clothing, the sacrifice of leaving my sweet Omega wasn't worth it.

Gareth handed me half a sandwich that made my stomach rumble with excitement. "So I think it's safe to say we need to ask for courting leave," he commented. "I doubt any of us are going to be of use for the next few days, and it seems Bailey-Rose is already noticing the draw to be close to us."

"Remind me how long we get?" Warrick asked. "I know the Scent Matchers gave us a whole book on this stuff, but for the life of me, I can't remember any of it."

"Two weeks," Ulysses answered. "We get two weeks for initial courting and a month after bonding. Do any of you have something in the next two weeks that would prevent us from taking our leave?"

I shook my head. "No, I finished up on my case yesterday. The others I have on my schedule aren't pressing, and the court dates are months away."

"Glad to see they put a priority on human rights and

disabilities," Gareth muttered. "Have you told your dad yet about Bailey?"

"When exactly would I have had time to have that lengthy conversation?" I asked, raising a brow and then looking down at Bailey-Rose.

Gareth mumbled something under his breath and wandered around the room, looking at the various paintings on the wall. The guys knew my father and I weren't on speaking terms since I chose to be part of this pack. It had been arranged for me to join another group of powerful, affluent men in a sort of old-world advantageous corporate marriage. Not only had I refused to be part of this pack my father built with his buddies, I walked away from the chance of being a partner in his law firm. To add salt to an already angry wound, I chose to work as a public defender.

Unlike my father, I didn't become a lawyer to make a profit. I chose this life to help those who everyone turned their noses up at. The disabled, immigrants, and the poor were equally deserving of my help as those who could pay a million-dollar retainer fee. I used my time in law school to learn all I could to go toe to toe with companies like my father's. They were the giants that would squash the little guy with the seemingly endless supply of money and staff. The trouble is when the opposition knows all your tactics, they don't work as well.

However, when I did gather the mental capacity to call my father about Bailey-Rose, the only thing he would care about was her last name. Everyone knew the Thatchers. Infinery Petroleum was a massive company that had a choke hold on many other industries. Interestingly enough, my father had no idea I was now tied not only to the Thatchers but the Fords as well who owned the other half of Infinery.

Not to mention the Shaws through Warrick, even though his relationship with his parents was as strained as mine.

None of that mattered to me. I found the family I wanted and a job I loved which has given me the inner peace I lacked. Now to add the cherry on top of the perfect life I live was Bailey-Rose. What more could I possibly want out of life?

"Okay, so we all agree to take our courting leave, but that means we need to figure out what the fuck it means to court our Omega," Warrick pointed out, pulling me back to the present moment. "Why do we even need to court her? It's obvious how strong the connection is between all of us."

Vili shocked me by smacking Warrick upside the head. "How dare you say such thing."

Our cheerful Numolandian was never one to get upset about things. He was the one we could always count on to take the worst situation in stride with a smile, finding the silver lining. Clearly, when it came to our Omega, the rules had changed.

"She deserves it all," Vili announced. "To be wooed, dazzled, showered with gifts, and treated like a princess. No, I will not hear you speak about not courting."

Warrick rubbed the back of his head, looking a little dazed and utterly confused at the outburst. "Hey, chill, V. I didn't say we shouldn't court her, I just wasn't sure what that looked like. Most things I remember about courting in the books was building the connection between the pack and their new Omega. Seeing as she wouldn't let us leave tonight, I'd say we're well ahead in that department."

"I see what you're saying, but just because we connect through scent does not mean she will be happy. Our precious flower must be comfortable in our home, delighted with the nest which we do not have, and build trust with us as her Alphas. This take time, you no rush something so important," Vili explained.

As if a lightbulb of understanding flicked on in Warrick's head, his eyes widened, and he nodded. "Ooooh. Now I get it. This isn't about making sure we're the right match for her and vice versa, it's about figuring out how to build a life together."

"*Exakt*," Vili cheered.

The outburst caused Bailey-Rose to make the most adorable sleepy grumbles as she released my arm and rolled over. With Pearl in her grasp, she curled around the stuffed octopus like an anaconda burrowing into the pillows. Free, I shifted away slightly, tucking a soft lavender blanket around her, ignoring the pain of my arm coming back to life. Once I was sure she would stay asleep, I slipped off the bed.

"I sorry," Vili apologized in a low whisper. "Sometimes my head forgets, and the words rush out before I even think."

Clapping him on the back, I gave him a reassuring smile. "It's fine. I wasn't willing to make her move and risk waking her up, but I really wanted to get out of these clothes."

Not a moment later, Ulysses was handing me my clothes and pointing. "Her bathroom is through there."

I took my time, splashing water on my face and using the facilities as my bladder screamed at me now that I was standing. Once refreshed and relaxed, I joined the others in her sitting area where the food was located.

"Vili made a good point," Ulysses said, breaking the comfortable silence. "We don't have the nest set up, but in a way, I feel like that is a good thing. Rosie is one Omega I know who's as particular as hell about how her space is set up. Setting up the nest together might be a good group bonding activity."

Warrick's hand shot up like a child in a classroom. We all just looked at him for a moment, but when it was clear he wouldn't speak unless we called on him, Gareth took pity on the man.

"Yes, Warrick, I see that hand. Did you have something to add?" Gareth teased.

The raised hand turned quickly into flipping Gareth off as Warrick lowered the limb. "As a matter of fact, I do. I think the group idea is great, Lys, but how do we all feel about taking Bailey-Rose out on individual dates?"

We thought that over for a moment, but I didn't need to think about it all that much. To me, it made perfect sense. Bailey-Rose needed time to get to know each of us as a person and as a pack. It would also be a great way to show her things that made us individuals.

"I'm all for it," I stated.

Vili nodded excitedly. "Yes, I love this plan. I have many ideas that most of you would hate, but maybe she like, yah?"

"What if our idea means taking her out of the city and would need to stay overnight?" Gareth asked. "Do we all go?"

That question had me scratching my jaw as I turned over all the different angles of that question. "I think that depends on Bailey-Rose," I reasoned. "If she doesn't want to be away from us that long since the codependency is the worst during the time before bonding, it might be best for us to come. However, I believe we're all adult enough to give you two space and entertain ourselves."

Everyone added their agreement to what I'd just said, which seemed to relieve Gareth. "Great, because I was thinking of taking her out to the original Watson Ranch for a day or two."

"Hey, two birds, one stone. None of us have been out

there either," Ulysses added with a grin. "Then we can meet your grandmother you talk about all the time and see where you grew up."

"I've been meaning to have you guys come out one weekend, but it just never seemed to work out. Oh, and trust me when I say, once you've tasted my grannie's cooking, you'll never want to leave," Gareth warned as he sat back in his seat with a proud smile.

"Then it's settled. Tomorrow we will ask for our leave so we can focus all our attention on Bailey-Rose for the next two weeks," I confirmed then proceeded to dig into the plate of food waiting in my lap.

BAILEY-ROSE

My dreams were filled with visions of the most perfect pack of Alphas coming to rescue me from the cursed tower I'd been locked away in. They whispered sweet words as they lovingly stroked my skin, making me believe it might almost be real. The craziest part of it all was Ulysses making an appearance and sweeping me off my feet. Together with his packmates, we rode off into the sunset where the happily ever after I'd always wanted waited for me. Now as my stomach grumbled and my bladder screamed at me to get up, I had to admit defeat. No longer could I stay in this magical world. Instead, once again, I'd be forced to face the reality of my life alone, unwanted, and broken.

Rolling onto my back—or should I say attempted to—I ran into something hard and warm. Instantly, arms wrapped around me, and I was submerged into a warm summer afternoon sitting on the patio with a glass of cool lemon sweet tea. Even more shocking is when the perfect summer moment started to purr. Snapping my eyes open, I found my cheek plastered to someone's bare chest.

Holy shit, it wasn't a dream!

The reality of what occurred yesterday came crashing back into my brain. Ulysses had been in my room, there was a pack of Alphas who were my scent matches, and I had a cardiac episode in front of them.

Wait... why was one of the Alphas in my bed?

Movement like someone else was stirring in my bed told me there might not just be one of them here with me. Popping up like a meerkat searching for danger, I glanced around my room, finding not one or two of them but four. Gareth was holding me, Warrick was to my back, and Vili was sprawled like a starfish on the foot of the bed. I spotted Yun-Sun sleeping on my sofa but didn't see Lysse. As if thinking of him was all it took to make him appear, the bathroom door opened. Out walked the man I'd been pining after for years, wearing only a pair of boxers.

Fearing he'd see me gawking at him with my eyes about to bug out of my head, I collapsed onto the bed. Unfortunately for Gareth, I forgot he was between the mattress and me. A grunt burst from him as I practically body-slammed into him, causing Ulysses to notice that not only was I awake, I'd just assaulted his packmate.

"Fuck, baby girl, you're stronger than you look," Gareth grumbled as he peered at me with sleepy eyes. "We need to work on a better plan than a full-body tackle if you need to get up."

"Sorry," I squeaked. "I got a little disorientated having people in my bed. I panicked."

Gareth nuzzled my hair and kissed my head before releasing me. "That's fair. We didn't really discuss sleeping over before you passed out."

I was going to ask him why they stayed, but hands scooped me up and lifted me out of the bed. The tang of orange quickly followed by the warmth of milk chocolate told me it was Lysse who decided to extract me from my nest. His skin was silky to the touch which I didn't think would be possible with how much time he spent outside. Yet everywhere I let my fingers wander over his chest and shoulder was incredibly smooth. Realizing what I was doing, I snatched my hand back, clasping it to my chest like I'd been caught doing something wrong.

Lysse chuckled and turned on the bathroom lights before setting me on the tile floor. "There's no need to be shy, Rosie. What's mine is yours to do with as you please."

Struck dumb as my tongue became glued to the roof of my mouth, I just stared at him. How my eyes stayed in my head, I'll never know, but go me for not making this weirder than it already was. He just stood there watching me with such an intense expression that made me want to melt, so I gave him two thumbs-up. "Cool beans," I blurted.

Horrified at what I'd just done, I darted for the door that led to the toilet and slammed it behind me. Feeling like I might just throw up due to my embarrassment, I slid to the floor and dropped my head to my knees.

"Oh God," I groaned. "Could I be even more of an idiot?"

A knock sounded on the door. "Rosie, you good?"

"Oh yeah, doing super-duper," I answered, grabbing the safety bar and hauling myself up. "Be out in a sec."

His snort of laughter told me the dripping sarcasm had come across loud and clear. Pulling myself together, I did my business and marched out ready to face Ulysses head-on, but he wasn't there. Apparently, he was fine letting me be alone in the bathroom after sounding like a deranged idiot, but not when my heart monitor went off. Taking advantage of the alone time, I brushed my teeth, but looking in the mirror, I noticed there was a slight mark on my face telling me I'd drooled in my sleep.

Great, now not only did I act like a moron as I tried to give a sleeping person the Heimlich maneuver, I probably slobbered all over them too. God, I've been awake for all of five minutes, and it's already a disaster of a day. Glancing at the clock, I noticed it was six thirty in the morning, causing my jaw to drop in shock. Never have I claimed to be a morning person. In fact, it went against everything I stood for to be awake right now.

What time had I fallen asleep to feel so well-rested? You know what, I don't want to know the answer to that. It will only make me upset since I'm pretty sure I didn't have dinner. No wonder I was so hungry.

As I looked in the mirror again, I noticed I was still in my dress and shorts from last night. I should probably be relieved by that, but it was simply another acknowledgment of my epic fail of an introduction to these men I was supposed to spend my life with. Cracking open the door, I peered into my bedroom, trying to take stock of what was happening before I entered.

"Rosie, what exactly are you doing?" Lysse asked as he moved from where he'd been standing.

Okay, so he didn't really leave like I thought. He just knew I'd kick him out if he tried to creep in while I was in the bathroom. Clearly, I was going to need to put in some ground rules if this was going to become a regular occurrence. I cleared my throat, stood tall, and tried not to show that I was being weirder than normal.

"Nothing... just not used to having men I'm not related to in my bedroom," I answered, opening the door fully.

Ulysses raised a brow as he took a step forward, causing me to back up a step. "Does that mean you think of me as someone you're related to?"

"What?" I asked, not following his train of thought as I continued to back up while he advanced one step at a time. My retreat was halted when I bumped into the wall, allowing Lysse to cage me in with his broad body.

He reached out and gently wrapped a hand around my throat, stroking his thumb over my pulse, making me shiver.

"You said you weren't used to people you weren't related to being in your room."

It was hard to process what he was saying as his scent, touch, and the sight of his bare skin left me in a daze. Then the bastard had the audacity to lean in and whisper in my ear with an edge to his voice that made me want to melt.

"Now, Rosie," he continued, his hot breath on my neck. "I distinctly remember being in this room. With you as you painted while your brother and I read comic books. So does that mean you view me the same as your brother?"

Like hell, I viewed him the same as Crew.

"N-no," I stammered. "You are definitely not like my brother."

"Good..." Ulysses pressed a kiss just below my ear, "... because the intentions I have toward you are anything but brotherly."

My chest tightened as my heart rate sped up, and my breathing became more rapid. I tried to calm myself down since the last thing I wanted was for my monitor to go off and ruin the moment. Ulysses gazed down at me with a heat in his gaze that I'd dared to dream about as I scratched an itch. I might not be able to have a heat, but that didn't mean I couldn't get horny. Sex was great, but it didn't happen often for me, so I was left to tend to my own needs.

Before I could think better of it, my hand connected with Ulysses' chest, fingers splayed wide to touch as much of him as I could. A possessive sound erupted out of the Alpha before me as he stepped closer, pressing me between him and the wall. Lysses' hand gripped my hips and lifted me until we were at eye level. Wrapping my legs around his waist to secure myself to his body, I used one hand to free his hair from its loose bun. It fell to his shoulders in a thick sheet of blond silk that would make any woman jealous. Leaning in, I caressed my cheek along his neck. I wanted his scent on my body, proving I was his while leaving mine on him marking him as taken.

"Rosie," Ulysses bit out. "You are making it rather challenging to be a gentleman."

"Hmm," I hummed, then nipped at his ear. "Since when have you ever been a gentleman around me?"

That comment seemed to be what made Lysse snap. A hand fisted the hair at the base of my neck and pulled, forcing me to look up at him. Without a second thought, his lips were on mine as our bodies melded together. I could feel his other hand on my ass, gripping it so tightly I wondered if he might leave a bruise. My fingers sank into his hair to make sure he wouldn't pull away from me.

Feelings of need welled up within me like I'd never experienced before as I ground my pussy against his abs. Forget a six-pack, this Alpha of mine had an eight-pack, and I planned to use it to my advantage. With a nip on my lower lip, Ulysses demanded I allow him to deepen the kiss, and I did so eagerly. My years of pining and watching from a distance were over in this one moment. The universe knew how much I craved this man, and in the most perfect twist of fate, he became mine.

Ulysses moved his hand from my ass to my lower back, changing the angle so my clit had better contact with his skin. Pulling back from the kiss, he tucked my head to his neck and whispered in my ear, "Rosie, I want you to rub that perfect pussy on me. You're going to keep doing it until I tell you to stop."

I let out a shaky breath that sounded more like a whimper as I nodded, unable to speak.

"That's my good girl," Ulysses purred as he rolled his

hips in a way that had me mewling with pleasure. "Now ride me 'til you can't take it anymore."

There was a split second of hesitation as I questioned what the fuck I was even thinking dry humping this man like it was my only purpose in life. Thankfully, that doubt ended the second I felt Ulysses' mouth on my neck, teasing my skin with his teeth. He didn't bite, more like let them drag along my skin, making my pussy pulse with desire.

Fuck, if this is what it was like before we bonded, how much more intense would it get?

My body needed the release he was providing me as I rocked in a steady rhythm against him. However, it wasn't enough. I had too many clothes on to get the friction I needed. A soft whine slipped out as I dug my nails into his skin, desperate to achieve the promised climax.

As if Ulysses knew exactly what I needed, he turned to set me on the counter. Sliding his hands around my ass, he rucked up my dress, tugging it over my head. Next, I let out a surprised yelp as he grabbed the front of my leggings and ripped them open at the crotch. Once he felt enough fabric was out of the way, he wrapped me around him tightly. Instead of pressing me to the wall like before, he laid me out on my bathroom sink counter.

"I thought I could let you have control, but it seems I'm just not a strong enough man for that," Ulysses whispered.

Not having the brain power to follow what he was saying, I wriggled under him, trying to find that friction I'd been teased with. Everything came to a screeching halt when his lips wrapped around my nipple, and he gently tugged at it over my bra. Euphoria swept through my body at the feel of his hard silk-covered cock making contact with my soaking wet pussy. A cry of pleasure burst out of me as the head of his cock collided with my clit. Now this was exactly what I needed to reach the promised land of orgasms.

Ulysses buried his face in my neck, clutching me to him as he thrust against me. At this point, I lost all capacity for reason or giving a fuck we might be heard. All I cared about was what was happening between my legs with a man I'm fairly certain I've loved for a long time. The grunts and heavy breathing coming from Ulysses spurred me on as I reveled, knowing he was enjoying this as much as me.

Then came the moment when I stood on the edge of the cliff, waiting for that last push to fall headlong into pure pleasure. Trying to help, I ground against him as he rutted into me. Ulysses seemed to think my assistance wasn't needed and clamped his teeth on the muscle that ran between my neck and shoulder to hold me still. That was all it took to send me rocketing off the cliff so hard my vision started to blur as my body locked up. Pure joy flooded my body once I climaxed, and a scream of delight soon followed. Lysse roared, leaning back, and hot ropes of cum landed on my stomach. I watched when he gripped the knot at the base of his cock, giving him the sensation of knotting all Alphas craved.

Flopping back on the counter, I couldn't help but smile and giggle. That was the best orgasm I'd ever had, and we hadn't even had sex. God, how much have I been missing out on wasting my time with losers who took pity on the sick, sad Omega no one wanted. The moment abruptly stopped when the bathroom door crashed open, and my other four Alphas tumbled in.

"Oh my God, what happened? Why is she on the counter? Did she faint in the shower?" Warrick asked in rapid succession.

Confused, I slowly sat up, realizing how precarious my

position was, as I almost slid off and crashed to the floor. Vili grabbed my arm to steady me then froze as he stared at my chest. Forgetting I didn't have a shirt on, I looked down as well. There in the fabric of my bra was an outline of where Ulysses' mouth had been and the peak of my nipple right in the center. I flicked my gaze back to Vili's, and a slow smile bloomed on his face.

"Our pretty lady is fine," Vili announced. "Screams of joy, no?"

Heat burned across my face as he helped me stand, and Ulysses offered me a damp washcloth. "You could say that."

Vili let his hand slide down my arm until it gripped my wrist to show me my monitor. It was flashing a warning that my heart rate was too high, but it was still in sleep mode so it didn't make any sound.

"How..." I started to ask, but Vili beat me to the punch by showing me his phone.

"Your eldest brother insisted," he explained. "Was his only rule a good one? This isn't the moment you want them rushing in on."

The mere thought of Eli bursting in here while I was half naked, post orgasm, with cum on my stomach would have been horrifying. "Oh God," I moaned, covering my face with both hands.

"I don't think you want him to show up either," Gareth interjected, a smirk on his face as I peered through my fingers. "Come on, guys, let's give our girl a moment to collect herself now that we know she's okay."

Ulysses took my hands, pulled them away from my face, and dropped a kiss on my lips. "Take all the time you need, Rosie. Crew texted me that two of the guest bedrooms were set up for us to use."

Nodding, I watched them all head out, still mortified I'd

been caught with Lysse. Then again, if I was going to have five Alphas I was matched to, it was only a matter of time before something like this happened. However, not even twelve hours into the relationship might be a record. Hopping off the counter, I grabbed a claw clip, tossed up my hair, and turned on the shower. It took a little effort to wriggle my way out of these torn leggings, but it was a helpful reminder that I hadn't dreamed the whole thing. Of course, the drying, tacky globs of cum on my skin made that pretty clear.

Once clean, awake, and refreshed, I wrapped myself in a bathrobe. My room was empty, but their scents lingered causing me to draw in a deep breath. A wave of sadness flowed over me when I realized I was alone, and fear started to creep around the edges telling me they wouldn't be coming back. It felt so silly to be this upset when I've just met these men. Head hanging, I shuffled my way to the closet and randomly grabbed things off hangers, not caring what they were. Why would it matter? It's not like they were going to stay with me once they realized how much work I was. Better not to get overly attached.

Ha. Who was I kidding? There was no way I could ever be happy if it weren't with them. While it was rare, I'd heard stories of Alphas who turned their backs on the Omega they were scent matched with. It was hell for the Omega. Some never recovered and took their own lives. Others existed as empty shells of a being wandering aimlessly through life, having lost the most important thing to their existence. These Alphas didn't seem the type to leave someone for greener pastures, but that didn't mean all of them would want to build a relationship with me. Yeah, they said all the pretty words yesterday, but meeting your Omega or Alpha for the first time is overwhelming. Instinct took over and swept you away, creating the beginning urges to bond.

Letting out a sigh, I trudged back out, headed right for my bed, and scooped up Pearl. Nuzzling her close, I felt better but not enough to stop me from crawling back into bed. My movements were halted as arms wrapped around my waist, and I was hauled back out of bed.

"Nope, sorry, my little dumpling, but you can't go back to bed. We've got lots to do today," Warrick said as he hoisted me over his shoulder. "Lys warned us that if you were left alone for too long, you'd sneak back into your nest. Good thing I made it in time."

BAILEY-ROSE

To keep from slamming my face against his body, I braced my hands on his back. They slipped with his movement so it was more like I was groping his ass. Warrick didn't seem to mind. If anything, he put a little extra sway to his step to make me grip harder.

"Where are we going?" I asked, trying to keep up with the abrupt commandeering.

"First, we're taking you out for breakfast, then you're going to come over to our home so you can see the place, and after that, I'm not too sure. It won't take us long to think of something, though," Warrick informed me. "I should give you a heads-up, though. Each of us put in for our courting leave, so we'll be around all the time for the next two weeks."

"You did what?" I gasped as Warrick jogged quickly down the stairs. "Why would you take leave when we all live in the same area? Isn't that meant for those who need time to relocate?"

Warrick paused when we got to the bottom of the stairs and set me on my feet. Taking both hands, he squished my cheeks together, giving me fishy lips. "Who could resist a face like this?" he asked with a wide smile. "Look, it's clear that you're at risk of experiencing scent withdrawal, another reason we all stayed last night. We'll take the two weeks and build our relationship to the point you're ready to bond with us or at least comfortable enough to live in our home."

That wasn't the answer I expected him to give me. "Wait," I tried to say, but with my face all squashed up, it came out all slurred. Shoving away his hands, I took a step back, needing to have a clear head for this conversation. "You really want me, even if it means dealing with all the restrictions?"

With a frown on his face, Warrick cocked his head. "What restrictions?"

"Ah..." I started to answer, but then I saw Crew coming down the stairs, and I wasn't going to talk about this in front of him. "Never mind, you said something about going to breakfast?"

Warrick didn't look convinced but let it go as Crew swooped in and hugged me. "Morning, LouLou. I can't believe these guys managed to get you dressed and awake this early."

"Guess it happens when you go to bed before dinner like a grandma," I muttered, struggling to get out of his headlock.

Crew laughed and planted a sloppy kiss on my cheek before letting me go, doing his best to embarrass me. "Aww, my little LouLou is such a grumpy kitty when she's forced to be up early. Oh, because I'm pretty sure none of them will say anything, you might want to have a second look at your choice of clothes. Not sure plaid and checkered print really go together, but you do you, LouLou."

Flipping my brother the bird, I hurried off to the hall bathroom. After I flicked on the light, I saw what he was talking about. I was wearing pink and blue plaid shorts while the top was an oversized peach and white checkered T-shirt with peaches randomly appearing in some of the white squares. I looked like a toddler who was determined to dress herself no matter what it looked like.

"Okay, I seriously need a do-over on this day." I groaned. "How can everything be going so wrong?"

The heat of someone coming up behind me with the added scent of sweet tea warned me that one of my guys was in the bathroom with me. "Baby girl, what exactly do you think has gone wrong so far?"

Lifting my gaze, I looked at him in the bathroom mirror. "Everything."

He leaned against the bathroom wall, arms crossed, watching me. "Yeah, you're gonna need to lay it out for me because this has been one amazing morning for me so far."

"Even after I body slammed into you?" I challenged.

Gareth grinned. "Baby girl, waking up with you in my arms and crawling all over me is not something I'll ever regret. Was the wakeup rather jarring, sure, but you're cute, so I'll let it slide."

"How can you say that after I drooled on you?" I demanded.

"Oh, it wasn't just me. You also left your mark on Yun-Sun," Gareth added.

I tossed my hands in the air and sank to the floor, head in my hands. "God, I'm a disaster."

A moment later, a body slid down next to me and wrapped an arm around my shoulders. "Bailey, I'm gonna need a little insight here because I want to make sure we didn't somehow give you the impression we were expecting a superhuman Omega. Everyone has drooled in their sleep at one point or another. In high school, I played football and got tackled more times than I can count, not to mention kicked or stepped on by cattle. Having you crash into me was like getting hit with a pillow. Okay, your elbow was a little sharp, but there's not even a bruise to show anything happened. So forgive me if I sound like a dick, but I think you're being a little hard on yourself here."

Unsure how to even respond, I rested my head on his shoulder, mulling over his words. "I don't want to cause any more work for people than necessary," I finally admitted. "All my life, the people around me have had to be given a list of things to be aware of, or Crew had to come along to keep an eye on me. It was so hard to make real friends who didn't care about my family name and run at the first sign of how damaged my heart is. After a while, I stopped trying and accepted I would only have my family who would love me no matter what."

"Hmm," Gareth hummed as he nuzzled my head. "Never being an inconvenience is a hard task to achieve. I'm guessing even if I tell you not to worry about it, you won't take that to heart."

"At this point, I feel like it's something I do without even realizing it," I added. "It's like telling someone not to breathe or blink. How do you simply stop doing something you don't even realize you consciously do?"

"I think it's something we will all have to work on together," Gareth reasoned, pressing a kiss to my temple. "Now that I understand how you view things, it will help me to reassure you. Same with the others... we're your Alphas, pack for life. I know it won't happen overnight, but one day you'll learn to trust us when we say we don't see you as anything but perfectly ours."

With a soft sniffle, I wrapped my arms around his neck and hugged him tightly. "How is it possible that you're real? I keep thinking this is a dream, and I'll wake up to find this was all a product of my lonely imagination."

"I'll be real with you, baby girl. I pinch myself constantly to make sure this is really happening. Things aren't going to be perfect all the time... it's just how things work with people. However, when it comes down to it, I know we're all meant to be a family, and I'll do whatever it takes to keep us together," Gareth assured me as he looked me right in the eye. "Now, take a moment and go change into something that makes you feel totally confident and comfortable. When you're done, meet us in the living room, and we'll head out for a fun day with your pack."

Grabbing onto the ounce of bravery I gathered during this conversation, I leaned in and kissed my summertime Alpha. He tasted as sweet as his scent promised with the brightness of lemon making my nose tingle. The soft touch of his hands spanning my back made me feel safe and secure in his hold as our kiss deepened. After a moment, he pulled back his gray-blue eyes, bright with intentions that had me biting my lip.

"Go. Change. Now," Gareth ordered with a stern tone I didn't really believe but wanted to respect.

"Right," I agreed with a jerky nod.

Not so gracefully, I jumped to my feet as my knee got stuck in the fabric of my oversized shirt. Thankfully, Gareth had excellent reflexes catching me, but we both crashed to the floor again. Mortified that I'd turned into a baby giraffe who couldn't even manage to get to her feet, I groaned. However, Gareth started to laugh, and it was so infectious I couldn't help but join in, realizing how ridiculous all this was.

The bathroom door opened, and Warrick popped his head in. "Sorry, I couldn't take it any longer. My FOMO was going crazy. You two good?"

"For all our sakes, I think you should help Bailey to her feet," Gareth suggested.

Needing no other encouragement, Warrick stood before

me, hooked his hands under my armpits, and hoisted me up. Once I was securely on my feet, he released me and offered Gareth a hand, who took it and hauled himself to stand next to me.

"You all right to make it to your room without one of us?" Gareth questioned, suddenly a little unsure by the look he was giving me.

"Don't worry, I can send an SOS signal from my monitor if I need help, but I think I got this," I shared.

Both men looked at me for a moment then Gareth motioned for me to go ahead of them. Feeling cheeky, I blew them a kiss before dashing off toward the stairs. Glancing over my shoulder, they both had a dopey smile as they watched me. That had me grinning like a fool that little old me could have an effect on them like that.

Bursting into my room, I found Eli sitting on my bed, head in his hands. It brought me to an abrupt halt. "Elee?"

Hearing me, his head shot up, and I saw his eyes glassy with tears. "B, I thought you were heading out for breakfast?"

"I decided to change, knowing we'd be in public," I offered, motioning to my clashing clothes as I walked over. Dropping to my knees, I rested my hands on my big brother's knees. "What's wrong?"

He gave me his best attempt at a smile, but it didn't meet his eyes as he stroked a hand over my head. "Nothing, B, nothing's wrong. In fact, you might say things are amazing. My precious baby sister found her pack. Now she's finally going to have all the love she deserves five times over."

"Elee, don't," I chided. "Don't pretend, not with me. You and I don't do that with each other. Brutal honesty, remember?"

"B," Eli said, letting his thumb stroke my cheek. "I will

always be your big brother, a man you can count on to be in your corner no matter what. If you need an ear to listen or a shoulder to cry on, I'm a phone call away. However, some things will have to change. From now on, the first call you make when you need help is to one of your Alphas. In no way does that mean I won't drop everything to be there, but I can't be number one. My role has been to protect, guide, and raise you until it was time to take a step back for those who were meant to walk life alongside you."

My chest got tight at the emotions that rioted inside me. "I never agreed to that."

"It's the brutal truth, B," Eli countered.

"You make it sound like I'll never see or spend time with you. My family is everything to me. I'm not going to disappear," I said, trying to figure out why this felt so final. "Like you said, we're family, and that will never change. Let's be honest... since Dad died, you've been there for me through everything. Sure, I might have them, but saying I won't ever need you is stupid."

"B, the person I'm talking to when I say those things is me. You and the business have been my whole life, and now that you won't need the same things from me, I'm not sure what to do with my life. Of course, I knew this day would come, but fuck, this just came out of nowhere. Ignore my melancholy, I'm just processing the fact I won't be needed the same way," Eli admitted. "When Dad knew he wasn't going to last much longer in the hospital, he made me promise you would never be alone. He wanted to make sure you always knew he loved you and had a father in your life. So I suppose I took on that role, and now I'm coming to terms with something all fathers face one day. The day when I'm not the most important person in your life anymore."

Throwing myself at Eli, I hugged him tightly, trying to show him just how much I loved him. "You will always be an important person to me. No matter what happens in my life, there will never be a time I don't need you in it. Things are changing so fast, and I don't know what to do with this either, but knowing no matter what, you're here, gives me all the courage I need to take the leap. Don't think of this as losing me because that's just not possible. Instead, view this as a chance to invest in yourself, find a pack, build a family, love someone who needs your unending self-lessness."

I sniffled as I continued to hug the shit out of my brother to the point I'm sure I was cutting off oxygen, but he simply held me as tightly. "Elee, out there is an Omega just like me, wondering if there is ever going to be someone to love them. They are out there, I know it. You are too gifted at loving someone not to have a match waiting."

"The same is true for you, B," Eli whispered. "Don't let the lies the world has told you steal the joy you're sure to have with these men. I see the way they look at you, and they're already under the spell you unknowingly cast by being you. So don't waste a second more with me. It's time you get started on this new chapter of your life. Know that I'll always be cheering you on as I always have."

Releasing my hold Eli, he stood then gave me a smile that reached his eyes before heading out of my room. I took a moment to sit there as I processed the moment that had happened between us. Part of me was upset that I didn't think about how this would affect the rest of my family. Crew always hid his deeper emotions in playfulness while Eli bottled them up until he had a moment alone to face them. If I hadn't caught him, I'm not sure I'd ever know how hard this was for him to see me start a new life.

Still a little off balance by the realization Eli dropped in my lap, I entered the living room. All conversation stopped, and their attention was honed in on me. My first instinct was to freeze then consider bolting, but I met Vili's gaze and relaxed at the sweet smile he gave me. Rising from his seat, he walked over, took my hand, and pressed a kiss to it like I was the princess in some book.

"You look lovely," Vili complimented. "Like a summer flower blooming and gracing us with its beauty."

My cheeks heated as I dropped my gaze and tapped the tip of my white Mary Jane on the tile floor. "Thank you, Vili."

Since it was summer, I decided to keep the pink and blue plaid shorts on but add a white tank top that had a cute pink Peter Pan-style collar on it. To finish off the look, I decided to wear pink ruffled socks to connect the whole style together. With the addition of a simple pastel blue purse, I was ready for my day out with the guys. As Gareth instructed, I felt adorable and utterly confident dressed in this outfit. I might look like something that came out of a little girl's storybook, but I felt like a million bucks.

"Are you hungry?" Vili asked as he laced our fingers together. "We thought breakfast out would be fun."

Hearing the promise of food, my stomach growled loudly, answering the Alpha's question for me. "Breakfast sounds perfect," I said, gently squeezing his hand.

The others rose to their feet, and Ulysses led the way to the front door. I wasn't sure if they realized it, but almost innately, they formed a circle around me. Warrick walked on my left while Gareth and Ulysses took the lead, and Yun-

Sun fell in behind me. Taking them all in, I noticed they wore fresh clothes.

"How close do you guys live from here?" I questioned.

"Oh, about fifteen minutes with no traffic, twenty-five to thirty during rush hour," Warrick informed me. "I went back home last night when we decided to stay and grabbed clothes for us."

"About that," I cut in. "What made you guys choose to stay? Not that I'm not glad you did, but some might think that's awful fast. Plus, I wasn't even awake. I passed out, and as you've now all experienced, it takes a *lot* to wake me up."

Ulysses stopped next to a blacked-out Hummer. Gareth pulled out his keys, and the vehicle's headlights blinked as it unlocked. I suppose I shouldn't have been surprised that Gareth would have a car no one expected him to own. It seemed to be the theme of his life.

"Well, sweetheart, you fell asleep on Warrick's lap. So we felt it was best to call it a night and let you rest. I fully planned to place you on the bed, tuck you in, and leave a note letting you know we'd be back in the morning," Yun-Sun explained. "The challenge to that was you refused to let us leave you. If one of us weren't touching you, then seconds later, you'd be whining so incessantly there was no way we'd be able to walk away."

My jaw dropped. "I whined? You mean like an *Omega* whine?" I asked, resting my hands on my burning cheeks. "I don't ever whine."

"Oh trust me, Rosie, you let out a whine so insistent it took three seconds for all of us to be glued to your side, which was exactly what you wanted," Ulysses added with a smirk so cocky that I wanted to wipe it off his face.

I opened my mouth to say something sassy, but I stopped and remembered that this wasn't my childhood friend anymore. Ulysses was a respected man in the oil industry and one of my Alphas. Instead, I just crossed my arms and scowled.

"Your brother is correct. You are like an angry kitten," Vili murmured. "So ferocious, yet adorable even with your claws out."

Now I was slack-jawed at Vili's comment, unsure what the hell to even say to that. Vili, however, had no problem leaning in, brushing our noses against each other in an Eskimo kiss. The action had me giggling like a schoolgirl, and all my irritation vanished. My stomach voiced its irritation at being kept from the promised meal, spurring us to climb into vehicles.

I figured we'd all climb into one, but it looked like most of them drove here separately, so it only made sense for them to drive them back. Gareth opened the front passenger door for me and gave me a hand when the step to get into the damn thing was higher than I expected. Once I clambered into the seat and got buckled in, I waved a stern finger at the vehicle owner. "Don't even think about making some kind of short joke," I warned. "Yes, I'm tiny, but it's never stopped me from getting even with someone who teased me about it."

Gareth held up his hands as if he was warding off an attack. "I would never dare to comment about your height. However, I was considering whether it might be wise to add an extra handle or step to make the task easier. Would it offend you if I made some accommodations?"

Honestly, I had to think about that for a moment. If I had an extra handle or even a step to use, I could have gotten in and out of the Hummer just fine. It's not like I could ask him to trade in the car to get something closer to the ground. That would be crazy talk.

"Is this your everyday car?" I asked.

Gareth hit the button to start the car, and it rumbled to life. Rock music blared from the radio, and he scrambled to turn it down. "Shit, fuck, goddammit... sorry about that."

I covered my mouth to hide the fact I was laughing at him.

He cleared his throat as he buckled his seat belt. "As for your question, this is the car I drive pretty much every day."

"Then if you don't mind making it a little easier for me to ride in your tank, it would be appreciated," I said, trying to peer over the dashboard.

"Should I get a booster seat too?" Gareth teased.

I glared, pointing a finger at him. "Don't push it, buddy. We might be scent matched and destined to be together, but you have yet to earn the right to make short jokes."

"Duly noted, baby girl. I won't let it happen again," Gareth assured me.

Satisfied with that answer, I turned to stare out the window at the beautiful summer day.

Maybe this day wasn't turning out to be so bad after all.

Warrick

Our breakfast location had been left up to me—not sure why they thought I would have the pulse on the restaurant industry. Yeah, my family was a major player in this field, but I didn't like the politics of it all. Lucky for them, I did know of a few spots that would be perfect from doing my market research before opening the bar. The Giddy Grill was known for their top-notch food and setting, making it the perfect place. I called and asked if they had seating for all of us, knowing it was a smaller restaurant. My hope was to get a table on the patio that looked out over the city community garden. They promised to try, but no matter where we sat, the food would be killer.

"Our little kitten is perfect, yah?" Vili commented as he sat there smiling like a fool.

Perfect was an understatement. I'm not sure a more stunning woman could ever exist. Bailey-Rose was pure sunshine, and her smile was infectious to the point I'm not sure anyone could be upset around our Omega. Of course, the fact she was a petite walking color explosion with her hair and choice in personal aesthetic all created such a vibrant life that I was itching to know better. I wanted to learn everything there was to know about the Omega who has appeared in our lives.

"We are one damn lucky pack," I agreed. "Shit, V-man, I don't even know what to do with all the feelings that are happening right now. All I want is to snuggle with her in bed all day, but then I also want to know everything she hasn't done yet and check them off the list. Hell, if I could go on national television and tell the world that she's ours, I would."

"Yes, I have big feeling too. She makes my heart explode," Vili agreed, then turned to look at me with a worried expression. "Why would people say she is broken? I see nothing wrong with her."

"I don't know what it's like in Numoland, but here in Preidon, people see anything less than perfect as wrong. It sounds like the Matchers wouldn't take her because they don't want her birth defect to be passed on to any children she might have. It's sick and disgusting, but Preidon has always cared more about appearances and wealth than anything substantial," I explained. "You know, sometimes I question why we didn't look at living in other countries."

Vili shifted in his seat as he started to fidget with the spinner ring on his finger. "Preidon, like all places, has bad things, but they are less than other countries."

We learned pretty quickly that Vili didn't like to talk much about life back in Numoland. If we ever asked, he'd change the subject or give us basic answers that didn't really tell us much. From what I was gathering, he didn't fit into the social circle his family lived and worked in, so they sent him away under the pretense of starting this international branch. Well, it was their loss because Vili happened to be one of my favorite people. I could always count on him to join me in having a bit of fun or exploring new places. Windermere was the largest city in Preidon, providing us with lots to do.

Bailey-Rose's family lived in the upper-crust part of town where gated communities or estates with large properties were. It made it feel less city but kept them close to all the major corporations they ran. The Giddy Grill was on the northern side of the city, so it took us longer than it should have, being a weekday, but that was the city life for you. There wasn't parking close to the restaurant, but the parking garage wasn't too far, and it was such a lovely day, a walk would be nice. Hell, anything would be nice if our cutie was doing it with us.

The sight of Bailey-Rose leaping out of Gareth's Hummer and the owner of said Hummer rushing forward to catch her was priceless. She would have been totally fine. It wasn't that far to the ground, but the look on Gareth's face —priceless. With a grunt as she crashed into Gareth, the valiant knight kept our darling Omega safe from the perils of her exit strategy.

"What are you doing?" Gareth demanded as he placed her on her feet.

She looked up at him, perplexed, and I just watched and waited to see how this would go down. It could turn one of two ways. I was betting the reaction Gareth was about to receive wasn't what he thought it would be.

"Getting out of the car," she answered. "What did you think I was doing?"

Gareth rubbed a hand on the back of his neck as he studied her. "Leaping out of a car like that isn't a smart choice, baby girl. What if oil had been on the ground, or you landed funny and twisted your ankle?"

"I'd pick myself up, dust off my ass, and remember to be more careful next time. Why are you making this seem like I almost stepped off a cliff?" Bailey-Rose challenged with hands on her hips.

It took everything in me to tell him to shut the hell up and not say what I'm sure he was about to say. Gareth always meant well, but many times what came out of his mouth made him sound like an asshole.

"Bailey, your safety and well-being are now at the top of my list of things to worry about. As one of your Alphas, it's on me to keep you in one piece," Gareth pointed out.

With a quiet groan, I palmed my face, knowing that statement was going to fly like a lead balloon.

"On you? Is that so?" Bailey-Rose snapped. "So the fact that I've been looking after myself for the past twenty-five years means nothing? That now I have you five, suddenly I'm a delicate flower too fragile to even be breathed on?"

"Bailey, tha—" Gareth started to speak, but our sweet, gentle Omega snapped out a hand, cutting him off.

"No, you listen. On second thought, all of you better listen up because I will only have this discussion with you once," Bailey-Rose warned, looking each of us in the eye. "I might have a heart defect that limits me in many areas of my life. However, what it doesn't make me is a woman who needs five men to protect her from the world. I'm well aware of my limitations... they get thrown in my face every day. What I will not tolerate is the men I'm supposed to be living with for the rest of my life fearing every move I make. So much life has been taken from me, don't make me feel like you're stealing more of it by trying to be overprotective."

Feeling it was the safest course of action, I raised my hand. Bailey-Rose shifted her mesmerizing dual-colored gaze to meet mine. She studied me for a moment, then let out a sigh, waving for me to speak.

"I agree with everything you just said, but I do have one question," I said, trying to keep my voice calm even though panic was beginning to rise. "You said the men you're *supposed* to be spending the rest of your life with. Are you telling us that if we can't agree to get a handle on our protectiveness, you won't be our Omega?"

This had everyone snapping to attention, eyes fixed on the woman before us who held our fate in her petite hands. Bailey-Rose dropped her gaze and wrapped her arms around herself like she was trying to keep from falling apart. "I can't live my life with people who only see me as broken, fragile, and sick. There is more to me than a broken heart. I deserve to be loved just like anyone else, and if my one scent match can't do it, then I'll make a life on my own in peace."

Pain ripped through my chest at the thought of her walking away. It sounds crazy, seeing as we've only known the woman for half a day, but that is the power of finding your match. She is the person who was meant to complete my, no, our life, to fill the void no one else ever could. For her to think we wouldn't be able to love her unendingly means either we fucked up or that behind the bright colors and smiles, our precious Omega has been tricked into believing she's not worth loving.

Unable to simply stand there staring at her, I rushed forward, dropped to my knees, wrapped my arms around her waist, and buried my face against her stomach. "No," I rasped. "Don't, don't you dare give up on us that fast. Bailey-Rose, you are the most perfect being to walk this planet, and we aren't worthy of you being our Omega. Please, please give us a real chance to show you who we are and learn how to be a family together."

Her arms circled my head, returning my hug. It gave me hope we hadn't fucked this up too badly. We took for granted how happy and joyful our sweet, tender-hearted Omega seemed and didn't bother to question it. She'd balked this morning when I carried her downstairs. Gareth said the matter had been handled, so I didn't question it, but I should have pressed him about what happened.

"You're right, Warrick," my sweet angel shared. "My fear of letting you guys get too close only to throw me away makes me lash out at you. While I do really fear being locked away in a glass cage, I shouldn't just expect you guys to be the ones who will do it."

"Rosie, being rejected or hidden away aren't the only two realities you face," Ulysses pointed out. "As new as this is for you, it's the same for us. With the flip of a switch, you gained five Alphas, but we also gained an Omega. Sure, it might seem we have the simple part of this, but there are five of us all feeling the possessive high that comes with finding your scent match. It's one of the reasons they give us courting leave. This way, we have a chance to settle into a new way of life without having to deal with the normal chaos of life."

Feeling Bailey-Rose's hold on me loosen, I took the opportunity and stood. Not letting her go far, I tucked her against my side. Over my dead body was I going to let her walk away from us. I didn't care if I needed to beat some sense into my packmates, nothing was going to push our Omega to the point where she needed to walk away.

Ulysses' words seemed to make an impression on my sweet Care Bear. I could feel her relax against me as if the fight-or-flight mode she'd been in was now calming down. Bailey-Rose nodded her head, accepting all of us might have overreacted slightly.

Gareth stepped up and held out a hand to her with a pleading look. "I'm sorry, baby girl. I've been waiting for this day for what seems like forever, and the thought of you getting hurt on my watch is terrifying. Remember when I told you this wouldn't always be easy between us? As long as we're willing to fight for each other and forgive mistakes all of us are bound to make, I know we'll be happy together."

The man was right. There is no such thing as a perfect relationship, and to assume there is was downright stupid. People are flawed with scars of their past that dictate how they act in the future. Some things can be relearned, while others might require some grace and acceptance. I knew why Gareth was so scared of Bailey-Rose getting hurt, but that was his story to tell.

"You're not the only one who needs to apologize," Bailey-Rose said, taking Gareth's hand. "I could have handled things better. Instead of assuming the worst, I should have explained my fears and not just lash out at all of you. None of you have given me any reason to believe you'll treat me the way so many others have, and for that, I am truly sorry."

Unable to control the relief I was feeling, I scooped my Care Bear up and hugged her tight as I spun in a circle. "God, just when I didn't think you could get any cuter," I mumbled against her neck. "Thank you, Care Bear, for trusting us enough to give this relationship a fair shot."

The giggle that bubbled out of her had my heart melting. "Care Bear... I like it. That's my favorite so far."

Lifting my head to meet her gaze, I couldn't hold back the smile that took over my face. "Yeah?" She nodded with a hum of agreement. "All right then, Care Bear it is."

The moment was broken as her stomach rumbled, reminding us why we were even in this parking garage. Not bothering to put my girl down, I marched off toward the elevators feeling like nothing could bring me down. Today has certainly had its ups and downs, but that's life. It's not about how many arguments or disagreements that happen in a relationship but how you resolve them. Leaving things to fester and anger to grow helps no one, but speaking your mind, as well as being honest with the group, prevents negativity from growing.

"Where are we going? I don't think I've ever been on this side of the city before," Bailey-Rose asked.

Hitting the button for the ground floor once everyone stepped into the elevator, I answered, "We're in the northern part of the city that used to be the suburbs when Windermere was still a small city. Once it grew, this area became surrounded by factories and skyscrapers, but this small pocket of the downtown area managed to keep its roots. You know the farmers' market they have all summer long? Well, most of the people who sell produce, honey, or spices grow them all here in this neighborhood."

Stepping out of the elevator, I released my hold on Bailey-Rose, leaving her to stand next to me. Her eyes went wide as she took in the massive garden you couldn't see from the side we pulled in on. It was about the size of a football field and had various plots that different families or groups tended to. While each section was technically looked after individually, no one would let a plot go to waste.

"Oh my goodness, this is amazing." She gasped. "Are we allowed to explore and see what people have done?"

"Of course, it's open to the public," I assured her. "Let's eat first, then we can wander all you like."

Bouncing with excitement, she clapped her hands together, grinning up at me. "It's magical, like it's a secret fairy garden tucked away in the cold concrete city. I wish I'd brought my sketchbook with me. It would be so fun to draw in a place like this."

Reaching out, I tucked a lock of hair that had fallen into her face behind her ear. "Sounds like we'll just have to come back another time. It's not like we're that far away. I'm sure there will be plenty of opportunities for you to sketch all you want."

When people talk about someone being the embodiment of joy, I now understood what they meant. Bailey-Rose was beaming as bright as a ray of sunshine at the prospect of coming back here. It showed me how I'd lost the appreciation of simple things that so many take for granted.

"Come on, Rosie, if we don't get you moving, you'll say screw it to breakfast, and we'll lose you to the garden," Ulysses said, grasping her hand and tugging her along.

BAILEY-ROSE

Breakfast was divine not only because we got to sit on the balcony overlooking the garden but the food was outstanding. The restaurant tried to use as much local produce as they could incorporate with their meals. The guys all ordered substantial dishes—omelets, eggs benedict, traditional sausage and eggs—making me feel slightly guilty for wanting to pick something that was practically dessert.

"Sweetheart, order what you like," Yun-Sun urged. "None of us will judge you for your choices. Think of the next two weeks like we're on vacation. Let loose, and enjoy the time we have to be free of normal responsibilities."

I chewed on my lip as I considered what he said before admitting the truth. "Lysse already knows this, but I have a *major* sweet tooth. Like I would prefer to live off all things sweet and delicious than suffer through eating a leafy green vegetable. Of course, with my health, I'm always careful, but given the chance, my go-to isn't gonna be the healthy option."

They all smiled and some chuckled, but none of them seemed at all bothered by this. Reassured I ordered strawberry cream waffles and about died at the fact there was a scoop of strawberry ice cream sitting proudly in the middle of the pile of fluffy waffles. It was almost too pretty to eat, but once I tasted it, there was no way I could let it go to waste.

"Oh, I might also mention that I'm not the world's best at

cooking. I know some packs who are career-orientated like yourselves appreciate having their Omega fill the typical homemaker role. However, I should be upfront and honest and say I grew up with a cook and housekeepers looking after me."

"No worry about that," Vili said, waving a hand. "We too use both those things. They have weekends off so we cook then, but otherwise, it's done for us."

My shoulders sagged in relief as I blew out a breath. "Oh, thank goodness. I'm not hopeless by any means, but to go from just learning to look after myself to caring for all of us would have been rough. I fear there would be many burned meals and ruined laundry because of simple mistakes."

"Rosie, we are blessed as a pack that each of us has an excellent-paying job on top of coming from families that are well-off. This has given us the freedom to hire help around the house if you're comfortable with that. I should also add that as a pack, we never wanted to strip our Omega of the life they'd been living to fit our needs. You're a talented artist who deserves to continue down the path you started. Crew mentioned the art studio space they gave you for graduation and your hopes of turning it into a gallery for yourself."

I nodded, poking a chunk of strawberry with my fork. "Originally, I wanted it to be a space where local artists could show their work. So many amazing artists are in our city, but the art community is all about who you know, how much money you have, and the last thing they care about is the art."

"Why do you say, *originally*? Has your dream changed?" Warrick asked, leaning forward and resting his chin on his hand.

It was becoming apparent to me that Warrick had a keen ear and was quick to pick up on any underlying emotion in my words. I shrugged, not wanting to admit why I was doubting myself since it seemed so stupid at this point. "When I told others about the idea, no one seemed to think it was a smart choice. They thought it was foolish of me to take on people who probably wouldn't sell, costing me money in the end."

Warrick's face scrunched up as if my words had offended him. "Why the hell should that matter? Forgive me if this sounds crass, but you're not doing this for the money. You're plenty well-off with whatever inheritance you're going to get, that if this happens to be a passion project, then so be it. What you want is to give people the chance to be discovered, right?"

"That's exactly what my goal is," I blurted, slamming my fork on the table in my excitement. "When Papa Addy died, a trust was set up for me that I got access to when I turned twenty-one. Even without the allowance I get from that, what I earn selling my art is keeping me more than comfortable. Of course, I've never had to pay rent or other things like most people my age do, but still, it will never be about the money for me."

The conversation petered off after that outburst, making me feel a little self-conscious. I *hated* talking about money. Yes, it gave my family every opportunity to provide the best care, even trying a few experimental programs that made all the difference. I respected the life money has given me, but it's also caused me heartache, especially when you find out that people only want to be your friend in hopes of getting close to your brothers, who are some of the most eligible bachelors in Preidon. My personal goal has always been never to take the life I've been blessed with for granted or let money turn me into a snob who looked down on those with less.

"Bailey," Gareth started, then paused as if he wasn't sure he wanted to ask his question. "First, let me just say we know you've had a recent breakup. I will try not to ask about it because I'm afraid I'll end up in jail if I know who it is. However, I would like to know if he's the one who told you your idea was stupid?"

Was I that easy to read?

It didn't surprise me that they knew about the breakup, considering Crew invited Lysse over to snap me out of my funk. I hated to admit that Gareth was right—Randall had been the one to stomp all over my dreams. Before I went off to finish my semester on campus, I'd told him all about my dreams since my family had been so excited about the plan. Of course, my family would always think whatever I came up with would be brilliant, even if it wasn't. They just liked to see me taking a risk and trying something new, which is why I turned to my boyfriend. I thought he would be a logical sounding board, but the second I finished explaining, he didn't hesitate to tell me what an idiot I was. That had stung and made leaving for school a little easier, but I never thought it would lead him to cheat on me.

"He was the loudest to object to the idea," I answered. "A few other classmates and a teacher seemed to agree with him. As part of our final project, we needed to present a business plan to the class to prepare us for when school was over. You might say I got the harshest feedback."

Yun-Sun rested a hand on my thigh to offer me his support. "Sweetheart, if people always listened to what others told them, think of all the things we'd be missing from the world. Every person ahead of their time in art, music, or technology has been told they were crazy for trying at least once. To me, it means your idea might be something groundbreaking and just what this city needs."

The sincerity in his voice had my heart swelling with hope. He made a valid point—this was something every dreamer faced. We saw what the world could be and the possibilities that might be around the next corner, while many kept blinders on to focus solely on their goal, never allowing something to pull them from their course. For me, the world had never been black and white, not when you weren't sure if you'd live long enough to experience it all. I leaped at every opportunity I thought I could manage. My biggest challenge was people who held me back with the belief they were helping, only focusing on the limitations my condition forced on me.

"That is an excellent way to look at things," I agreed. "I feel like I need to have that put on a pillow or framed somewhere so I can remind myself of it when I start to doubt again."

The grip on my leg tightened as Yun-Sun smiled at me. "Don't worry, sweetheart. If you ever need to be reminded again, I'll be happy to do so. Everyone desires encouragement from time to time. It's only natural to question something that's never been done before. I know I can speak for the others when I say whatever you need to make this dream happen, we'll help."

With hope blooming in my chest at his words, we left the restaurant and headed down to the garden. Since it was a weekday, there weren't many people working in their little plots, but those we met were happy to share what they were doing. My fingers itched to take pencil to paper and sketch the older woman softly singing to herself as she weeded, surrounded by lush flowers and spices. This place was a snapshot of an authentic, simple life in motion—a bubble in the hustle and bustle of the city where you could slow down and breathe.

"You know a plot just opened up one row over," a man commented, pausing in his efforts to secure the toppling tomato plant. "Nice young pack had been tending it, but one of the Alphas got a job offer in another city they couldn't turn down. You lot seem the sort to fit in around here. All you'd need to do is fill out the application."

Surprised by the offer, I looked at the guys, unsure of what to say. We were on our first date as a pack, and committing to a plot here seemed like a major step in our relationship.

Sensing my panic, Ulysses wrapped an arm around my shoulders, hugging me to him. "Thank you for letting us know," he said. "We'll talk it over and see if that's something we have the time to dedicate to. None of us would want to take the opportunity from someone who's been waiting to get a plot here and not be able to give the garden the time it deserves."

The man looked us over and gave a grunt before returning to his plants. For the life of me, I couldn't tell if that was a sound of approval or disapproval at Lysse's answer. Before I could pester the man about it, I was guided back toward the parking garage.

"What do you say we head home so you can check out the place?" Ulysses offered. "There are two options for where the nest could be set up. It's totally up to you which one works best. Once we know what room we're working with, then the fun begins where you get to design it."

"You were looking for an Omega but didn't have a nest put together?" I questioned. "That seems a little bit like you didn't believe you'd find one."

"Says the woman convinced she could live the rest of her

life in bed so long as she had enough Peeps to eat," Ulysses countered.

"Dammit, Crew," I muttered. "Always telling people things they don't need to know. Man doesn't understand the term 'privacy.' "

"Oh, don't get your blankets in a twist, Rosie. You know Crew and I have always been close. He told me that as his best friend before discovering we were scent matched," he chided.

Scowling, I poked him in the ribs where I knew he was always ticklish. "That does nothing but prove my point. Just wait until he has his own pack, and I get to spill all the dirty details I know about him."

Ulysses snorted, trying to cover up a laugh before dropping a kiss on my head. "Oh, Rosie, don't ever change. You are perfect the way you are."

The drive was shorter than I expected, but then again, everyone was at work. When we pulled up to the house, I was impressed to see it was set back from the street with lots of trees around the property, providing some privacy. My first sight of the house had me intrigued. The home was wildly modern, looking as if a child with building blocks put it together. With so many shapes stacked on top of each other, I didn't have a clue what to expect inside. Ulysses pulled up to a row of garage doors that all began to open, allowing the four cars to park. There were three more already in the bays, making me curious who had a second vehicle. By the looks of them, they were probably fun cars, not something you drove every day.

I managed to get out of Ulysses' car without any mishaps. Then again, being a more normal four-door car, I wasn't at risk of falling out of it like before.

"Come with me, kitten," Vili urged as he grabbed my hand and hurried out of the garage. "You need the full experience, so the front door is best."

His excitement was infectious, so I let him take the lead as we climbed the five steps to the front door, or doors since there were two. Vili typed in a code, and the door gave a cheerful chime as it unlocked. Turning both handles at once, Vili shoved them open, revealing the main entryway. The space was open and bright with many windows to ensure the home was filled with light. Stepping into the foyer, I saw a curved staircase on either side leading to the second floor.

"Welcome to your new home, my sweet kitten," Vili announced, tossing his arms wide in a grand gesture. "Come, I show you all the rooms. First, we have main room or, as you call it, the living room."

Taking a step down from the tiled entryway into the living room with lush carpet, I stared up at the vaulted ceiling with three rows of windows, making it seem like there was no wall at all. A massive flat-screen television hung on the wall over the fireplace. Before it was two sectional sofas, creating a U-shape with a large stone coffee table. This whole home screamed that men lived here, but I had to say they did a decent job decorating it. Green plants scattered around the space, and when I ran a finger over a fuzzy-looking leaf, I knew it was real.

"Come, come," Vili called, waving me to join him. "Formal dining, which we don't use, but I think that will change now we have you. Then behind this door is one of my favorite rooms."

Walking through the door he held open, I found myself in a stunning kitchen set up with all state-of-the-art appliances in all stainless steel. The room bowed out in a crescent moon, allowing space for a breakfast nook. It was also where the patio doors were, giving you access to the paved brick area with a table and lounge chairs. I spotted a grill as well, making me wonder if the guys or the cook they hired used it.

Unable to linger longer, I was whisked off to the next room, which turned out to be a library with a pool table. There was also a small bar set up with various bottles of liquor and the tools to make any drink you could think of. It makes sense since Warrick is a bartender as well as a bar owner. So far, this room felt the most lived in, like they actually spent time in here with each other.

I was soon on my way upstairs where, at the top, it opened up to another living room. Comfy overstuffed couches and armchairs were arranged, with windows on three sides of the room to make it inviting. The view of the backyard was stunning, and it made me so happy that whoever built this house made an effort to appreciate it.

"Our rooms are down either hall," Vili pointed to the right. "This side is Ulysses, Gareth, and one open room. The other side is Warrick, Yun, and me."

I frowned. "Lysse said there were two rooms for me to pick from."

"Yes, the second choice is up," he answered, pointing to the ceiling. "First, I think you should see the room here, then we go see the other."

With a shrug, I followed him to the end of the hall. He opened the door and ushered me forward as he flipped on the light. The room was empty save for a few boxes stacked along one wall. It was painted a light gray color that matched the hallway with white trim. I wasn't all that impressed with the room until Vili pulled back the curtains on one wall. This wasn't just a giant window—the whole wall was made of glass, giving you a breathtaking view of the backyard. Now I could see why they'd think an Omega would appreciate this space.

"What do you think, Care Bear?" Warrick asked as he joined us, the others following on his heels. "There is a connecting bathroom as well. In fact, all the rooms have their own en suite. It's one of the reasons we loved this house so much."

I turned slowly, taking in the space and trying to picture it with more color, plus lots of pillows and blankets. It was a beautiful room, and I could turn it into something spectacular, but I wasn't fully convinced.

"It's really lovely. The wall of glass is everything I could hope for in a space. However, I think I should see the other option before settling," I shared.

"Would you do me the honor of escorting you?" Yun-Sun asked, offering me his hand.

Blushing, I placed my hand in his, allowing him to guide me down the hall to the opposite end of the house. There wasn't a room on this side, but instead, another flight of stairs that led up to what I would have guessed to be the roof. Yun-Sun glanced at me over his shoulder as he turned the door handle to the room, making me giddy with excitement. Tossing it open, I was momentarily blinded by the sun as its light poured over me.

I trusted Yun-Sun to guide me into the space since I rubbed my eyes to get them to stop watering. Then a shadow crossed over me, and I was able to get my senses under control. Carefully, I opened them to find Yun-Sun looming over me, using his body to give me shade. Most of the time, I found being so short irritating, but right now, I don't think I ever felt more cherished.

Before I could second-guess myself, I popped up on my toes, closed the small space between us, and kissed him. "Thank you," I whispered.

A bright smile appeared on Yun-Sun's face, making his eyes sparkle. "You are most welcome, sweetheart. Will you be all right if I move?"

Biting my lip, I nodded, feeling shy at the moment we were sharing over something so simple as the sun. What I wasn't prepared for when he stepped to the side was the sight of the world's most perfect room. Gasping, I covered my mouth with my hands as I slowly turned, trying to take in everything. As a little girl, I always dreamed about what my nest would be like, how I wanted to design it, what color it would be, or what I would fill it with to make me feel cozy and safe.

Nothing I came up with matched the beauty I was surrounded by in here.

At first glance, you would think this space was supposed to be a greenhouse or a sunroom with the way it was constructed. The fact that my feet were sinking into the plush carpet that covered the floor gave me the first clue. It was so soft and luxurious I wanted to lay down and starfish on it so I could touch as much of it as possible. A shimmering chandelier hung from the center of the ceiling and cast prisms all over the room like shimmering fairy dust. The ceiling came to a point almost like a circus tent, but it was made of glass held together by white wooden seams in a pattern that reminded me of a beach ball. Three of the four walls were also glass with elegant woodwork forming the arching centers, making a bold statement. Gauzy curtains were gathered in the corners of the room, willing to offer some privacy. However, with the way it sat behind the house's main structure, you couldn't see it from the driveway, and the trees blocked any nearby house from peeking in.

Dumbfounded by the space, I couldn't even speak as I passed the guys to check out the two doors in the room's solid wall. One opened to the bathroom with double sinks, a massive shower, and a hot tub pretending to be a bath sunk into the floor. The second door revealed a closet about the same size as mine at home with all sorts of storage. It was perfect—every single detail about this room was absolutely fucking perfect.

When I rejoined the others, they looked at me with hope and excitement, making me realize they'd been waiting for my reaction. The only thing I could do was let out a sob as I tried to express what I was feeling. Their expression changed to worry as they circled me, trying to offer reassurance, not knowing what upset me.

"Baby girl, if you don't like either of the rooms, then you can have your pick of ours. Please don't cry. If we need, we'll move and find a home we all love," Gareth assured me as he stroked my hair.

I hated when I got overwhelmed—my body's first response was to cry.

Happy—cry.

Sad—cry.

Angry—cry.

Hell, the first time I had an orgasm, I fucking cried, and that went over so well. Men love it when they have a weeping woman in their bed after they thought they just gave you the world.

"Talk to us, Care Bear. We can't fix it if we don't know what's wrong," Warrick pleaded.

"N-nothing," I managed to hiccup out. "It's perfect... everything is perfect. It's so beautiful."

There was a collective sigh as my guys relaxed and wrapped me up in the best group hug I've ever experienced. To be surrounded by them, their comforting scents filling my nose, I began to calm. Somehow we ended up sitting on the floor in a mess of limbs and one snotty Omega at the center. Vili pulled a cloth hanky out of his pocket and offered it to me. I'm not sure there could be a more precious man than him at this moment. Taking it, wiped my eyes ad I blew my nose, glad I wore waterproof mascara.

Ulysses rested his chin on my shoulder as he nuzzled behind my ear. "Welcome home, Bailey-Rose."

BAILEY-ROSE

ventually, once I'd convinced everyone I was truly fine, we returned to the house's main level and spread out on the giant sofa. To my amazement, the chaise lounges on the end could be moved to fill in the gap and create one massive sofa bed. Warrick disappeared for a bit, but when he returned, he had pillows and blankets galore. The second he dumped them on me, I squealed with delight since they carried their scent. He'd gone from room to room and collected something from each of them for me to snuggle with.

"Are you trying to make the rest of us look bad?" Gareth grumbled.

Warrick just fluttered his lashes at him. "I don't know what you mean. Everyone knows Omegas love pillows and blankets to nest in no matter where they are."

"Let me guess... you actually read the book the Matchers gave us last night, didn't you?" Gareth accused.

"No! No fighting," Vili cut in. "Silly thing to fight over. Leave it be."

Both Alphas stared at each other for a moment, then Gareth let out a huff and flopped back on the couch. Unsure how to navigate what just happened, I occupied myself with arranging the goodies Warrick brought me until I was satisfied with the outcome. Surrounded by my Alphas, their scent grounded me in a way I didn't realize I needed. Logically, this home might be mine, but Omegas were a fussy bunch when it came to our spaces. As wonderful as this house might be, it wouldn't be my home until the nest was finished perfectly.

Yun-Sun offered me a tablet with The Snuggery website pulled up. This was a store every town had filled with anything and everything you could possibly need to start or update a nest. I took the offered device, but I wasn't sure what exactly he expected me to do with it.

"Whatever you want is yours, sweetheart. There is no limit, no rules, no idea we can't entertain, so don't shy away from what you truly want," he explained.

I looked from the tablet back to Yun. "Why do I need to buy all new things when I have a nest back at home?"

"We will, of course, move your clothes and personal things here," Ulysses answered. "But it would mean the world to us as your Alphas if you would allow us to provide what you need for a nest here in the house. I know it might seem silly to you, but that will always be your room at your parents' estate. We want to create something that's just for us."

It was hard to argue that logic. I knew how important it was to an Alpha to provide for his Omega. That need was hardwired into their system, and to say no would be cruel.

"Okay, I'll go shopping if I have to," I agreed with a dramatic sigh.

"Do you want our help, or should we put on a movie to watch while you look over the options?" Gareth asked.

"No, you guys can put on something you want to watch. Handing me this and telling me to go crazy will send me down a rabbit hole that's going to take me a bit to come back out of. Once I have things somewhat narrowed down, then you can help me figure out what will work best in the room," I suggested.

The guys didn't need much convincing, and soon some action movie was playing while I dove into the beautiful world of nesting. For those who aren't an Omega, a nest doesn't really make sense. They don't understand the need to build a space in their home where they can retreat when the world becomes too much. By nature, Omegas need to be grounded by their Alphas, environment, and internally for peace of mind. At the core, our purpose is to offer comfort and emotional support to our pack as well as ensuring other Omegas or Alphas are born to keep the cycle of our world going.

When a pack has an Omega, each member bonds to the Omega in one way or another, creating a united force. It also provides the Omega with protection, assistance in caring for offspring, and companionship that Omegas crave. Alphas and Betas are also drawn to community living, which is why packs form in the first place, but they don't *need* it the same as Omegas do. If an Omega is left to fend for themselves with no support or care, they suffer physically and mentally. Being lonely could actually kill an Omega and cause them to give up any effort to keep living which, in turn, could result in suicide or trauma-induced illness they don't recover from.

My doctor had warned my family to keep an eye on me for these issues since I was at a mature age and still hadn't found a pack. It was the major reason Crew and Eli worried about looking after me on top of the heart defect. The nest I built at home meant so much to me because it was my safe space, the one place in my life where I controlled every aspect. I could hide away from everything but not fear going mad, knowing my brothers were around if I needed them.

Now that my pack found me and I was going to be moving into this home, I could understand the importance of making a fresh start. The nest I built at my parents' home was what I needed to fill the hole in my life where a pack was supposed to be. With that void no longer in the equation, it gave me a new perspective and vision for this space. Many would say my current nest was childish and I should grow up, but that room needed to be filled with all the joy I could manage. It was a reminder that even if the world seemed like a cold, callous place that only saw me as imperfect, there were still good things about it.

Looking up from the tablet, I took a moment to study each man I was matched to. I so wanted to believe they would stay with me forever, but other than my brothers, no one had kept their promise. Each time this fear spilled out of the shadows of my insecurities, I tried to remind myself it wasn't true. These men were created to bond with me and I for them. How could something destined since birth not work out?

"You good, baby girl?" Gareth asked, making me realize I'd been lost in thought, staring at him blankly.

"Yup," I answered a little too loudly with a slight squeak. "Just got lost in thought, is all."

Fingers combed through my hair, making a moan slip out at how wonderful it felt. "Anything you want to talk about?" Yun-Sun asked.

Did I want to talk about how I was feeling? Part of me felt like I'd caused enough drama today with my outburst in the parking garage that it would be better to keep this to myself. Then, on the other hand, they'd been pretty insistent about sharing how I was feeling.

"Just a little overwhelmed," I answered. It wasn't the whole truth, but it wasn't a lie, either. I simply didn't feel up for another deep soul-searching conversation.

Yun-Sun plucked the tablet out of my hands and set it

on the coffee table. "Then I think it's best for you to relax. We are in no rush. These next fourteen days are all about enjoying time together as well as preparing the house. It should be fun to plan out your room, so if it feels like too much work, come back to it later."

"That sounds like a good idea, but when this movie is over, I get to pick the next one," I said, leaning against Yun-Sun's shoulder.

"You got it, Care Bear," Warrick assured me with a wink and thumbs-up.

Wriggling around, I tried to get comfortable, but with the height difference between Yun and me, it made it challenging. He must have gotten irritated with all the shifting because the next thing I knew, he scooped me up and settled me between his legs. My head now rested on his chest, and I was securely nestled as he tucked one of the blankets around me. The final touch was for him to loosely wrap his arms around my waist and drop a kiss on my head.

"Better?" Yun-Sun inquired, a smile in his tone.

Peering up at him, I grinned. "Perfect."

"Sweetheart, can you promise me something?" Yun-Sun asked, and I nodded, urging him to continue. "Don't ever be afraid to ask any of us to snuggle if you need a hug or any other physical contact that will help you settle. Believe me when I say we're all craving the chance to hold you at any opportunity we get right now. I have no idea if that will shift for either of us as our bond grows, but for now, it's all I can do to control the urge. If I had it my way, you wouldn't be walking anywhere around this house. I would carry you just to keep you close. Anyway, all I meant to say is as we learn about each other and what you need from us, never fear asking for it outright."

I'm not sure Yun-Sun had any idea how lethal words like

that were. If he kept talking like that, I would be madly in love with him by tomorrow, if not in the next hour. Okay, I was half in love with him already, but I couldn't tell what part of that was the high of finding my matches or not. Either way, this Alpha was proving himself to be one hell of a lawyer with that silver tongue of his.

"I'll try, but I'm not the best at asking others for help," I admitted.

Yun-Sun pressed a tender kiss to my forehead. "It's okay. We'll just be checking in a lot more until we can help you realize asking for something won't upset us. Honestly, I'm not sure there is much we would ever say no to."

"If it's dangerous or the chances of her getting hurt are way too high, then I have zero issue saying no," Gareth interjected. "Otherwise, Yun is right. We want to give you the fucking world, baby girl. You deserve all that life has to give, and we plan to make that happen."

These Alphas were determined to make me melt into a puddle of goo. If I ever had hopes of keeping my heart protected, they were quickly fluttering away like the butterflies in my stomach.

"Hey, Care Bear," Warrick called, nudging my knee with a finger. "What do you think about spending the afternoon with me tomorrow? I'd love to take you to the bar, show you where I work, then maybe we can go out for dinner?"

I started to say yes but then paused to look at the others. "Is it okay for me to just spend time with one of you?"

Ulysses snorted. "Rosie, just because we're a pack doesn't mean we need to do everything together. I think it's important for you to have a relationship with us all individually as well as a group. When we all go back to work and fall into a routine, having an individual relationship with each of us will help make you more comfortable. Some days

Warrick will be around more or Vili if he chooses to work here instead of his office. Not to mention when the time comes for us to be intimate, we might appreciate some alone time with you." He pointed out with a smirk on his face. "However, I want to be clear that none of us have a problem if group activities happen, but none of us are romantically interested in anyone but you."

At the mention of being intimate, my body started to tingle as I remembered what happened between Ulysses and me this morning. Then my imagination went wild at the prospect of the others joining in. It was extremely common for packs to have intermingled relationships. Obviously, not always as was the case with my own pack, but it usually happened that a romantic pairing would occur between Alphas and Betas before they found their Omega.

The real question was, would my poor little heart be able to withstand that much stimulation? Guess there was only one way to find out, and I would be more than happy to experiment, given the opportunity.

"Thank you for telling me that," I said once I realized an awkward lull had gone on for far too long. Turning my head, I looked at my sweet cinnamon-candied Alpha. "Warrick, I would love to spend the day with you tomorrow. Although I should warn you, I've never been to a bar before, so I hope I don't embarrass you."

"Oh, Care Bear, you could try, but I don't get embarrassed by much," Warrick assured me. "Once you've seen how drunken idiots act, you realize you're not doing so bad at life."

The others murmured their agreement on that nugget of advice.

"That just leaves what you'd like to do about tonight," Yun-Sun pointed out. "We can hang here, have dinner, then head back to your parents' home to sleep. Otherwise, you can have your pick of beds to sleep in with or without the Alpha who uses it."

"Hmm... I didn't really pack to sleep over," I murmured as I plucked at my lower lip in thought. "Although if we aren't going anywhere until the afternoon, we could swing by the house."

"I have idea," Vili declared in an excited voice. "We spend evening here, then return to your home to sleep. This way we all get to have breakfast together before you go. While you have fun, we will pack your clothes to bring here. No more problems."

Each of them pinned their gaze on me, waiting for what-ever answer I was going to give. "You shouldn't have to pack up all my things, especially when I'm not even there. Wouldn't that be awkward?"

"Because why?" Vili challenged. "Soon you will have all the things here. Eventually, we will see you in the clothes or in no clothes at all. Why be odd?"

"I-I have no answer for that," I admitted once I failed to have anything else to say. "Okay, if you four are fine with doing that while Warrick and I are gone, I won't stop you."

Vili and Warrick cheered then high-fived each other reveling in the excitement. Seeing them so happy about me moving in gave me the boost I needed to get back to my search. Crawling over Yun-Sun, I grabbed the tablet and let the delicious-smelling pastry of a man settle me back between his legs. A contented sigh escaped me as he stroked his fingers through my hair as I dove back into my search.

When dinnertime rolled around, we ate out on the patio, which is also when I discovered they had a pool set off to one side. I loved being able to swim and float for hours during the summer. It was something I'd always been able to enjoy since it wasn't as taxing on my heart. Their personal chef made a delicious stir-fry with chicken and steak over a bed of fluffy rice. The guys all had a beer or glass of wine with their meal, but Warrick made me a special mocktail to enjoy.

"This, m'lady, is called a strawberry breeze," Warrick announced as he set the fizzy drink in front of me. "I thought tomorrow it might be fun if I teach you how to make a few different recipes. That way, when you visit me at the bar, you don't have to feel left out and get something tasty. Who knows, maybe I might even make up one and call it the Care Bear after you."

"Really?" I gasped, practically bouncing in my seat.

He chuckled and tucked a finger under my chin to tilt my head up to meet his lips in a sweet kiss. "Really, and it will be sweet like you."

Just when I didn't think these men could make me melt more than I already had, they went and made a liar out of me.

"Come on, man, give the woman a chance to eat before you get all mushy," Gareth teased. "Look at her. It's a miracle she hasn't slid right out of her seat with that dreamy expression on her face."

Warrick flipped Gareth off as he nuzzled another kiss to my lips before taking his seat. The others dug into their meal, but I had to sit there and contemplate the meaning of life for a moment as I convinced my body we could still function while swooning. Taking a big gulp of the drink Warrick made me, I was surprised at how bubbly it was. It tasted amazing, and the carbonation danced on my tongue, but I made the fatal mistake of breathing in, causing the bubbles to go right up my nose.

Momentary panic ensued as I wasn't sure if I could swallow in time or spew the drink everywhere. I managed to swallow, feeling the burn all the way down before I sneezed so hard I rocked the patio chair, making it spin and face the other direction. As luck would have it, my legs were too short to stop the movement without slouching down to extend my leg, which I did. With the chair's movement stopped, I now had to scooch myself to the edge of the chair and shuffle my way back around to face the others.

The waft of chocolate and orange told me Lysse had come to help me out, making me even more embarrassed. "Ah... you good there, Rosie?"

Flopping back, I looked up to find him peering down at me. "Does it look like I'm good?"

"Hard to say... you always look good to me," he answered with a cheeky grin. "Care for some assistance, or would you like to deal with this on your own? Wouldn't want you thinking I'm doubting your abilities."

This was the Lysse I grew up knowing and fell madly in love with as an awkward teen. Well, clearly I was still awkward, but now I didn't have to hide how I felt about him.

"Lysse, you and I both know you're going to help me whether I want you to or not. That's how things between us have always worked," I reminded him. "Now chop-chop, I'd like to eat tonight."

"Wow, it's a really good thing we are getting you out of that house. You sounded *way* too much like Crew just then. The world can only handle one of his kind at a time," Ulysses warned as he turned me to face the right direction and shoved the chair closer to the table. "You know if I get a pillow—"

"Okay, thank you for your help. You can feel free to sit back down now," I ordered, cutting off what he was about to say.

Gareth tried to cover the fact he was laughing at Ulysses but failed. The shaking shoulders gave him away. "Looks like you haven't earned the right to make short jokes either," he managed to say.

"Let me guess... you tried and got your ass handed to you?" Ulysses asked, taking his seat, to which Gareth nodded. "Yeah, I should have guessed she'd shut me down, but I wanted to test the waters and see if I was in the clear."

"Guys, I'm well aware of how short I am and the limitations that are bestowed upon such special people," I informed them, pressing a hand to my heart for added effect. "Do you want to know why people are always scared of us tiny folk? We've learned to be scrappy and find ways to accomplish what you giants do so easily. So make all the jokes you like, but don't blame me when retaliation sneaks up on ya."

The table erupted into laughter, and I couldn't help but join them. I knew I sounded silly, but the more they underestimated me, the easier it would be to plot my revenge. Even a Care Bear knows how to cause a little mischief.

BAILEY-ROSE

The following morning I awoke covered in various limbs that belonged to my Alphas, each of them needing to have some sort of contact with my skin. It took some juggling, but we managed to figure it out, only for it to fall apart at some point in the night, leaving me with this puzzle to wriggle out of. It should have been uncomfortable to use Vili's calf as a pillow, but the man was as soft as the marshmallows he smelled like.

A knock on my bedroom door was the only reason I decided it was worth getting up. Otherwise, I would have laid there enjoying the peace having all my pack resting beside me. As carefully as I could, I managed to get out of the snuggle pile and leap onto the floor without stepping on anyone—*go me!*

Grabbing my robe off the bench at the foot of the bed, I wrapped myself in it before opening the door. It wasn't like my brothers hadn't seen me in my pajamas before, but I'd put on a nightgown that clung to certain things. My guys had loved and hated it all at the same time, but damn, they couldn't keep their hands off me, so I counted it as a win.

I opened the door mid-yawn, and instead of Eli, I found my mother standing there. Shocked, I blinked at her a few moments before flinging myself into her arms. She caught me and twirled around, hugging me tightly.

"Mom, what are you doing here?" I asked once we came to a halt.

"Shh, let's go to my sitting room and talk," Mom whispered. "I need some one-on-one time with my daughter before her Alphas wake up and steal her away."

Nodding excitedly, I clasped her hand as we headed to the other end of the house where my parents' rooms were located. Mother's sitting room was a perfect representation of who Jolene Thatcher was. Everything was made with light, warm-colored wood with cream cushions and mountains of pillows on the two small sofas. A cart with coffee and everything else we would need waited for us when we entered. Mother pulled me down to sit beside her on one of the sofas, knocking various pillows onto the floor. None of this bothered my mother—she was far too excited to hear all about what was happening with me.

"Did you really think we wouldn't come home after hearing you found your scent matches? Darling, I thought you knew us better than that," Mother scolded. "Now tell me everything. I want to know every detail. Eli and Crew were no help when I peppered them with questions."

I could only imagine how that went. Those two were useless when it came to telling Mother the information she felt was important. Crew would suffer through answering the best he could, while Eli wouldn't bother to retain such silly things when the root of the matter was simple. So as mother poured herself some coffee and prepared a cup of tea for me, I started with Randall dumping me.

"Darling, I don't want to know about Randall," Mother cut in. "He was never going to be good enough for my baby girl, but I guess he proved that to you himself."

"Are you going to let me tell this story or not?" I challenged. "This is an important part of why Ulysses even came over that day."

Mother pouted but sat back against the pillows and let

me continue. Not really having had the chance to share this news with anyone who wasn't there for it all to happen, it was fun to gush over this with my mother. No one was better at having the best reactions at the right places as I told my tale—a gasp here, snicker there, and clapping at the description of the room where I was going to build my nest.

"Oh, darling, this is all so exciting." Mother sighed, letting her hands flutter for added drama. "It's like something out of a storybook. Who would have ever guessed your childhood friend you've pined after for so long would end up being one of your true loves? These are the moments I wish my beloved Adrian was here with us. He would have been so proud of you and the woman you've become."

I could see her eyes getting glassy with tears as she talked about my father. Now having met my guys, I couldn't even fathom losing one of them, and we've known each other for barely two days. My mother was with Papa Addy for almost thirty years before he died. It gave me a new level of respect for her and Daddy Rawr to continue their loved one's legacy. Resting my hand over hers, I gently squeeze it, letting her know I was there. She gave me a watery smile and dashed away the tears that slipped out.

"He truly enjoyed Ulysses, you know that, right? Whenever the three of you palled around, he would tell me how much safer you were with them both looking after you. I know he would be so pleased to find out he's one of your scent matches," Mother shared, holding my hand in hers. "This is all I ever wanted for my children... to find the love I have and had with both your fathers. There is nothing greater in this whole wide world than having people you love experiencing life with you."

"Mom," I admonished her as my voice caught with

emotion and tears welled up in my eyes. "Now you're gonna make me cry."

She quickly took my cup from me and set it down before wrapping me up in a hug only a mother can provide. Her comforting sweet scent of honey and orange blossom gave me a sense of home that nothing else could. It triggered so many wonderful memories of growing up in this home with two doting fathers and a mother who was always there to be our cheerleader. Unable to hold back my tears, I clung to the last moments of being that child because once I walked out of this sitting room, I was a woman who had her own family to build and look after. The feeling was bittersweet, but every person alive has to face it one day.

"Shh, my darling, it's going to be an amazing adventure for you," Mother soothed. "Never forget that just because you have your own pack and life with them doesn't mean this won't always be your home. Rawlly and I are only a phone call away if you ever need anything. That will never change no matter what happens in life."

We stayed in her sitting room and talked. Well, I talked, she listened. It was exactly what I needed to share my fears and concerns in a safe place where I wouldn't be judged for voicing them. My mother was attentively engaged but didn't chime in and allowed me to get everything I was feeling out in the open. When I finished, the weight of keeping all that fear and worry inside lifted. It made me realize just how much I'd been carrying around.

Mother cupped my cheek as she studied me. "Darling, all of this is completely normal. No one said just because you're scent matched, everything would be perfect. Does it give you a better shot at a happy life together? Of course, but it doesn't change the fact that we are still human with our own scars and issues from the past."

She pulled me into another hug, rocking side to side like she did when I was a child. "Give yourself and them some slack. Trust yourself, my sweet girl. You've always had an internal compass that leads you in the right direction. There will be bumps along the way, but once you and your Alphas develop trust in each other, everything will smooth out."

"What if I get worse?" I whispered. "What if I can never have kids because my body can't handle it?"

That caused my mother to pause, and I sat up to look her in the face. Her calm demeanor had shifted to one more rigid and serious. "Bailey-Rose Thatcher, did something happen that I don't know about?"

"Nooo," I said hesitantly, drawing out the word. "I went to see Dr. Arbour when I got back from school, and he shared his concerns again about me having children. He tried to bring up that new experimental surgery, saying it had the potential to give me more freedom to the point I don't have to wear the heart monitor."

"You know that I support your choices, whatever they may be, when it comes to your condition. It's your body, your life, and any risk involved is one you have to take on, not me," Mother expressed as she clutched my hand tightly. "However, if Dr. Arbour continues to bring up the surgery, isn't it at least worth looking into?"

"That's just it. I did look into it. It's open heart surgery where they need to take my heart out of my chest. Then they add material to strengthen the weak spot in my heart where the hole was as a baby. Once that is done, they remove the malformed valve that doesn't work well and replace it with a new valve," I explained. "That's if the person doesn't have a genetic disorder that makes them fundamentally weaker than the average person or a rare blood type causing it to reject any tissue that doesn't match.

Mom, they would have to find a human tissue donor with my blood type because a pig or cow would be rejected."

I hadn't wanted to be so blunt about this, but the only way for her to understand why I was terrified to do this was total honesty. Mother nodded, her eyes welling up with tears as she tried to keep her composure. Her biggest fear after losing Papa Addy was that the same thing would happen to me. Of course, Papa Addy didn't have the exact same situation I did—I was far worse off. When Dr. Arbour told me there was a chance I could have a practically normal life with this surgery, I was ecstatic. Then I did the research and realized the seventy-percent chance an average person with my condition had dropped to fifty. If the genetic aspect of my heart condition wasn't a factor, I had so many more options.

As of right now, I had three.

Stay as I am monitoring my heart, taking medication, and keeping a quiet lifestyle.

Then there was a full heart transplant, which no one was sure I would survive due to the high chance of rejecting the heart.

Finally, there was this new repair surgery with its own risks but more of an option than replacement.

It was a hard pill to swallow the first time this was brought up two years ago, but the risks and results hadn't gotten better in that time. Not enough people needed the surgery for them to advance the process and anticipate the problems during recovery.

"Do they know?" Mother asked, her voice a soft whisper.

"About my heart? Yeah, I had an episode right in front of them ten minutes after meeting them. With one little nip on my neck, my body was so overwhelmed with sensation and need, I crashed. Crew had to give me an injection to slow my heart back down," I answered, flopping against the pillows. "Talk about a crash course."

Mother chuckled, knowing how people reacted when things like this happened. "While I'm glad to know you didn't try to keep it a secret about your health, I was more so asking if they knew about the surgery option?"

Rolling my head to the side, I looked at her. "It's hardly been two days. How exactly was I supposed to bring up something like that? Besides, I'm not doing it."

"Okay, you make a fair point on the timing," Mother agreed, nodding and biting on her perfectly manicured nail. "Have they asked you about kids?"

Sitting up straight, I narrowed my gaze on my mother. "Why?" The guilty look on her face had me a little worried. "Mother, what haven't you told me?"

She shifted, plucking at her dress absently, and refused to look me in the eye. "There was no reason to tell you right away, being so young and already rejected by the Scent Matchers."

"Mother," I snapped.

"If you have any children, they will be excluded from the database just like you were. The Scent Matchers refuse to allow a genetic defect to continue and affect further generations," Mother admitted. "The only reason your father didn't face the same issue was his diagnosis came later in life, well after we were bonded. Then your condition was worse so our family got put on a list."

"But Eli," I said as the realization hit me.

"Don't you worry about him. I have that well in hand whenever he's ready to admit he wants a family of his own. Which I'm hoping will be sooner rather than later now that you're going to be well looked after by your pack. No matter how I tried, he refused to accept he was your brother, not a third father... Lord love him," Mother grumbled. "You two are peas in a pod when it comes to looking after each other. The first thing you're worried about after I tell you that no child of yours will be matched is to worry about Eli."

She had a point. I didn't really process the fact she just told me that my children would suffer the same fate I had. Raking my fingers through my hair, I blew out a breath, not even sure how I was supposed to feel.

"I don't even know if kids are an option," I argued.

Mother shrugged. "Darling, no matter what happens, you still deserve to know all the facts, as do your Alphas. What you as a family choose to do is up to you."

"Well, that just made everything clear as mud," I mumbled, scrubbing my face with both hands as my stomach complained. "Any other major news I should be aware of before I get dressed and head down for breakfast?"

Tapping her chin as she hummed deep in thought, I rolled my eyes, knowing she was messing with me. Standing, I dropped a kiss on her cheek. "Love you, Mother, and thanks for coming back home to check on me. I really needed some mother-daughter time."

"Darling, there isn't anywhere I'd rather be right now than supporting you in this new phase of life," she assured me. "Now go get ready for the day, I can't wait to meet these men who are going to be part of our family."

Leaving her sitting room, I felt better and lighter, but at the same time, I worried about telling my new family that kids might not be an option. *Why couldn't things just be simple?* For once in my life, I'd really love to face a problem with a solution everyone could be happy about.

Warrick

Breakfast turned out to be an interesting situation with the surprise of meeting Bailey-Rose's parents. They arrived early this morning and were beyond excited to meet us all. Jolene insisted we call her Jolene, Mother, or Mom, whatever we felt comfortable with. Rawlins was a far more reserved man with kind eyes and a soothing voice who gave you his full attention when you spoke. It was intimidating, even though I knew he didn't mean it to be.

Seeing Crew and Rawlins side by side, there was no denying they were father and son. However, I could see hints of his mother in him as well, but more so in personality. Bailey was an exact copy of her mother, seeming only to share one eye with her biological father. It made me curious to know what his personality was like and if Eli took after him. We spent most of the meal answering questions and talking about our families—many of whom they knew in passing. The upper crust was a small community, and everyone had at least been introduced to one another at some point.

With breakfast finally over, Ulysses shared the plan that I was going to be taking Bailey-Rose out for the day while they packed things up.

"Oh, that's a brilliant plan," Jolene said, clasping her hands in excitement. "If you boys don't mind, I'd like to be of any assistance. That way, I can make sure she has everything she needs."

"Thank you, I think that will be a big help," Yun-Sun agreed. "Our plan was just to take everything we could find, but I'm sure we'd miss something important."

This answer seemed to please Jolene to no end, making Rawlins chuckle and pat her hand affectionately. "Dearest, please don't run them ragged. They might be our sons-in-law, but let's not overdo it on the first project together."

Jolene scowled at her Alpha in an expression I've seen my sweet Care Bear use once or twice already. It seems it wasn't only in personality that she took after her mother.

"Rawlly, are you telling me not to be bossy?" she questioned.

"Not at all, dearest. I would never use such a word," Rawlins assured her. "All I meant is you take everything on with such gusto it's hard for others to keep up."

My brows rose at the artful way he'd just worked around the accusation by stating the same thing in a different way. It was a mystery to me why he wasn't the man in the boardroom running things instead of leaving it all to Eli. With a shrewd mind like that, you'd think the man would crave the challenge.

"Rawlly," Jolene cooed. "You know better than to sweet talk me like I'm some egotistical CEO. However, if you feel like I'm going to be too much for these young men to handle, you can always join us and supervise."

Gareth started coughing as he choked on his coffee, and Vili started to thump him on the back to help. That whole interaction was a look into our future, of that I had no doubt. Bailey-Rose was a total sweetheart, but it was the rule of nature to make something deadly so enticing you couldn't help but be drawn to it. I had the feeling once our Omega got her feet under her when it came to us as a pack, we'd all be in trouble. That being said, today was my day to start collecting points in my favor for when I inevitably do something stupid.

Clearing my throat, I looked over at Bailey-Rose seated next to her mother, trying not to smile. "Do you need to grab anything before we go, Care Bear?"

I watched as she did this cute head tilt as she thought about my question. "We're going to your bar for the afternoon then out to dinner, right?"

"That was my plan, but I'm happy to change things if you have something else in mind," I offered.

"No, I think it will be a great day. I just wasn't sure if I'd need to change for dinner. Do you have a place picked out?" she asked.

A grin tugged at my lips. I wanted to tell her my plan so badly, but the surprise was going to be so worth it. "I do have a place in mind, but you'll be fine wearing what you've got on now. The only thing is you might need a sweater."

Last night she tried to kill us all with this soft pink silk nightgown that rippled over her body like water. When she caught us all staring, it was all I could do to behave myself when her nipples made an appearance. Everything in me wanted to know what it would feel like to tease her until she came only using her nipples. Yet I wasn't going to take that leap until she made the first move. Even then, I was terrified I was going to fuck up, make her heart go haywire, and we'd be taking a trip to the hospital instead.

I was beginning to learn that calling her Care Bear might be the best way to describe not only her personality but style. Everything about her was adorable, colorful, and simply made you smile when you saw her. With her being short and petite in size, it was a fine line to walk between being childlike and an aesthetic. Case in point, today she was wearing lavender short overalls with strawberries on them and a mint green crop top that showed the barest hint of her stomach. Bailey-Rose was a walking rainbow of cuteness, and I wouldn't change a damn thing.

"Okay, give me a sec. I'll run up and grab something," she said, getting up from the table and kissing her mother's cheek before hurtling off to her room.

The atmosphere at the table changed drastically with her exit. Jolene, who'd been nothing but a bundle of warm, motherly energy, shifted to something that had me sitting up straight as she pinned me with her piercing green gaze.

"Warrick, I'm going to say this to you, but the rest of you better listen carefully," she stated, casting the others a quick glance. "I love all my children the way only a mother can, but there is a special connection between a mother and her daughter. Bailey-Rose is a rare one-of-a-kind woman. I expect you to treat her with the utmost respect not only because she's your Omega, but if you don't, I will be the person you deal with. Trust me when I say that isn't something any of you want. Don't let the fact I'm an Omega and a philanthropist fool you. I've single-handedly destroyed companies, foreign governments, and made a leader of a cartel wet himself. I won't stand for anything less than my baby girl being treasured and loved more than anyone in the world. Have I made myself clear?"

My head bobbed in answer before I could even think about the action. Coming from a powerful family, I knew when to take a threat seriously or if they were bluffing. Jolene Thatcher was by no means bluffing, and I had zero doubts she could do everything she promised.

"Yes, ma'am," I blurted. "You have my solemn vow that I will spend my life making sure your daughter knows how absolutely perfect she is to me... *us*," I corrected quickly, feeling flustered.

With one more soul-searching gaze, the terrifying woman smiled, and the ominous energy vanished. "Oh, I love that. Now just to make sure you're aware Bailey-Rose can't drink, not with the medication she's on."

Taking a deep breath, I relaxed into my seat, rubbing my sweaty hands on my jeans. "Yes, she already shared that with me. My plan is to help teach her what to order at a bar or even make at home so she doesn't feel left out. There are hundreds of options for her with ingredients all bars carry."

"How sweet... isn't that just wonderful, Rawlly?" Jolene asked, leaning against Rawlins and resting her head on his shoulder.

Her Alpha pressed a kiss to her head before answering. "Yes, my dearest. It seems these men are exactly what our little girl needs."

"We want to give her everything," Vili announced, his tone gruff with irritation. "It makes me angry like a volcano that so many people didn't try. Our sweet kitten can do anything if given the chance to figure out how. No imagination, these people, so boring and selfish."

Jolene's smile grew even bigger at Vili's outrage. "Quite right," she agreed. "So many people focus on what she can't do instead of simply making adjustments. Then again, as you aptly put it, people are selfish and couldn't possibly put themselves in another person's shoes."

"I would love to have her make a list of all the things she's always wanted to do, then figure out if there's a way to make it happen," Yun-Sun added. "Kind of like a bucket list but more so focused on missed opportunities."

Jolene jostled Rawlins in her excitement. "Oh my God, I don't think they could be more perfect if they tried. Rawlly, our little girl is all grown up with a pack of her own, moving out, and starting a life full of adventure and romance."

The Alpha took his partner's abuse with the hint of a smile tugging at his lips. Rawlins might be a reserved man by nature, but it was obvious to see how much of a relief it was to know that Bailey-Rose had people to surround her with love.

Faster than I anticipated, Bailey-Rose entered the dining room where we all still sat. She had a purse slung across her chest and a fuzzy pink sweater in her hands. "Ready to go?"

I pushed back my chair and stood, casting a glance back at the others to make sure they didn't need me for anything before I left. Bailey-Rose seemed to take this hesitation as reluctance.

"Unless you want to stay here," she offered. "It's fine. We can all work on packing my things. Seems silly to make you guys do all the work."

"Absolutely not," Jolene said as she jumped to her feet, cutting off any further argument. "You and Warrick are going to have a fabulous day while leaving the packing to me. Young lady, I don't want to see you back in this house until tomorrow when you come over for tea and to tell me all about your evening. Now go, spend time with your handsome match, and have fun."

"All right, Mother, you win." Bailey-Rose sighed, giving into her mother's wishes.

Honestly, I'm not sure anyone could argue with that woman when she made up her mind about something. It made me wonder once more what Bailey-Rose's other father was like. It seems the option was to ask and see if my Care Bear was up for sharing that part of her life with me.

Reaching her side, I offered my arm in a gentlemanly manner, getting an approving wink from her mother. Feeling rather good about myself, I flashed my new mother-in-law a bright smile and guided my girl out the front door.

This time, when we drove over, we made sure to bring all the vehicles that could hold boxes. All of us except me, that is. I made sure to leave last and park my little Pac-Man where it wouldn't be seen.

The anticipation of her seeing what our ride was had me almost skipping over to the car. It was my one indulgence and happened to be my most prized possession. Finally, when we rounded Gareth's Hummer, she spotted our ride for the day. Coming to an abrupt halt, she just stared at it, jaw falling open as she looked from me to the car.

"Oh my God, it's so cute," she squealed, letting go of me and rushing forward to look. "Please tell me it has a name. It has to have a name."

"I call him Pac-Man," I answered with a shit-eating grin.

Before breakfast, I came out and put the top down on my little vintage Fiat 500. This left it in the perfect position to show off its cream-colored seats that paired so well with the bright sunny yellow that made up the rest of the car. It was a rolling ball of sunshine I knew my Care Bear would love.

"That is a perfect name," Bailey-Rose agreed then hesitated. "We're taking this to drive for the day, right?"

"Care Bear, do you honestly think this little guy can hold more than one box? It would be useless to leave it here for them," I pointed out. "Hop in. We're going for a ride."

The shrill sound of her excitement almost had me flinching, but the joy of seeing her so excited made the hearing loss worth it. Feeling the need to show off, I vaulted over the side of the car, landing in my seat before reaching over and buckling in my girl. This brought us face to face, and I couldn't resist the urge to kiss her. The way her cheeks were pink with excitement and her dual-colored eyes sparkled made her irresistible.

I'd planned for it to be a simple peck on the lips, but

Bailey-Rose had other plans. When I tried to pull back, she grabbed my T-shirt, refusing to let me back away from her. Not one to argue with a woman, especially one who smelled like summer nights and romantic moments, I happily gave in. My hand cupped her face, tilting it up so I could deepen the kiss and nibble at her lower lip. To my surprise, she instantly opened up, surrendering herself to me. A bigger man might have been able to slow things down, but I was no such man. I was so weak for this woman it was fucking nuts.

With a growl, I pulled myself together enough to pull back and rest my forehead against hers as we caught our breath. "Holy shit." I panted.

"You can say that again." Bailey-Rose chuckled. "That was amazing. I don't think I've been kissed like that in my life."

Lifting my head, I looked into her eyes feeling like I was king of the world. "Well, I hope you're ready to be kissed like that for the rest of your life because you are addictive."

The bloom of pink on her cheeks at my words did something to me that I'd never experienced with a person before. I wanted to wrap her in my arms protectively, yet at the same time, I wanted to ravage her until she was screaming my name. Both were so primal and polar opposite, it felt a little scary to be so out of control. That was the last thing Bailey-Rose needed. She deserved Alphas who could control their natures and didn't fall mindlessly into rut.

"I think we better go before I take this too far," I whispered, pressing a kiss to her nose.

She hummed her agreement and let me click the seat belt into place before doing the same for myself. Starting the car, I was rather thankful it was a stick shift. That meant I needed to give it my full attention, and it would keep my hand busy. Backing out of the spot, I pulled my shit together, and we were off. I planned to take the long way to the bar, but I thought it might be better to spend time with her someplace more public.

A few minutes later, Bailey-Rose threw her hands up and let out a shout of joy as we sped down the highway. It was intoxicating to see her enjoying the small moments in life, soaking in the sun, and her beaming smile. Much to my family's disdain, I've always been a hopeless romantic, but I never truly believed I could have a romance like you saw in the movies.

This stunning woman beside me was determined to prove me wrong.

God, what the hell had I done to deserve such a woman to be my scent match?

"Boss, what are you doing here? I thought you were on courting leave?" Drew, my manager, asked when I entered the bar.

Stepping to the side, I revealed Bailey-Rose who'd been trying to hide behind me. "Drew, this is Bailey-Rose Thatcher, my scent matched Omega. Bailey-Rose, this is Drew. He's my right-hand man who runs things when I'm not here. I would be lost without this guy, and I was lucky to con him into working for me."

Bailey-Rose smiled and gave a small wave. "Hi."

Drew looked from her to me with wide, shocked eyes. "Holy shit, she's like a walking, talking ball of cotton candy."

"Back off, man, she's my ball of cotton candy," I warned, wrapping an arm around Bailey-Rose's shoulders, cuddling her close to me.

The Beta threw his hands up in surrender but wouldn't stop grinning. "Don't you worry, boss. I'm a bonded man. My Alphas would kick my ass if I dared let my attention wander."

"Good, because I really didn't want to have to fire you," I admitted, relaxing slightly. "If you could do me a solid and pretend I'm not here, that would be amazing. As you mentioned, I'm on courting leave, and this is supposed to be a date. Oh, and we're going to take the training section of the bar so I can teach her about mixology."

Drew flashed me a thumbs-up as one of the servers called for him. "Duty calls… gotta make sure this place stays standing until you come back."

I hadn't been kidding when I told Bailey-Rose I was lucky to have that guy. He was my secret weapon to success that no one would ever guess since he was a Beta. Somewhere along the way, our society as a whole seemed to forget that Betas could be wildly successful, given the chance.

Returning my attention to my shy little Omega, I interlaced our fingers and led the way to the back of the bar. The Fat Mule was the culmination of all the dreams I'd had of one day owning my own bar. In all reality, it was two bars in one. The front of the house was an easy-going, chill cocktail bar to grab a happy hour drink and eat. Many sofas and armchairs were organized in little groupings to make it feel more intimate. When you passed through the dual barn doors in the middle of the bar, it changed into a cheeky, fun, playful nightclub with neon signs and a disco ball. Like a mullet, it was business in the front, party in the back.

While the name of the bar stayed the same, I created two logos to match the feel of each space. The more business side of things was a copper mule mug that was knocked over with ice, lime, and mint spilling out of it. As for the night-club, I had an artist draw me up a mule dancing under a disco ball with a Moscow mule mug in one hand raised high above its head like it just doesn't care. This way, when advertising was done, people knew which side of things the deals fell on.

"Warrick, you came up with all this?" Bailey-Rose asked as I showed her around the place.

I gave a little huff on my nails before rubbing them on my shirt. "Why, yes... yes I did. So far, it's been rather successful too. Seems I picked up more from watching all the failures my siblings and other family members made in business, allowing me to avoid doing them myself."

Bailey-Rose wandered around the bar's club section, looking at all the random art painted on the exposed brick walls. It made me think I should have her add something to the building. None of us had seen what her style was like other than the gloomy self-portraits that hung on her bedroom walls. Something told me that wasn't a fair glimpse into her artistic eye.

"Are these all local artists or did you commission them?" she asked, pausing to stare at one section that was like a psychedelic trip of swirling colors.

"Local. I put out an ad and picked artists I thought would fit the vibe I was looking for. It was really fun to see what the city had to offer," I shared. "What about you? Would you like to add your mark on The Fat Mule?"

Whipping around to face me, her expression full of excitement, she rushed forward and gripped my hand. "Do you mean that? I could absolutely create something that would be perfect for this space."

I gripped her chin with my free hand and leaned down to softly kiss her perfect lips. "I would never joke about art with you. Even having just met you, it's clear how much it means to you. I would be honored if you wanted to bless my business with your talent. You can even pick where you want to put it."

She practically vibrated with excitement in my grasp, popping up on her toes to kiss me. It caught me so off guard that I almost fell backward, but I managed to save the moment by twirling her as I peppered her face with kisses. The laughter that bubbled out of her was the sweetest sound I could imagine. Setting her on her feet, I brushed her hair out of her face and simply studied her for a moment.

"What?" Bailey-Rose asked.

I shook my head and smiled. "Nothing, just can't believe I get to have you in my life."

She blushed and dropped her gaze, making me grin like an idiot. There was something powerful about seeing my effect on her. It made me want to do it again and again to ensure I wasn't dreaming.

"Come on, let's go make some drinks and create some magic," I urged, knowing if I didn't give us an activity, I was going to test out how soundproof my office was.

BAILEY-ROSE

Never did I think there was so much science that went into making cocktails. Warrick was a patient teacher explaining the tools, ingredients, and how to balance the flavor of a drink. He even laughed when I shook a carbonated cocktail and shot the cover off the shaker and out into the dining area.

Time flew by as we laughed and talked about anything and everything that came to mind. Warrick was such a warm person it was effortless to spend time together. In many ways, it felt like I'd known him for years instead of days. My hope was it would be just as easy to connect with the other men in my pack. Talking with my mother helped immensely, but the fear of them deciding I was too much work or held them back still lingered.

"Okay, so we've decided to make the drink an experience," Warrick said as he wrote on a fresh sheet of paper. "You said your favorite summer treat is a snow cone, which I think is brilliant. We have an ice shaver that can whip up what we need in no time. Give me a moment to collect all these ingredients from the back storage, and we'll get this vision of yours created."

Dropping a quick kiss on my nose, he rounded the bar and headed into the kitchen. Having gone to help him carry other things we needed, I knew the storage for the whole place was off the kitchen next to the walk-in freezer. Unsure what to do, I noticed how messy and chaotic everything was, so I started to clean up.

The main bar for The Fat Mule took up the whole width of the building. There were five stations to serve from while one end of the bar was for table orders, and the other end where we were was for training. It allowed the trainee to be in the thick of things and help but not be on the front lines since the kitchen access was right there, preventing people from trying to order. Never having been in a bar, it was fascinating to watch the bartenders making drinks three or four at a time, never forgetting what they were doing. Warrick and Drew ran a well-oiled machine, and all their employees seemed to respect them.

Things were getting busy since happy hour started a little over a half hour ago. I did my best to ignore what was going on, feeling nervous to be back here without Warrick. What if someone asked me to make them a drink? I didn't know the first thing about whipping up a real cocktail. My anxiety shot through the roof when I looked up and came face to face with Randall.

"Bumblebee, what the hell are you doing behind the bar?" Randall demanded, his expression full of worry, confusing me even more.

I opened my mouth to say something, but before I could manage, he marched around and ducked under the bar. Grabbing my wrist, he flipped up the section of the bartop and tried to drag me after him.

"Randall, stop," I pleaded, digging in my heels.

It didn't matter what I wanted, Randall was six foot two and built like a linebacker with all the hours he'd spent in the gym. Either I followed after him, or there was a risk I could get seriously hurt. I'd never seen Randall like this before. He'd been sweet, kind, and understanding about my condition with his brother in a similar situation as myself. This was a darker side of the Alpha I'd dated a mere week ago.

"No, Bailey, you don't belong in a place like this. What would your brothers say? Hell, what would your parents think if they knew you were working at some seedy bar?" Randall challenged, coming to an abrupt halt, so I crashed into him.

Catching me, he sighed, closing his eyes as if trying to calm himself down. "Why are you doing this to us? You finally came home, and everything was going to be perfect. All that stood in the way of our happily ever after was your need to finish school. Now that's all finished, we can move forward," he murmured, brushing his fingers along my jaw.

Fear raced through me at the possessive and terrifying look in Randall's eyes. "Why do you even care? We aren't even dating anymore, not after you cheated on me," I whispered harshly, not wanting to cause an even bigger scene as I tried to pull my arm free. "I'll ask you once more, Randall. Let. Me. Go."

"Let you go? Cheated on you? Bumblebee, what are you saying?" Randall questioned, utterly confused. Then his grip tightened on my arm, making me whimper as his gaze hardened. "Why are you acting like I'm the bad guy? Did you tell your brothers about what you saw? Are they the ones who told you we broke up?"

"They didn't need to tell me anything," I sobbed, struggling to free my arm. "Randall, I mean it. Let me go, or I'm going to make you."

"Make me? Bumblebee, you can't even handle having sex. What makes you believe you could fight me off? Furthermore, it's your fault I had to sleep with that Beta bitch. Why do you think I needed to fuck her? Could it be because my girlfriend can't meet my needs?" Randall shot back, verbally slapping me in the face with one of my biggest fears. "I did that for us, and now you've decided that we're done? Sorry, Bumblebee, I don't remember ever agreeing to that. I was just giving you time to cool off. I know how emotional you get. I hoped we could talk like adults, let me explain the sacrifices I was making for you... for *us*. Clearly, it was a mistake to leave you to your own devices after being free to do as you pleased while at college. Now I'm going to have to fix things until I get my sweet submissive Bumblebee back."

The normally calming scent of freshly roasted candied pecans had a burned tang to it as Warrick appeared. Gone was the warm, fun-loving man I'd spent the day with. In its place was a furious Alpha whose commanding energy was crackling in the air around me.

"Get your fucking hand off *my* Omega," Warrick bit out through clenched teeth as he squeezed Randall's wrist, causing my ex to flinch and let out a grunt of pain.

The second I was free, Warrick used his grip on Randall and shoved him away before scooping me up. Instantly, I wrapped around him like a koala burying my face in his neck, only then realizing I was whining. My body shook as the adrenaline and fear coursed through my body, causing my breath to come out in shuddering gasps.

"Your Omega? What are you talking about? That's my girlfriend. She doesn't have anyone but me." Randall scoffed.

"Wrong, asshole," Warrick stated. "Bailey-Rose has a scent matched pack now, so any relationship you were delusional enough to think you had after cheating on her is over. Scent matched pairings trump any other previous claim on an Omega. End. Of. Story. Now get the fuck out of my bar. You aren't welcome here, and if I find out you so much as wave at Bailey-Rose ever again, I'll have you arrested."

"You would really send *me* to jail over a defective Omega like her?" Randall challenged. "Do you even know who I am?"

"Yeah, someone who's about to be arrested if you don't leave *right this second*," Warrick threatened, a growl coating his words, making me whimper at the anger behind them. "Drew, deal with this prick. I'll be in my office if the police arrive."

"It doesn't matter... she is my girlfriend," Randall bellowed, accompanied by the sounds of him fighting off whoever was trying to remove him. "You'll see the truth before long. She'll come back to me. I know she will."

Keeping my face tucked against Warrick's skin, I felt him turn and walk away from the situation. A few moments later, Warrick sat on what felt like a couch and instantly started to purr as he stroked a hand up and down my back.

"Shh, it's okay, Care Bear, I've got you," he murmured, kissing and nuzzling his cheek against my hair. "I'm so sorry that happened. I should've had you come with me to the back. Trust me when I say he will never be allowed in this bar ever again. In fact, I think I have enough connections in this city that he won't be able to eat anywhere that isn't fast food."

"He hates fast food," I mumbled.

"Perfect, then I'll make a few calls later tonight, and by tomorrow, he'll be blacklisted," Warrick assured me.

Sitting up just enough to meet Warrick's gaze, I needed to see if he was serious. The determined expression told me I had nothing to worry about. My Alpha was pissed and looking for revenge.

"Warrick..." I started, then decided I wasn't sure I wanted to know the answer.

He leaned forward, resting his forehead against mine. "What is it, Care Bear? No matter what you have to tell me, I'll listen. You can also ask me anything, and I'll answer you honestly, of that I promise. I don't ever want you to be worried about sharing what you're thinking or feeling."

I clutched his head in my hands, using his reassurance to ground me. Everything inside me wanted to believe he meant every word he said, but Randall's words were like barbs in my heart. How could I have been so wrong about him? Never in a million years would I have thought Randall capable of this kind of cruelty.

"What if he's right? What if I'm not enough?" I rasped. "There are five of you... if I can't even manage to be enough for one Alpha, how can it be possible with my own pack?"

One of Warrick's hands slid into my hair at the base of my neck then fisted. With a gentle tug, he drew my head back until I was looking up at the ceiling, my neck exposed to him. I could feel his lips as they brushed over my skin and his hot breath which had me shivering with need. The sensation of rough fingers caressed my bare leg until they slipped under my shorts and stopped at the crease where my leg met my body. A moan floated out of my mouth as he skimmed the edge of my underwear line, teasing that sensitive skin, yet so far from where I wanted him.

"If he can't see what's right in front of his face, then he's the one who will never be enough," Warrick said, his lips dancing along my skin as he spoke.

"So what if we have to make sure we don't overdo it? Personally, I think that gives me the perfect excuse to take my time and enjoy. Every. Single. Inch. of your body," Warrick added, making sure to punctuate that last part with teasing kisses as he brought me closer to him. "Tell me, Bailey-Rose, did that man worship you the way you deserve to be worshiped? I'm betting that man is a selfish asshole who only cared about what he got out of sex."

Using his nails ever so slightly, he dragged them along my thigh as he removed his hand, making me gasp. Warrick then slipped his fingers under my shirt, letting his thumb sweep over my nipple as his large hand wrapped around my ribs. I felt so small compared to him, yet I don't think I've ever felt safer. When his hand in my hair finally released its hold, I dove in for a kiss, nipping at his lips to give me what I desperately needed.

Warrick didn't hold back as he feasted on my mouth. It was intense, heady, and everything I never knew I wanted. There was a click, and one strap of my overalls slipped off my shoulder, soon followed by the other. With no hesitation, Warrick shoved up my shirt, exposing my cream-colored silk bra. When he hooked a finger over the edge of the cup and pulled it down, he broke our kiss, dipping his head to catch my nipple in his mouth. Tossing my head back, I arched, giving him the access he wanted, trusting his one hand splayed in the middle of my back would support me.

When he switched to the other side, I cried out, rocking against him, needing to feel more. Just like with Ulysses, my skin burned with desire I'd never experienced with any partner. It was like they had the magic touch to coax what they wanted out of me, and I wanted nothing more than to please them.

"So beautiful," Warrick whispered as he kissed along my breastbone, where I had a scar from past surgeries. "I could listen to your little moans and gasps all night long. God, just imagining you sprawled out in my bed as I found every spot that made you cry out would be heaven. You have no idea how perfect you are, do you, my sweet Bailey-Rose?"

His teeth bit down on the meat of my breast, and I wanted nothing more than for him to mark me. The bond that can be created between an Alpha and an Omega was so intimate, unique science couldn't explain it. For years, they've tried to understand why there was a primal drive for Alphas to mark their Omegas, for us to carry their scent along with their mark, proving we belonged to them and no one else. Once that bond is made, it can never be broken— those two are bonded for life.

Some Omegas experience being able to *feel* their Alphas on a more emotional level. While Alphas have been known to locate their Omega no matter where they are, it's like they have an internal tracking that's always fixated on their bonded partner. Each experience is different, special, and seems to be what the individual needs. Betas can also experience the bond through an Alpha's mark, but the Betas can't initiate the bond. It's only through the Alpha's bite that the experience is created.

In our world, the bonding mark is like being married for eternity. You are now one with that person or pack, allowing you access to everything the Omega's Alphas have to offer. As always with Betas, there's an extra step, and the Alpha needs to make a declaration in writing that the Beta is bonded to them in all ways. This is why it's so important never to take being marked lightly and is seen as the ultimate commitment to each other. So why was I on the verge of begging Warrick to mark me after only a few days? It was too fast. No matter how badly I wanted to believe otherwise, we didn't know each other.

As if he could tell I was distracted, he pinched my nipple, making me shout and grind against him. "Don't get lost on me now," Warrick cautioned, letting his finger swirl around my nipple. "I'm not often a man who gets possessive or jealous, but right now, I don't want to share your attention with anything else."

Holy shit, why was that so hot? No one ever talked to me the way these men seemed to so naturally. I was hardly ever seen as the sultry, sensual goddess they viewed me as. Most people tended to pat me on the head like I was a puppy, happy to stick by their side as they walked through life. There was no doubt in my mind that Warrick saw me as a woman.

"What do you think? Have I teased you enough to chase away the lies that bastard dared to utter in front of me?" Warrick asked as he tugged down the front of my overalls. "Fucking hell, Care Bear. Do you even realize how strongly you're perfuming for me? Could it be that your body realizes how needy you are even if you don't?"

My brain was in a cloud of euphoric feelings that I didn't even notice how strong my scent was. It permeated the room to the point now that I noticed I could taste it on my tongue.

"I feel hot, so hot, and I want to be touched. No, I crave being touched by you. Please don't stop," I answered, rambling, not really sure if I was answering any of his questions.

Righting me so I was facing him once more, he grinned as he nuzzled his nose against mine. "Shh, Bailey-Rose, let your Alpha take care of you. Let me give you everything you need and deserve."

He caught my lips in a hungry kiss, but it felt like he was still holding himself back. Then in an abrupt move, he gripped my hips, lifted, spun me to face the other direction, and set me back down. With a hand on my chest, he urged me to lean back against him.

"That's it, my precious girl. Forget everything but what's happening right here between us. Nothing else in the world matters but you and me right here," he said as his other hand glided down my stomach and slipped under the band of my underwear. "I'm going to do my best to give you everything you need and not set off any alarms."

My brain didn't give a flying fuck about what he was saying with his fingers so close to where I was desperate to have him touch. It got to the point I rolled my hips to see if I could get closer, which earned me a chuckle from my Alpha.

"That's not letting me take the lead now, is it? Be a good girl, and you'll be rewarded..." Warrick paused to nip at the shell of my ear, "... I promise."

Already melting at his words, he started to purr as he nuzzled against my neck that I willingly exposed to him. Again, here I was practically begging him to mark me, but Warrick was nothing but a gentleman who kissed and nipped my offered column of skin, acknowledging the gesture. Then any rejection I might have felt was thrown out the window as he let his fingers slide over my pussy. I could feel how slick I was for him and how my body molded to his touch, opening to him like a flower in the sunlight.

"*Fuck*, I can feel how wet you are for me," Warrick praised. "So eager to please me, are you, precious girl? I did promise that good girls get rewarded, and I'm nothing but a man of my word."

In a fluid motion, he sank one finger into me, and I nearly blacked out with the intense pleasure that flooded my body. He'd gotten me so turned on with simple touches and dirty words that for him to make me come was going to be child's play. He languidly stroked that finger in and out of me, using the heel of his palm to apply pressure to my clit. Proving he was a man above other men, he located that certain spot every woman has at her core, guaranteed to bring on the fireworks.

Unable to stay as relaxed as I was at the start, my nails dug into his arms as the orgasm began to build. Closing my eyes, I tried to slow my breathing, but it was in vain as Warrick added a second finger and picked up a little more speed. Cries of pleasure poured out of me as the pressure from the impending climax built. Finally, when the dam broke, I let the feeling sweep me away, allowing my body to do as it pleased, unable to fight the natural response. Warrick slowed his movements but didn't stop nudging that happy button, causing my muscles to spasm in delight. Then they stilled, but he didn't remove them. Instead, it was almost like he simply enjoyed having them there to mark his territory.

"You, Bailey-Rose, are everything I ever hoped for and so much more," Warrick murmured, removing his fingers. "There is nothing I would change about you because, to me, you are flawless."

As if to add to that statement, he proceeded to place those two fingers in his mouth and suck them clean. He hummed like tasting me was as delicious as dessert, which I couldn't fathom, but it was fucking hot. Boneless and sated, I snuggled with Warrick on the couch in his office. After a bit, he helped to put my outfit back together and wrapped me tightly in his arms.

"Promise me if Randall ever tries to corner you again that you call one of us right away. I don't like the way he looked at you. It was almost as if he believed he was entitled to have you," Warrick said in a serious tone. "I think we need to give you a panic button or see if we can add a different setting to your monitor to page us if there's a problem."

"As much as I don't want to agree, I think it would make me feel safer too," I admitted. "Would you be upset if we did dinner another time? I think I'd like to go home and be with everyone else for the evening."

Warrick tucked some hair behind my ear and smiled. "We have the rest of our lives to go on dates, so I don't mind one bit. Plus, I feel like this is something we might want to share with the others sooner rather than later, just so they know to be aware."

Yun-Sun

The move had gone as smoothly as any move could. Jolene was a driven taskmaster, but she was detailed and organized in everything she did. Each box was labeled with what was inside it on the top and side so no matter how you stacked them, you could find it easily. Since the majority of it was her clothes, we stacked those in the closet while the others were lined up against the outside.

We hadn't had the chance to go over final selections with Bailey-Rose about setting up the room, but I made the executive call to at least get basics so the room could be used. Looking at all the things she'd picked out gave me a rather interesting look into her mind. It was creative, abstract, and honed in on finding maximum comfort.

"Are you sure this is the one she would have picked?" Gareth asked from the top of a stepladder. "I didn't even know a bed like this existed. Thank fuck the ceiling has enough wood to it that we can mount it properly."

It had been a risk to pick this bed out of the three she saved, but this one showed it had been viewed twenty times. That told me it was the one she really wanted yet didn't think we would go for. I knew it would take a little adjusting for her to realize that this room is *hers*. No matter what she wanted to do with it, we would back her one hundred percent. Omegas needed a space that met their personal needs, and the only person who could make that happen was Bailey-Rose.

"Trust me, this is absolutely what she wants," Ulysses said, handing up the rope to Gareth.

We'd already put together the mint green loveseat with a matching pair of armchairs and a pastel pink coffee table shaped like a daisy. I made sure we had plenty of hangers and organization for the closet. That might have been me putting my own desires for order in the chaos that was this room, but it couldn't hurt. Other than bedding so she could sleep here tonight, I didn't get any additional accessories for the room. As long as she had a place to relax, sleep, and store her clothes, we could manage. Tomorrow we'd all go to the store for her to pick out whatever pillows and blankets might be needed.

"Okay, that was the last rope. Now we can wrestle that mattress into place," Gareth announced as he hopped off the ladder.

"I said sorry," Vili muttered as he tied the lilac canvas border to the ropes creating the space to put the round mass off fluff. "Excitement took over, and I had to open."

Gareth patted Vili on the shoulder. "It's okay. I'm just teasing you. Even if you left the mattress shrink wrapped, it still would be a bitch to get in a hanging cradle of ropes."

"You think she let us join her tonight?" Vili asked. "I want to snuggle our kitten in her nest and sway gently in the air."

Vili, at his core, was a hopeless artist who saw the world and all its possibilities, much like I think Bailey-Rose does. Maybe it was their creative mind that gave them the ability to see what we linear-minded folks didn't. It was strange how our pack was such a blend of opposites. Half of us were detailed rule followers who worked by the book, while the other half saw the world in gray, lines blurred, and nothing was ever permanent. Yet somehow, it worked to create a family who made each other better.

Warrick and Vili reminded the rest of us there was more to life than accomplishing the next goal. Especially now that we had Bailey-Rose in our lives, I could easily see how work would become something I resented for taking me away from her. My work was important, but it didn't need to be all I cared about—like my father. Our family owned one of the most prestigious law firms in Oldstead, the second largest city in Preidon. It had been assumed I would join my father since I was the only male to be born into our family.

"Hey, you gonna help us or what, Yun?" Gareth called, pulling me from my thoughts.

Immediately, I grabbed a section of the feather-stuffed poof that served as a mattress for the round floating nest I'd ordered. It was unlike anything I'd ever seen. A network of woven ropes created the base covered by a thick canvas that served as a boundary to keep whatever was inside from falling out. One section of the structure was left open so people could easily get in and out of bed.

"Hold on, let me grab the damn thing," Ulysses grunted. "Were we supposed to put this in, then hang the ropes?"

There was no answer as we struggled to get this unwieldy mass into a moving target.

"Are you seriously asking that question *now*?" Gareth muttered. "Look, I was in charge of getting the eyes anchored in the ceiling, that's it. Did anyone bother to read the instructions all the way through?"

We all paused, realizing the answer to that was no. "I was working on the coffee table," I pointed out. "You three were supposed to manage this."

"Fucking hell, the damn thing won't stay still," Ulysses

snapped. "Vili, let go of the mattress and see if you can keep this damn thing in check."

Dripping sweat with copious amounts of swearing, we managed to get the fucking thing in the net we'd hung. It looked like a giant ball of marshmallow fluff was trying to escape, oozing out of the space between the ropes. The picture online made it look way more inviting, but at this point, I'd take the win that it was where it was supposed to be. Dropping to the floor, I sprawled out, my breathing labored and my heart feeling like it was going to pop out of my chest.

"God, that shouldn't have kicked our asses that badly," I commented. "Someone find the instructions and tell me we didn't do this the hardest way possible."

"Oh, I found it," Vili exclaimed, waving the papers in the air. "Ah, I see... I see, there are two. One, if you want to use different mattress, then this for goose-down nesting poof. Let's see what the poof one says."

Vili's handle on the Preidonian language was excellent, but his reading and writing skills weren't at the same level. He managed brilliantly, but there were times he'd come find one of us to help him navigate something he didn't know. I admired the man. Never once did he seem embarrassed or ashamed that he couldn't figure out a word or phrase. He used to tell me that no matter what age you are, learning a new language is the same as for a child. You start small and build. No one shames a child for not understanding something, so why should his being an adult matter?

"Ah, yes, this better idea," Vili mumbled, nodding his head. "They say hang half, put poof, then finish the rest. Seems much better idea, and I didn't make harder by opening poof." The room filled with our groans at this news.

"Next time, one person reads the whole thing before we

even get started," Gareth suggested. "Then they can tell people what to do and split up the work."

"So I shouldn't mention that there is still the gauze covering that has fairy lights sewn into it to drape?" I asked, knowing the answer as I shoved up on my elbows.

Ulysses and Gareth flipped me off, but Vili seemed rather excited. The discussion was sidetracked as all our phones went off. Pulling mine out of my pocket, I saw it was from Warrick.

WARRICK:

Hey we're heading back to have dinner at the house. A situation came up and Bailey-Rose wasn't up for it after that.

I frowned, not liking any part of that message.

YUN-SUN:

Is she okay?

WARRICK:

I think so, she just seems worn out. It had been a great day until her ex decided to make an appearance.

ULYSSES:

WHAT! That fucker dared to approach her after what he did?

WARRICK:

Guys, I'll fill you in when we get home. I'm bringing all the stuff we were going to use to make the drink we created so we can experiment in peace. You guys need to be willing guinea pigs and try whatever she puts together.

GARETH:

Done and done. You know you didn't need
to ask that. We can't say no to the woman.

VILI:

I be good guinea pig, she can feed me
anything.

ULYSSES:

War, you promise she's okay?

WARRICK:

From what I can tell, yes, but I don't know
her well enough to know if it's an act. Gotta
run, can't be texting and driving, precious
cargo and all.

YUN-SUN:

Drive safe, see you when you get here.

Looking up from my phone, I locked eyes with Ulysses, knowing out of all of us, he'd be the one to do something stupid. I'm sure his history with Bailey-Rose made matters like this worse for him, and I was ready to hunt the bastard down for even looking at our girl.

"I think I should call her brothers," Ulysses stated.

Reaching over, I gripped his arm tightly, using the touch to ground him. "Maybe you should wait. Let's get the whole story before we escalate matters. I'm not saying you shouldn't, but, Lys, if they ask you what happened, we don't have much to tell them."

He dropped his gaze and nodded. "The thought of that man even breathing the same air as my Rosie makes me want to punch him in the throat."

"Trust me, I don't even know a thing about the fucker other than he hurt our girl. However, I'd be right behind you to give him two black eyes so he can't even look at her," Gareth shared as he stood and started to pace the room.

Vili looked at all of us with concern and a little uncertainty. No matter how rude or mean people were to him, Vili treated everyone with kindness. I wasn't sure if he was the type of man who would throw punches. Then again, it wouldn't be good if we were all hotheads ready to charge to war at the drop of a hat.

"Now is no time to worry about things that don't matter," Vili announced, all traces of his uncertainty gone and replaced with total confidence. "My kitten is upset, so we prepare to make her feel safe and cared for. Running off to punch stupid people is not going to help. It will only make our pretty lady sad. So we need pillows, blankets, big hoodie, and something sweet. Oh! I will make my cocoa. Yes, that will work best."

The three of us looked at each other, rather confused by this change in attitude. We had strong personalities in our pack, but Vili was our go-with-the-flow champion. To see him giving orders was odd as much as it was heartwarming.

"I'll grab a hoodie and the pillows off my bed," I said, holding out a hand to Gareth for him to pull me up. "Where should I bring it all?"

Vili cocked his head as if he didn't understand what I was asking. "Here," he answered, pointing to the bed. "This is her nest, no?"

Okay, I deserved that look. Of course, it made sense to establish this space as warm and comforting from the start. "Yup, you're absolutely right."

"Look, I know this might be a stupid question, but is there such a thing as too many pillows in a nest? As we all know, Warrick likes to pretend he's an Omega with the mountain of pillows he has on his bed. Should I take them all, save one, or what?" Gareth questioned.

We contemplated that question for a moment. I wasn't sure how we would even fit in the space with how the poof took up so much room in the netting. Before any of us could react, Vili launched himself onto the bed with only a soft *ooph* to let us know he was fine since he was lost from sight. The bed started to sway, but whatever Vili was doing seemed to deflate the poof somewhat. Eventually, the bed began to take shape, and I was shocked to find how large the sleeping space was. It could easily fit all six of us and more, but it was perfect for us to snuggle up with our Omega.

Looking like he'd just been put through the air-fluff cycle in the dryer, Vili's hair stuck out all over the place with his glasses skewed on his face. However, the man's giant smile had me thinking he might be making this his permanent sleeping place.

"This is magnificent," he shared while fixing his glasses. "So cozy and very, very soft and fluffy. This perfect for our sweet little kitten."

Ulysses chuckled and clapped me on the back. "Come on, guys, let's gather what we need while Vili makes the hot cocoa. Oh, V, make sure you put lots of marshmallows in the cup. Rosie can never get enough of them."

As we headed down, I glanced at my watch. With work traffic, we had about fifteen minutes to get this set up and be downstairs to grab her. Taking off at a jog, I hurried to my room and slid to a stop in front of the shelf that had all my hoodies folded and stacked neatly. More than once over the years, people have commented on my particular need to keep everything in order, but I didn't see a problem with it. So what if I color-coordinated everything and sectioned out by season? It gave me comfort to know I knew where everything was, so when I needed to find something in a pinch, I knew right where to look.

Instinctively, I went for my old college hoodie, the one I've had the longest and was worn from use. The original navy color was a little faded, but the embroidered emblem of Monarch University of Law was damn near perfect, except for some slight fraying on the thread. I'd been so proud to wear this crest, making me one of the few lucky enough to earn the right to wear it proudly. The memory became slightly tarnished after finding out my near-perfect academics and glowing recommendations hadn't been the true factor for my admittance. The donation my father gave to the school to build the new library had. Thankfully, I didn't learn that until my last year so I could live with rose-colored glasses and enjoy my experience.

Brushing a finger over the flaming wings of the butter-fly, I couldn't help but feel a little nostalgic. There had been another group of men I thought I was going to call my pack, but when I announced my intention to work as a public defender in some fashion, they treated me as if I'd died. They ignored me and never answered my calls, emails, texts—none of it. Those assholes hadn't wanted *me* for a pack brother but the connections I could provide for them. Not a day goes by that I don't think how lucky I was to dodge that bullet and find a pack who supported me so unequivocally.

Clearing my throat, I headed out of the closet and collected the three pillows on my bed, leaving one to sleep with if I ended up in my own bed tonight. Sleeping as a pack the past few nights has been a new and wonderful experi-ence I didn't think I'd enjoy as much as I did. At the last second, I grabbed the knitted blanket my grandmother made for me when I graduated high school. Not only was it warm and cozy, but it wouldn't lose its scent with how long I've owned it.

Back in Bailey-Rose's room, I awkwardly tried to place the pillows around the outer edge without falling into the damn thing. Then I unfurled the knitted blanket but paused and pulled it back out of the bed, choosing to place it to rest over the back of the couch. That way, whenever she sat here, one of us would be close to her whether we were home or not. Gareth stumbled into the room with a mountain of pillows in his arms, blocking his vision. Hurtling forward, I grabbed the one that fell before he tripped over it.

"Here, let me take some of those," I offered. "Don't tell me these are all from Warrick's room."

"There's one of mine in there somewhere," he said, tossing the pillows into the nest, clearly not planning to spread them out. "Okay, they're all in, but I'm not sure we can fit more. Well, not without losing her in there for good. I'll be worried the pillows will smother our little Omega as it is."

Ulysses arrived carrying one pillow and two blankets but paused when he saw the state of the nest. "I thought this might be a problem. Why don't I set these to the side so if she wants to hang out on the couch or something, she has things to snuggle with there."

With that agreed upon just in time, an alert that someone was heading down the driveway caused our phones to buzz. The security feed showed Warrick's bright yellow car with Bailey-Rose resting her head on his shoulder. Even with this grainy footage, I could tell she was drained. Whatever happened took a toll on our Omega, and I didn't like it one bit. I might practice civil law, but I knew criminal law just as well growing up in the house I did. So if I wanted to commit a crime and get away with it, I knew what steps to take. Let's hope it doesn't come to that, but it would be a cold day in hell before I ever let someone mess with *my* Omega.

The three of us hurried down to the main floor, where Vili was already waiting with a small silver tray. I did a double take when I saw the mug would take two hands to hold for anyone, let alone our girl. It was also in the shape of a marshmallow with a cute little smiling cartoon face. Taking Ulysses' advice to heart, mini pastel-colored marshmallows were piled high to the point some fell onto the tray. I couldn't help but smile, seeing how fast this woman had wrapped us around her delicate fingers. The best part was none of us gave a shit. We were happy to do whatever it took to make her know how we felt. This was what it meant to find the other half of your soul—you're complete for the first time in your life.

So with that thought, I opened the front door and marched out to collect that missing piece. Knowing she was struggling even the slightest had my protectiveness rising from vigilant to overbearing. Everything in me needed to know she was okay and safe within our home as soon as possible. Before my brain could catch up to what my body was doing, Bailey-Rose was in my arms, clinging to me as I nuzzled her hair, purring my reassurance.

"You're home now, sweetheart. We've got you," I whispered, pressing a kiss to her temple.

BAILEY-ROSE

Wrapped up in Yun-Sun's arms, I felt protected. Not that I didn't feel safe with Warrick—he's the only reason I hadn't let Randall's words send me into a spiral. Yet there was something about this stoic Alpha that grounded me. It was as if he took my underlying anxiety and calmed it, allowing me to breathe easier. Maybe my connection with his scent to happy moments of my youth brought that on, but all I know is I didn't ever want him to leave me.

Once we were in the house, another hand brushed down my back soothingly. "Hey, Rosie, Vili's made his famous hot chocolate for you."

That had me perking up enough to lift my head and see the cutest mug overflowing with multi-colored marshmallows. Yun-Sun kissed my cheek, warning that he was going to put me down. He didn't let go of me, though. The weight of his hands on my shoulders let me know he wasn't far.

Vili beamed at me as he offered up the beverage. "This, my kitten, is famous family recipe. My *mormor* taught me how to make it and no one else," he leaned in and whispered. "I was her favorite grandchild."

You couldn't help but smile around Vili. He was filled with joy and all the good things life had to offer. Even though I was feeling out of sorts after today's events, I returned his smile easily as I took the mug from the tray. There were so many marshmallows in the way, I was forced to eat some of them first, a hardship I was willing to suffer.

"Come on, baby girl, let's get you settled on the couch where you can manage that sugar rush more easily," Gareth suggested, holding out a hand to me.

Shifting my hold on the giant mug, I got a solid grip on it before threading my fingers with Gareth's. He guided me down the step into the living room and over to the nest of sorts I'd made the other day. It seemed I was already leaving my mark on this house. As if I was as light as a feather, he grabbed my hips, lifted me, and plopped me down in the middle of the blankets before removing my sandals.

Using my tongue, I collected a few more marshmallows to munch on as the guys settled in a semicircle around me. Gareth on my right, Vili on my left, Lysse dead center, and the other two filling in the gaps on either side. I wasn't looking forward to this conversation as it meant I had to tell them what happened. The last thing I wanted to do right now was to relive the moment. It didn't matter that I had them now—rejection and betrayal weren't something you brushed off because you found something better.

"War, why don't you tell us what you know and give Rosie time to actually taste the hot chocolate before talking," Lysse directed.

Warrick nodded and leaned forward to brace his elbows on his knees. "I had to run into the stockroom to get a few things for the drink we were going to make. Care Bear here decided to call it Clouds and Daydreams, but we hadn't built it yet to make sure it was the right combination. I was only gone for a max five minutes, but when I returned, she wasn't at the bar where I'd left her. Instead, some fucknugget had his hand on her, yelling at my Omega in the middle of my goddamn bar. That man is lucky he walked out of there alive the way I saw red."

Hearing the rage in Warrick's tone made me feel guilty

and embarrassed. Randall had not only caused a scene in The Fat Mule, he repeatedly shared his opinion on how beneath him he felt the place was. Not once had I defended Warrick's hard work or argued that Randall was wrong in his thinking. I'd just crumbled under Randall's hold and thought only about myself.

"Pretty lady," Vili whispered as he cupped my jaw and urged me to look at him. "Why are there tears?"

I hadn't even realized I was crying until he used his thumb to wipe it away.

"There is no need for tears. You are safe now with family," Vili explained. "Warrick's anger is not for you, my sweet kitten. Do not take it to heart. He is upset for you and at himself for letting this man close. Nothing is your fault."

Hands took the mug from me, but I was trapped by Vili's caramel-colored gaze, looking more serious than I'd ever seen. His sweet, comforting scent hand me nuzzling against his arm, picking up the slight honey of the graham cracker and smooth milk chocolate brought together with a perfectly golden marshmallow, gooey and perfect inside. Vili was my kindred spirit in that regard. Like me, he preferred to see the good in the world around us.

"Randall..." I started but stopped, unsure how to even begin to share what I was feeling. "He said such terrible things, untrue things. Warrick's bar isn't a shithole or seedy, but I didn't correct him."

Licking my lips, I fisted the blanket someone had put on my lap, using it to bleed off some of my anger. "He can say what he likes about me, most if it is true, anyway, but Randall should never have spoken about Warrick's accomplishments like that. It's just wrong."

"Oh, my kind, gentle kitten, Warrick isn't like this because of that," Vili murmured, sadness filling his expression. "No, he wanted to break Randall's wrist for daring to touch what is most important to him, to all of us. Business comes and goes, things happen, you move on, rebuild. Yet, when it comes to people we care about, that is a different story. Like taunting a lion through the bars, not knowing the door to the cage is open. Only the lion's willpower and control keep it from killing the fool with the stick."

The guys shifted, and Warrick was now sitting next to Vili so he could look me in the eye. "He's right. I don't give one flying fuck what that man thinks of my bar. Hell, he can write a terrible review, slander me on social media, or whatever else makes him feel like the big deal he believes himself to be. I told you in my office that *you* are what's important to *me*, no matter what."

Tears were now streaming down my face. How could I be such an idiot to think Warrick would be upset with me over such a small matter? The more time I spent around these men, it caused me to realize how tainted the view I had of myself was. With a gentle tug, Vili urged me to curl up on his lap as he hugged me tightly. As self-realization took hold and the pain of that knowledge hit me, Vili held me together. He swayed side to side, singing something softly in a language I didn't know but was beautiful. With slow, deep breaths, I let his scent become my soul focus as it brought me back to a memory as a child...

"There's my Bean," Papa Addy exclaimed as he scooped me up in his arms. "What's the matter? Has Crew been teasing you again?"

I shook my head, sniffling as I looked into his eyes that matched one of mine. "Why do I have two colored eyes, Papa? No one else does, and they tell me I look funny. One boy said his mother told him it was a mark that I was a bad person, and that's what made my heart weak too."

Papa carried me over to the fire we had going out in front of our beach house and took a seat. We went there every summer for two weeks just to be a family. It was Papa Addy's favorite place to go and mine too. There were other families with young kids who came every summer, and we would play on the beach together.

"Bean, I want you to listen carefully to me, okay?" Papa said in his serious tone. Nodding, I crossed my heart to prove I meant it. "This world is full of people of all different colors, shapes, sizes, and ages. If you looked closely enough, you'd find something odd about every single person who's ever been born."

I gasped. "Everyone?"

"Yup, everyone, Bean," he assured me. "Some of these differences might be obvious while others aren't, but they're there, trust me. Now do you want to know what I think about the people the universe blessed with being a little odd?"

Eagerly I nodded my head. "Mm-hmm."

"Well, this is only my opinion, but so far, I haven't been proved wrong, so keep that in mind. People like you, who seem a little different on the outside or face health challenges, are some of the best humans I know. Life for them isn't always easy, but nothing will hold you back if you learn to love what's different about you. I mean, if really, truly, down to the core of your being you embrace what makes you stand out, then what anyone else thinks won't ever matter," Papa explained. "Now I won't say it's easy, but that is the journey you must take if you want to be the best version of you that you can be. Sometimes on this journey, you might get lost, lose your way, and believe something that isn't true about yourself."

My eyes grew wide with fear. "I don't like getting lost. It's scary when I don't know where I am."

"No one likes getting lost, but sometimes we don't even know

we're lost. So the moment you figure out that you let someone tell you that being odd is wrong or bad and believe it, is the instant you come to find me, Daddy Rawr, your mother, or your brothers," Papa said, tapping my nose with a finger, making me giggle. "Do you know why you need to find us?"

"Because you love me just the way I am," I answered, repeating the phrase all my parents said as they tucked me in at night.

Papa pressed a kiss to my forehead. "That's right, Bean, and along the way, you'll find others who don't see your differences, loving you like I do. People who want to change you or make you feel bad about yourself have never learned to love themselves. So many people in this big world around us never learn how to do that, but I think people like you were created to teach them how. When they see you confident and embracing what makes you stand out, they will see it's possible too."

"You really think I can do something that special, Papa?" I challenged, a frown creasing my brow.

Papa chuckled and reached over to hand me a roasting fork with two giant marshmallows on it. "Yes, my baby Bean, you were born to do lots of special things. Never stop dreaming and always see magic in the clouds."

Eventually, I calmed and snuggled deeper against Vili as my tears dried. *How could I have forgotten that conversation with Papa?* He was so adamant about never letting me see myself as anything other than Bailey-Rose, his beloved daughter. Hearing that advice again now as an adult, having lived through so many people telling me what I could or couldn't do, I realized I'd lost my way. Now that I knew I was lost, it was time to turn to the people who valued me for who I was at the core. Lifting my head, I met Vili's gaze, full of compassion and affection.

While I've only known these men for a few days, there's never been a moment I felt they pitied me or found me lacking. They were overprotective and cautious when it came to some things, but that was out of fear of the unknown, which had nothing to do with pity. Taking both hands, I adjusted Vili's glasses back up his nose before leaning in to kiss him.

It was a sweet kiss full of promise, hopes, and new beginnings—all things I hoped to build with this pack and each of the Alphas in it. The purr that emanated from this gentle soul was a balm to the exposed wounds of my heart, easing the pain and giving me hope that I might be able to repair the damage. I might not be as strong and confident as I thought, but that doesn't mean I couldn't be. Anything was possible with the right people in my corner and the willingness to make a change.

"Thank you," I whispered, nuzzling my nose against his. "I needed to come to terms with a few things, and you helped me see that. Yet, I'm a little sad that your cocoa has probably gone cold now."

"Kitten, that is the smallest of worries," Vili assured me. "I will hand you to Lys before he explodes and make you new cocoa."

Confused by what he said about Ulysses, I started to ask, but Vili stood in one fluid motion and deposited me on the man's lap. With a wink and a smile, Vili was off to the kitchen, and I was left to face the rest of my incredibly worried Alphas.

Lysse wrapped his arms around my waist and buried his face in my neck, taking deep breaths of my scent. Everything about his body was rigid like he was ready to jump up and run off to do something. With each inhale, he relaxed until finally, he pressed a lingering kiss on my neck before lifting his head.

"Sooo..." I started, unsure what to even say to them. "I don't know what to share or tell you about all this. Where would you like me to start?"

"Let's start simple," Yun-Sun suggested. "I think it would help to know if he dumped you or you broke up with him?"

Gareth scoffed, smacking Yun-Sun lightly with the back of his hand. "You call that starting simple?" He then turned to me. "Let's go with how long you were together?"

"We were friends for a few months. I didn't trust he was really into me. Then officially dating for about six months, the longest I'd ever had a boyfriend," I shared, plucking at a loose thread on my shorts. "As for Yun's question, well, I don't really know. I thought sleeping with another woman was a pretty clear indicator he was done with me. Then again, I did scream and swear at him before storming out of his apartment, so I can see why he thinks I broke up with him there in the bar."

"I'm sorry, baby girl, back up one second," Gareth cut in, motioning for me to rewind. "You caught him in the act of having sex with another woman?"

Not really wanting to talk about it, having finally gotten the image out of my head, I nodded.

"Fucking piece of trash. I hope his dick rots and falls off," Lysse mumbled under his breath.

I covered my mouth to keep from laughing at the seriousness of his tone and how ridiculous the threat was.

"Okay, so dated for six months, then showed up one day and found him banging another chick. Is that the basics of it?" Warrick asked, rubbing his temples like he had a headache.

"Ah… well," I started, then paused to take the mug Vili offered me.

This time there was a more reasonable amount of marshmallows, allowing me to take a sip. While the cocoa was hot, it didn't burn my tongue, which allowed me to get the full experience of this cocoa. The flavors exploded in my mouth, making me moan and go back for a second sip so I could savor it longer this time. No wonder his grandmother didn't give this recipe to just anyone—it was lethal and in the wrong hands, would be deadly. Never had I been so impressed with a mug full of liquid as this.

"Wow," I finally said after my third gulp. "This is incredible. I don't think I've ever had something this amazing before."

Ulysses grabbed the mug with my hand still wrapped around it and stole a sip before I could even try to stop him. "What the hell? Not cool, man, so not cool."

"Holy fuck," he blurted. "That shit's amazing."

There was the sound of a smack, and Ulysses hissed, letting go of the mug.

"Don't steal from her," Vili scolded. "You want some, I give you some, but use words next time. They say I don't speak so good, then you do stupid thing like that. No manners."

Ulysses looked like a scolded child while Vili marched back to the kitchen, mumbling like an agitated grandmother. My sweet Alpha didn't get ruffled by much, but it appears he would rally to my defense. Sneaking a look at Lysse, I stuck my tongue out at him, making a face.

"Rosie, I suggest if you don't want me to put that tongue to good use, then keep it to yourself," he warned.

Instantly, I sucked it back in and hid behind my cocoa. Warrick might have given me a few O's in his office, but damn, it didn't do anything to curb the need these men stirred up in me. A moment later, Vili returned carrying a tray with five mugs on it, ensuring everyone got their own. There was even a little pitcher that he used to top off my mug, still glaring at Ulysses.

"Now you have your own, but you didn't deserve mallows, so you don't have them," Vili informed Lysse before taking his seat and sipping his own cocoa.

Watching the way these men interacted reminded me of my brothers—they were a real family to each other. It was the way packs should be, and I hoped it stayed that way. However, I'm not naïve enough to believe there can't be issues within a family unit—even within my own family, there were fights. What mattered was how they ended.

"Sweetheart, I believe you were about to tell us another piece to the puzzle," Yun-Sun said, bringing us back on track.

I slurped up another marshmallow before diving back into my heartbreak. "When I found him with the other woman, I'd been gone for the past three months. The final project for my Fine Arts master's degree had to be done in person on campus. Up until that point, I'd been doing school online to keep my stress low. Also, with my many doctors' appointments, it was easier not to find specialists in another city. For this final project, however, there was no other choice, I had to go, but Randall encouraged me to embrace the experience."

"I'll bet he did," Gareth grumbled.

Dropping my gaze, I traced a finger around the rim of my mug as I continued, "We video-chatted most days, and things between us seemed good, or so I thought. In my effort to get the project done and presented to the Fine Arts faculty, I ended up being able to come home three days early. I have a key to his place, so it wasn't like it was unusual for me to pop in unannounced. Seems he didn't think I would show up randomly, or he wouldn't have been so careless."

Lysse squeezed me tighter in a comforting hug. "Rosie, you have nothing to feel bad about in this situation. His giving you a key meant you had every right to show up there whenever you wanted. If he didn't have anything to hide, then none of this would have been an issue. Randall is the one who fucked up, not you."

"Yeah, well, the only reason he was fucking her is because I can't have sex like a normal person. You guys have seen how easy it is for me to set off my monitor. No one wants to deal with that in the heat of the moment," I muttered, then chugged the last of my hot chocolate like I was taking a shot.

"Care Bear, have you already forgotten our afternoon delight? There were no alarms going off on my watch," Warrick reminded me.

The guys whipped their heads to look at Warrick then back at me. Vili had a pleased smile on his face as if he fully supported the fact Warrick and I fooled around. Yun-Sun looked a little uncertain, but Gareth didn't look happy.

"What the hell does that mean?" Gareth demanded.

A little taken aback, Warrick's eyes went wide. "Are you asking me to give you a play-by-play?"

"No, but you were at the bar which isn't the most private location," Gareth reasoned.

"Wooow," Warrick said, drawing out the word as he set down his mug. "What's next, are you going to ask me if I let others watch? Made her scream loud enough everyone knew what was happening in my office? Or maybe you want to be a real ass and ask me if I pushed her to fool around while she was upset and vulnerable?"

Gareth recoiled like he'd just been slapped. "What? No, I would never assume you would do something like that."

"Then why are you treating me like we did something wrong? You didn't say shit to Ulysses when he had her screaming on the bathroom counter, why now?" Warrick challenged.

Gulping like a fish out of water, Gareth attempted to answer the question but couldn't seem to find the answer.

"Stop it," I snapped, drawing their attention. "Warrick was nothing but a gentleman and knew exactly what I needed to hear and feel to keep from spiraling. Randall threw some of my biggest fears in my face when he told me the woman he was banging was a hooker. Since he couldn't have sex with me the way he wanted, he found it with other women he paid, or at least that's his story. None of that matters, though, because I wanted... no begged for everything that happened between Warrick and me."

Gareth looked guilty as hell while rubbing the back of his neck, unsure whether to meet my gaze or not. "Being Alphas makes you overprotective, quick to leap to conclusions or fix problems, but I don't ever want you accusing each other of something so awful as taking advantage of me. Gareth, do you truly believe that Warrick wouldn't do everything possible to keep me safe while I was with him today?"

"Of course, I don't believe that," he admitted, shoulders slumping. "I'm upset because I wasn't there to protect you, and something bad happened. Fuck, every time I think I have a handle on this issue, shit like this comes up, throwing it in my face."

Now I was totally confused.

When Gareth met my gaze, I could see the pain in his eyes. "I had a little sister, she died, and it's my fault."

GARETH

Callie's face flashed before my eyes the moment I brought her up. Her head of wild curls always looked like a rat's nest, no matter how our mother tried to tame it. We had matching gray-blue eyes and a thirst for adventure that ultimately took her life.

I couldn't look at Bailey if I was going to make it through this story. No one but our immediate family knew what really happened and how I wasn't there to keep her safe. My mother always tells me she doesn't blame me, but I know it's not true. Every time she looks at me, I see the pain it causes, so I've distanced myself from my parents. I still worked for the family business, but my department rarely ever needed to interact with the corporate office or the CEO. Hell, I've barely been back to the ranch unless it was work-related.

"Callie was ten and hell on wheels," I shared, smiling as I remembered her facing down an ornery bull that wouldn't leave the holding pen. She feared nothing, and I admired that about her. "She was barely big enough to help us on the ranch, but damn, if she wasn't determined. One Christmas, one of my fathers finally got her a 4-wheeler that was small enough for her to handle. I still remember the squeals of joy when she took off the blindfold and saw it sitting in the garage. She wasn't allowed to use it without one of us there to make sure she didn't flip the damn thing or get tossed off. I raced around the ranch with her, almost getting frostbite, but it was worth it to still have that memory."

The warmth of that memory helped me to continue. It was as if my little sister was here, helping me to share my pain.

"My two older brothers are about ten years older than me and sixteen years older than Callie. They didn't want anything to do with her, finding her bothersome to their adult lives. Our dads worked in the city all week and came home on the weekends. This left me and Mom to look after Callie, which was a full-time job most days," I explained, needing them to understand how important Callie was to me. "She was my shadow, always following me around the ranch, helping me with chores. We even did our homework together in the evenings so I could help her with her math. The girl had a brilliant mind, but damn, when it came to numbers, she was hopeless."

I chuckled, rubbing my forehead, trying to keep from letting my emotions get the best of me. Thankfully, no one tried to interrupt me or ask questions. That would have been my undoing, but they just let me struggle my way through this.

"It was spring, and the cows were starting to have their calves so I was helping the ranch hands keep watch when I wasn't in school. Callie found a new trail she wanted to explore on her 4-wheeler, but I couldn't go with her, not to mention it had been a super rainy season, and the ground was a sloppy mess. There had been plenty of instances of the bordering dirt caving in down by the river. We kept the cattle close instead of letting them wander the grazing fields as it was too risky, and lost cattle meant money taken out of our workers' pockets.

"Then one Saturday rolled around, and the weather had been decent for a few days but not enough for the ground to firm up. That didn't stop Callie from begging me nonstop to go with her so she could explore. Our mom had gone into the city that weekend to join my fathers. It was our parents' anniversary, and they wanted to spoil my mother. I was in charge of Callie with the help of Mrs. Cook, the elderly neighbor who kept an eye on the two of us if our parents were gone or out for the night. The day had been like any other but for two cows going down struggling with birthing twins. You guys probably don't know this, but it's not uncommon for twins to happen. But it is odd that both went into distressed labor at the same time." Pausing, I took a shaky breath knowing what came next.

I'd only ever told this story twice before...

Once to my parents.

Second to the police.

Now I was telling my pack, exposing who I was and how I failed the one person I was supposed to protect. Tears burned in my eyes, but I refused to let them fall. I'd already spent years of my life mourning my sister in private moments, but I couldn't bring myself to let my pack see just how weak I was.

"We were light on help that weekend. A big cattle sale was going on, and they were auctioning off cattle we couldn't butcher. Our brand never sells meat that's been given antibiotics or growth hormones. Yet cattle get sick, so we care for them as any rancher would then sell them off to recoup something from them. Even at the age of sixteen, I was trained as well as any ranch hand, so they came to find me. It was all hands on deck. If we couldn't help these cows, then we could lose the mother and the babies, which would be a major blow. As we worked for hours, an awful storm rolled in out of the blue, rained buckets... even hailed some.

"We managed to save all four calves and the mothers, but when I returned to the house, I found Mrs. Cook asleep in the armchair and no sign of Callie. My heart sank, and I knew... I knew what she'd done. Running to the shed we kept the 4-wheelers in, I saw hers was missing, so I hopped on mine and started looking for my baby sister. Two hours later, I found her at the bottom of a steep ravine where the ground gave out under her 4-wheeler and rolled all the way down the hill. She was still trapped under it, but no matter what I did, I couldn't bring her back." With those final words, I couldn't hold back the sob that tore out of me as the memory of that moment felt as fresh as the day it happened.

Then I was wrapped in the warm, comforting scent of summer roses. My mother and Callie loved to put freshly-cut roses on the dinner table for as long as they bloomed. It's how I knew it was finally summer, school would be over, and the fun would start. After Callie died, there were no more roses. Yet it seemed the universe decided I was going to be blessed with an Omega who reminded me of my baby sister in all the best ways.

Shifting so Bailey could stand between my legs, I rested my head on her chest, listening to her heart. She claimed it's broken and fragile, but to me, it's fucking perfect because it is still beating in her chest, proving this woman I was head over heels for was very much alive. There was nothing more important to me than keeping her that way. I wouldn't fail Bailey-Rose the way I'd failed Callie on that fateful day. The others might think of me as an ass or overprotective, but I knew what it felt like to fail and lose someone you love forever.

"Gareth, I'm so sorry," Bailey-Rose whispered, pressing kisses to my head. "I know how hard it is to lose someone you love. The pain never really goes away. When the tiniest moment can bring back all that loss and sorrow, making it feel as fresh as the day it happened. So please don't hide how you feel or try to brush it off until you can deal with it in private. Let me share that moment with you so you're not alone in this pain. Those feelings can become so over-whelming, and if you don't let them have their moment, it will crush you. Will you trust me to be there for you, Gareth?"

Her question was so simple and yet at the same time terrifying. *How can I burden her with my pain when she has her own to deal with?*

"I can try," I answered honestly, pulling back to see her face. "You have so many things to worry about... how can I ask you to take on my issues?"

The tender smile on her lips and the way that dual-colored gaze cut through me had me taking a sharp breath.

"That's the thing... you aren't asking me to do this, I'm offering," Bailey-Rose countered. "Think of it this way... I'll share some of my struggles with you to free up room for me to take some off your plate. Then we each have less of our own but feel that we're helping each other."

"Deal! But I can't promise I won't still react if I feel you're in danger," I warned.

She shrugged. "It takes time to retrain your brain in how it responds to things. Nothing changes overnight, and I know I'm not going to do well giving up some control over things either. Yet if we are patient and understanding with each other, soon this will become the new normal."

Lifting a hand in the offer of a handshake, she grinned and took it. "Well, then I, Gareth Lee Watson, promise to have open and honest conversations about how I'm feeling when it comes to keeping my family safe."

"Likewise, I, Bailey-Rose Thatcher, promise to come to

one of you when my self-doubt raises its ugly head." Holding up a hand to stop me from speaking, she continued, "In addition, knowing how important my safety is to you and the reasoning behind your reactions, I won't call you out on it unless it's unreasonable, and we need to talk about it right then and there."

I shook my head as I chuckled to myself. "Damn, you're as crafty as your mother, you know that?"

"Where do you think I learned it from?" she countered, then gripped my head, turning it up to look at her.

The way I could get lost in her gaze was unlike anything I thought possible. As a man who never believed in the fairy tales people told about soulmates, I was now well and truly converted. When her lips met mine, I groaned, savoring her taste and the feel of her in my arms. With every passing second I spent with her, this woman was becoming my whole world. You can't tell me that isn't something magical, and there's no way it can be explained with science. Scent is only one part of the bonding process. It didn't create anything more than a need to be around the person. Yet here I was on the verge of telling this woman I was falling madly in love with her if I wasn't already.

Bailey pulled back from the kiss, making me almost pout, but seeing the expression of a woman who's thoroughly been kissed on her face had me grinning. "Well, baby girl, it seems we've come to an understanding."

"Hmm," she hummed, a little too dazed to speak.

"Hey, what do you say we put all this serious stuff to the side and let us show you something fun?" I asked, combing my fingers through her hair, brushing it off her face.

"I think that is a fantastic idea," Bailey-Rose agreed, taking my hand so she could attempt to pull me to my feet. "Are the rest of you coming?"

That was all the others needed to hear before setting aside their cocoa and standing.

Guess that's a yes.

BAILEY-ROSE

areth led the way upstairs, still holding my hand which I was grateful for. I tried to keep how the story about his sister made my heart ache. So many things about the way Gareth reacted to various situations made so much more sense now. Of course, my episode after he nipped my neck would send him spiraling. Then there was the overre-action of me jumping out of the car. It was obvious Gareth carried around so much guilt about his sister that those emotions were bleeding out into other areas of his life. Now here I was, a woman he was charged with looking after who was sick and at risk for many things. I just hoped he would keep his end of the deal and be honest with me.

When we got to the base of the stairs that led to my room, he stopped to look at me. "I'm going to have you close your eyes while I carry you up to your room. Then when I give the order, you can open them but not a moment before, or you'll ruin the surprise."

My curiosity was running wild as I nodded eagerly. Gareth scooped me up in a bridal hold, giving me a warning look, so I slapped my hands over my eyes as promised.

"Not that I don't trust you, Rosie, but I think two of us are going to go ahead so we can block the view if you cheat," Lysse said, poking my side, making me giggle.

Excitement flooded my system to the point I wondered if I was bouncing in Gareth's hold like I thought I was in my head. The flight of stairs seemed to never end, and I was about to jump out of my skin if they didn't hurry up. Finally, I was set down, and hands rested on my shoulders.

"Okay, baby girl, you can look," Gareth whispered.

Dropping my hands, I let out a shriek of elation and raced over to the giant hanging nest. Without hesitation, I flung myself into the pile of pillows and blankets the guys had filled it with. Laughing, I rolled around in the fluffy mess like a kid in the season's first snow. This was *glorious*.

When I saw the bed, I thought there would be no way they'd go for it. That, and I wasn't sure if the ceiling with all the glass panels would be able to hold something like this. Not only had these men taken it upon themselves to get me the bed of my dreams, but they set it up and filled it with bedding that smelled like them. I had a room with a bed so I could sleep in our pack home with my Alphas. This was the beginning of our forever, and I was over the moon, so much so that all the excitement and acrobatics set off a warning buzz from my monitor.

It wasn't a full-on alarm but a warning I was getting close. Most of the time, this was how I managed to avoid what happened in the living room on our first meeting. Then again, I'd been highly emotional since things happened with Randall, which caused my normally low resting heart rate to be higher than my typical. Flopping onto my back, I closed my eyes and took slow, deep breaths, working to slow down my heart rate. My senses were flooded with the aroma of my Alphas—chocolate, blue-berry, cinnamon, graham cracker, and sweet tea with that tang of lemon—the perfect way to cool off during the summer.

The more I thought of my guys, the calmer I became, but another problem I didn't think about arose. Their scent was starting to become lost as I began to perfume, sending out a come-hither call to my Alphas. Jerking upright, I found all five of my men with their gaze locked on me, noses flared as they took in my wantonness. I gulped loudly as the mental picture of them stripping out of their clothes and coming to join me played out.

The calmness I'd been trying for flew out the window as I locked gazes with Yun-Sun. My cool, calm, and collected Alpha looked like he was on the verge of snapping. The energy around him shifted slightly, causing me to feel a little on edge. It was almost like I knew something was about to happen that I needed to be aware of, but I couldn't quite put my finger on what it was. His normally warm, sweet scent of blueberry and melted butter became more tart. It wasn't bad or off-putting, it just had a sharper edge to it than normal.

Slamming his eyes shut, Yun-Sun's hands fisted as he turned on his heel. Before I could say anything, he marched out of the room with the others right behind him, leaving only Warrick and me behind.

"What just happened?" I asked, sliding out of the bed and heading for the door.

Warrick caught my hand, shaking his head when I looked back. "Let them cool off, Care Bear. They left for a reason, and you need to respect that."

"I don't understand," I pressed.

Letting out a sigh, Warrick urged me to sit with him on the cute mint-colored loveseat. "Do you know what rut is?"

"It's the Alphas version of a heat," I answered.

"In a manner of speaking, yes. Unlike an Omega, Alphas have no trigger or warning when rut rises. Some Alphas have them more often than others... it's rather individual. During this time, they become filled with hormones that make them slightly unpredictable, possessive, and flooded with the urge to dominate. When an Alpha is in full rut, it can last a day, two, or even three in some cases. They will be single-mindedly focused on the need to protect their Omega, becoming unreasonably aggressive to those not part of the pack. It's one reason when this happens, they are asked to stay home," Warrick explained.

With this new information, I pictured the way Yun-Sun looked at me, saw how I felt, and the change in his posture. "Are you saying he's in rut now?"

"I'm not sure, Care Bear," Warrick admitted, wrapping an arm around my shoulders and hugging me to his side. "The way he reacted to you perfuming makes that seem likely. I know I said there aren't triggers, but it's common knowledge that when Alphas find their scent match, it can trigger an Omega to go into heat and the Alphas to experience rut. Some say it's nature's way to ensure the bonding will happen while everyone is lost to their base needs."

I looked up at Warrick, concerned. "I've heard from other Omegas going through a heat without an Alpha is torture. They claim to have medication to help, but it doesn't always work. If Yun is in rut and chooses to face it alone, will it be awful for him?"

"Not as awful as he would feel if anything happened to you," Warrick murmured, pressing a kiss to my forehead. "The guys are with him, and they will know how to help. This isn't the first time we've been through this, but I will say Yun is one who doesn't have rut happen often."

He might be telling me things would be fine with his words, but the tone of his voice said something different. I chose to trust my pack—they'd been together longer and knew what needed to be done. However, it firmed my resolve to figure a way to make it safer for me to be intimate with my Alphas. Sex was an important dynamic in any relationship, but with Alphas and Omegas, it was a necessity.

"Hey, I have an idea," Warrick announced, leaping to his feet. "Why don't we unpack some of these boxes and start getting you settled in? You're gonna need to find pajamas to sleep in eventually, so why not now?"

"What if I just sleep naked?" I asked, trying to keep an innocent expression on my face.

Warrick's eyes almost bugged out of his head as he coughed from practically swallowing his tongue, making me burst into laughter. "Bailey-Rose, you sassy minx. Don't say things like that unless you really mean it," he chided.

I fluttered my lashes at him as I stood, then brushed past him, running my hand across his chest. "Who says I didn't mean it?"

"Holy shit, I'm in trouble," Warrick muttered, running his hands through his hair as I giggled to myself all the way to the closet.

After an hour, Vili and Gareth joined us in our quest to get the basics put away. I'd handled the boxes with my undergarments, not wanting to push Warrick further than I already had. He needed a full five minutes after that sleeping-naked comment before he felt safe enough to be in the confined space of the closet.

"Is Yun okay?" I asked.

Vili gave me a bright smile and nodded. "Yes, he and Ulysses are making dinner. Yun just needed fresh air... our pretty lady's scent was too enticing."

"So he's not in rut?" I pressed.

"Well..." Gareth started then paused as he pulled down a box from the stack. "He might have if he didn't take a suppressant. We're having him be cautious for now since we all know that while drugs are helpful in these situations, they don't always work as expected. Giving him some time to clear his head and the meds to kick in is just being cautious."

Frowning, I hung up the dress I'd pulled out. "Why would he need to take anything? Would it be bad for him to go into rut?"

They all stopped what they were doing and looked at each other as if unsure who should answer the question. The task seemed to fall to Gareth since he was the one who faced me while the other two took backup positions. I didn't like that at all. It made me feel like whatever I was about to be told was going to piss me off or scare me.

"You asked me before if going through rut would be painful for the Alpha if he couldn't act on the urge to mate. Physically, it wouldn't cause harm, well... other than feeling like you have massive amounts of adrenaline pumping through your veins telling your brain there is something out there that desperately needs your protection. Now that we have you, our sole focus during rut would be to make sure you are always within our sights. Even better would be having you close enough to touch at a moment's notice," Gareth shared, reaching out to take my hand as if to prove what that would be like.

"Okay, that all makes sense, but I get the feeling that's not all of it," I reasoned.

Gareth took a second to wet his lips before continuing, shifting from foot to foot, "No, that isn't all of it. Generally, Alphas who are lost in the rush of rut tend to devolve slightly and become aggressive toward those who they feel threaten their pack or Omega. What Yun-Sun is worried about and why he's refusing to allow the rut to take hold is the need to dominate and breed. I'm not saying any harm would come to you or that any of us would ever put you in a situation where you'd feel forced or taken advantage of. Our fear is lost in that state of mind... would we notice if you were in medical distress? If the worst happened and you needed help, no one outside the pack would ever be allowed in the house. Our job as your Alphas is to keep your care and safety at the top of our list. Right now, there are just too many unknowns."

Shocked by this answer, I didn't know what to say at first, but an idea popped into my head. Without saying a word, I exited the closet and hurried to the bedroom door. I wasn't sure if they would try to stop me, so I wasn't taking any chances. As quickly as I could, I made it down the first flight of stairs and was just about to start on the second when an arm wrapped around my waist.

I'd been thwarted.

A squeak escaped me as I was scooped up and found Vili was my captor. Surprised, I didn't even argue as he started to carry me back toward my room. Shaking my head clear, I found my voice and two thoughts to rub together.

"Vili, wait," I blurted. "Please take me down to the kitchen along with the others so we can talk this out as a family."

Vili peered at me, his disapproval made more pronounced with the way his glasses had slid down his nose. "Bailey-Rose."

He almost never used my name, so I knew this was probably going to be a losing battle.

"We do this for you, to keep safe, not upset you," Vili pointed out. "Yun ask for time, make sure medicine working before he see you."

"But it's been an hour. Does the medication take *that* long to take effect?" I challenged.

His gaze seemed to be staring into my soul as I waited for his answer, "I will do this for you, kitten. But only if you promise to leave if I say so and go right to the nest. Deal?"

My objective wasn't to upset or make things harder for Yun—quite the opposite. The idea I had would help twofold if, by some luck, what I needed was possible.

I nodded my agreement, but Vili clucked his tongue disapprovingly. "Use words, kitten."

Seeing this stern side of Vili was becoming something I found rather sexy. When it wasn't directed at me, that is.

"I promise if being around Yun is not helpful and you tell me to go back to my room, I will," I agreed.

The sound of feet pounding down the stairs had us both looking down the hall to see Gareth and Warrick running full speed ahead. When they spotted us, the brakes went on immediately.

"What the hell, Care Bear. You just up and vanished," Warrick grumbled, crossing his arms as he scowled. "After everything Gareth and I told you, why would you disregard that in favor of heading downstairs?"

It was as obvious as a neon sign that all my guys were worried about what might happen with Yun. I fully understood what concerns they had, but if he took medication and I was no longer perfuming or thinking dirty thoughts, then it should be just fine. Plus, I think it would put an end to this unnecessary tension if I could simply talk to them.

"Because I think I have a solution to all this," I stated.

"Reeeally?" Gareth asked, sounding rather skeptical.

"I said what I said. If you want to know more, then we're going to have a family discussion," I announced. "Vili and I agreed that if he told me to go back to my room because it was too hard for Yun-Sun, I would. Now, can we please do this?"

No one looked thrilled, but they gave in all the same. Vili set me down, and we headed for the main floor to find my other two Alphas. Soothing classical music floated through the air coming from the kitchen. When we entered, Yun's head snapped up, finding my gaze instantly. I could still feel something was off about him, but it wasn't anything like before he stormed out. It was almost like I had the inkling of a thought, but it wasn't quite fully developed yet into words.

"Why is she in the kitchen?" Yun-Sun snapped, shifting his gaze to the three men behind me. "Didn't you explain what's going on?"

"Oh, we sure did," Warrick shared dryly. "How about you try telling our girl no when she's made up her mind? Go on, tell her to march her cute ass back upstairs."

Yun-Sun gripped the counter, looking at me warily but didn't move. Ulysses, however, had no issue setting down the knife he was using, wiping his hands, and heading right for me.

"Wait, hold on," I blurted, holding out my hand, knowing Lysse would have zero issues throwing me over his shoulder. "What if we all went and talked to my doctor?"

That seemed to surprise Ulysses enough to stop a mere few inches from me. I quickly sidestepped away from all the guys putting the sliding door to the patio at my back. I wanted to be heard, but I also wasn't going to create a situation that would cause someone to do something they'd regret.

"The reason you're separating me from Yun is because you're worried about something going wrong. My whole family has gone to classes at the hospital where my doctor works for CPR and other emergency care for people like me.

I want you guys to feel confident living life with me, and this is something simple I can offer. Dr. Arbour has been looking after me since I was born. If there's anyone who can answer your questions, it's him," I reasoned.

Yun-Sun seemed to finally relax and walked around the counter but leaned against it instead of coming closer. "Thank you, sweetheart. I think that will help immensely to ask questions and get some answers."

"I also plan to ask if there's anything we can do about making it safer for me to have sex," I informed them. "It wasn't something I really worried about since I thought Randall was fine with how things were. I'm not willing to have you guys hide from me because you're worried about hurting me. I refuse to let our lives start like this."

Ulysses closed the distance between us, cupping my face in his hands. "You make a lot of good points, Rosie. We need to find better ways of dealing with situations that arise because it's not going to change, and rut is something that will happen to all of us at some point. Tomorrow we can call and set up something. However, until then, can I ask you to respect Yun-Sun's request to keep some distance from you for tonight?"

My gaze shifted to Yun-Sun and the heartbroken expression on his face for even having to ask. "Yes, I can do that for tonight."

"Bailey-Rose, I know you and your brother well enough to pay attention to *how* you say things," Lysse warned. "If the medication hasn't suppressed his rut, then we might need to make other arrangements."

"We'll see," I countered. "I'm not trying to be difficult, but I think you need to have a little more faith in me and Yun-Sun. There is no way to know if things will go badly, but none of you are even willing to test the matter. I've known him for a few days, but it's obvious to me that he prides himself on the level of self-control he holds over his actions. He thinks before he speaks or acts not in a way that makes you feel judged but shows his sincerity. No one can say Yun does anything in an impulsive manner, and that doesn't change just because of raging hormones."

Ulysses smiled as his thumb stroked my cheek. "I can see why you think we're doing this because we don't trust him with you. Interestingly enough, that is far from the truth. We trust Yun to always put your best interests first. However, there are factors that come along with falling into rut that can't be prevented no matter how controlled or intentional of a person you are. As you said, it's only been a few days of us being a pack, making us far more unpredictable during rut. Once you are bonded to the pack, it will be another story, but unmarked, it makes our possessive nature run rampant."

He searched my face for a moment, and not finding what he was looking for, a crease appeared between his brows. "Why do I feel like none of that changed your mind?"

I shrugged. "Probably because it hasn't, but you don't need to change my mind. It's clear that this is an important matter to all of you, and because I care about my pack's feelings, I will take your warning to heart. Just let it be known that I think you're all being overdramatic about this."

With a frustrated sigh, Ulysses pulled me into a hug. "God, I forgot how stubborn you are, Rosie. Brick walls give more than you do when you've made up your mind."

"What can I say? I've had to prove a lot of people wrong in my life," I shared. "You've got to be stubborn to fight back when people think they know what's best for you. I'm not saying I haven't been wrong and I should have listened, but nine times out of ten, I turned out to be right."

"So that's why the universe knew you had to be so cute," Lysse teased, chuckling to himself.

Glancing up at him, I rolled my eyes. "The universe owes me... that's why I'm so adorable. It helps me get away with being a stubborn ass like now." That got the others to laugh, and the tension in the kitchen finally broke.

Pulling out my phone, I scrolled to my doctor's cell number and hit dial. On the second ring, Dr. Arbour answered, "Bailey-Rose, is everything all right?"

"Everything is fine with me, but I do need your help. You see, I found my pack," I shared. "Any chance you have time tomorrow to chat with all of us?"

"I always have my staff block out two hours in the afternoon for lunch. Come by at one, and I'll see what I can do to help them feel more confident in looking after you," Dr. Arbour said.

I smiled brightly at the guys. "Sounds good. We'll see you tomorrow at one."

BAILEY-ROSE

As we drove to the hospital, I gazed out the window, watching the city go by. The city of Windermere had one of the country's best heart hospitals, which was quite fortunate for my family. From the moment I was born, we had the best of the best keeping me alive, and Dr. Arbour became like a grandparent to me over the years. I saw him more often than I did any of my other extended family, but it made sense since they lived in other states.

The sensation as my phone buzzed in my pocket had me sighing. I pulled it out to see four more texts and two missed calls from Randall. With everything that happened yesterday, I couldn't deal with this too, so I shut the damn thing off shortly after talking to Dr Arbour. When I turned it back on this morning, I was flooded with progressively intensifying text messages and a few ranting voicemails.

RANDALL:

Bailey-Rose don't you dare ignore me. I know you turned your phone off and I expect a call when it turns back on.

RANDALL:

Why haven't you called me back? I called yet again and you hung up on me so I know your phone is working.

It's them isn't it? They are telling you not to talk to me. Trying to keep me from my goddamn girlfriend. Those so-called Alphas don't want you, they don't love you. Not like I do.

Bumblebee I'm sorry, I shouldn't be yelling at you, it's them I'm mad at. Please, please call me back Bumblebee, it's all a huge misunderstanding. They are lying to you, the person you're meant to be with is me.

Reading these made me sick to my stomach, so I deleted the voicemails and the texts, ensuring I didn't have to ever look at them again. Fingers combed through my hair, drawing me to meet Yun-Sun's gaze and settling my nerves.

I'd done as he requested and left him to wander the main level of the house while I hung out upstairs. The guys rotated spending time with him so he didn't feel lonely, per my demands. If he wanted to keep some distance to be safe, that was fine, but I didn't want it to feel like a punishment, so I had the guys all sleep in their own rooms. That led me to getting practically no sleep, but I wasn't going to say a damn word about it, adding more guilt onto Yun's shoulders.

Unsurprisingly, Ulysses snuck into my room somewhere around four in the morning with Vili right behind him. The moment I was sandwiched between them, I finally got some real sleep. It wasn't enough, but it was better than the fitful catnaps I'd been able to manage. The others lasted until seven before making their way up to my room—even Yun-Sun. It would seem he felt the medication was working, and he was no longer worried about falling into rut.

"You look tired," he murmured.

I gave him a tired smile and let my head rest on his

shoulder. "Other than the apartment on campus, where I stayed for three months, I've never lived anywhere else. It will take me a little time to adjust to new sounds and a different bed. Although I think that bed might be more comfortable than the one I've been sleeping on."

"I'm glad you like it, sweetheart. When I saw how many times you went back to view it, I figured it was the right call. It was important to me that we got you settled in our home in an efficient manner." He pressed a kiss to my head before whispering in my ear, "Call me selfish, but I wanted you to be all ours and in our home. Maybe when we're done with this, we can head back and take a nap together."

That had me purring in approval, snuggling against him as he stroked his fingers through my hair. I must have dozed off because the next thing I knew, we were parked at the hospital, and everyone was getting out of the car. Rubbing my eyes, I tried to wake myself up so I didn't worry Dr. Arbour or the guys. With a quick, sharp slap to my cheeks, I took a deep breath and hopped out of the car.

Vili snatched up my hand and intertwined our fingers as he swung our arms in time with our steps. His lighthearted actions made me smile as we entered the hospital's lobby I knew all too well. We took the elevator up to the sixth floor, where Dr. Arbour's office was located. Nurse Harlow, Dr. Arbour's right-hand woman, sat at her desk typing notes from a chart she was looking at. Her head snapped up when she heard us entering, and a smile bloomed on her face when she stood to greet us.

"Bailey-Rose, you little gem, how are you?" Nurse Harlow asked, stepping up to give me a quick hug. "I hear congratulations are in order. The doctor told me you found your pack."

My cheeks hurt with how big I was smiling as I nodded,

too excited to even speak. Turning to the side, I gave my best magician's assistant impression as I showed them off, waving my arms. Thankfully, the guys had their shit together and were able to introduce themselves as I remained a grinning idiot.

"Hello, I'm Warrick Shaw," he greeted, offering his hand to Nurse Harlow. "These are my pack brothers Ulysses, Vili, Gareth, and Yun-Sun. It's an honor to meet someone who's been looking after our girl until we could find her."

Nurse Harlow blushed at the compliment and charming smile Warrick was gracing her with. I wasn't worried about Warrick's flirtatious nature. Not only because I knew Nurse Harlow was a bonded Beta, but I had zero doubts about his feelings for me. Of course, it didn't hurt that he gave me a cheeky wink, letting me know he was simply being sweet for my sake.

"Ulysses, I thought that was you," Nurse Harlow exclaimed, giving him a hug before moving on to the rest. It was sweet of her to be so excited on my behalf, but Dr. Arbour's staff has been there through it all with me over the years.

"I can't tell you boys how grateful I am that you found each other. There isn't a more deserving soul alive than Bailey-Rose," she gushed, quickly wiping at her eyes. "When the Scent Matchers refused her, I was about to march down to their headquarters and give them a piece of my mind. People can't choose how they were born, and they shouldn't be punished for it."

"Well, none of that matters now, does it?" Dr. Arbour said, his deep, even voice cutting right through the bullshit.

Shifting to face him, I smiled as he gave me a side hug, patting my shoulder affectionately as he towered over me. "Hey, kiddo."

Dr. Arbour was in his fifties with super short salt and pepper hair and kind brown eyes hidden behind the same pair of small square glasses he always wore. He didn't have his normal white coat on, making him seem more relaxed with his dress shirt sleeves rolled up.

"Come on back, and we'll have a chat," he said, nodding to the others as he guided me down the short hall to his office.

This wasn't the first time I'd been in this room, but it always struck me as if it felt like he was either just moving in or moving out. Boxes with books and files were stacked in the corner behind his desk. The only thing he had hanging on the wall was his medical license and diploma. Thankfully, since he held meetings in his office, he had a small seating area to accommodate his patients. The couch wasn't big enough to fit us all, so Gareth pulled me onto his lap, and Yun-Sun took the chair next to Dr. Arbour.

"Well, gentleman, where would you like me to start?" Dr. Arbour asked, clapping his hands together.

In a twist I didn't see coming, Vili pulled out a folded sheet of paper that seemed to be a list of questions. He handed it over to Dr. Arbour, and he looked it over. He nodded and gave affirmative grunts at this or that before sitting back and crossing his leg over the other, ready to get down to business.

Grabbing the coffee cup from the side table, he took a swig before speaking. "First, I would like to know if you understand the condition and complications Bailey-Rose has?"

Everyone nodded, murmuring their agreement.

"Excellent, that makes covering all your questions easier. Now a running theme I see in all these is how best to help when a crisis arises. I'm sure Bailey-Rose has told you her family took some classes I offer to help with these concerns. It would be my professional opinion that all of you do the same. Are any of you currently certified in CPR or any other immediate medical response?"

Gareth raised his hand. "I am. Working in warehouses and on the ranch, we require everyone to get that certification and keep it up to date."

"Very wise of you," Dr Arbour commended. "It's important for one of you to know and feel confident in this while you wait to get into the classes. I'm not saying you need to live in fear that something will happen. Bailey-Rose is a model patient when it comes to looking after herself. Always takes her medication, sticks to the diet, and follows the rules any doctor gives her. However, not having a plan in place would just be foolish, so I applaud you all for meeting with me to ensure Bailey-Rose is well looked after."

Ulysses leaned forward, clasping his hands together as he spoke, "I'm well aware of the battles Rosie has been through in her life, and she had an episode right in front of us the other night. We froze. If Crew and Eli hadn't been there, it could have been so much worse. The duty of keeping her safe is now passed to us, and we're flying a little blind."

"That is to be expected. No one is ready for something like this unless they have to be. Each case for each person is different. The genetic factor in Bailey-Rose's case presents challenges we don't find with others. What you need to keep in the forefront of your mind is to remain calm. If you allow yourself to freak out and spiral, you will be of no help to your Omega. Not to mention a body in flight mode won't be able to process the situation the way you need to. There is no running away from the problem... you must face it head-on," Dr. Arbour explained. "You are the only lifeline she has if something goes wrong. It's a heavy burden to bear, but you're all Alphas built to protect and nurture your Omega. I have zero doubt you'll manage just fine once given the tools."

A tension I hadn't realized was running through all my guys seemed to dissipate at this encouragement. Another Alpha, one specifically trained in this area, was telling them it would be okay. Part of me felt sad they'd had so much stress and worry over this that I couldn't help them find peace with.

"Now, moving on to the matter of heats…" Dr. Arbour paused and shifted slightly, taking another swallow of coffee. Almost as if this topic made him ever so slightly uncomfortable.

I suppose it made sense. He's been looking after me since I entered the world. Now having to talk about heats, sex, and all that went with it might be somewhat awkward for him.

"I told them I can't go into heat, that it would be too much for my body," I added, trying to help him out. "Is that still your opinion on the matter?"

Dr. Arbour met my gaze, and I saw the moment he decided to plead his case. Everything in me wanted to tell him to leave the matter be, but they had the right to hear his idea even if I would never use it.

"As things stand currently, yes, but there is another option," Dr. Arbour said, shifting his attention to the guys. "In the past few years, there has been an advancement in surgery that would allow us to make some much-needed adjustments to her heart. We could fix the valve that isn't working properly as well as add in a new type of mesh that her body won't reject. This would be major surgery since we need to remove her heart from her body entirely to make the repairs."

The guys all shifted their attention to me, and I was met with various levels of shock, confusion, and hurt.

"Were you going to tell us about this?" Ulysses asked, his tone laced with a hint of accusation.

Letting out a heavy sigh, I shook my head. "No."

None of them liked that answer, and it was written all over their faces.

"Dr. Arbour, please tell them the risk involved with this life-changing procedure," I requested, knowing they needed the full scope.

"Due to her diminished stamina because of her condition and the high likelihood of rejection if the valve we use isn't a perfect blood-type match, we're looking at a sixty percent success rate of her making it through surgery. Depending on how the surgery went, it could drop to fifty percent of her making it through recovery," Dr. Arbour answered truthfully. "I want to make it clear that this is the only option available to us. She would never be able to survive a heart transplant, and we've exhausted all other avenues with medication and therapy. There might come a day that no matter what her feelings are on the surgery, it will be the only choice to try and save her."

The room fell silent as the guys wrapped their heads around that thought. When the silence stretched on for too long, I knew I had to redirect this conversation. Getting up from Gareth's lap, I stepped to the side so I could see all my guys. Their expression matched the ones they had that first day in the living room.

"Hey, this is not the end of the world," I reminded them. "I can still live a full and happy life with all of you without this surgery. Please know I wasn't keeping this from you for any malicious reason or because I didn't trust you. This simply isn't an option to me, so why bother to bring it up? I would much rather know I have ten, twenty, thirty more years with all of you than risk the chance at fifty to sixty odds. So I might not be able to have a heat or give you biological children. If we want a family, there are other ways of doing that. Even with this surgery, I'm not sure if I want to have kids. The likelihood of them being born with my genetic disorder is high. However, we all know there are kids out there who need a family to love them, so children are still possible."

The fear in their expression faded somewhat, but they needed to hear it from Dr. Arbour before they'd believe me. I looked at the man who's saved my life more than once over the years and gave him a pleading look. He pulled off his glasses and rubbed the bridge of his nose, letting out a frustrated grunt.

"She's right," he admitted, using his tie to clean his glasses. "While I keep pushing for the surgery to make her life easier and allow her to do more things, it's not to the point where I believe she's in danger. The younger and stronger she is will give us far better odds, but I'm not at the point where I feel justified in pressuring her into it. I'll have you know it's something I'm rather upset about, young lady. I even tried to speak to your mother about this after hearing she was in town, but she told me to respect your choice."

Go, Mom. I knew she would back up my choice after I explained the situation.

"Duly noted," I commented, returning to the couch where Ulysses snatched me up. He hid his face in my neck as he hugged me tightly. "So going into heat is too risky, but is there anything we can do or that I can take to make having sex easier?"

The way all the guys inhaled sharply and tensed at this question made me laugh. They were acting like I didn't tell this man everything about my body. Hell, to get out of the hospital, you have to announce when you fart, poop, or piss, depending on the surgery. Talking about sex was the least of my worries.

"Is there a particular concern? Are the suppressants making you too dry for intercourse?" Dr. Arbour questioned, making Warrick choke on his own spit and causing a coughing fit.

"No, it's more the challenge of keeping my heart rate low enough not to set off my monitor," I shared. "Oh, and we had a situation where one of them was going into rut, and they were concerned about me being able to handle that much aggressive affection."

Had I purposely phrased that to make the guys uncomfortable? Yes. Did I get the best reaction out of Yun-Sun doing it? Also yes. The poor man looked like his eyes were about to pop out of his head. Nice to know it wasn't the fact they thought he would hurt me but were scared he'd fuck me into cardiac arrest.

Dr. Arbour nodded and rubbed his chin in thought. "There might be something we can try, but it's not going to be something I'll feel comfortable with you using long-term. Think of it more as a patch while I do some research to find a more permanent solution. I can give you a mild beta blocker that's mixed with anti-anxiety medication to keep your heart rate lower. The combination will allow you to still give into the heat of the moment without overdoing it. However, the tricky part is how to administer the medication. You need it to be fast-acting since this isn't something you should be taking all the time."

As the good doctor mused over this thought, the guys

seemed to perk up a bit at the idea of worrying less about sexy times.

"Ah," Dr. Arbour shouted, slapping a fist against his other hand. "An inhaler... it will be perfect. That will deliver the small dose you need and dissipate out of your system in a shorter time frame. I think even for young folks in love, three to four hours is long enough... hmm?"

Now it was my turn to blush. I didn't mind talking about the subject in general, but for Dr. Arbour to tease me about being a wanton hussy going at it for that length of time seemed uncalled for.

"I believe we can make that work," Gareth answered with a smirk tugging at his lips.

Dr. Arbour chuckled and pushed to his feet. "I'll get in touch with my people in the pharmacy wing and see if we can't whip that up in the next few days. Think you'll be able to wait that long, or do I need them to work over the weekend?"

"No," Vili assured. "We shall take time to savor our pretty lady."

"I have no doubt," Dr. Arbour said, laughter clear in his words as he shook their hands. "Bailey-Rose has my direct number. If you gentlemen have any questions, feel free to reach out."

"Thank you, doctor. This has been really helpful," Yun-Sun added, giving the doctor a slight bow.

With a farewell wave to Dr. Arbour, I left the office with the guys right behind me. Nurse Harlow smiled, wiggling her fingers in acknowledgment, but pointed to her headset so I knew she was on the phone. We all piled into the elevator, but no one really said much as we descended. While we ended our conversation on a lighter note, I knew the guys were still processing the information about the surgery.

The second the doors opened, I dashed forward then spun to look at them. "Hey, you guys mentioned something about going to The Snuggery today and grabbing some things to decorate my room. Still up for the adventure?"

"Did you say you were tired?" Gareth countered.

I shrugged. "I'm getting a second wind. Besides, I don't want this to be what you guys stew about when we get home. If we all go do something fun, then it will change the mood."

They all looked at each other for a moment then Vili clapped his hands together and cheered. "To The Snuggery!"

That got everyone to smile, which led them to give in to my request, but I had a sneaking suspicion I'd win nine times out of ten.

Vili

My heart nearly burst with joy as we entered the giant warehouse full of everything and anything you could imagine for an Omega. The *only* reason you ever stepped foot in this place was if you had an Omega in your pack. For a moment, before we found my sweet darling kitten, a kernel of fear had started to grow in my heart. What if there wasn't an Omega out there meant for us?

"Look out, world's best Omega coming through," Warrick yelled as he raced past with a cart.

It took me a second to realize that Bailey-Rose was in the cart's basket with how fast it flew by. Her peals of laughter filled the air as she tossed her hands up like she was on a roller coaster. Gareth's face fell into a frown, but I caught his arm before he charged after them.

"She is fine," I said when he glared at me. "Let them play... he be careful."

Realizing he was reacting to this for the wrong reasons, I watched as Gareth took a deep breath. "You're right, and I'm guessing one of the store employees will scold him the moment they see what's going on."

That wasn't why I stopped him from putting an end to their fun, but if it would keep him from lashing out, I'd take it. I slapped his back comfortingly before heading down the aisle after them. Our first stop was to the customer service area, where we could get a tablet with all the items in the store loaded on it. Bailey-Rose could pair it to her account, pull up everything she saved, and it would provide us with the location of the items.

"Remind me why we gave into doing this when we all know how tired she is?" Ulysses muttered under his breath. "We're so fucked if none of us can tell her no to things."

"No, this good idea," I shared.

My three pack brothers looked at me in surprise. "Really? How so?" Yun-Sun questioned.

Taking a moment to sort out my thoughts, I tried to explain, knowing my ability to communicate clearly was a challenge I often wanted to scream in frustration, knowing how I spoke made me sound like an idiot. It wasn't anyone's fault but my own. I came here knowing nothing about the language, so I had a lot to catch up on.

Since the day I was born, I'd been taught to take owner-ship of my mistakes. They aren't anyone else's problem to deal with, just mine and mine alone. My parents were always such cold, detached people who viewed everything as a transaction. The way they interacted with people was brusque, to the point, and without emotion. Wealth provided them with a comfortable life, but it also made them callous. No one wanted to be their friend out of the goodness of their heart, or that's what they believed.

Everyone whispered behind their backs, wondering if they were actually human or robots. One of the many ther-apists I had growing up believed that to compensate for how disliked my family was, I chose to do everything to have people like me. I'm not sure I agree with that being the root of why I was so different, however, I'm sure it played a large factor. My goal in life was to make everyone I came in contact with feel they'd been seen, that I would remember them, and they would think fondly of the face that got them to smile, relax, and feel I had time for whatever they needed. This mindset is what connects me to my pretty lady. We share the same heart in this matter, but damn, I wish I didn't sound like such a fucking idiot when I spoke.

"How we worry for our kitten, she worries for us," I explained. "I think our kitten fears news of surgery will cause more worry, and we'll become obsessed keeping her safe. Already we have talks about this with little things, now we know bigger problem. So bigger response."

Ulysses paused to consider what I'd said. "So she's worried if we go back to the house, we'll want to talk about the surgery, maybe try and convince her to do it."

Shrugging, I tossed up my hands. "Only guess, but yes, I think what you say."

"*Guys, hurry up,*" Warrick shouted from the end of the row.

Ulysses chuckled as Gareth rolled his eyes, but Yun-Sun still seemed a little lost in thought. I fell into step beside him, hoping he might share with me what was going on in his brilliant mind. While I haven't told the guys much about my family, I knew Yun-Sun and I shared similar issues with our parents. Likewise, Yun-Sun chose to be his own person, and that led him to us.

By the time we reached the service counter, Yun still hadn't shared his thoughts, so I let the matter drop. He'd open up if he needed to, and the past twenty-four hours had been a roller coaster of feelings and hormones. I didn't blame him for wanting some time to understand how *he* felt about what we'd learned.

"Hello there, how can I be of service to you today?" the woman behind the counter asked.

Warrick smiled at the woman and leaned against the counter. "We're here to do some nest shopping, and our girl has a profile on your website. Could we get one of those tablets that helps you find stuff in the store?"

"Certainly, I'll just need the young lady's name to look up her account so I can pair it with the tablet," she said, her gaze shifted to Bailey-Rose, no longer in the shopping cart.

"Oh..." Bailey-Rose seemed surprised by this. "Could I just log in myself?"

The woman frowned slightly. "That's not how the system works. Look, you've already given us the information on the website to start an account, so you're not telling us anything we don't already know. It's for your security that we do it this way."

Not liking how this woman spoke to my precious kitten, I stepped up and rested my hands on Bailey-Rose's shoulders. "Do not speak to her like that," I stated.

There weren't many times that I let out the part of myself that proved I was my parents' son. However, to defend the person I treasured more than anything in my life, there wasn't anything I wouldn't do. My kitten's head tipped back as she looked at me with wide eyes, and her lips parted in surprise. Giving her a smile full of every emotion I felt for this stunning woman, I dropped a kiss to her forehead. Once I felt my girl was settled, I turned my attention back to the employee.

"You want name, I give you name," I offered, my voice cool even to my own ears. "Vili Rantala, there is account made."

When we first started our scent matching quest, I created one wanting to prepare myself for when the day came. I studied all there was about making a warm and comforting home for a new Omega. So far, we'd been doing well with Bailey-Rose, but I would take nothing less than the best for our Omega. Our pack had more than enough money to do whatever it took, and I planned to apply that thinking to this shopping trip.

"I'm sorry, did you say Rantala?" another woman asked, stepping away from the shelf she'd been stocking and joined in the conversation. "Forgive me, I couldn't help but over-hear. Would you be related to Henning Rantala, the founder of Silveda?"

"Yes, he is one of my fathers," I answered in a soft voice.

"Oh. My. God," the woman squealed. "Tanya, radio Philip and tell him we have a VIP and his pack in our store."

When Tanya didn't move fast enough, the woman clapped her hands urgently. "Right now, Tanya."

"No, no, this not needed," I assured the exuberant employee.

In an odd way, it was hard to take reactions like this when all my pack brothers were people of note to society. She, of course, brushed me off and stepped up to Bailey-Rose, causing me to tighten my hold on her ever so slightly. I didn't want to alarm my sweet kitten, but I'd learned long ago to be prepared for people to act irrationally when they found out I was rich. While I might want to fill the world with light and joy, leaving it a better place than I found it, people were unpredictable. Something shifted the second I realized I'd found my scent match. Not generally an overly dominant Alpha in daily life, the *need* to protect my Omega had become a major driving force in every action I took.

"Forgive Tanya. We have procedures to follow, but I understand not wanting to give out your name when you're bonded to someone of his status," the woman said kindly, taking Bailey-Rose's hand in hers. "Thankfully, we do have a system set up for situations like this that will make your shopping experience more enjoyable."

In a move that shocked the woman and me, my kitten

yanked her hand free. "You know what, I don't think we need your help or a tablet. Thank you for your assistance, but we'll be off to do some shopping."

The woman blinked at her then looked up at me, utterly confused. "Thank you, as my kitten say, we go shop now," I explained and started to turn away.

"Wait one moment, please," a man called, running over in his three-piece suit, making him look like the odd man out in this setting.

Bailey-Rose looked at the man, her expression annoyed. "Look, we just want to shop like normal people. I don't want to sit in the fancy rooms, drinking champagne as I click on a computer screen and you pull my order. That isn't fun nor does it give me a chance to really look at the item before buying it."

"Yes, I understand that, Miss Thatcher... it's noted in your file. Would you allow me to offer one of my staff to handle the things you personally pick out? That way, you don't have to worry about a full cart or something being on a shelf you can't get to?" The man asked as he tried to catch his breath. "Forgive me, our elevator is out of order, and I had to race down five flights of stairs."

This seemed to make our girl soften toward the man. "No, I'm sorry. Your staff wouldn't let me just log into the tablet so I didn't have to tell them who I was, and I got frustrated with them. Then I upset my Alphas, and they tried to fix the issue I was blowing out of proportion."

"Not at all, Miss Thatcher," he assured her. "Our goal here at The Snuggery is that every Omega or pack gets to enjoy shopping in our store however they want, not to mention you're one of our largest stockholders. Please take this tablet I connected to your account and take all the time you want in the store. I'll have one of my staff along to assist you shortly."

I took the offered tablet when Bailey-Rose didn't accept it, allowing the man to scurry off. We all turned to look at our Omega who was apparently full of surprises. She didn't meet our gaze, just tucked some hair behind her ear and tapped the toe of her shoe on the tiled floor.

"Baby girl," Gareth started, but she held up a hand to stop him.

"When I tell you the whole story, you're all going to laugh." She sighed. "Come on, let's talk and shop while we're still alone."

Warrick grabbed the front of the cart she'd been riding in and dragged it along. "So does this mean we still can't race around the store like that old man said?"

"Yes," Gareth and Ulysses snapped.

A smile tugged at my mouth, but I tried not to let them see, knowing it would only make this a bigger issue.

"Okay, geez," Warrick grumbled.

We ambled down the aisle full of lamps in all kinds of shapes, sizes, and styles that lined the shelves. Not wanting to push the matter, I simply drifted along, pausing to look at this or that. The others seemed to be following my lead, leaving our Omega to be the one who filled in the blanks.

"It was an accident," Bailey-Rose finally blurted. "I got a rather large sum of money on my sixteenth birthday from the trust my papa set up for me. My teacher took the opportunity to use that to teach me about managing money, learning about the stock market, and even had me bidding on things in a fake program to get a so-called *real* experience."

"So where did the accident come into play?" Yun-Sun questioned.

She sighed and faced us. "I thought I had a handle on how things worked. Daddy R always said when you're starting out, you pick companies you like or use. Then you know you're supporting something you benefit from in more ways than one. Well, you all saw my room. I shop here far more than I should, so it was a no-brainer. The problem was when I put in how many shares I wanted to buy, I thought it was the spot where you put how much you wanted to spend. Well, I put the number, and the next thing I know, I'm getting a call from The Snuggery corporate office asking to meet with me."

"What percent of shares do you hold, Rosie," Ulysses asked.

"Umm… four percent," Bailey-Rose answered. "The only people who own more are the actual owners and founders of the company."

I let out a bark of laughter and pulled my darling kitten into a hug. "You are perfect, kitten, so very perfect."

Who else at the age of sixteen could end up having a stake in a company like The Snuggery? Other businesses had tried to come into the nesting business, but none of them matched what this place could provide. Bailey-Rose was probably richer than all of us, and that's without her family's money. This marvelous woman stumbled into the best scenario possible. Now I understood why she didn't want to draw attention to herself in the store. She never meant to end up in this position, but she was making the best of it.

"Why not sell the stock as soon as you figured it out?" Warrick asked.

Gareth scoffed and slapped Warrick on the shoulder playfully. "Oh, man, that would have been the worst thing for her to do. You clearly don't know how the stock market works."

"I like to deal with the tangible," Warrick admitted. "Why pay for something you can't really see, touch, or interact with? Nah, I'll stick with the real deal any day, but I'm glad one of you understands in case she has questions."

"Oh, don't even worry about that. I've hired all the right people to make sure I don't do something like this again and to manage what I'd already done," Bailey-Rose shared. "Now, can we let this go and get our shop on?"

Letting out an excited whistle, I scooped her up and plopped her back in the cart. "You, my pretty lady, will ride in style, and we have fun." Glancing at Warrick, I caught his eye. "Slow, with us, please."

With a grin and a thumbs-up, we spent the next three hours wandering the store. True to the suited man's word, we had a helper with us the entire time, switching out full carts and getting our selections set up to be dropped off at home. Now that we knew no matter what we did in the store, they wouldn't stop us, it gave Warrick and me the permission we needed to make the most out of this trip. After seeing how much fun we were having, Ulysses decided to loosen up a bit and play a little.

"No, no, Lysse," Bailey-Rose called out before there was a yelp.

A large high-sided bin filled with pillows was left in a section to restock a display, and Ulysses just tossed our girl into it. There was enough room so the pillows weren't spilling out, but she sank into the mass since they were so soft and squishy.

"Lysse, how the hell am I supposed to get out of here now?" she called, her voice echoing from deep within the bin.

I tapped Warrick on the shoulder and gestured for him to help me up. When I bent over the edge, Warrick gave a shove, and I too ended up in the pillow quicksand. Weighing more than my kitten, I sank fast and was worried I would squash her. So what more was there to do than dive into the pillows to find my trapped Omega?

When I spotted her and the rosy color of her cheeks, I couldn't hold myself back. Instantly, my lips were on hers, and I slid my tongue over her bottom lip, urging her to let me deepen the kiss. I only needed to ask once as she submitted to my request. The sound of her moan had my hands slipping under her shirt, stroking her soft, smooth skin. Her scent wrapped around us, making it so all I could think, see, or smell was her, only her, my precious kitten. When she started to purr for me, I thought I would come in my pants right then and there. For an Omega to purr is a rare quality, and only those who believe they're completely safe, loved, and treasured by their Alphas feel the urge to share that joy with their pack through purring. It was a sound I savored, and I wished I could bottle up this feeling of being invincible by just hearing it.

A bang sounded on the side of the bin. "Okay, you two, cut it out. This fucking thing is like a megaphone broadcasting everything that's happening in there," Gareth informed us.

I laughed, burrowing my face in my kitten's neck, holding her tightly against my body. There was no way she couldn't feel how hard I was for her, how desperately I wanted to make her mine in every way. But I would be patient. I hadn't lied when I told the doctor I wanted to savor each and every inch of this woman. Only when she reached the point of desperation in her need to come would I give her that climax, and it would be one she'd never forget.

"You done?" I asked, lifting my head to look her in the face. "I think we have enough, maybe too much."

The smirk on my kitten's face was sinfully sexy. "There is no such thing as too much. Remember, I have a whole house to add my flair to, not just the bedroom."

"So, more shopping?" I challenged, seeing how tired she was. Being trapped in a pile of pillows didn't help her any, nor did the fact she wasn't on the move trying to keep herself going. "I think you need a nap, sleepy kitten."

"Yeah, I think I need a nap too," she agreed, proving it further as she yawned. "If we don't get out of the pillows soon, I might just nap here."

"Easy to fix, no problem," I announced.

Popping up, I grabbed the sides and flipped over to land on the floor. I motioned to the man who'd been assisting us and pointed to the bin. "We take it all."

"Certainly, I'll get it emptied right away," he said.

"No, we take it *all*, whole thing as is," I explained, stopping him from grabbing the bin. "We will bring up for you, she decided to be done."

He hesitated then determined it was above his pay grade and headed off.

"Um... V, what are you doing?" Warrick asked.

"Our kitten comfortable and half asleep. She wants to stay there so we take it all home," I answered. "You guys disagree?"

They all shook their heads, smiling as they grabbed hold of the bin, and we got to rolling.

BAILEY-ROSE

When I woke up, I found myself still in the pile of pillows, but there was no noise like I would expect if we were still in the store. Stretching, I knocked a bunch of pillows off and discovered I was in our home. I had no recollection of us leaving The Snuggery or arriving home, where I had been unloaded and placed in this mountain of fluff. Wiggling out of the nest, I reached the edge of whatever was holding the pillows, and it buckled under my weight. This caused me to ungracefully roll out into the middle of the floor.

I closed my eyes and held my breath, waiting for someone to comment about my entrance. When I didn't hear anything, I glanced around to discover I was in one of the side rooms that didn't have a purpose yet. All the items we bought were in boxes and bags along one wall waiting to be given a home.

Vili entered with a mug in his hands and a charming smile on his lips that had me remembering just how soft they were. "My kitten is awake."

Combing my fingers through my hair, I tried to get it to calm down after all the static buildup from the pillows. "How long was I asleep?"

"About two hours," he answered, offering me a hand. "I came to wake you. If you keep sleeping, then you not sleep tonight."

I let him pull me to my feet and accepted the sweet-smelling tea. "Good call. I've been known to overdo it on the naps and throw my whole sleep schedule off. Although I'm not sure what schedule I really have these days."

Vili cocked his head. "Why is that?"

I quickly covered my mouth as a yawn overtook me. "Sorry," I mumbled, sipping on the tea, hoping it would help clear my head.

"Come, let's sit with the others," Vili suggested as he grasped my hand.

Like a duckling to its mother, I followed along, shuffling my feet as I tried to drink and walk. I hissed as some of the tea sloshed over the side and ran down my arm, but it didn't stop me from getting another taste. Vili clicked his tongue disapprovingly at me and snatched the mug away, causing me to pout.

"I will give back once sitting," he assured me.

"What kind of tea is it? I don't think I've had anything quite like it," I asked.

"Serenity is the name I gave it," Vili shared.

Shocked, I dug my heels in, which had Vili jerking to a stop. "Wait, it's a blend you came up with? Meaning I can't find it in a store?"

He smiled and hummed his acknowledgment. "I love tea, so I experiment. This is a favorite, and I only share with you."

That had me grinning like a fool as we joined the others, relaxing in the living room and watching some sports game.

"Well, look who finally woke up," Gareth teased, patting the spot next to him. "Seems like that nap did you wonders, baby girl."

Slipping my hand from Vili's, I joined Gareth who apparently decided against me sitting next to him. Instead, I was snatched up and curled into a ball to be cradled on his lap. He nuzzled his nose into my hair, breathing in my scent. "God, I love how small you are. It's like you're our own personal Omega teddy bear to snuggle."

I preened under the affection, loving every second of it. Why Omegas were built to thrive off this sort of interaction, I'll never know. What I do know is now that I was getting major doses of it every day, I felt complete. It was as if I was a flower, and my Alphas were the sun which gave me vital nutrients I needed to grow. To my delight, the soft vibrations of my purr echoed in my chest as I nestled into a more comfortable position.

Gareth kissed my head a few times before he sat back and returned to watching the game. It was hard to stay awake when I felt so content, but the aroma of the tea had me cracking an eye. There was Vili offering the enticing drink he'd made just for me. Admitting defeat, I sat up, but Gareth wasn't having that. He widened his legs and settled me between them so I could lean back against his chest. This way, I could sit up to drink my tea safely and continue to cuddle.

"Are you hungry?" Warrick asked, scooching forward so I could see him. "You didn't really get any lunch."

I grabbed Gareth's wrist and looked at his watch. "Dinner should be happening shortly, right? I think I can wait until then."

"That's why I'm asking, Care Bear. It's ready when you are," Warrick explained. "We can relax and eat in here unless you want to sit at the table?"

"Nah, here is great," I said, but a yawn caught me halfway through. The guys looked at me skeptically. "What? Can't a girl be tired? We did a lot today."

Ulysses frowned. "Would you say today was too much?"

Ugh, I knew I shouldn't have said that. Of course, they would read into it, believing I pushed myself too hard.

"No, today wasn't too much," I argued, but they weren't buying that story. "Honestly, it's because I didn't get a good night's sleep. It might have been a little too much for that reason, but normally, this would be no trouble at all. Personally, I think it has more to do with the fact that so many changes have happened in the past few days. Think about it. I moved, met all of you, and my normal routine has been blown sky-high, which is why they give us this two-week leave, right? Remember what Dr. Arbour said? I know what I can handle and how to care for myself. I'll just go to bed early."

Ulysses didn't seem convinced and surprised me when he set my phone on the coffee table. "Then could it be that you didn't sleep well because Randall has been blowing up your phone?"

Even as he asked the question, the damn thing buzzed with Randall's name appearing on the screen. "He's still texting?"

"Texting, calling, leaving voicemails... the whole deal," Gareth added. "Baby girl, why didn't you tell us this was happening?"

I looked at the phone then my guys. "I-I didn't think he'd keep trying. Last night, I turned it off so I didn't have to deal with them. We just broke up, and everyone processes that differently, so I figured he'd wear himself out when I never responded."

"Rosie, this is harassment," Ulysses stated. "I'm of the mind to call the police about what's happening."

"They won't do much," Yun-Sun interjected. "We certainly can make them aware of the problem, but for right now, he hasn't done anything."

"Then what do you suggest we do?" Gareth demanded.

Yun scratched his jaw as he stared at the phone. "I think Bailey-Rose has a point about this being a new revelation for him. My thought is we turn off her phone and leave it be for a few days. There's no reason for her to need the phone while we are all with her, and for that same reason, I don't think Randall will be a danger to her. He's mad and lashing out, but if he persists, we will absolutely go to the police. However, as I said, that is my opinion, sweetheart. If you want us to go to the police about this now, then that's what we'll do. This is your life, and you know this man better than us."

Chewing on my lip, I thought over everything I knew about Randall. The person I saw in the bar was unlike anything I'd experienced over the time we were dating. While I realized now that I didn't love Randall, he'd been the closest thing to it. He'd always been understanding about my condition, or so I thought. Nothing in our time together gave me any reason to believe he'd hurt me. Yes, the moment at the bar had been scary, but I put myself in his shoes. If I'd shown up somewhere not expecting to see him, and he was acting strange and telling me we weren't together anymore, then I'd be equally as upset.

"Let's go with Yun's plan," I decided. "I would feel awful if I brought in the police and made a big deal out of this when there was nothing to be concerned about. Let the man cool off while we forget all about him and enjoy the time we have together. We'll just let my brothers know they need to reach out to you guys if they need me since they'd be the only people who call me."

Ulysses picked up my phone, turned it off, and tossed it to Yun-Sun. "Tuck that away someplace safe, and for now, we'll forget all about this."

This seemed to settle everyone's concerns enough for Yun-Sun and Warrick to get up and head to the kitchen. Moments later, they came back with bowls of food and handed them out. I gazed down at what looked like a cross between a pasta salad and a regular salad. Kale wasn't my favorite, and this dish was loaded with it. Stabbing a twirly noodle, I popped it into my mouth. I was delighted to find whatever dressing they used was flavorful and had a good kick. As subtle as I could, I ate around all the greenery in the bowl, just going for the bits I liked.

"Baby girl," Gareth whispered in my ear. "Don't think I don't see what you're doing."

I froze and slowly peered up at him. He cocked a brow, looking from me to the bowl, then back to me again before he narrowed his eyes.

"I really don't like kale," I mumbled, dropping my gaze and poking at the stuff. "Everything else is really tasty, but there's so much kale in my bowl."

"You know that kale is good for your heart, right?" Warrick interjected. "I've been studying what foods are best for those who have cardiac issues, which is why I made this dish. Slowly, I want to add more things to the restaurant menu, so I know you have things to eat and drink there."

Hearing him say that made me feel like a dick for not eating the meal as is, but there were some foods that no matter how good they were *for me,* I didn't like. "I appreciate that from the bottom of my heart, but I really can't stand kale."

Warrick gave me a sweet, understanding smile and pulled out his phone. "That's totally fine, Care Bear. I'll just add it to the list of things you don't like."

"You're keeping a list?" I questioned, trying to peek at his phone.

"Yup, it's a short one so far, but it helps me to keep things like that written down. In fact, I made it a sheet all of us can access. That way, if there's ever any doubt, we'll have something to reference," Warrick shared, showing me his phone.

How the hell could men be this sweet? It's almost as if they were created from all the best parts and none of the bad.

I started to tear up, but instead of letting my emotions get the better of me, I shoved a forkful of kale in my mouth. The bitter taste was so jarring, it was all I could focus on. Unable to stop the reaction I had to the stuff, my face scrunched up, and I swallowed as fast as I could. Grabbing my tea, I gulped it, desperate to get the nasty taste out of my mouth. The guys all chuckled, alerting me they were all watching this situation go down.

"Damn, Rosie, you really don't like that stuff, do you?" Ulysses teased.

My instant response was to glare and flip him the middle finger.

"Any day, any time, Rosie. You say the word, and I'll happily fuck you," he countered, his voice getting deep and raspy with desire.

I sucked in a breath, feeling my neck heating up with embarrassment and need. My skin started to feel a little itchy like my clothes were suddenly too much for my skin to handle, making me squirm.

Hands clamped on my hips, holding me still. "Baby girl, keep that up, and you're going to make me come all over your perfect ass."

Holy hell, I was in trouble. I needed to calm down, even though that was the last thing I really wanted to do. Just the thought of Gareth and Ulysses taking me at the same time had me panting. Then fingers pinched my nose, making me gasp, only to find a mouth full of kale being shoved into it.

All thoughts of sexy times came to a screeching halt as I gagged on the roughage in my mouth.

"Easy, kitten," Vili soothed, cupping my jaw. "Look at me, please." I did, and when I met his gaze, I seemed to calm, knowing I was fine with my Alphas here. "Chew or spit, which one?"

Vili moved his hand from my chin to hold it in front of my mouth, helping me to connect the dots on what he was saying. *Did he honestly think I would spit food into his hand just because I didn't like it? Also, why the hell was that so damn romantic and sweet?* I shook my head and chewed it enough to know I could swallow the lettuce in one gulp. Seeing my choice, he grabbed his glass of water and offered it to me once I got it down.

"Slowly, kitten," Vili cautioned. "Choking on salad is a terrible way to die."

The image of that on my tombstone struck me so funny I couldn't hold back my laughter. In a move only I could ever manage, water shot out of my nose and sprayed all over Vili. Horrified, I slapped a hand over my mouth and nose, trying to keep what was left in my damn body. Vili just blinked at me a few times before erupting in laughter, taking a napkin and drying himself off. The others joined in, and Warrick ran toward the kitchen only to return with towels to clean up the floor.

"That was, how do you say it? Ah, some funny shit," Vili commented, still chuckling as he used a special cloth to clean his glasses.

After having finally swallowed the water, the flood of apologies came rushing out. "Vili, I'm so sorry. I can't believe I snotted water at you. God, this is so embarrassing."

"Kitten," Vili chided as he slid a hand around the back of

my neck. "There is no need to be sorry. I am fine, you are fine, nothing to worry about."

"But…" I argued, trying to give words to my emotions.

Vili seemed to have a different plan as he pulled me into a kiss. It was a sweet, tender kiss that seemed to settle whatever rioting worries were rattling in my head. "My sweet kitten, it will take more than a little water from your nose to chase me away."

"I so don't deserve you guys," I whispered, resting my forehead against his.

Vili grunted disapprovingly as he pulled back enough to look me in the eyes. "Wrong, you have it backward. We don't deserve a precious gift such as you, Bailey-Rose." He gave me another kiss that was over too quickly, making me pout.

He merely smiled and nuzzled his nose against mine. "I can't get you excited. We just got you to calm down, kitten."

My brows shot up. "That's why you ninja attacked me with kale?"

"Fucking brilliant if you ask me," Gareth muttered. "Baby girl, the way you were squirming and starting to perfume, I'm not sure any of us could have held back. I thought you were on a suppressant?"

"I am," I blurted defensively. "Maybe it needs to be a stronger dose now that I've found my pack."

"Warrick, make a section on that sheet for a list of questions we need to ask the doc," Yun-Sun urged. "We had a lot to ask him today, but I'm sure there will be plenty more."

Gareth slid out from behind me and started to gather the bowls from the guys. When he caught me watching him, he winked. "We're fine, baby girl. I picked the short straw for kitchen cleanup while the house staff is taking two weeks off. Figured it might be best to keep it just us for now."

How he'd guessed that I was sitting here thinking he was

upset with me, I'll never know, but whatever the reason, I was thankful. I'd never been one to feel this insecure, but the opinion of these five men meant the world to me.

"Okay," I answered, snagging a pillow to cuddle with.

"Care Bear, come sit with me so we can snuggle," Warrick invited, holding out a hand. "I hate to admit it, but I'm getting jealous of that damn pillow."

That made me snort as I chucked the pillow at him. "Here, if you're so jealous, you can have it."

Warrick caught the pillow with ease only to set it aside, pop up from his seat, and tackle me. We rolled so I ended up on his chest out of harm's way. I laughed as Warrick nuzzled into my neck, only to tease me as he blew a raspberry against my neck. The vibrations had me squealing and wiggling in his hold with how much it tickled.

"I give up!" I gasped when he started to tickle my side. "We can snuggle all you want."

Letting his head fall back to the couch, Warrick grinned triumphantly at me. "Ha, I win."

Still trying to catch my breath, I flopped across his chest and let the sound of his steady heartbeat thumping in my ear slow my own. "That was a dirty trick. Did Lysse tell you I was ticklish?"

"Nah, just took a wild guess. You seemed like the type of person to be ticklish," Warrick answered.

Crossing my arms, I rested my chin on my hands so I could look him in the face. "I have a *look*... hmm?"

Warrick shrugged. "Pretty sure it's a rule that anyone as adorable as you has to be ticklish."

I rolled my eyes at that but couldn't keep the smile off my face.

"Kitten," Vili said after a lull in the conversation. "Earlier when you woke up, you telling me about not having schedule. Then mentioned your routine changed. Would making new schedule help?"

Turning so the side of my head rested on my hands, I considered his question. When I first got back from college, I was so excited to start realizing my dream, started building my art studio and created paintings of the millions of ideas floating around in my head. Then Randall happened, and the spark to create had fizzled out. Now my mind was so consumed with these men and spending as much time with them as possible, I'd all but forgotten about my plans.

"All of you work outside the house, right?" I asked.

Of course, I knew Warrick had the bar, but I didn't really know what day-to-day life was like for these Alphas of mine.

"For the most part," Ulysses answered. "Vili works from home a few days here and there, but I think we can all agree that nothing is set in stone. We knew that once we found our Omega, things would adjust, but we haven't hammered all that out."

I nodded, trying to visualize what *normal* life would look like once these two weeks were over.

"*Omae*," Yun-Sun called, drawing my attention. "What plans did you have for yourself after college? I know finding us was something you didn't think would happen, so it only make sense you have aspirations to chase."

Hearing him ask me that question made my heart flutter in a way that had nothing to do with my condition. It proved once more that they saw me as capable and didn't want me to lose out on my desires for my life. Many Omegas knew once they joined a pack, their life was now centered around taking care of their new family. That's not to say they couldn't push for more or that their pack was forcing them to give up everything. Yet when you grow up being taught this is how things are done, you don't tend to question it.

"I think I might have mentioned that my parents gave me a studio for a graduation present. To call it a studio might be a little misleading. It's a space that I can turn into a gallery and have a private area for me to work. My dream is to have a place to display local artists, those who no one will take a chance on," I shared, sitting up.

Warrick maneuvered me off his chest to sit beside him, curled up, with his arm wrapped securely around my ass. There was nothing sexual about it, more to offer security and to make it clear he didn't want me going anywhere.

"Over the years of exploring this city, I've found so many amazing people in it. Each time I asked about their journey or dreams, it's always the same thing. No one will give them the time of day unless they have a following or money to buy their way in," I explained, my tone bitter. This was one subject that could get me heated every time it was brought up. "There's no reason for things to be like that. Art is subjective, and not every artist will have a massive market, but when their art finds the right person, it will impact them in a way no one else can. Many simply need to be discovered, given the space to find those people who resonate with their art. We create what our souls inspire, and no one should tell you that isn't good enough."

The silence as the guys all stared at me with shock and awe had me tucking my hair behind my ear as I dropped my gaze. Now I've gone and done it. I'd gotten on my damn soapbox ranting like a crazy person. Well, people have always said that artists are an odd bunch, so I guess I'm totally living up to that standard.

"I think that is amazing," Warrick announced before sitting up to hug me tightly. "God, it's crazy how perfect you are for us, Care Bear." He pulled back, holding my shoulders, his expression becoming serious. "Whatever we can do to help you accomplish this goal, just say the word. I know money isn't an issue, but I'd be more than happy to spread the word with my connections in the restaurant and hospitality world. Just think, if we could get you on the map as a hotspot destination for people traveling, you'd have the perfect opportunity to find buyers willing to take a chance. Not to mention, once I get you to do your piece on the night-club wall, it will be great advertising."

My jaw dropped at the intensity behind his words and how he practically vibrated with excitement.

"He's right, baby girl," Gareth interjected. "This dream of yours deserves to be given any and all chances to succeed. Not only for you and your art but to inspire others to follow their dreams."

Vili nodded his head excitedly and clapped his hands together. "Yes, this is good all good ideas. Maybe I make special line of jewelry that only is sold at the studio. Kitten, you and I shall create a collaboration."

"I can help you make a contract that is favorable to you and your guest artists. I'm sure there will be some hoops to jump through with insurance, but we will figure it out together," Yun-Sun assured me. "It might also be advantageous to put together a buyer's contract as well, something that ensures their painting and artistic copyright is protected."

Overwhelmed, I merely sat there stunned at how easily they were onboard with this idea. Not only that, but understood exactly what I was trying to accomplish with this dream. "R-really? You guys think this is possible? Randall—" I stopped speaking the moment I said his name, knowing it would upset them to finish that thought.

Ulysses stood, walked over to me, and cupped my chin as he held my gaze. "That idiot clearly didn't know you at all, Rosie. Never have I met a more determined person than you. If this is what you've decided to do, then I pity the person who tries to stand in your way."

"You mean that?" I asked, my voice hoarse with held-back emotions.

He bent down, our noses brushing and the heat of his breath on my skin. "Every. Single. Word."

As if to add proof to his words, he sealed them with a kiss that stole my breath and left me wanting more as he pulled back. He stroked his thumb across my cheek simply staring into my eyes. "Bailey-Rose, trust that I will never lie to you. You might not always like to know what I have to say, but whatever comes out of my mouth will always be honest and true. That is the type of relationship I want between us."

"Me too," I blurted.

Ulysses smiled, his expression so tender and loving. "Good, I'm glad we agree. Now do we need to get you something else to eat? Speak now because I fully intend to put you to bed early."

A shiver ran down my spine as the Alpha side of Lysse was taking charge. "Can I have more of what was made without the kale? I really liked the dressing that was on it."

"I'll see what I can do," Ulysses answered with a quick kiss before heading to the kitchen.

Sitting there on the couch, Warrick curled around me, and with what I can only guess to be a dopey smile on my face, I sighed.

My life was turning out to be pretty damn perfect.

BAILEY-ROSE

With some artful negotiations on my end regarding the time they deemed I should go to bed, we settled on eight o'clock. My argument was that after having taken a nap, if they let me fall asleep too early, I'd be up at the crack of dawn throwing off my whole sleep schedule. Not that I really had one at this point, but it was the best logic to use to make my point. One movie and bowl of birthday cake ice cream later, I was scooped up in Gareth's arms and deposited in my room.

"Be good, baby girl, and go to sleep," he warned. "Tomorrow we're going to check out the studio space and figure out what needs to happen to turn your dream into reality. Pretty sure you don't want to be half asleep for that."

As if on cue, I yawned so wide it made my jaw pop. "I can barely keep my eyes open, so I don't think sleep is gonna be a problem."

Sliding his hand around my throat, Gareth used his thumb to tilt my head back for him to kiss me. My hands fisted his shirt, trying to draw him closer to me, but he didn't move an inch. With a playful nip on my lip, he took a step back, a smirk on his perfect lips.

"Tease," I muttered.

"Oh, baby girl, if there is a tease in this room, it's all you," Gareth countered with a chuckle. "Your scent alone brings me to the edge of my control. Once your doc gets us those meds, I plan to make the most out of those three hours."

I sucked in a harsh breath at his promise, my imagination running wild with what he might do during *those three hours.*

"Now that, baby girl, is me being a tease," Gareth stated as he walked out of the room, leaving the door wide open to let me watch him swagger down the stairs.

My libido, which had been kept in check my whole adult life, was rattling the bars of its cage more and more. These Alphas were going to be my ruin, and I was quickly discovering how little I cared. It would be one hell of a way to go while lost in passion and lust with my men as they sent me to heaven. Fanning myself, I dropped onto my ottoman, needing a moment to compose myself. Once I knew my legs would support me, I headed for the closet and plucked a silk nightgown out of a drawer.

Another yawn took over as I changed, proving that no matter how riled up I might get, sleep was going to win out. Bleary-eyed, I shuffled to the bathroom, brushed my teeth, and called it good enough. I was on my own, at least for part of the night, since the guys weren't ready for bed so early. There was no doubt in my mind some of them would drift up here, so I left the door open—a clear sign I was more than happy to welcome them in my bed should they want to join me.

Crawling into my nest, I groped around for Pearl, eyes no longer able to remain open. Finally, I latched on to one of her tentacles, dragging her to me so I could wind myself around her as I did every night before finding the guys. With a sigh, I nuzzled one of the pillows that smelled like Warrick and let sleep take over.

The feel of a hand brushing up my leg had me stirring. Soft kisses soon followed the same path, making me moan when those lips reached my inner thigh. Before even being asked, I shifted onto my back, widening my legs slightly, praying they would continue. The huff of laughter teased my skin as those hands slid under the silk of my nightgown, sliding it up my body. I shuddered at the kiss pressed to the top of my mound, making me whimper, desperate for them to move a little lower to where my clit ached.

"Please," I begged. "It's too much."

There was no reply, only the feel of my nightgown being pulled up and off my body. It wasn't enough. I was so hot, and my skin felt so sensitive. The lightest brush of his fingers, lips, and even his breath was almost too much for me to handle, but I didn't want it to stop. I needed more.

A whine escaped me as a finger traced from my clit down to my asshole, which had me arching, chasing after the touch.

"No!" I cried when the hand pulled back. "Pleeease. Please touch me, lick me, fuck me, anything you want. I just need you."

When the touch didn't return, I thrashed, searching for whichever Alpha was here with me. With a gasp, I sat up, my eyes snapping open, desperate to find where they'd gone. Finding there was no one in my nest, I rushed to exit the bed only to crash to the floor when my limbs refused to cooperate. The feel of the carpet which I'd found so soft and luxurious, felt like sandpaper on my skin. This clued me into the fact I was naked, so someone had to have been in here.

"Why are you hiding from me?" I asked, shoving up on shaky arms to look around my room again. With hardly anything in it, there weren't many places to hide, and the bathroom and closet doors were open.

"I don't understand what's happening?" I sobbed, curling up into a ball.

The heat of my body was unbearable, and the rough feel of the carpet made it impossible to remain where I was. Delirious, I crawled toward the door that I thought was to the bathroom. Once there, I would fill the tub with cold water and submerge myself. It would help—it had to help— because I couldn't take the sensation of being burned from the inside out much longer.

In my misguided efforts, I picked the wrong door. Instead of the bathroom like I thought, it was the entrance to my room. My hand slipped on the first stair, and I was unable to stop the forward motion as I slid down to the landing. Thankfully, I was already on the floor so while a completely ungraceful move, I wasn't hurt. A scent hit my nose, and instantly, a whine erupted from me as my body refused to listen to anything I was telling it to do.

"Bailey-Rose," Vili shouted. "Guys, come *now*."

The sound of thunder coming toward me had me curling up into a ball. Then a hand tentatively brushed my shoulder, and I whimpered.

"Did I hurt you?" Warrick asked, his voice panicked. "She's burning up. Do we need to call an ambulance?"

I reached out a hand in hopes that one of them would take it and relieve some of my suffering. Fingers wrapped around my hand, gripping it tightly, making me moan and drag the hand to my chest.

"Oh fuck," Gareth swore. "How can she be going into heat? I thought she was taking something to prevent this?"

"Obviously, whatever it was isn't working," Ulysses snapped.

Rolling on my back, I took the hand I held and brushed it over my nipple, hissing at how mind-blowing it felt. Yes, this is what I needed. "Please touch me," I begged, rubbing myself against any skin I could of my Alpha.

The hand was yanked out of my grasp, making me sob at its loss.

"Yun," Gareth's voice sounded dark, almost threatening. "If you don't let go of me and walk away right now, I'm going to do something all of us will regret."

"Get out of my way, Gareth," Yun-Sun growled. "She needs me, and I'm not going to leave her like that. Pack or not, our Omega's well-being will always come first."

"I agree with you, which is why I'm standing between you two. Look, you're in rut and barely holding it together with the suppressants. Can you honestly tell me you wouldn't do the same thing if the roles were reversed?" Gareth challenged.

The energy coming off these two men was intoxicating. I could feel it ripple along my skin, teasing me to the point I let out a soft moan, my hand drifting between my legs. My pussy was soaking wet, allowing my fingers to glide over my sensitive, needy clit. That slight touch alone had me orgasming, a scream tearing out of my throat as my body shuddered.

"Enough of this," Yun-Sun roared. "Decide right now. Either trust me as a member of this pack to protect what is ours or knock me out, lock me in my room, and I'll pack my shit in the morning."

"You don't fucking mean a word of that, and we both know it. Right now, your caveman brain is in control, making it impossible to take you at your word," Gareth countered. "I trust Yun-Sun with my life... with her life. This rut-headed idiot, not a chance."

The sound of a struggle had my head drifting in that direction. Yun-Sun was being held back by Ulysses and Gareth as he struggled to get to me. When his wild, spice-brown eyes met mine, I reached a low whine full of pleading and called out to him. In a rather impressive move, he freed himself from the others and scooped me up, cradling me to his bare chest. Instantly, I wrapped my arms around his neck, pressing myself to him.

"Alpha, will you help me?" I whispered. "I don't know what's happening to me."

Yun-Sun started to purr as he nuzzled my shoulder. "Leave it to me, sweetheart. I will take care of everything."

Then he started up the stairs, and the door to my bedroom slammed shut, followed by shouting on the other side. Yun-Sun spun, and my back was pressed to the door's cool wood, making me sigh.

"I've got her pressed to the door so if you want to hurt her, by all means try and get in here. I know I'm in rut, but there's no way Bailey-Rose could handle all of us at once. Let me handle this for both our sakes, or it could only make things worse," Yun-Sun warned, then turned his focus on me.

"You can't know how you'll respond to her being in heat. If all of us are there, we can make sure no one goes too far," Warrick argued.

Brushing his nose along mine, Yun-Sun spoke softly for only my ears, "Bailey-Rose, I need you to tell them you trust me even if I'm in rut. They won't believe me, but they might listen if it's you."

It took my hazy brain a minute to figure out what he was saying, but the dots finally connected. "Stop, please," I called out, hoping they would hear me. "I trust Yun-Sun to do what's best for me, rut or no rut. Believe in the man you know him to be because, at the core, we don't change who we are."

The sounds coming from the other side of the door quieted, and Yun let out a breath of relief, resting his head on my chest. Finally having the contact I needed, my head started to clear, giving me more control over my body. I let my hand stroke down the back of Yun-Sun's neck, between his shoulder blades, until I couldn't reach any farther. The purring returned, and the vibrations set my skin ablaze causing my breath to hitch.

"Sweetheart, do you have any idea why you're going into heat?" Yun asked between pressing kisses along my collarbone.

"No," I answered, my voice barely more than a puff of air as I let my arms fall to my side resting against the door, opening myself up to him.

"We need to stop this from going any further. Do you have a fast-acting suppressant?" Yun pressed.

A groan of pleasure rolled out me as his tongue laved over my nipple. "I-I think so, but it's hard to think when you do things like that."

"Do what?" he inquired, flicking his gaze up to mine. "Oh, you mean this?"

This time he went for the opposite nipple, sending a jolt of electricity through my body right to my pussy. If I'd thought I was wet before, I'd been wrong. I was a damn Slip 'N Slide, and Yun's washboard abs were the perfect friction for my eager clit. Yun's hand gripped my ass so hard I wouldn't be surprised if there were fingerprints left behind. It felt glorious to know he was leaving a mark on my body showing his claim over me. That feeling emboldened me enough to nip at the skin just below his jaw.

"Sweetheart," Yun growled out, stepping away from the

door, creating a little more space between us. "If I'm going to prove to myself and the others that I can handle this, you can't go provoking me. I need to see if you have a suppressant while my medication is giving me the ability to hold back. Where should I look?"

"Bathroom," I started, then paused to collect my thoughts. "There is a pink metal chest with the medical symbol on it. All my medication should be there."

Yun carried me to the bathroom and set me on the counter. Biting my lip, I tried not to whimper at the loss of his touch, but he was right—I needed to stop what was happening. Setting the case on the counter, he opened it and expanded the trays of medication.

"What am I looking for here, sweetheart?" Yun asked.

Grabbing the box, I slid it over and noticed a packet of pills that shouldn't have been in there. It was the daily dose of suppressant I clearly hadn't taken for the past two days. No wonder this was happening. With everything going on, my normal routine of taking my meds before bed had clearly gone out the window. I tossed them on the counter so I wouldn't forget again and dug through the bottom of the case to find the ready-to-go suppressant pen.

"This one burns like a bitch when injected," I shared. "Think you could take my mind off it?"

Yun-Sun grabbed my hips and slid me to the edge of the counter. "I'm sure I can think of something to distract you with."

Wasting no time, Yun buried his face between my legs and sucked sharply on my clit. This had me instantly coming so hard my vision started to darken. Using the last two brain cells left, I hit the button on the pen, injecting the medication. I hissed as it felt like acid was being forced into my bloodstream, but Yun-Sun did his damnedest to make it easier on me. Two fingers slid into me and immediately found that spot that had every woman quaking with pleasure. The soft clicking stopped, letting me know all the medication had been administered.

Chucking the used device into the sink, I used both hands to grab Yun's head so I could grind myself on his face. "God, yes," I cried out. "Just like that. Oh fuck, fuck, fuck."

The next orgasm slammed into me like a tidal wave, sweeping me under the water, making me feel weightless even as it tried to drown me. My body slumped back against the glass of the mirror, the coolness almost burning my hot skin.

A vibration at my wrist told me what I already knew, Yun had rocked my fucking world.

BAILEY-ROSE

Eyes closed, I focused on the marble countertop under my hands as a way to ground myself. It was much harder to get my heart to calm the fuck down when it was still doing flips from the orgasm I'd just experienced.

"*Omae*," Yun-Sun murmured, his voice full of concern as he brushed hair out of my face.

Cracking open an eye, I saw his worry and took a moment to wet my lips before reassuring him, "I'm fine... more than fine after something like that. Just give me a sec to catch my breath."

He gingerly gathered me up and carried me to my bed, where he climbed in and stretched out beside me. Twisting, I pressed my ear to his chest just over his heart so I could use it as a metronome for my own. Soon, the boiling heat abated somewhat, giving me a little relief and clearer thinking.

"What does *omae* mean?" I asked, tilting my head to look at him.

Yun grabbed my leg and hoisted it over his hip, pressing us as close as humanly possible. The feel of his rock-hard cock pressed against my belly sent a shiver through me. Instinctively, I rocked against the fabric of his sleep shorts, eliciting a deep rumble from Yun. He buried his face in my neck, letting his teeth scrape along it.

"It's a word from my family's native language," Yun-Sun shared. "Translated, it means 'you.' However, the way it's written shows that it has a much deeper level of intimacy. It's not simply you, as in hey, you over there." Yun paused to kiss up my neck until we were nose to nose. "This means *you are mine.*"

With that declaration, he caught my lips in a searing kiss that had me moaning and clinging to him. Yun's tongue flicked along my bottom lip, coaxing me to open for him. Eagerly, I deepened the kiss, my hips rolling in time with the fervor of our make-out session. One of Yun's hands smoothed over my ass and dove between my legs, stroking my pussy. I didn't realize his true motive until he used my slick to tease at the entrance of my ass. That was one area where none of my other sexual encounters had broached. I wasn't against the idea by any means, just uncertain, having no experience.

I broke the kiss as I tossed my head back, crying out at the ecstasy flooding my body from his finger pressing past the entrance. My skin broke out in a sweat while my breathing quickened.

"Looks like someone is enjoying themselves," Yun crooned as he slipped the digit back out only to collect more slick. "Tell me, sweetheart, do you like your perfect little round ass to be fucked?"

The feel of his finger getting deeper this time had my eyes rolling back in my head. No words came out of my mouth when I opened it, only sounds of pure enjoyment. Yun chuckled, nipping at my ear. "I'm going to take that as a yes, but we will save that for another night. A time when I know I can focus all my efforts on making you scream as you come over and over again on my cock. However, I'm in rut, and that is making me feel selfish. The need to claim your pretty pink pussy as it begs for my knot isn't something I can fight against."

Like a fan to a smoldering ember, Yun-Sun's words ignited the needs of my heat, regardless of the suppressant. "Then take what's yours and claim your Omega," I urged, letting my hand glide down his chest until I hooked a finger on the waist of his sleep shorts. "Bind me with your knot and fill me with your cum, *Alpha*," I purred, wrapping my fingers around his throbbing cock.

Yun's eyes shifted into something more primal, and I knew his rut was winning out. Grabbing my wrist, he yanked my hand off his dick and rolled me onto my stomach. I started to lift my head to see what he was doing, but a hand wrapped around my neck, keeping me firmly in place.

"Stay just like that," Yun-Sun ordered. "I'm going to fuck you, have no doubt about that, but we are going to do this my way."

I nodded the best I could with his hand still on my neck, but he knew what I was doing. He let go of my neck to stroke his fingers down my spine, over the round of my ass, and all the way down to my heel. Then his touch vanished, but I could hear the rustle of him removing his shorts, and that had me squirming, rubbing my legs together in anticipation.

When I felt him straddle my legs, I couldn't help but let out a small whine, unable to wait patiently for what my body needed so desperately. Yun slid a hand under my hips and lifted just enough to get a pillow under my stomach. Taking a moment to massage my ass, letting his thumbs brush over my pussy had me panting.

"No more teasing, I beg you," I gasped.

Hot breath along my skin and the brush of Yun's cock along my ass as he leaned down was nearly my undoing. "What is it that my Omega needs?"

"You, I need you," I mumbled, arching my back, hoping I could get closer to his dick.

"*Omae*," Yun chided. "Tell your Alpha exactly what you need, and I promise I will give it to you."

This man was going to make me lose my mind if he didn't hurry up and shove his fucking cock in me. If he wanted me to tell him exactly what I needed, then my heat-driven brain would be more than happy to tell him.

"Alpha, I want you to slam your cock into my pussy, filling me with every inch you have. Then I want you to fuck me into this mattress and see if it can really withstand what we're going to put this bed through. Finally, I want your knot locked so deep in me that we become one person as you flood my body with your cum," I stated.

The man above me had gone stone-still, but I watched as he fisted the blankets, telling me that I'd gotten to him. Now we would truly see if Yun-Sun, in full primal rut, turned into the mindless animal the others thought he would.

Yun's mouth latched onto my neck, and his teeth scraped the sensitive flesh just under my ear, where I could feel my pulse. For a brief second, I thought he was going to actually mark me, placing his permanent claim on me, binding us together for the rest of our lives. Instead, he gripped the flesh and began to suck on it sharply, making me grunt at the burn. With the force he was using, I knew the hickey he was leaving would be dark and last quite some time. When he was finished, he kissed the spot tenderly.

"Until you are ready to be bound to me, I will make sure this mark is always here as a reminder of my intention to make you mine," Yun said, his voice deep and husky as he parted my ass cheeks and speared me with his cock.

The sensation of him thrusting into me and stretching my walls which gave in, eagerly accepting everything until his hips met my ass was mind-blowing. Unable to stop the scream of delight at finally being filled, I buried my face in the blankets and fisted whatever I could grab onto. Yun kissed along my shoulders as he uncurled my hand so he could thread his finger overtop, gripping tightly as he stretched my arms straight out in front of me.

"That's it, sweetheart. Let the others hear how good I'm making you feel," Yun praised, slowly rocking into me. "Fuck, I never imagined how amazing this would be to have your pussy wrapping around my cock. Nothing else will ever be good enough after experiencing this."

Yun showered whatever skin he could touch with kisses as he shifted his legs wider to get a deeper stroke. I gasped, clutching his fingers in my grasp as Yun sped up. The sound of wet flesh slapping together filled the room, along with my constant stream of moaning gibberish. Any time I tried to get him to speed up or fuck me harder, he would slow and pull back.

"What did I say, sweetheart?" Yun asked once he'd stopped fucking me, and turned my head to look at him. "We are going to do this my way. Now be my sweet, perfect Omega, and let me take care of you."

When I didn't say anything, he raised a brow and started to pull out of me.

"No," I cried, grabbing his thigh with my free hand. "I'll be good, I promise. Just keep fucking me."

Yun kissed my forehead as he slid back in achingly slow. "That's my girl. Now you wanted me to fuck you into the mattress, right?" I nodded eagerly. "All right, but the only way that's going to happen is if you focus on relaxing and let me do all the work. Let my heart take the brunt of this so I can give you everything you asked for and know you're safe."

That final request had me melting into my nest, realizing how this man cared so much about my happiness and well-being. *How could I not do as he asked when the request was to fulfill my desires?*

"I submit to your care, Alpha," I whispered, trying to blink away the tears threatening to fall.

Yun-Sun adjusted us slightly with another pillow supporting my hips, which allowed him to wrap my arms close to my chest and hold me snuggly to him. Now that all the weight was removed from my body, it allowed him the freedom to move as he needed. His cheek brushed along mine, nuzzling me tenderly.

"Are you ready for me, sweetheart?" Yun-Sun asked.

I wriggled my ass since it was the only part of my body I had any control over. "More than ready," I answered.

Yun-Sun pulled back almost to the point he'd slip out, but just before that could happen, he slammed into me. A shout was forced out of me at the impact, but I loved the feel of it. Yun hid his face in my neck as he made good on his promise and drove me into the mattress. There was nothing for me to do but feel every stroke of his hard cock hammering in and out of me. He was thicker than anyone else I'd ever been with, but the slight burn as my body adjusted only made it more real. There was no way for me to mistake this for a dream.

While the power stayed the same, he started to shorten his thrusts, alerting me that his knot was starting to expand. A slight panic grew in my chest like the flutter of butterfly wings. I hadn't told Yun that this would be the first knot I'd accepted. Randall hadn't wanted to knot me until we were bonded, and the other two guys were flings I didn't want to be attached to.

As if Yun could tell my mind was wandering, he nipped at my neck. "Omae, you are allowed to be nowhere but in this moment. Right now you are all mine, and I want your mind to be filled with thoughts of me, nothing else."

One of his hands shifted off my upper arm to tease my nipple. He gave it a slight tug which in turn caused me to moan loudly.

"That's my girl," Yun-Sun praised, kissing along my jaw. "Tell me, sweetheart, whose cock is buried deep in your pussy?"

Ensuring I knew the answer, he slammed into me and rolled his hips in a move that had me seeing stars. "Yours, Alpha."

"No, not Alpha," he corrected. "Say my name. I want to hear you say it as I make you come all over my cock."

Again he swirled his hips as he rolled my nipple between his fingers. All the stimulation set off a chain reaction of sparks that led to detonation. "*Yun,*" I screamed as the orgasm exploded within me.

Fireworks appeared in my vision, followed by my body going tense as everything contracted around Yun's cock. He fucked me through the orgasm drawing out every second of pleasure he could.

"Fuck!" He growled as I felt the knot pressing against the walls of my pussy. "I'm going to knot you so deep, it's going to make a permanent spot just for me inside you. No one else will be able to claim that part of you. It's all mine."

Somewhere in my brain, I felt like I should be worried about him talking like that. Yet the knowledge he was in rut reminded me that what he was saying was driven by his base needs. While I wasn't a fool to think there might not be moments the guys want me to themselves, our nature was to be a pack, to share one Omega.

All thoughts stopped as the pressure from his knot reached the point it pushed past what I could handle. "No, it's too much," I whimpered, trying to wriggle out of his hold and free myself before it was too late.

The feel of teeth on the back of my neck, just under my hairline, instantly had me motionless as Yun roared his completion. It was as if he'd latched on to a pressure point that caused my body to go utterly limp. There was still a slight panic as the knot continued to push my limits, but while there was pressure, it wasn't painful. Once my body realized this, the panic started to subside, turning me into a limp ragdoll in Yun's hold.

I could feel his ragged breath on my neck as Yun's cum started to fill my womb. This was it, the moment I was well and truly knotted for the first time. Now he was breeding me, marking me from the inside out with his claim. A wash of cooling energy spread through my body as this moment met the needs of the heat I'd landed myself in.

Carefully, Yun released his hold on my neck, loosened his arms, and rolled us so we were lying on our sides. "Holy fuck, that was amazing," I blurted.

Yun-Sun started to purr, sending shockwaves of pleasure through my body. Over the years of not being able to have consistent sex, which wasn't ideal for such a hyper-sexual being as an Omega, I'd bought toys to play with. Right now, being filled with Yun's knot and combining it with the vibrations from his purring, the man turned into a damn silver bullet. I rocked slowly, testing how much movement I could make without hurting either of us. Yun hissed, both hands clutching my breasts, letting me know it was a good sound.

I have no idea how long we laid there teasing each other, letting aftershocks of our orgasms spark through our bodies. He'd managed to make me come again, clamping down even tighter on him, which wrung out even more of his cum.

"*Omae, please* take mercy on me," Yun gasped. "I can't take much more of this mind-blowing torture."

That put a smile on my face to know this was driving him as crazy as it was me. Reaching up, I pulled him down to kiss, enjoying the feel of his lips against mine. "I suppose I can let you have some rest," I teased. "It seems you're rather addictive. Now that I've had a taste, I can't seem to stop wanting more."

Yun cupped my cheek and kissed me deeper this time but cut it shorter than I would have liked, pressing his forehead against mine. "Bailey-Rose, I need you to know there's no turning back after this."

Slightly confused, I frowned, but he continued before I could ask what he was talking about. "You, my stunning Omega, own me, body, mind, and soul, bonded or not. From this day 'til forever, I'm going to need you in my life. So forgive me for the days I become an overbearing Alpha because there isn't anything I wouldn't do to keep you right here with me forever."

My heart melted and burst at the same time upon hearing those words. "I don't plan on ever leaving you or the others. This is where I was always meant to be."

"*Omae,* I can't deny how I feel, and I know for scent-bonded matches, feelings develop faster. However, I need it to be clear that I don't expect you to feel the same as I do right now, but I'm unable to lay here with you like this and not say it," Yun rambled in a hurried manner, only to pause and take a deep breath. "I've fallen in love with you, Bailey-Rose Thatcher. I can't wait for the day we become a bonded pair and live out our lives together as a pack."

Taking Yun-Sun's hand in both of mine, I kissed the top of it and twisted as far as I could to meet his gaze. "You and the others are more than I ever could have dreamed of. I know that all of you are quickly becoming people I can't live without, but I don't know if that's considered love. What I know beyond a shadow of a doubt is I belong to all of you, and I wouldn't trade that for the world."

Yun kissed me in a way that had my toes curling, and I moaned into his mouth. He held nothing back from me, pouring his feelings into that kiss so there was no questioning what he'd said to me.

"Sleep now, sweetheart. I have a feeling it won't be long before my cock wakes you up again," he warned, tucking me close and lulling me to sleep with his purrs.

Ulysses

Sleep eluded me to the point I gave up and walked out to the upstairs living room. I flopped on the couch, turning on the television but keeping the volume low in case the others were sleeping. A few minutes later, Gareth joined me, looking like a grumpy bear that had been woken up early from hibernation. When his leg wouldn't stop bouncing, I finally muted the random show neither of us were watching to face him.

"Something on your mind?" I asked dryly.

Gareth dropped the thumb he'd been chewing on. "You know there is."

"Maybe it might help if you talk about it," I suggested.

He just glared at me. "Really, that's your solution to this? Talking? Gee, thanks, Dr. Phil."

"If you're going to be an ass, then do it in your own room. I got here first, and I don't need your crabby ass making this night even more delightful than it already is," I remarked and turned the volume back on.

Gareth snatched the remote and turned off the television. "Okay, look, do you really think Yun was serious about leaving? I can't get him saying that out of my head. Did we push too far? What if he resents us from now on, and this moment haunts us for the rest of our lives together?"

I groaned as I slouched, letting my head fall back on the couch. This was exactly what had been keeping me up. I'd been right there holding him back, not trusting he would look after Rosie, and he called us the fuck out on it.

"There's no way to know until whatever's going on up there is over," I said, raking a hand through my hair. "Fuck, man, out of all the ways I thought our pack would hit a rough patch, this certainly wasn't it."

"What?" Gareth demanded, sitting up to look me in the face. "Why would you assume we'd have trouble?"

Shrugging, I looked up at the ceiling. "The four of you have been living together longer and worked out a routine. Then I was finally able to quit traveling, but I wasn't here more than a few days before finding Rosie. Now there are two of us throwing a wrench in the ecosystem. Not to mention fearing resentment for knowing our Omega so much better than anyone else in our pack."

"Dude, how long have you been worried about moving into this house?" Gareth pressed.

I flicked a glance his way and was surprised to find worry written all over his face. The man was genuinely concerned about why I'd felt that way. Many only saw the brash, sarcastic side of Gareth, not this man who cared about those who were important to him more than anything.

"It's not a big deal... people worry," I argued. "I think it's rather normal to question your choice when you get paired with a group of people you don't know all that well. Yeah, we've been a pack for a decent amount of time, but for me, it's been weekends and random days here and there. So yeah, I was worried I wouldn't mesh the same way all of you seem to so effortlessly."

Gareth shook his head with a huff of laughter. "You didn't see it because things always went so well with you around, but the four of us didn't get along." He held up a hand to stop me from speaking. "Let me explain. Yun-Sun's whole purpose in life before Bailey-Rose was work. The man was never home, and when he was, he'd set up camp in the library or his room. Warrick and I probably saw each other the most on a daily basis. Problem is that our personalities clash in so many ways, it's a miracle he's still alive. Vili did his best to keep the peace, but he was out of the house before the sun was up and went to bed by eight. That's why he started to work from home randomly. It was to keep an eye on things when either Warrick or I had coinciding days off."

Everything he said had me rather speechless. I didn't even know how to begin to piece together what that even looked like. "I don't understand."

"Yeah, it took me a few weekends to figure it out myself. Then when Bailey-Rose entered the picture, I knew I'd been right," Gareth commented. "The simple fact is that our pack didn't function the way it should have because you weren't there. God, that sounds so fucking cheesy when you say it out loud."

I couldn't argue with that, but it made me curious to hear what led him to that conclusion.

"It started with noticing Yun would set aside work and make sure he could be part of things while you were in town. At first, I thought it was merely out of respect for the effort you were making for the pack. Then I realized you and Yun connect on a level that none of us do. Warrick wasn't being a pest and always in my business or personal space because you knew how to make him feel purposeful around the house. Vili didn't need to be on guard, so his lighthearted side shone through *way* more to the point of it being infectious." Gareth stopped and rubbed the back of his neck as if embarrassed. "I sound like a damn chick talking about all this. What I'm saying is that the Scent Matchers put us all together for a reason, and it doesn't work without all of us. Bailey-Rose just proved all of that with her mere presence. Nothing has been as smooth sailing for our pack as it has the past week."

What he was saying made a fuckton of sense and also shed light on why he was so worried he'd messed up with Yun. If not having me around caused issues, then it's safe to say that any of us not being part of the pack would create the same problem.

"I don't think Yun is leaving," I shared, causing Gareth to let out a sigh of relief. "There is no way he would leave Rosie before tonight, and I doubt after being intimate with her, there'd be a reason strong enough in the world to make him leave her side. However, I do think there might be some tension between him and the pack. Yun was right to challenge us the way he did. If he believed he could control himself around Rosie, we should have backed him up."

"What about all those stories we hear on the news? Alphas crazed with rut raping or hurting Omegas who have volunteered to help them through it?" Gareth challenged.

I thought about that for a moment. "I would have to double-check, but I would bet none of those Alphas were in a stable pack or had a scent matched Omega. It's like what Rosie was trying to tell us. Yun-Sun's first and only concern, no matter what state of mind he's in, is to keep his Omega safe. It's a biological response that's ingrained in us since the first Alpha was born. We are protectors and caregivers, and Yun is one of the most noble men I've ever met. Sadly, we failed him... we failed both of them tonight," I admitted, slamming my fist on the arm of the sofa. "If we hadn't stopped Yun, he would have been able to help her faster instead of leaving her there naked and whimpering on the fucking stairs."

"God, the way she was perfuming, it's a wonder any of us kept our heads, but I agree. We did fuck up royally tonight," Gareth said, dropping his head into his hands. "So how do we fix it?"

Rubbing my brow, I gave him the best answer I could think of. "*We* don't. This problem started because we didn't trust him, so I think the smart move here is to apologize and see what he has to say on the matter."

Gareth nodded and gave an agreeing grunt, then pushed to his feet. "Well, I guess there's nothing to do until one of them emerges. Now I just need to find some earplugs so I'm not jerking off every time I hear her screaming as she comes."

That got me to smirk as I considered how lucky I was to be on the other side of the house. "You could sleep downstairs... might have a better chance of getting some rest. That pillow nest of hers looked pretty comfortable."

"Right," Gareth scoffed. "Then I'll be humping the pillows because they're all covered in her scent. Damn, I'm so jealous of Yun right now, getting to make all those sounds come out of her. Fuck, I might come just thinking about it."

With that, it was my cue to leave. "Whoa, man, we're close, and I'm sure we will get even closer as time goes on, but right now, you busting in front of me after the heart-to-heart we just had is a bit too close."

Gareth laughed as he rubbed his neck, clearly embarrassed. "Sorry, my mind is all over the place right now and probably said more than I should have. I'm gonna go now. See you in the morning."

I watched my pack brother trudge down the hall back to his room. "Huh, looks like I was right... talking about things did help. Guess those months of watching Dr. Phil while stuck in the middle of nowhere did help."

Just as I turned to head to my room, I was caught off guard as an unmistakable scream echoed down the stairs. "*Yun!*"

Looks like Gareth wasn't the only one who was going to be suffering from blue balls tonight.

BAILEY-ROSE

The feel of someone's fingers tracing over my skin was the first thing I noticed as I awoke. That was quickly followed by a satisfying ache between my legs. A smile tugged at my lips, remembering being woken up at least twice before this to Yun sliding his cock inside me. The first time, I let him run the show since my body was so tired I could barely keep my eyes open. Yun rolled me on my back, hitched my legs over his hips, and fucked me back to sleep. I don't remember much of that round other than the sweet words he whispered in my ear.

"Rest, my love," Yun urged. "I'm sorry. I tried to hold back, to wait longer, but I had to feel you again."

I don't know how long he fucked me, but there were only flashes of pleasure as he made me come more than once before knotting me again. The second time, I woke to the sensation of his cock hardening inside me as if he never removed it from the last fucking. While my heat—or whatever you want to call it—was subdued, the natural libido of an Omega was alive and well.

Reaching to cup Yun's face, I pleaded my case. "Let me make you feel good this time."

"Sweetheart, you make me feel good just by holding you," Yun countered. "Even feeling the softness of your skin along mine is enough pleasure to satisfy my needs. There is no reason for you to worry about me in that regard."

"What if it will give me joy to reciprocate the attention

you've been giving me?" I reasoned as I pushed him to lie on his back. "Please."

Yun groaned, throwing an arm over his eyes. "How can I say no when you look at me like that?"

A grin of satisfaction bloomed on my face as I crawled between his legs. Instantly, he was shoving up on his elbows, ready to tell me this would be too much for me, but I cut off any words as I swallowed him. I'd only ever given a blow job about twice in my life, so I wasn't all that skilled. However, my goal was to make this all about him, showing him how much I cared about his happiness as much as mine.

Yun flopped back on the bed, and the most delicious noises came out of his mouth as my mouth and hands worked him over. I was unable to take every inch before I started to gag, so I used my hands to make up the difference. Omegas were made to be fucked, and it didn't take much for our vaginas or assholes to be ready for use. Our throats weren't quite the same way. From what I've heard from other Omegas, it took time to develop your blow-job skills. On the other hand, Yun seemed to be thrilled with what I was doing, so I continued.

"Fuck, sweetheart, your mouth feels amazing, too amazing. If you don't stop now, I'm going to come in your mouth, and I'd much rather fill up that pussy of yours even more," Yun managed to get out as his legs began to shake.

Giving his cock one last good suck, I let it pop out of my mouth, eliciting a growl of pleasure from my Alpha.

"Come here and sit on my cock so I can hold you as we come," Yun directed, crooking a finger at me.

Desire flooded my body at his words, causing my pussy to gush at the mere thought of his cock entering once more. Slowly, I crawled up his toned body, dropping kisses on his skin as I went. Even knowing I was playing with fire, I let my wet pussy drag along the length of his cock, which backfired on me. With a yelp of surprise, Yun grabbed my hips and slid me under him so he could once more fuck me into the mattress.

"Such a naughty Omega, teasing her Alpha while in rut," Yun chided, nipping at my ear as he fucked me hard and fast, the pressure of his body holding me still and safe under him.

By the time he knotted me for the third time, filling me with his essence, I was drenched in sweat and felt like a wrung-out rag. My heart thundered in my chest hard enough, I looked at my monitor to make sure I wasn't pushing the limits. It was elevated, to be sure, but it was also quickly coming down as Yun purred, curling around me and cradling my body against his.

I watched as his fingers curled around my wrist, lifting my arm so he could see the monitor. "That was a little too close for comfort, sweetheart."

"The important thing is it's going down on its own," I shared. "Where things get dangerous is when it doesn't."

A kiss was pressed to my shoulder. "Still, I let my control slip that time."

"If we're going to be placing the blame on anyone, it should be me. I provoked you," I countered. "We won't have to worry about this much longer. Once the medication Dr. Arbour prescribed is ready, everything will be fine."

Yun grunted, clearly not pleased with that answer. If he had anything more to say on the matter, I don't remember, having drifted back to sleep. This was the most physical activity I'd experienced in a long time, and my endurance wasn't what it should be.

Clueless as to how long I slept after that to this moment when Yun's touch roused me, I felt rested, so it had to have been awhile. The brush of his lips on my shoulder had me purring as my Omega love bucket was overflowing with all the affection I'd received through the night.

"Good morning, sweetheart," Yun whispered and kissed my cheek.

Letting out a small groan of complaint, I slowly stretched, testing how my body moved and felt. Muscles I had no idea were there protested the movement but did as they were asked. Rolling to face Yun, I nuzzled my cheek to his chest. "Morning."

"How are you feeling?" he asked, the question tinged with his worry.

I tilted my head back and cracked open my eyes. "A little sore but in a good way." This seemed to perplex the Alpha, making me smirk. "It means last night wasn't just an amazing dream I had, but it really happened."

"Oh, I can assure you it really happened," Yun said with a chuckle. "The scent of sex is so thick no one would mistake what happened here, not to mention that the sexiest Omega I ever laid eyes on is naked and covered in my cum."

As if to prove his point, he slid his hand between my legs and swiped them over my pussy. When he lifted it to where I could see, his fingers were covered in slick and milky-colored cum. Now that he'd drawn attention to it, I could feel the sticky mess all over my legs, even on my ass and lower back.

"Okay, that's kind of gross," I admitted, my nose wrinkling at the sight. "Sounds like we need to test out the giant shower in my bathroom."

"Couldn't agree more," Yun said and slid out of bed. He then grabbed my ankles and dragged me toward him, making me yelp. Before I could even protest, he scooped me up, headed for the bathroom, and deposited me on the marble bench in the shower.

Looking around the space, I counted six showerheads on two of the walls and a huge square showerhead that spanned most of the ceiling above. "How the heck are you supposed to know how to turn all this on?"

"This control panel," Yun pointed out as he tapped the black square just outside the shower door. "Here, you can set the water temperature and how many showerheads you want to use. The water won't start coming out until it's reached the right temperature so you never have to worry about getting in a cold shower."

My jaw nearly hit the floor at this information. "That has to be the most genius thing anyone's ever created."

"You can thank Warrick. He had this system in his house and refused to live in a place that didn't have it installed. Although now that I've learned how nice it is, I don't think I could go back, either," Yun admitted.

A warning beep sounded three times before the water erupted out of the main overhead shower faucet but I was safe where Yun had placed me. Now I was blessed with the sight of one of my Alphas walking toward me with water running down his body like a real-life wet dream.

Once out of the spray, he ran a hand over his face before he held it out to me. "Care to join me, or would you rather watch?"

Biting my lip, I had to actually think about that question. Then the itching of the drying fluids on my skin had me placing my hand in his. As fluid as a dancer, he pulled me to him and spun us both under the cascading water which was the perfect temperature. He tenderly combed my hair out of my face, pressing a kiss to my forehead as my hands rested on his chest.

When he pulled back, it was to grab a loofa and coat it in the scentless shower gel. It was common for bonded Omegas to use all unscented items because their Alphas craved their natural perfume. In a surprising move, Yun took my hand and began to wash me. When he reached my chest, Yun kneeled, bringing him closer to eye level with me. The loofa ran down the center of my chest, where I knew the raised skin from my scar ran down to the top of my belly button.

My first surgery was when I was just over a year old. That was the beginning of many over the years to repair various things. Medical procedures got better over time, and the surgeries were less invasive, but as a child, there was so little space to work they did what was necessary. Most of the time my scars didn't bother me. In fact, I forgot about them until I caught someone staring. Yet, for some reason, standing here with Yun's full attention focused on the outward proof of my flaws, I felt vulnerable, stripped bare under his gaze.

He raised a hand, reaching out to touch the puckered skin, but I grabbed it before it could make contact. "Don't, please," I whispered, unsure if he could hear me over the water falling around us.

Yun frowned but nodded and continued to wash the rest of my body. The sweet moment between us had been shattered by my insecurities, and I didn't know how to fix it. When he finished, I stepped away to grab the shampoo and wash my hair. I couldn't gather the courage to look at Yun, knowing he must be upset with me for rejecting his touch. The heat of his body came up behind me, and his comforting blueberry scent permeated through the water, telling me how close he was. When the shampoo was rinsed out of my hair, I grabbed the conditioner, but Yun plucked it out of my hand.

I started to turn around, but he gripped my shoulder, halting my movement. Submitting to his command, I stood just as I was until he started to massage the conditioner into my hair. My legs almost collapsed under me as he moved with confidence, using his hands and a wide-tooth comb to work through my loose waves, ensuring they were free of tangles. Hidden by the water, tears rolled down my cheeks as I was once more shown what it meant to truly show love to someone. I could tell my request not to touch my scar bothered him, but he was putting that aside to care for me.

The gentle tug on my hair had me tilting my head enough to let the water wash over it, rinsing the conditioner out. Once Yun decided my hair was clean, he walked away, and the shower turned off, leaving me to stand there. I waited, praying he'd say something, let me know what was going through his mind, but there was only silence. Gathering my hair over one shoulder, I started to wring it out, hating the feel of water dripping off my hair onto my skin. Eyes focused on the tiled floor, I turned and took a few steps forward, only to be blocked by a large fluffy mint green towel being held out.

"Come here, sweetheart," Yun instructed. His tone held some emotion in it, but I couldn't quite place what it might be. My head thought it sounded angry, even slightly irritated, but my heart refused to believe that based on his actions.

Thankfully, the towel was as soft as it looked because I wasn't sure I could handle something rough right now. Yun wrapped it snuggly around me then reached out to take another towel someone handed him. My head snapped up, meeting Ulysses' gaze. He stood there in low-slung sleep pants, looking tired and slightly distressed about something. I looked between him and Yun, confused why he suddenly appeared in the bathroom. Neither of them said a word as Yun, who had a towel wrapped around his hips, worked at drying off my hair. The confident movements as he gently squeezed out the water led me to believe this wasn't the first time he'd done something like this.

"Will your hair be all right if we don't dry it right away?" Yun asked.

Far too anxious to care about something stupid like that, I nodded, unable to speak as my mind raced, leaping from one worst-case scenario to another. Yun took my hand, threading our fingers together, and gave it a soft squeeze as he led me out of the shower. Lysse hurried forward to drop slippers with a big pink puffy heart on them at the entrance to the shower for me. I stepped into them, allowing Yun to draw me out of the bathroom.

There in my bedroom waiting were the rest of my Alphas. Each of them looked like they'd had a rough night, still dressed in loungewear. Finally, I found my voice as my fear and anxiety peaked.

"What's going on?" I questioned.

Yun drew me to stand in front of him, my back to the guys facing the large full-length mirror they'd gotten me. The others gathered behind so they could see my reflection in the mirror, and I could see them here with me.

"Bailey-Rose, do you still trust me?" Yun asked in a soft voice only I could hear.

Licking my lips nervously, I nodded.

"I need you to say it out loud, sweetheart," Yun urged.

Closing my eyes, I took a deep breath, trying in vain to calm my anxiety. Even though I was worried and this situation made me uncomfortable, I knew in my soul Yun would never do something to intentionally hurt me. "Yes, I trust you."

Quick as a flash, Yun tugged on the towel wrapped around me, causing it to fall in a heap at my feet. I gasped and instinctively wrapped my arms over my chest, trying to cover my nakedness. A whine of distress slipped out to which Yun responded by wrapping me up in his arms and resting his head on top of mine.

"Shh, *omae*, you're safe," Yun soothed. "We are here in our pack home, standing in your room, surrounded by your Alphas who will stop at nothing to protect you. There is nothing to fear, Bailey-Rose. You are encompassed by nothing but love and support."

Taking a shaky breath, I looked into the mirror and focused on the faces of the men who gazed back at me tenderly. He was right. I had nothing to fear from these Alphas—they were mine, and I was theirs. I had no doubt that being naked around all of them would soon be a common occurrence, or at least I hoped it would be. Feeling more confident, I dropped my arms and stood there bearing it all, trusting Yun had a point to all this.

"Tell me what you see," Yun instructed.

Brows scrunching together, I tilted my head back to stare at him. "I don't get it."

Yun gave me a sweet smile, dropping a kiss on my head before using his hands to return my focus to the mirror. "It's simple. I want you to look straight ahead and tell me what you see in the mirror."

Still not truly understanding the point of this, I let out a sigh and looked at what was before me. "I see someone who got out of the shower and needs to brush her hair, and it might also be a good idea for her to shave the next time she's in the shower."

"You can see deeper than that," Ulysses scolded. I flicked my gaze to where he was standing just to the right of Yun, surprised at him calling me out. "Rosie, I know you and how you see the world. Pretend you're looking at someone you want to paint to bring that life into your art."

A different kind of panic bubbled up inside me. "I-I can't," I rasped out.

"Why is that?" Yun asked, his voice calm and grounding as he rested his hands on my shoulders.

Tears burned as I shook my head. "To look at someone the way I do when I paint is to strip away the mask and reveal what's under it. You're asking me to stand here and emotionally crack open my chest, letting all that I have hidden from even myself spill out in front of all of you."

Yun brushed my hair to one side so he could kiss the spot where he'd left his temporary mark. "I refuse to accept there is a flaw you have that we can't accept. No one is perfect. Every one of us has our own battle scars. Yet I believe with all my heart you're the only one in this pack who's strong enough to wear it on her chest." As he spoke that last sentence, he let the tips of his fingers glide between my breasts.

Unable to stop myself, my eyes slammed shut, refusing to watch this man accept something I've fought to embrace as part of myself. It wasn't the scar I hated—it was the questions. Once people found out about my condition, then everything about the interaction changed. Within a matter of seconds, Bailey-Rose was gone only to be replaced by the girl with the bad heart. Few people took the time to get to know me past that fact. I went through a phase where I tried to hide it all the time, but that became more work than it was worth. No matter what I did, eventually, people found out the truth.

I felt Yun step in front of me, the feel of his hands running down my arms to land resting on my hips. At the feel of his lips on the base of the scar, my eyes popped open, my hands grabbing his shoulders to push him away. "You don't need to do that. Honestly, it's not a big deal."

His gaze met mine, and I could easily see he didn't believe a word I'd said. "Try again, sweetheart," he said, pressing another kiss between my breasts. "This time, tell me something I'll believe. If you can do that for me, you'll be rewarded."

A hand gripped my neck, urging my head to look up. I already knew it was Gareth, his unmistakable sweet tea scent made me wish I had a glass to help soothe my parched throat. Gareth's gray-blue eyes were full of compassion and affection as he held my gaze. "Baby girl, we are doing this for a reason, even if it seems like we're trying to torture you. It's become clear to us that you don't truly see the woman we do, and that is simply not okay with us. Now be a good girl and listen to your Alphas."

BAILEY-ROSE

My heart ached upon hearing Gareth's words. He was right—this did feel like torture. As if these men were going out of their way to make me experience pain I didn't want to face. Rationally, I knew that wasn't true, but when your mind and heart were at war, it was seldom your heart that won.

"Wh…" I paused, clearing my throat as fear constricted it. "What if *I* discover something about myself in all this I can't accept?"

"Not possible," Warrick said as he took my hand.

Gareth let his hand slide to my shoulder so we were still touching, but I could look at my sweet, sugary Alpha.

Warrick leaned in and kissed the tip of my nose. "Even if it were possible, then the five of us would help you find a way to appreciate all aspects of yourself. Bailey-Rose, when you were created to be part of this world, I have to believe every piece that makes up who you are was fated to be just as it is. Now, turn those stunning artist eyes to the mirror and tell me what you see about the woman I'm fairly certain I'm in love with."

A tear slipped out as Warrick's words knit together a piece of my shattered heart next to the one with Yun's name on it. Warrick brushed it away, stroking my cheek comfortingly before he gestured for me to look in the mirror. With a soft sniff, I gathered the courage to face off with myself and find the woman these men could see.

I stared into the dual-colored eyes that reflected back at me, noticing there was a brightness to them. In a way, they seemed more alive, vibrant, and while a little fearful, there was strength. Pulling my focus back slightly, I looked at my face. There was a pinkness to my cheeks, giving me a healthier glow, or it could have been from the heat of the shower.

When I took in the whole picture, I found Yun kneeling before me, the side of his face pressed to my stomach with his arms wrapped around me. Warrick was to my left, his pinky hooked to mine in a show of solidarity. Gareth stood tall, guarding my back, his hand still on my shoulder with his thumb absently stroking my skin. The second my attention shifted to Ulysses, he laced his fingers with mine, reassuringly squeezing my hand. I couldn't spot Vili, but he appeared as he came around Ulysses and sat in front of the man who'd blocked his view. Vili curled his hand around my calf and kissed my hip, letting me know he was here with me just as the others were.

How could I be afraid of anything when I had these men right here to protect me?

"I see a woman who has five men who are absolutely crazy about her," I shared. "Men who have shown her that she's never seen what real selfless love looks like."

"Good girl," Gareth praised, then sucked my earlobe into his mouth, causing me to inhale sharply. "This time, tell us what you're good at."

Thankful for the direction, as slight as it was, it seemed to make this whole thing less overwhelming. "I'm an artist," I stated.

Gareth clicked his tongue in disapproval as he pinched my nipple, making me yelp. "More, baby girl. I want to hear you boasting about yourself. Say all the things people would consider rude, self-gratifying, or even cocky."

Yun shifted, releasing his hold on me to move more to the side like Vili was. This meant I was once more on full display as I gazed into the mirror.

"I'm an artist, a damn good one," I announced. "My skill is to elicit emotions from anyone who looks at my paintings. I can capture the *moment,* if you will, encapsulating emotion and movement, and draw them in with the way I splash color across the canvas."

Fingers glided up my leg to tease the outside of my pussy. "Beautifully said, kitten," Vili applauded as he swirled a single finger around my clit. "Keep going... say more. Tell us everything."

My legs shook slightly as a soft moan slipped from my lips. Gareth grasped my neck once more, holding me against his body, offering his support. Warrick took my hand to help balance me just as Lysse did.

How the hell am I supposed to be able to think straight, let alone talk with Vili teasing me?

"I can't cook well, but I'm a fabulous baker. My mother taught me, but soon I had to look elsewhere to learn more since I surpassed her skills. Spoiling my family is one of my favorite things to do. They do so much for me that I take every chance I can to shower them with gifts that make me think of them," I said in a hurried rush as Vili's finger traveled from my clit to sink inside me.

The moment I stopped, so did his finger. It was obvious now the only way I was going to get the reward at the end of this was to do as they asked.

"Those are amazing qualities that you should be proud of, Bailey-Rose," Warrick pointed out, lifting my hand to kiss the back of it. "Tell me, Care Bear, are you proud of yourself?"

"I'm proud of many things," I started. "I've lived longer than any doctor predicted I would. Graduated college top in my class with people begging to buy the work displayed in my end-of-the-year project. I—"

My words were cut off as a second finger joined the first, along with Vili's thumb brushing over my clit. When I tried to continue, no words came out, just breathy moans and whimpers as Vili teased me.

"What were you saying?" Ulysses asked as he massaged my breast, letting the rough skin of his hand bring my nipple to a peak.

"I have five sexy-as-hell Alphas who are determined to shatter me in the best way possible," I managed, fighting to keep talking so all this was worth it in the end.

The sensation of someone probing my asshole was nearly my undoing. Instantly, my legs no longer wished to offer any kind of support, and if it weren't for the guys, I would have crashed to the floor. Gareth caught me around the waist while Vili placed himself directly under me, his shoulder preventing me from total collapse.

"You're doing amazing, Rosie. What I need you to do is open your eyes, look right at yourself, and repeat what I say. It's important that you don't just say the words but mean them," Ulysses instructed. "Let me know when you're ready."

Nodding, I took a second to compose myself before meeting my own gaze once more. "Ready."

"I am strong and resilient."

Licking my lips, I swallowed, knowing I wasn't ready for this, but there was no backing down now, so I repeated the phrase. Ulysses kept giving me one affirmation after another, each of them becoming harder to say to myself.

"I am at peace with my appearance."

"I-I…" Pausing, unable to speak, I was overwhelmed by the power of these phrases. That and the combination of these men showering me with love, support, and encouragement as they stirred my body with their touches was going to be my ruin.

One wouldn't think having a man with his fingers in your pussy, sucking on your clit, while another was knuckle deep in your ass, introducing you to a whole new level of pleasure would be exactly what I needed right now, but it was. Gareth's possessive hold on my throat as he purred, stroking my pulse point, grounded me as did Ulysses with the occasional jolts of welcome pain to clear away the panic these words induced. Warrick had latched himself onto my other breast, letting his hot tongue swirl around my nipple then sharply suck on the tender flesh, making my whole body shudder.

"God, look at you all flushed, need in your eyes, and those sexy sounds coming out of you," Ulysses said as he gripped my chin, turning me to look at him. "You have one more affirmation to say, and then you can have your reward. Think you can manage it?"

Eagerly, I nodded my head only to cry out as Yun pulled his fingers out, leaving my ass empty and pulsing with the energy of a climax it was being denied. He stood, pressing a quick kiss to my lips. "You need to focus now, sweetheart. Finish this task, and I promise we will finish what we started."

Before I could beg for him to finish me *now,* he left my field of vision, making me whimper. Then Vili also slid his fingers from my pussy, and I watched him stand as he licked them clean. To my dismay, everyone but Gareth removed their hands from me, cutting off their touch and forcing me to focus solely on the next phrase given to me.

"Repeat after me, Rosie," Ulysses ordered.

Taking a shaky breath, I looked in the mirror and said a truth I'm not sure I ever truly believed. Tears rolled down my cheeks as my hands fisted in determination to make it through this affirmation. "My mind, body, and soul deserve love and respect. Furthermore, I allow myself to feel deeply and openly, choosing happiness."

A sob burst from me as I covered my face with my hands, unable to keep facing this raw version of myself. I'd done as they asked, cut through the bullshit to face the truth of what hid underneath. Within seconds, I was surrounded by my Alphas, their scents and warm bodies shielding me from any danger. They started to purr all at once, and I could *feel* how proud they were of me. Kisses were showered over my skin, and hushed words of love and praise were whispered in my ear. Then I was scooped up only to be laid out on a soft blanket.

Everyone curled around like a pile of puppies. I also realized they'd stripped out of their clothes so our skin pressed together in the most fulfilling way. Vili lay facing me, his fingers tracing the features of my face while Gareth was at my back, face buried in my neck. Warrick laid above my head, a smirk on his face as he combed his fingers through my hair.

"You really are so goddamn fucking adorable, you know that?" Warrick murmured.

A smile tugged at my lips. "I think someone has mentioned that a time or two."

He tweaked my nose. "Troublemaker."

I was about to give my rebuttal, but Vili had other plans

as he hooked my leg over his hip and let his cock brush over my pussy. My attention instantly focused on Vili's caramel-colored eyes which weren't obscured by his glasses.

"Would you like your reward, kitten?" Vili asked in a tone far too innocent for the situation. "Or no..." He ventured when I remained silent, pulling away.

In a move I rather impressed myself with, I hooked my heel behind Vili's knee, grabbed his shoulder, and impaled myself on his cock. "Yes, I would very much like my reward."

Vili beamed at me for a second then he caught me up in a searing kiss rolling on his back. Much like the kiss we shared in the pillow cart, it was demanding. I wanted this man just as much as he wanted me. Hell, who was I kidding? My Omega ass was ready to ride whichever Alpha of mine even hinted at the idea. Thanks to his attentive moments before, I was lubed and ready to rock this man's world.

Just when I didn't think things could get any more perfect, hands brushed down my back to massage my ass. The sensation of cool liquid being poured right on the crack had my head popping up to look over my shoulder. Gareth was kneeling there, coating his fingers in something he poured out of a nondescript bottle.

"Figured we could see how things go. You seemed to enjoy your ass being played with," Gareth explained. "If it's too much, we can stop."

"What about my heart?" I questioned.

"Same rule applies... if it's too much, we'll stop. We keep asking you to trust us with things, but we haven't done the best job of returning that favor. You know your body best, so we'll take it slow, but we won't know until we try, right?" Gareth countered.

Excitement prickled along my skin as I grinned at Gareth. "Sounds like the perfect plan to me."

"It seemed to work best if I could pin her down. The less moving she did physically seemed to help balance out the effect of the adrenaline surges," Yun offered.

Hearing Yun talk about what happened between us last night was a little strange, but I understood his reasoning. Most packs didn't have boundaries when it came to sex, nakedness, and being open about what occurred between partners. All it took was one heat, and every member of the pack was witness to a massive gangbang for three to five days. My awkwardness came from living a life far more sheltered than the average Omega.

"Kitten, what is best for you?" Vili asked, tucking my hair behind my ear. "Stay on top, be bottom, or have Gareth keep you still?"

Was that even a real question? What Omega wouldn't want to be sandwiched between her Alphas' naked bodies?

"Yun's right. I can relax and let go, keeping myself calmer if I don't have control," I answered.

Gareth came to the side and draped his body over the middle of my back, trapping me between them but allowing him access to my ass. His weight set off some instinctual thing in my brain that had me going boneless. Vili nipped at my lower lip, drawing me back into kissing him while rolling his hips in a gentle rhythm. The more intense our kiss got, the same happened for the fucking. When we fell into a steady pace, Gareth began testing the waters. Before Yun so rudely abandoned his work, he'd had two fingers working that hole as deep as they could get. This allowed Gareth to work back up to that in no time.

The sensation of Vili in my pussy as Gareth fingerfucked my ass was euphoric. There were so many sensations my mind didn't know where to focus, leaving me in this limbo-like state. I could feel everything at once, but I wanted more.

"Gareth," I whimpered. "I need more."

"You think you're ready for another finger?" he challenged.

I shook my head wildly and peered over my shoulder at him. "I want you to sandwich me between the two of you as you fuck my ass. Please, Gareth, I need to feel you... fingers just aren't enough."

"Warrick, how's her heart rate?" Gareth asked.

"It's high, but that's to be expected. However, it's staying pretty consistent at the moment," Warrick informed the guys.

"Baby girl," Gareth said, kissing between my shoulder blades. "I'm going to believe you when you say you can handle this, but I need you to know if something happens, I'm not going to be okay."

My heart melted hearing him being so honest. Gareth was keeping his end of the deal and being upfront with his feelings. I didn't want to push him, but goddamn, did I need his fucking cock in my ass.

"Why don't we just try having you both inside me, no movement, to test the waters?" I suggested. "Baby steps, if you will."

Gareth cursed under his breath as the blunt tip of his cock pressed against my entrance. "You clearly have no idea how bad I want to fuck you if you think I can pull that off."

"It's not that I don't understand what I'm asking," I countered. "This is me trusting you to take care of me."

His head dropped to my shoulder as Gareth chuckled. "Fuck, if this isn't irony at its best."

Slowly, Gareth's cock sank deeper into my ass. Forcing a

long, drawn-out moan from me as I arched into the feel. Having them both nestled inside me was a feeling that was nearly impossible to explain. How do you describe the feeling of being so full your mind rejected reality because it wasn't quite sure how I should be feeling? My breath came in quick, shallow movements as I tried to stay calm, but the overwhelming explosion of sensation made it challenging.

"Breathe, kitten," Vili encouraged, guiding my head to rest on his chest. "Listen to my heart. Follow my breathing."

"Tell me how high it got," Gareth ordered.

A hand slowly grasped my wrist, stroking the inside of my forearm. "It's eighty-one."

Gareth nuzzled my neck, purring as he stroked his hands down my arms. "Baby girl, this is too much. I know you wanted this to work, but there's no way I could live with myself to continue when there's too high of a risk. This isn't to say once we get the medication from the doc, we can't try again, but not right now."

Hiding my face in Vili's chest, I knew he was right. I'd been lost in my need and high off the fact my Alphas were desperate to be intimate with me. My instinct was to give them what we both wanted, even if it might be pushing the limit. Gareth pulled out as I writhed at the pleasure coursing through my body at the simple movement. Once he was free, Vili sat up, cradled me in his lap, and began to rock into me.

Arms wrapped tightly around his neck, I clung to him as Vili's hands grabbed my ass using them to set the pace. He'd rock forward while simultaneously pushing me further on his cock so each stroke hit deeper without being rough. Even though Vili was the one I was fucking, the rest of my men let me know they were there, peppering my body with kisses and gentle touches. A hand fisted my hair and tilted my head back so Ulysses could kiss me. I might not be able to fuck more than one Alpha right now, but that wasn't going to stop them from showing me it changed nothing between us.

Vili's mouth latched onto my breast, licking, sucking, and scraping his teeth over my nipple. The rocking became more urgent as I felt Vili's teeth digging into the flesh of my breast, tongue flicking my nipple. My fingers were buried in his hair, ensuring he wouldn't be able to move from that spot. I was so close to coming, teetering on the edge, pleading for that one thing to cast me in the river and sweep me away.

Two fingers entered my ass and matched the tempo of Vili's movements. That was all it took for me to fall head-long into the euphoria only these men seemed to bring me. I cried out, screaming into Lysse's mouth, and he cupped my face refusing to let me go, drinking down every sound I made. Even as Vili's knot expanded, making it harder for him to move, he kept up the rocking motion. Just as I thought I couldn't handle more, a second orgasm hit as the knot stretching my walls pressed on the perfect spot to keep me coming forever. The fingers in my ass started to curl down, working in tandem with Vili's knot, causing a third climax to slam into me and my body to shake uncon-trollably.

Ulysses released my mouth just in time for me to gasp for air and attempt to give them a warning. "I-I I'm going to pas—"

Shit, I was too late. God, I hope they don't call an ambulance for this.

Vili

Terror unlike anything I've felt in my life speared through me as Bailey-Rose collapsed in my arms. My fear was so strong I swear it stopped the orgasm I was having in its tracks.

"Bailey-Rose," I barked as I tilted her back so I could see her face.

Her skin had gone ghostly white, her breath shallow, and the monitor on her wrist buzzed its warning.

"What does it fucking say," Gareth snapped as Ulysses grabbed her wrist.

Confusion was written all over the man's face as he looked from my kitten's wrist back to her lifeless expression. "It's eighty... wait, it just dropped to seventy-nine."

"So does that mean it's her heart?" Warrick questioned.

Anger and fear clawed at me as I tried to figure out how best to deal with the fact I was fucking knotted to her. Using two fingers, I checked her pulse using the clock on the wall above the bathroom to time it right. Her monitor wasn't lying. In fact, it had dropped to seventy-eight, and her breathing was evening out on its own.

Shifting so I was kneeling, I laid her down on the blanket, but in the surprising turn, my knot loosened. It wasn't by much, but it was enough to carefully work it out of her, even if it was excruciatingly painful for me. In my mind, nothing mattered right now but making sure my kitten was safe, and whatever pain I had to endure was inconsequential. Once free, I collapsed to the side, curling up in a ball, protecting my dick from touching anything else.

"Holy shit, Vili, are you okay?" Gareth asked, reaching out to touch my shoulder.

I blocked his hand, shaking my head. "Don't worry about me, tend to kitten."

Tentatively, I reached between my legs to see if holding the knot would make it feel better. Biting my lip as I roared at the pain, which had me seeing stars, told me that was a stupid idea. Flopping on my back, my skin covered in a cold sweat, and I let the damn thing rest on my stomach. It pulsed like it had its own heartbeat.

Fucking son of a bitch that fucking hurt.

Mental note—never *pull out a knot unless absolutely necessary.*

Holy hell, why wasn't that taught in school or mentioned by I don't fucking know—anyone?

A cool cloth was placed over my head, to which I groaned at how good it felt. Cracking open my eyes, I found the most beautiful sight I could have ever hoped for. "My kitten," I crooned, brushing my fingers along her cheek, needing to know she was really there. "You scared us."

"I'm so sorry, Vili," Bailey-Rose said, turning to kiss the palm of my hand. "It's all my fault you're like this. If only I'd noticed before it got to the point I passed out so you didn't worry and end up like this."

My brows knit together. "What didn't you notice?"

Dropping her gaze and tipping her chin down so her hair fell, it blocked me from seeing her face. My precious girl was hiding from me as she shouldered all the guilt that didn't belong to her. This was something I wouldn't allow for a second longer. Slowly, I sat up, hissing at the pain as my dick shifted to lay on my thigh, the damn knot still inflated.

My movements caught Bailey-Rose's attention, causing her head to snap up, meeting my gaze. Once I was sure I'd remain sitting upright, I cupped the face of the greatest treasure of my life. Seeing her face as I made her come over and over again was like living art. Everything about her was breathtaking, and I couldn't, no, wouldn't let the moment we shared be tainted by how it ended.

"I will ask again, kitten. This time, you answer," I instructed, my voice firm but kind. "What didn't you notice?"

The guilt that shimmered in her exotic-colored gaze had me wanting to punch something while also fighting the urge to cradle her in my arms. Someone had put the belief that whatever she was about to say was her fault, and in my gut, I knew that wasn't the case. If anyone was at fault, it was me. My selfishness is what drove me to continue fucking her after Gareth bowed out when, in reality, everything should have ended there.

"You see..." she started then paused.

"Kitten, I'm not mad. I'm worried," I assured her.

Bailey-Rose nodded or tried to, forgetting I was still holding her face. "It's been a little while since I've eaten, then adding in the fact I went into heat. Well... kind of went into heat," she rambled. "Sorry, that's not the point. The point is I pushed my body too far and didn't sleep or eat enough. It causes strain on my heart in a different way, creating an intermittent arrhythmia. Normally, this is only something I worry about when I've been sick with a fever, dehydrated, and don't have much of an appetite. Going into heat is pretty much like having a fever on steroids."

Hearing this caused me to believe I deserved the pain I

was in right now. *How the fuck did we forget to ensure our Omega had eaten?* The moment we heard the shower running in her room, one of us should have prepared breakfast to bring up. Our fear over upsetting Yun-Sun had created an even bigger problem.

"Do you need anything?" Was the first thing out of my mouth. "Medicine, doctor, sleep, food? Tell me, kitten, how do I fix it?"

Her gaze dropped to my lap, where my cock rested, and then back up. "I should be asking you that. They said you've been laying here for a half hour in horrible pain while I was passed out."

"Forget me. You are more important," I said, releasing her face to wave off the concern. "This will end."

My kitten gave me a skeptical look, which I ignored until she reached out to touch the aching reminder of my selfishness. Quick as a snake, I grabbed her arm. "I'm sorry, kitten, it is sensitive."

"Let me help you," she pleaded. "I can fix this. I know I can."

A pulse shot through my cock, making me groan with pain as a spurt of cum leaked out of the tip. "You probably can fix, but I deserve the pain for failing you."

"What?" Bailey-Rose demanded as her face scrunched up. "Why on earth would you need to be in pain? How did you fail me?"

"Alphas put Omegas first, *always*. I not put you first this morning, which made you pass out," I explained.

"That's on me too," she challenged. "I know how my body reacts under stress, and I pushed the limits. You all trusted that I'd tell you if I couldn't handle something, and I didn't. That's on me, not you, Vili."

My sweet, kind, forgiving kitten didn't understand, and

that's fine—she shouldn't. The entire reason for Alphas to exist is to protect Omegas from the dangers of this world. I'd seen firsthand what it looked like when that didn't happen. My family pack once had two Omegas, my mother and another woman, Eden, who they found themselves scent matched to after their pack had been established for a few years.

Eden was a soft-spoken, timid woman who came from a simple life and was thrown into the deep end of old money. People judged her for every mistake, not even taking the time to know the woman for who she was. As a child, I believed she was the mother that gave birth to me based on the love and devotion she showered on me. When I was seven, Eden got sick, and six months later passed away. My world changed forever, becoming so cold without Eden's warmth and love. This was the point I realized Eden wasn't my birth mother, and her pack never cherished her for the treasure she was.

Once I was an adult, I looked into the situation without my family knowing I learned the truth. My parents cared more about status and wealth so much so they hardened their hearts to a scent-bonded Omega. They didn't want to bring her into the pack, but the Scent Matchers wouldn't hear of it—scent matches weren't up for negotiation. If an Omega belonged to a pack, no matter when they were discovered, then they were obligated to provide for their match, which is what my parents did—they provided for Eden, but nothing more than was necessary. Eden became sick due to neglect and died a terrible death that could have been prevented.

Staring into my own scent matched Omega's eyes, I can't fathom how my fathers could have turned their back on Eden. In an instant, Bailey-Rose became my reason for living, but this slip had panic creeping in that I was more like my fathers than I'd like to admit. If I let this gentle and forgiving woman take away the pain I deserved, then what made me any better than the men who turned their back on Eden?

"My perfect kitten, you not win this argument," I warned her, brushing my fingers down her neck along her collarbone to her shoulder. "But I thank you for trying."

The determined look that crossed my kitten's face should have warned me she wasn't going to listen to a word I said. "Gareth, Lysse, can I have your assistance?" Both of my packmates walked over with curious expressions. "Would you be so kind as to make sure Vili doesn't move while I deal with his issue?"

To my shock, the two didn't even hesitate before grabbing my arms and pinning me to the floor. I quickly gave up trying to fight back with how painful it was to thrash around. "Stop this," I demanded.

"V, you're clearly in a shit-ton of pain. Why won't you let her help you?" Gareth challenged.

Out of all my pack brothers, Gareth should understand. "We failed... our Omega was in danger. This is my punishment."

"No, man, it isn't," Gareth murmured as his eyes softened. "It's not just you that you're punishing right now because it's hurting her too. Trust me, this isn't the path you want to go down. I've been there, and it's not something I'd wish on anyone. Let Bailey-Rose fix this, and you can make it up to her in another way."

The fear of turning out like my parents clawed at me, but Ulysses rested a hand on my shoulder, drawing my attention. "Vili, we all fucked up, not just you. Taking the full blame for this isn't right nor is it what Rosie wants.

We're human, man. This isn't going to be the last time we screw up, so forcing yourself to endure this much pain is pointless."

He was right. We, as a pack, fucked up—this wasn't all on me. It also proved to me that my pack was vastly different from that of my parents. None of these men would let me turn into the cold, callous examples of an Alpha I'd grown up seeing. "Okay, I will let my kitten fix this," I agreed. "Someone should hold legs... it is very painful. I don't want our kitten hurt."

Hands wrapped around my ankles. "We'll keep you both safe," Yun-Sun assured me.

Bailey-Rose straddled my legs, and the feel of her weight was comforting. Then the brush of her hair let me know what she intended to do, so I braced myself for the pain that was to come. Only none came. Instead, a cooling sensation traveled from the base of my cock all the way to the tip. Featherlight kisses like that of snowflakes falling on my skin told me that Bailey-Rose had been right—she could fix this.

The moment she took my cock in her mouth, the pain seemed to vanish. I flinched for a second when her hand wrapped gingerly around the base of my knot, causing me to groan from pleasure instead of pain. How my body knew the difference and responded in a much more favorable way, I have no fucking clue, but damn, was I thrilled. My kitten was on a mission to save me from pain and fix the problem she believed she caused. Her movements were efficient and simple, but it felt like heaven to me. I didn't care if she licked the damn thing like an ice cream cone for hours—it felt incredible. There was no need for fancy moves or tricks. All I wanted was to feel my Omega's desire to give me enjoyment, to know the feelings were mutual. The only thing that could make this even more wonderful was to have her pussy riding my face so we could both feel good.

"Oh God," I muttered. "Your mouth is heaven, kitten."

She hummed her enjoyment at my praise which had my hips bucking and eyes rolling into the back of my head. "Yes, more... more of that."

Taking me at my word, Bailey-Rose started to purr as she worked my cock with that delicious mouth of hers. The vibrations were my undoing, and I roared as I came, thrusting my hips up and shooting my cum down her throat. A squeak of surprise let me know I caught her off guard, but she adjusted like the perfect creature she was.

"Wrap your hands around his knot and squeeze it tight," Warrick instructed. "Don't worry, you're not going to hurt him. This will help more than anything."

She did as directed, hesitant at first, but with Warrick's encouragement, gave it all she had. Sweet relief as the pressure that had built up in my dick was released had me boneless under the attention of my precious kitten. It made me wonder if it ever would have gone away without her help.

"You did it, kitten," I shared and reached out to pet her head, the guys no longer needing to hold me down. "Come to me. I must kiss those lips."

Giving my cock one final suck, Bailey-Rose crawled up my body until I could wrap my arms around her and kiss the shit out of her. The past twenty-four hours had been a roller coaster of emotions, hormones, and speed bumps we hadn't seen coming. However, I had even more faith in this pack to become a family full of trust, love, and forgiveness.

As long as we were all together, the world would be a perfect place.

BAILEY-ROSE

After another quick shower with all the guys, we got ready for the day. First things first, they sat me down for a breakfast feast, even though it was well past noon. I couldn't argue, though, as crepes filled with strawberries and whipped cream were placed in front of me. There was also sausage and cheesy scrambled eggs to balance out the sugar. I wolfed the whole thing down and even got seconds of the crepes, revealing just how hungry I'd been.

"Damn, Care Bear, I think you ate more than we did," Warrick teased, dropping a kiss on my head as he refilled my orange juice. "Well, maybe not as much as Yun."

Yun-Sun had skipped the crepes, having gone straight for the sausage and eggs. No one was surprised about that, though, since rut caused Alphas to burn as many calories as heat did for us.

"So, are we still gonna go check out the studio?" I asked, popping the last strawberry into my mouth.

None of them answered right away, but I had a feeling they'd be reluctant to leave the house after all that had happened.

"What if we had a chill day here and went tomorrow? Maybe tonight we can go out to dinner someplace fun if you feel up for it," Lysse suggested. "Call us paranoid, but I want to be sure Yun's rut is settled, and there's no risk of you passing out or lapsing into heat again."

"I get your hesitation, but what if instead of staying at

the house, we go to a park or something?" I offered. "We could pack some snacks and lay out in the sun. This way, you guys could do something active if you wanted while I keep it low-key instead of being cooped up in the house."

Vili smiled brightly at this and clapped his hands excitedly. "This is best idea. Sun is good, same with fresh air, and maybe short walk. All things that relax."

"V-man makes a good point. Doctors encourage outings like this to help lower stress and promote wellness. Going to the studio would be a lot with all that we wanted to do, but this is a way to meet in the middle. Then if everyone is up for it, we can do dinner," Gareth said, seeming rather excited himself. "There's that awesome park with the lake and rowboats you can rent a half hour outside the city."

"All right, the people have spoken... a day at the park is the winner," Lysse announced. "Let's clean up from breakfast, gather what we need, and head out."

I couldn't help but smile at how everyone shot to their feet, grabbed dishes, and hurried to clean up. The kitchen was spotless in no time, and Yun was writing out a list of things we would need. "Warrick, you pack the cooler with drinks and snacks. Ulysses, you're the outdoorsman, so if you could grab what we'd need, that would be super helpful. Gareth might need help loading up the car if you can assist. Vili, I believe you got a yard game or two when we first moved in, didn't you?"

"Yes, I will get," Vili said, then started to leave but paused. "Anything else?"

"Not unless you know of something I missed," Yun-Sun commented with a shrug.

"Okay." Vili gave us two thumbs-up and left to accomplish his task.

"Sweetheart, gather whatever you want to bring, and

we'll get this show on the road," Yun instructed, jotting down a few things on the paper, most likely for himself. "As soon as we get packed, we'll head out. Thankfully, this time of the year, it's light out until at least nine, so we have plenty of time."

Giddy with excitement, I floated up to my room only to be met with the cloying scent of sex and noticed how the room was a bit of a disaster. I hesitated only for a moment before deciding to deal with that later. We only had five more days where the guys didn't have to work, and I planned to make the most out of it. An afternoon at the park was a far better use of time, and for the first time since I got back from college, I wanted to sketch.

The park was amazing and a place I'd never been to before. You could see the city skyline in the distance, but the hustle and bustle were gone, leaving a slice of blissful peace. There were two different sections of the park, but Ulysses was familiar with the place, so we agreed to leave our camp spot up to him.

He parked at the far end of the vast parking lot and took us down a paved walkway to the lake Gareth had mentioned. It was noticeably a manmade lake but still pretty with a pier that had rowboats, kayaks, and canoes floating, waiting for someone to rent them. People dotted the water as they made their way across the water's surface. Lysse brought us to a perfect spot with a few trees, a complete view of the lake, and an open grassy area to the right if we wanted to play a game. Most people were camped out on the other side, where the picnic tables and grills were located, leaving us to ourselves.

"Holy cow, Lysse," I said, laughing at what he'd brought for our afternoon. "You know we're only going to be here for a few hours, right?"

The man had a rattan mat rolled out with a pop-up canopy over it, offering shade. There were various styles of chairs they pulled out of bags and set up in a semi-circle. He even thought to bring a table and a fan if we needed it. What shocked me even more was the inflatable mattress he covered with a blanket and pillows from the downstairs nest thrown on it.

"Why are you even surprised, Rosie? How many years have I been going camping? It would only stand to reason I know the right way to hang in the outdoors. Just wait 'til I have this hammock strung up, then you'll never want to go anywhere without one," Ulysses teased with a wink. "Now get comfy... you're supposed to be relaxing."

Rolling my eyes, I grabbed my sketchbook and settled on the air mattress. Warrick joined me, curling around me like a cat, arms around my waist. It wasn't long before the man was softly snoring, making me smile. Flipping open my book, I scanned my surroundings, looking for the thing that would beg me to draw it. I landed on a woman paddleboarding on the lake, standing there strong and confident with a prosthetic leg attached to her knee. Joining her on the board was a golden-haired dog sitting tall as if they were the captains of the ship. The whole image spoke to me, and I had to capture it on paper.

Within moments, I'd lost myself in the sketch as I observed this woman. Her movements showed her skill as the paddle cut through the water, moving her across the lake. The serene look on her face as she navigated around the others who struggled to get their boats, betrayed this wasn't the first time she'd been on this lake. At one point, she stopped to help a young boy with his kayak, effortlessly dropping to one knee, her board hardly even shifting, as she showed him what he needed to do. All the while, her furry companion merely observed, never moving from its place.

"Care Bear, that's amazing," Warrick said, his voice filled with awe. "You got all that about her from this far away?"

I glanced down to see him awake and sitting up on his elbow to get a better look at my sketch. Instead of the woman being on a lake, I'd chosen to have her navigate through a canyon dressed in the clothes of an ancient warrior. Her hair flew in the wind, everything about her portraying the fighter she was and the inner strength that flowed off her.

"Some things you see no matter how far away they are," I answered, not really sure he'd understand, but I didn't know how else to explain it.

Warrick seemed to sit with that for a moment, staring at my sketch. "I think I get what you're trying to say. We are the product of the experiences we've lived through, and some of those moments continue to shape us long after the events happened. Am I close?"

My lips curved up in a smile as I leaned back against Warrick. "Yeah, I'd say that's a pretty great way to say it. Not every challenge in life has an end to it. There are so many who fight every day to exist. Even though it's hard, sometimes painful, and takes everything they have to simply get out of bed, quitting would make all the suffering they'd done pointless. Granted, there are those who feel there is no other choice, that life will only be filled with endless days of torment, and beg for it to end. The battle those people face is the hardest of all because there is no right answer or magic cure."

"Have you ever been in that place?" Ulysses asked, coming to sit on the edge of the mattress.

Yun-Sun, Gareth, and Vili joined, crowding us and squishing me to be the center of the circle they created. This clearly hadn't been meant for six people, but they didn't seem to care as long as they were close to me. I knew they thought Ulysses' question was going to be hard for me to answer, but I wasn't ashamed of my past.

"I never reached the place where I wanted to die," I assured them. "However, there were dark days when I didn't want to fight anymore. Anger and resentment at the restricted life that had been forced on me by this condition I never asked for was the lens I viewed life through. No matter how hard my family tried to get me to see the good all around me, I refused to let them change my mind. Everything turned into a fight. I refused to take my medications, eat the way I was supposed to, and for a week, I went without my monitor. Thankfully, I have a wonderful therapist my mother hired to work with me all through my childhood, knowing I'd need Dr. Libby's help in earnest at some point."

Pausing, I took a moment to look at each of the men surrounding me, offering their protection and support without hesitation. Their entire focus was on me, riveted to every word I spoke, proving with actions and not just words how important I was to them. How many times had Dr. Libby told me that the right people wouldn't be scared away by the baggage I brought with me? Clearly, the woman knew what she was talking about because not one of these men showed any sign this truth I was sharing changed their minds about me.

"I don't remember this," Ulysses murmured.

"That's because it happened when you left for college," I shared. "Thirteen was an ugly year in my life. Hormones kicked into high gear, my medication changed with every visit until we could find the right thing to balance teenage angst. The few friends I had were deeply involved with sports, started to flirt with boys, and discovered what their designations were. Because of the medication to stabilize my hormones, I didn't know I was an Omega until I was sixteen. Instantly, I was put on heat blockers and told I could never go into heat until they found a way to strengthen my heart."

A light seemed to go off in Ulysses' brain. "Is this why I never realized who and what you were to me?" He stopped and frowned. "Hold on, you stopped wanting to hang out with me and Crew around that time too. Did you know?"

Laughter burst out of me at his outlandish connection. "Of course, I didn't know. God, if I'd known you were my scent match, I would've never pulled away. I did that because I had the world's biggest crush on you, and I couldn't risk hearing about all the escapades with girls you had in college. Mind you, I was doing a lot better mental health-wise at that time, but I knew I was too fragile to handle much, so I decided not to risk it."

"Damn, if only I hadn't let you pull away so easily," Ulysses grumbled, combing his fingers through his hair.

Reaching out, I rested my hand on his thigh. "Lysse, we both needed time to grow up. There's no way I'd have been ready to deal with having a scent match so young. I believe with all my heart that things worked out the way they needed to for *all* of us."

"She's right. Hell, Vili only moved to Preidon three years ago," Gareth pointed out. "We might have always been meant to be a pack, but I can't imagine things going as well if we'd been put together that early. None of us would be at this point in our careers or reached the point where we chose to find a pack. For me, especially, that was a big mental shift."

The others nodded and murmured their agreement at Gareth's statement, making me smile. Sensing the conversation had ended, I decided it was time to move on from heavy topics.

"I feel like doing something fun. Vili, what games did you pack?" I asked.

Vili's face lit up as he shot to his feet and took off toward the car. The others followed suit, and I reached out to Gareth, who I expected would help me to stand. Instead, he scooped me up and nuzzled into my neck, tickling me with his stubble, causing peals of laughter to spill from me.

"Thank you for sharing that with us, baby girl. I just know that I love and treasure you all the more for it," Gareth said, brushing his nose along my jaw to whisper in my ear. "You are an inspiration, and I'm one lucky bastard to call you mine."

If I could have melted and turned into a puddle of goo at his feet, I would have. This man had a wicked mouth that could make me swoon one minute then beg him to fuck me the next. He knew what to say to get under my skin in the best way possible.

"Likewise," I said, keeping my voice low. "The calling-you-mine part, I mean. Not that you aren't an inspiration, I'm sure—"

Gareth put me out of my misery as he planted a searing kiss on my lips, shutting me up. My hands grasped his face as I returned the passion he was giving me. Everything about this kiss was flooded with emotions we struggled to say out loud, finding it easier to show the other instead.

"Hey, you two, are we gonna play a game or what?" Warrick yelled, laughter ringing in his words.

We broke apart, smirking at each other, but Gareth gave in and pressed one more kiss to my forehead before swinging me to cling to his back. My fathers and Eli were the only people who'd ever given me a piggyback ride in my life, but that had been when I was a toddler. However, I found I quite enjoyed wrapping myself around one of my Alphas as he held me securely before running to join the others in the open field.

When we reached the others, Gareth let me down carefully so I could see what was in the three duffle bags. "Is that a giant Jenga?"

"Yes, kitten, I have two sets," Vili announced, looking super excited. "We can have tournament, and winner picks prize, yes?"

Peeking into another duffle, I saw a rectangular board with a hole in it along with some bean bags. "That sounds like a great idea, but what is this?"

"We call it Cornhole," Gareth answered.

"Cornhole?" Yun-Sun questioned. "I've only ever heard it called Bags."

Gareth shrugged. "Guess it depends on where you learned it, but I think the game is still the same. Each team stands on the opposite side and tries to toss the bean bag into the hole. Whoever gets the most bags in the hole wins."

The mental picture of me tossing a bean bag only to hit one of the guys in the face, gut, or balls made me cringe. "I'm not so sure about that one. What's in the last bag?"

"Croquet, a favorite of mine," Vili shared, pulling out a wooden mallet. "It is a more complex game with balls, wickets, and become last one standing. Very fun, but takes time to learn."

Tapping my chin with a finger, I looked at the three options and settled on the one I had the best chance of winning. When growing up playing games with Crew, you took any advantage you could get against the irritating pain in my ass. Neither of us was overly competitive in life, but when it came to games, that was a whole other story.

"Jenga is my vote," I announced.

Apparently, there was no other vote needed as the guys instantly started setting up the two towers of blocks.

"Okay, we will have two people at each tower," Yun directed. "The two not playing will be the referees until the first round is over. The winners from the first round will pair up at a tower then those who lost will be referees. Make sense?"

Everyone agreed, and I walked over to a set of blocks, curious to see who would challenge me. Ulysses was well aware of my evil streak when it came to games, so he chose to be a referee.

Warrick sauntered over, rubbing his hand together with a grin. "Just so we're clear, I'm not gonna go easy on you because you're adorable, Care Bear."

"I wouldn't have it any other way," I assured him.

Ulysses walked over to us with a coin in his hand. "Heads or tails?"

"Tails," Warrick blurted.

"Then I guess I'm heads." I chuckled.

Lysse tossed the coin, caught it, and slapped it to the back of his hand. Warrick and I leaned in, eager to see the winner. A whoop of joy rang out from Warrick at the sight of the national flower, followed by a funny little jig.

"Tails never fails me," Warrick offered as Lysse and I gave him confused looks. "Now which block am I going to pick first?"

It was becoming clear that Warrick might be as competitive as me. Watching as he circled the tower plotting his first move, I could tell he was also developing a strategy. Finally, he tested an outer block to see if it would slide out freely, and Warrick set it on top when it did.

"You're turn, madam," Warrick said, bowing with a flourish.

While the man had been figuring out his plan, I'd been doing the same so I was ready to make my choice. Confidently, I freed a block from the second to the bottom row and added it to the top. Warrick's eyes narrowed as he studied me for a moment before making his move. Our game fell silent and more serious with each passing turn, each trying to figure out what the other was doing. Just as I eased a more precarious block from its spot, a loud crash and cheering from the other team nearly had me collapsing our whole tower. Thankfully, my hand held steady long enough to free the block. I let out the breath I was holding as I stacked the piece I'd freed.

Gareth was grinning from ear to ear as Vili clapped, not at all bothered that he'd just lost. When they set about rebuilding it for the next round, I absently circled our tower. I watched as Warrick tried to free a block that clearly held too much weight and grinned. Bending down had caused his T-shirt to slide up his back, revealing a smooth section of skin. The moment Ulysses took his eyes off our game to answer a question from Gareth, I brushed my finger lightly over the bare skin.

Warrick yelped as he flinched, then swore as the tower started to sway. "Shit, shit, shit," he muttered.

"Sorry, man, but you're gonna have to pull that block the rest of the way out," Lysse warned.

Dramatically, Warrick covered his eyes before pulling the block free, sending the whole thing crashing down.

"Damn, I totally could have pulled that off if that damn bug hadn't landed on me," Warrick grumbled.

My brows shot up, surprised he didn't call me out for the dirty trick. Warrick caught my eye and winked, letting me know he knew the truth but wouldn't sell me out.

"I guess it's my burden to bear being so attractive," he teased. "Come on, Care Bear, help me set this up for the next round."

Gareth proved to be a ruthless opponent, shamelessly using whatever tactic he could within the rules to make me mess up. I gave as good as I got, but I was no match to that man's wicked mouth.

"Come on, baby girl, slide that block out nice and slow. Make sure you wrap those pretty fingers around it nice and tight. You wouldn't want it to slip out now, would you?" Gareth taunted in a low, husky voice. "That's it, just like that."

My legs started to shake as I needed to stand on my tiptoes to reach the top of the tower. The second the block was out of my grasp, Gareth pressed himself to my back. His warm breath ruffled my hair which had it brushing along my neck, tickling me.

"That was good, baby girl, but let me show you a trick for getting something a little tight to loosen up for you," he said, his voice low with a slight rumble to it that almost had my legs giving out. "Look, see this one right here? First, you have to give it a little nudge to see just how tight it is. Once you know what you're getting into, then you have to coax it with gentle movements."

Gareth shifted slightly so his lips now brushed the shell of my ear, and his free hand rested on my hip, giving it a slight squeeze. Before I could stop it, a moan slipped out, and I slapped a hand over my mouth to keep any more from slipping through.

Gareth chuckled and used two fingers to push the middle block out the other side. "See that, baby girl. Once you get them to relax and welcome you, they are much easier to slide into."

My hands shook so badly, I knew there was no way I'd pull this off, but I was too stubborn to give in. I tapped a block to see if it would budge, and it shifted under the pressure.

"Don't tell me that's all you got, baby girl. Give it some real effort... thrust those fingers right in there," he urged.

Attempting to do as he suggested, I hit the wrong block with *way* too much force, and the whole thing swayed. I was so lost in the fantasies that Gareth was filling my head with I didn't notice it was heading right for us. Quick as a flash, Gareth wrapped his arm around my waist, lifted me off my feet, and spun us around so the block fell on him instead.

BAILEY-ROSE

A soft grunt coming from Gareth was the only sign that he'd had a tower of wooden blocks dropped on his back. Freeing myself from his hold so I could turn to face him, panic erupted in my chest.

"Oh my God, are you okay?" I asked, grabbing his arm to pull him free of the pile of blocks. "I'm so sorry. I should have gotten out of the way the second I knew it was going to fall."

"Hey, easy, baby girl... take a breath," Gareth soothed. "I'm fine, totally and completely fine. Those blocks weren't all that heavy, and none of them have sharp corners for this very reason."

I refused to let this go until I yanked up the back of his shirt and looked at his back with my two eyes. There were a few red marks from the blocks but nothing that gave me any concern. With a sigh, I pressed a kiss to each of the marks before wrapping my arms around his waist, hugging him as I rested my cheek on his skin.

"That was absolutely reckless, Gareth," I muttered.

He wrapped a hand around my wrist and drew me around so I could face him. "Baby girl, I don't give two shits how reckless it might be, but your safety comes first. Period."

"That's stupid. My life isn't more important than any of yours," I challenged.

Gareth cupped my face and smiled. "Not true... you are

the most important person to us. I know without a doubt I can speak for the others when I say this is a battle you will never win. There is only one of you, and there are five of us. You would be able to survive losing one of us, but none of us would ever recover from losing you."

I opened my mouth to argue, but Gareth tucked a hand under my chin and shut it. "Sorry, no matter what you say, none of us will agree. So what do you say to packing up here, grabbing some Chinese, and picking a movie to watch all snuggled up together?"

Everything in me wanted to do whatever it took to get him to understand that I could never survive without one of them. It was clear as day to me that each of them was a piece of my soul, and losing even one of them would leave me forever broken. There would be no way to fix that ailment unless science created a way to bring back a man from the dead. Yet I had a sneaking suspicion they felt the same way about me.

"That sounds perfect," I admitted, letting the matter drop for now. "What about the final round? You still have to go against Ulysses."

"Nah," Lysse said, gripping Gareth's shoulder. "Seeing the lengths this guy is willing to go to, I'll let him have the win."

"Fuck off," Gareth shot back, grinning as he shoved Ulysses. "Who's calling in the food? We can pick it up on the way back to the house."

"On it," Warrick called, pulling out his phone. "The usual place?"

"Make sure you triple the potstickers and crab rangoon. This little monster will eat them all before we even get a chance," Lysse warned, wrapping me up in a bear hug. "Anything else you want, Rosie? We always get beef and broccoli along with that chicken almond dish I know you like."

"I don't know, you might want to double up on those too if you're that worried about me eating them all," I muttered, trying to act upset even as I was soaking up the affection.

"Hmm…" Ulysses hummed, then scooped me up, tossed me over his shoulder, and headed back to our base camp. "War, better get two large orders of beef and broccoli since you're the only one who likes the almond thing."

"Almond Ding, not thing," Warrick corrected. "I'll get it sorted. There's a reason you guys always make me do the food orders."

I hung there for a moment, stunned that Lysse was tossing me around like a doll. Placing my hands on his ass, I pushed up to see Warrick on the phone and the others cleaning up the game like nothing odd was happening here.

"What do you think you're doing, Mr. Ford," I demanded.

His response was to pat my ass and chuckle. "Well, Ms. Thatcher, I'm ensuring my Omega doesn't get into any trouble. Seems she's rather prone to getting into mishaps lately… can never be too careful."

I groaned, rolling my eyes as I let my arms relax. "That is some of the most Alpha-sounding shit to ever come out of your mouth."

"Want to hear a secret?" Lysse asked as he paused, shifting me lower so my legs automatically wrapped around his waist, and we were face-to-face. "I really just wanted a little one-on-one time with my Rosie. Don't get me wrong, I'm happy to share with my pack brothers, and I see how happy they make you. Yet, sometimes, I simply want you to myself for a bit. Does that make me a bad pack brother?"

My love for this man only grew at hearing his concern.

"No, I don't think that makes you a bad pack brother. To me, it sounds totally normal for you to want some alone time with a person you care about. If you think about it, the others have also asked for one-on-one time with me over the past week."

Ulysses leaned in, kissing me with such tenderness it made me tear up. I don't know how long we stood there under the shade of a large tree with a soft breeze rustling the leaves above, and it didn't matter. In all the whirlwind of discovering this man was my scent match, meeting my pack, moving, and creating a new life with my guys, I hadn't really had time to realize my first and only love loved me back. Every person I dated was compared to this man, and I should have realized they were destined to fail when they didn't even come close. My heart belonged to Ulysses, Warrick, Yun-Sun, Gareth, and Vili long before I understood what that meant.

"I love you, Ulysses. I've loved you pretty much my whole life," I whispered, resting my forehead against his. "Thank you for coming back to me."

Lysse lovingly brushed my hair out of my face as the breeze picked up. "Rosie, there has never been a moment since meeting you that I wouldn't drop everything to be right by your side. I didn't understand why. No matter what happened in my life, you never left my thoughts. Now I do and fuck, am I a lucky bastard to have you."

Heat burned across my cheeks, telling me I was blushing and probably grinning like an idiot. I leaned forward and kissed him, wrapping my arms around his neck, pressing my body to his, needing to feel him so I knew I wasn't dreaming.

"Hey, you two," Yun-Sun called softly. "I hate to be the guy who cuts in on your moment, but everything's packed up."

My head snapped up, and I looked around, not that I thought Yun was lying but more so surprised we'd been making out that long. Ulysses let me slide down his body until I stood on my own but immediately took my hand, threading our fingers together.

"Yun, I'm sorry," I apologized. "You guys shouldn't have had to clean up everything after setting it all up."

Yun-Sun gently gripped my chin, urging me to tilt my head back and meet his gaze. "Sweetheart, it's no trouble. Don't fret over the small things. It was clear to us that Ulysses needed you, and we were more than happy to make that possible. We are a family, and that means we do things to support each other. Now if you'd like to help me out, Gareth is getting rather hangry."

I smiled as Yun dropped a kiss on my lips and headed for the car with the two of us right on his heels.

Sprawled out across Ulysses and Warrick on the couch, I groaned. "I think I'm going to burst."

Warrick placed a hand on my stomach and rubbed it, talking to it in a baby voice. "Aww, look at the food baby."

I swatted his hand away halfheartedly, only to squeal in laughter as he pulled up my shirt and blew raspberries on my stomach. A fart so loud it echoed off the living room walls rocketed out of me. It shocked everyone, including myself, but it wasn't long before Warrick started to snicker. He slapped a hand over his mouth to keep the laughter in, but it was too late. Gareth lost his shit a moment later, nearly falling off the couch, he was laughing so hard. This set everyone else off, and I joined in, refusing to let a normal bodily function upset this amazing night.

A knock at the door had us trying to pull it together, but it wasn't going well.

Yun stood and did his best to collect himself as he answered the door after the person on the other side knocked even more insistently. Wriggling around, I managed to sit up with Lysses' help, curious to see who was at the door. A middle-aged man dressed in a suit with the Scent Matchers emblem on the breast waited for Yun to sign whatever was on the clipboard. When he handed it back, the man in the suit gave him a letter, saying something I couldn't hear, but seemed serious. Yun said goodnight, giving the man a friendly wave before closing and locking the front door.

My gaze tracked Yun-Sun as he rejoined us, yet didn't take his seat. Instead, his whole attention was focused on the letter in his hand. "What is it?" I asked.

"The man said it's an official summons to meet with the Scent Matchers," Yun answered as he carefully opened the letter that was sealed with a sticker bearing the organization's emblem. He pulled the letter free, slowly unfolding it as he read, his brows furrowing. "They require our presence tomorrow, one o'clock, at the Windermere hub."

"What? Why?" Gareth demanded, holding his hand out for the letter. Yun-Sun gave it to him, seemingly lost in thought. "The fuck, we're to attend this meeting *without* Bailey-Rose? None of this makes sense, I've never heard of something like this before."

Ulysses took the letter out of Gareth's hand as he started to crumple it in his grasp. I read over Lysses' shoulder, trying to make sense of this as dread grew in the pit of my stomach.

"Gareth, you didn't read the whole thing," Ulysses pointed out. "It says right here, 'due to the unusual nature of matching, we require additional information before the scent match can be officially recognized.' "

"Hold on, who alerted the Scent Matchers we'd found our Omega?" Warrick questioned.

Yun-Sun paused in his pacing to raise a hand. "I did."

"Really? How did that go, and why are you just telling us now?" Gareth challenged.

Rubbing a hand over his buzzed hair, Yun sighed. "I didn't think it was a big deal. They were still sending us notifications of new Omegas and followed up on the email we sent about possibly adding in male Omegas. Seeing as we'd just found Bailey-Rose, I informed them that we no longer needed to use the database and to remove our pack from the system. I didn't hear anything back from them, so I assumed there were no issues, nothing to tell."

"How long ago?" Vili inquired.

"Ah..." Yun paused, pinching the bridge of his nose. "Oh, it was the day we moved her into the house. I got an alert on my phone, so I ducked into my room to answer the email from my computer."

Gareth dropped his head into his hands. "Oh, thank fuck. If there had been a major issue, they would have moved way faster than this to get their answers."

"It make sense," Vili interjected. "Kitten not in system, no, rejected from system. I think they want to know how we feel or if we know she rejected."

Gareth scoffed, flopping back against the couch. "Those elitist pricks don't deserve to know any of that stuff. Bailey-Rose isn't one of their clients, and it's not like it's the first time a pack has found their Omega on their own. The damn system has only been around for fifty years. We just went old-school."

"However, our pack was in the system," Yun-Sun reasoned. "Plus, you know they changed the laws that even in cases where packs and Omegas naturally find each other, they must be registered with the Scent Matchers. While I feel it's odd to be given short notice, there isn't a reason we can't go. I don't know about you, but I'm not going to risk there being an issue and giving them a reason to deny our bonding."

Fear struck me like an arrow to the chest. "C-can they do that?"

"I don't know, sweetheart, but I'd really rather not test the possibility. I'm sure all they want is to meet with us, hear our story, answer a few questions, and make sure everything is on the up and up," Yun assured me.

Ulysses pulled me onto his lap, cuddling me close, giving me the comfort I desperately needed right now. "Hey, I have an idea. We wanted to go to the studio, right? What if we went over after breakfast, took a look around the place, and while we have this meeting, you can paint? This way, you have a little breathing room and don't worry about us as you get lost in your art. I saw the way you disappeared into that sketch today. You haven't done any art since we showed up, so I bet your creative side is begging for you to let it free."

That did sound like a rather perfect idea. Being able to draw at the lake had pulled the cork from the bottle, allowing my creativity to run wild. "Sounds like a hard offer to pass up. I suppose if you guys have to leave me on my own, it's better to have my art than be all alone in the house."

"That's the spirit," Ulysses cheered, kissing my nose.

"There is nothing to worry about. This is all going to blow over, you'll see."

Everything in me wanted to believe him, but I'd be lying to myself if I hadn't been wondering when the shoe was going to drop. Things have been perfect, more than I ever could have dreamed of. It only made sense to me that it was time to wake up from the dream I'd been living. However, I would keep that line of thinking to myself and enjoy soaking up every second of my time with the men I was hopeless to live without.

"Can I suggest a movie?" I asked, twisting to look at the others. "It's a bit of an acquired taste, though."

This seemed to pique Vili's interest. "What movie, kitten? I love odd films."

"Ever heard of *Labyrinth*? It's an old movie with singing, puppets, and amazing costumes," I explained.

Gareth's mouth popped open in surprise. "That was Callie's favorite movie. I haven't seen it in ages, but I can promise I remember all the words to the songs. That girl would sing them at the top of her lungs randomly throughout the day, especially during farm chores." Gareth chuckled, rubbing his forehead. "God, I can still see her feeding the chickens, telling them they reminded her of the babe."

"What babe?" Warrick asked, his face showing true confusion.

"The babe with the power," I answered.

"Okay, what the hell... neither of you is making sense. What power could a baby possibly have?" Warrick said, exasperated.

Gareth grinned like a fool as he leaned in and pretended to whisper in Warrick's ear, "The power of voodoo."

"Voodoo? Now I know you two are messing with me,"

Warrick shot back. "There isn't a baby in the world who can practice voodoo."

"Oh, but one might if they were kidnapped by the Goblin King," I defended.

Warrick started to say something but stopped and pulled out his phone to look at something. "Fantastic, it's available on streaming so I can figure out what the hell you two are going on about."

Yun-Sun smiled and caught my gaze, giving me a wink, making me think he knew exactly what Gareth and I were doing. "Looks like your pick wins, sweetheart. Do we need anything before this movie starts?"

Ulysses set me on the couch and stood. "Let's at least get the remnants of dinner out of the way so we can make the couch into a bed."

"Smart man," Warrick said with a clap of the hands. "Tonight is a night of epic Omega snuggles. I can feel it."

"It's almost two hours long so we might need to rotate through the movie," Gareth pointed out. "Unless we want to decide whoever sits next to her now gets the fringe spots when we go to bed."

"Rock, paper, scissors?" Vili suggested, holding his hand up in a fist, ready to go.

Leaving the guys to determine the best course of action, I carried empty containers into the kitchen. Ulysses held the trash open for me, and I dumped my load into it.

"Hey, before you head back, I think you should have this so you can charge it for tomorrow," Lysse said as he pulled open a drawer and handed me my phone.

I'd totally forgotten the damn thing since I hadn't needed to worry about checking in with Crew or Eli if I went somewhere. Taking it from Lysse, I tried to turn it on, but true to his prediction, it just blinked low battery and shut off.

"You don't think Randall still believes we're together, do you?" I asked. "It makes no sense. I found my scent matches, and anything that happened before that would be over. Why would he even try to get me to come back to him and forget about you guys?"

Ulysses tucked me to his side and pressed a kiss to my head. "Just reading the messages he left you, it's clear that Randall might not experience being told no all that often. There could be other factors we don't know about or possibly a mental illness that makes him obsess or cling to things in his life. No matter what he threatens, there is nothing anyone could do to convince us to walk away from you."

He let out a heavy sigh, nuzzling his cheek against my hair. "If I'm being honest, I wouldn't have given you the damn thing back until you wore our marks. Then it wouldn't matter what anyone said or did, you'd be bound to us by a ritual that no one can break or dispute. All that aside, keeping you safe and knowing you have your phone with you tomorrow is more important."

"Then I'll charge it tonight, but I won't turn it on until we get to the studio. I don't want anything to ruin the perfect night we're having," I decided, setting the phone on the counter. "It can wait until the movie is over."

With a sweet kiss on my lips, Ulysses led me back to the living room, where everyone was waiting for me to join.

"Get over here, Care Bear," Warrick urged, patting the spot between him and Vili. "I need you here to protect me from the Goblin King."

Grinning, I skipped over to them and leaped into the

couch nest they made. Snuggled up between my two sunshine Alphas, all the worry that revolved around my phone faded away. It had been at least a year since I'd seen the movie, and I was just reminded how much I loved it. The moment *Magic Dance* came on, Gareth and I sang along, trading parts like we'd done this for years.

When the lightbulb went on for Warrick, he laughed, enjoying the joke. "Nicely played, you two. I walked right into that and didn't even know it."

"That's what made it all the more perfect," I admitted, grinning from ear to ear.

"Is that so? You like teasing me, is that it?" Warrick accused, then pounced, tickling me until I begged for mercy. "Mercy, you want mercy? Well, it's gonna cost you, Care Bear. I demand a million kisses. I'll even be nice and let you pay it off in installments."

I gazed up at Warrick, his citrine-colored eyes shimmering with love and laughter. "That will take me a lifetime to pay back."

"Huh, sounds like you're stuck with me for life then," Warrick said, diving in to get his first installment. "Only nine hundred ninety-nine thousand left to go."

"Excuse me," Vili interrupted, tapping Warrick on the shoulder. "Can we watch movie now? I must know if she saves the babe."

Letting out an overly dramatic sigh, Warrick released me and flopped back into his spot. "Gosh, V-man, never would have guessed you to be a cockblock."

Vili flashed him a smirk before scooping me up and settling me on his lap. He nuzzled a kiss to my temple with a soft chuckle. "Now you know. Start movie, please. We have much more to watch."

I had to cover my mouth as I giggled, seeing the look of betrayal on Warrick's face. "It's the quiet ones you have to watch out for," Gareth commented as he hit play, ending all further conversation.

BAILEY-ROSE

The studio was located in the heart of Windermere's art district. It was down the street from the acclaimed Museum of Modern Art, making it an incredibly sought-after piece of real estate. It was surrounded by boutique shops, galleries, and one of those paint-your-own-pottery places that held lots of classes and events. Many of the buildings had bright, colorful murals sprawling along the sides of the buildings. Two years ago, they'd started a campaign to make it the social media hotspot—a destination to capture the best pictures with interesting architecture, creative art, and a beautiful grotto with a gazebo covered in twinkle lights. All in all, an artist's paradise.

Amazingly, the hard work put into the project paid off, and Windermere Art District won an award for being a travel hotspot. It made me sad that everything that happened with Randall had kept me from coming to my favorite place in the city. From time to time over the past four years, I rented space at other studios to work on projects for school I couldn't do at home. Pottery wasn't my favorite form of art. I was passable at best, but it wasn't something I would invest in buying all the supplies when I knew I wouldn't use them long-term. Crew was the first to suggest seeing if there was a place to rent, and it started my love affair with this part of the city.

We pulled up outside the two-story, red-brick building with a wrought iron balcony wrapped around the front and side. I should have known this was the building they'd buy out of the ones I knew were for sale. It had been announced the owner was going to tear it down and build an expensive apartment complex, taking advantage of the boom in this area. The moment I knew that was what was planned, I got on the phone with anyone I knew who held sway in the city to put a stop to it as this building had enormous historical value.

"Wow, this is your parents' idea of a graduation gift?" Gareth asked, covering his eyes to peer up at the place.

I couldn't blame the man for having that reaction. When I opened the box with the keys in it, I thought I was going to pass out.

"They knew my dreams when it came to the gallery I wanted to start. It also might have something to do with the fact I was a one-woman army, determined to rescue this building from being torn down," I shared, pulling out the keys from my purse.

"Don't just leave us hanging, Care Bear. Did you win the battle?" Warrick pressed as we walked up to the thick wooden double doors.

Sliding the key into the deadbolt, I turned the key. When the bolt slid back, I did a silent happy dance as the reality this place was truly mine set in. Trying to keep my cool, I pressed down on the vintage handle and shoved the door open. My cheeks hurt as I smiled and entered the building I'd fought for.

Spinning around, I faced the guys, barely containing my joy as I answered Warrick's question, "You bet your ass I won. She's still standing, isn't she?"

"Did kitten swear?" Vili asked.

"Yeah, she sure did," Ulysses confirmed with a smirk.

"Look at her. That's the face of a woman who beat the pants off some unsuspecting man."

I rolled my eyes. "I did no such thing. Besides, I didn't do this *all* on my own. The whole neighborhood was up in arms about what this man wanted to do. This was one of the last buildings designed by a famous architect, Rosco Reign, who used his buildings to support the arts. In a way, you could say his aspirations for his work inspired my dream studio. Once I got the city to put a hold on things while the Historical Society did their investigation on my claims, the builder couldn't move forward. They even told him he couldn't pre-sell the apartments since, as it stood, the property wasn't zoned for residential. Without the final word from the Historical Society, they refused to change it should they claim it as a historical site."

Yun-Sun let out a low, impressed whistle. "That, sweetheart, is some brilliant thinking. Are you sure you never thought about being a lawyer?"

"Trust me, I never would have come up with that idea myself. One of the other fighters in this cause gave me the idea. I was just the one who had connections to people who would listen to what I had to say," I admitted with a shrug. "The last name Thatcher has its perks, but I hate to use them."

Warrick pulled me into a side hug and kissed my head. "Care Bear, this was absolutely the right time to use that power. Saving history, helping a community, and ensuring a legacy continues to support others? Yeah, I wouldn't lose any sleep over that man not getting his luxury apartments."

"Thanks," I murmured, hugging him tightly. "I needed to hear that."

"Hey, baby girl, why don't you take us on a tour? We still

have an hour before we need to head out," Gareth suggested.

"Would it surprise you guys to know I've never been in this building before? It's been locked up and sitting while the previous owner tried to get things settled with the city. I've peeked in the windows, but that's about it," I admitted.

Gareth reached out a hand to me with a grin on his face. "Then let's get exploring."

Since Warrick refused to let me go, I walked between them. My parents told me they had been working on it while I was away at school to ensure it was up to code and safe for me to use. The main area was open to the roof with windows everywhere, letting light flood in.

"I'm thinking this would make an amazing gallery space," I commented, taking in everything.

Yun pushed open a set of barn doors on a track, revealing an entire workspace setup. Gasping, I dropped the guys' hands to cover my mouth, tears welling up at the sight of my very own studio. Of course, I had one back at my parents' house, but it was a sitting room no one used that I took over. What I was looking at now put that studio to shame.

"Whoa..." Ulysses said, clearly as shocked as I was.

"Damn, if this is the gift game your parents have, we're gonna need some lessons," Gareth muttered.

Still too shocked to address their worries, I walked up to the shelves mounted on the wall stocked with every kind of paint known to man. Tool chests were set up as well, with drawers full of anything and everything I could possibly need to create whatever I wanted. While on campus, I'd started to explore more with oil painting, loving the different effects I could get with the thicker paint. Now lying in front of me were various palette knives, scrapers, and mixers with reusable paint palettes.

I saw a pottery wheel with a note taped to it, so I plucked it off and unfolded the paper.

JUST COULDN'T PASS UP THE CHANCE TO MAKE SURE YOU HAD SOMETHING IN HERE THAT I COULD MESS AROUND WITH WHILE YOU WORK. YOU MIGHT HAVE SPACE OUTSIDE THE HOUSE NOW, BUT YOU'RE NOT GETTING RID OF ME THAT EASILY, LouLou.
— LOVE, CREW
P.S. I CAN BRING GIRLS HERE, RIGHT, BECAUSE A MAN DOING POTTERY IS SEXY AS HELL!!

Laughing, I plopped down on the stool near the wheel, picturing Crew trying to impress a girl making an endless supply of ashtrays. Vili took the letter from my hand, glancing over it before he laughed too.

"Tell me, kitten, would this work?" Vili asked, gesturing to the note. "Is he lady killer of pottery?"

That had me laughing even harder, clutching my stomach. "God, no."

"Who's the lady killer?" Warrick inquired, snatching the note. "I mean, he has a point. Have you seen that movie? The one with that super-hot pottery scene."

"*Ghost*?" Ulysses guessed. "Wait, wasn't he dead the whole time?"

"No, that's *The Sixth Sense*," Yun-Sun corrected.

"Hold up," I cut in, waving my arms like a referee. "Ulysses was right, the guy does die in the beginning of the movie, but he knows it. The other one Yun is talking about, no one knew until the end of the movie."

"Huh, it's been ages since I saw either of them," Warrick mused aloud. "We should add that to the list of movie choices for movie nights."

"I'm game," I said, pushing to my feet. I grinned at the wheel again before exploring the space further.

Some of my favorite pieces were hung on the walls, but there was plenty of space for me to add more. Along one wall was a row of tall, empty metal-locking cabinets. I'm sure they were meant to keep whatever I was working on to be stored safely when I was gone for the night. When I came to a door, I opened it, assuming it would be more storage, but instead, I found a set of stairs.

"Hey, guys," I called over my shoulder. "There's more."

When we entered this studio space, I'd noticed the ceiling was what you'd expect for a two-story building. It had me wondering if my parents had opened up that front half, thinking, like me, it would be the gallery. Making my way up to the second floor, I was greeted by the sight of an office space of sorts. There was a simple sitting area with a full coffee and tea bar as if it was intended to be a space to meet with buyers or artists.

All the furniture was white and of a simple style with no personality. While my family was trying to give me the basics, they knew I'd want to decorate things myself, which I appreciated. In a corner set apart and walled off with iridescent walls was an office, or what could be turned into one. Right now, it had a desk, chair, and shelving behind it, but everything, including the walls, could be moved to another location, allowing me the freedom to do as I pleased.

Hands rested on my shoulders, and a sweet, chocolaty scent spiced with cinnamon told me it was Ulysses. "Well,

Rosie, it looks like we aren't the only people who think your plan for the future is brilliant."

Letting out a sigh, I leaned back into him, a little overwhelmed. "It's too much," I whispered.

"Why?" Vili asked as he stood in front of me. "Why too much, kitten?"

"All I have is a concept, and there's no proof it will work," I reasoned. "Anyone in the creative world knows choosing this for your living is always a risk. What if I do this, get people's hopes up, and then it fails so miserably I have to close the gallery? Then not only have I failed them, myself, but my family as well." Vili's expression was understanding, but I could tell he didn't agree with what I was saying.

Grasping my hand in both of his, he kissed the back of it. "Kitten, the only time you fail people is not even trying. Your family gave you foundation, a place to start, so now you must make it grow. Feed it your passion, shower it in determination, pluck out negativity, and trust the dream. It's okay to have fear, it makes you wise, but it can't take over the dream. This is the key... fear is good until it steals from you, but you have us. We won't let it win."

Turning my hand so it was palm up, he undid the band to my heart monitor and slipped it into his pocket. Confused, I watched as he pulled something out of his other pocket. It was a different monitor encased in silver with a band that had delicate-looking chains on it. In various spots on the chain was a heart with a letter stamped into it—one for each of my guys and a larger heart with what looked like a QR code etched into it.

"What is this?" I asked, even though it was obvious.

Vili kissed my wrist before releasing my hand. "Proof we are always here, kitten."

"What he means is that we have been talking to Dr.

Arbour. He alerted us to this new heart rate monitor technology. This isn't approved here in Preidon yet, so Dr. Arbour got us in the final product trial," Gareth explained.

Yun-Sun tapped the screen twice, waking it up. "Not only is it set to your specific thresholds, if it hits the danger range, an ambulance will be called, along with all of us getting notifications. That means it will give your exact location so the EMTs can find you, and we'll know too. We all agreed it was important for you to feel confident being here and running this place once it's open. This gives everyone peace of mind, and we hope it will do the same for you."

"The QR code was my idea," Warrick interjected. "It has all our numbers, what hospital to take you to, and to ensure Dr. Arbour is alerted about any situation. You've had to give up so many things in your life, but you deserve to have it all. We hope this will be a step in taking back some of the confidence others have stolen from you."

Unable to hold back the tears from earlier, I sniffled, clutching my wrist to my chest. "Thank you, thank you so much. You have no idea what this means to me, not only because of the added protection but the trust my Alphas have in me."

Arms wrapped around me as my pack converged into a group hug with me at the center, purring at the love and affection surrounding me.

Music filled the studio from the sound system I discovered had been installed thanks to Crew. He knew better than anyone how much I loved to lose myself in the lyrics as I painted. I stood in front of a large canvas, taking in the sketch I did and tapping the pencil against my chin in time with the song. The outline of five men in various places around a kitchen counter stared back at me. I wasn't sure how I felt about painting them since it was so different from what I normally chose to do. Most of my previous work had been of a single person, but this moment was seared into my brain.

One morning, I'd come down, but no one heard me enter the kitchen, so I watched as they worked. Yun-Sun was running the show, which I'm learning is the normal way of things, and they were trying to make an extravagant breakfast. Gareth and Warrick argued over the proper way to cook a poached egg. Vili was scooping flour into a bowl only to be knocked by Warrick dodging Gareth's attack. Flour exploded everywhere as the bowl flew across the counter and crashed to the floor. Ulysses had been cutting up fruit across from Vili and now had a face full of flour since the scoop Vili still had in his hand got flung in his direction. Yun-Sun was the only one not affected by this debacle, having just pulled bacon out of the oven, but the look on his face was priceless.

Warrick's solution was to grab more flour and toss it at the two who were still clean. Unable to keep from laughing, the guys discovered me standing there. Moments later, I got dragged into the situation as Ulysses snatched me up in a hug, smearing flour all over my face from his.

Now here I was trying to recreate the feeling of that moment as my pack was currently sitting with the Scent Matchers. I'd been hoping diving into a memory so perfect and full of love would keep my mind from thinking of all the terrible things that could happen. Grabbing the eraser off the table beside me, I started to fix a spot I knew wasn't working. The drag of my pencil over the canvas was comforting as I concentrated on shaping the bowl of flying flour.

The feel of a tap on my shoulder had me spinning around and jerking away, sending me crashing into the canvas. A hand grabbed me, keeping me from crashing to the floor like everything else did.

"Bumblebee, it's just me," Randall said, trying to soothe me.

Seeing him standing there holding my arm did nothing to calm the adrenaline racing through my veins. "Randall," I gasped. "What the hell are you doing here?"

"I'm sorry, I didn't mean to scare you. I tried to knock and call out, but you didn't hear me, leaving me no choice," Randall explained.

"That's not what I asked," I pointed out as I tried to blow hair out of my face. "I asked you *what are you doing here* in this studio you should know nothing about."

He reached out, making me flinch as he tucked the rouge hairs behind my ear. "Bumblebee, if you'd only answered your phone or responded to me, I wouldn't have had to come here. It's incredibly hard to get you alone since one of *them* is always with you. Those fuckers know you belong to me and are doing everything in their power to keep you hidden. Too bad for them I have connections in high places. I warned them not to fuck with me."

Nothing Randall was saying made sense. It's almost as if he was wearing a mask to look like the man I'd dated, but the words coming out of his mouth were nonsensical.

"I-I don't understand, Randall, why would they be keeping me from you?" I questioned, in hopes of getting some clue to his logic. "Those men you keep talking about are my scent matches, so why wouldn't I be with them?"

"No," he roared, yanking me closer. "You can't have a

scent match. You were rejected, and no one who's rejected has a pack out there waiting for them. It's forbidden."

Forced to place my hand on his chest or fall into him, I tried to keep as much distance between us. "I don't know what to tell you, Randall, but that's not true. I have a pack and five men who will be my scent-bonded Alphas."

"Lies, it's all lies. Don't you see they used something to make you think that, but it's not true," Randall said vehemently, spittle from his words hitting my face as he gave me a rough shake. "You're mine, Bailey-Rose. I picked you. They said I could have you because you're a reject, and no one will ever claim a reject. Who wants a broken Omega whose heart could stop working at any moment?"

Fear clawed at my throat as tears rolled down my cheeks, constricting my airway so all I could do was squeak my protest at the rough treatment.

"Shh, Bumblebee, don't cry," Randall cooed, wiping my tears with his sleeve. "I didn't mean to upset you by saying that, but it's the truth you need to face. See, I was rejected too. I had a pack, but they told lies about me and said I hurt our Omega to the point she ended up in the hospital. None of it was true. That bitch wouldn't let me mark her, said I scared her. No matter what I did, she didn't admit to the lie. If she'd just been honest, then I wouldn't have had to be so rough. They wouldn't even let me see her in the hospital, but none of that matters now because I found you."

Horror washed over me at his words, taking me back to when we met. "Are you telling me you didn't have a brother who was sick and in the hospital?"

"Well, in a manner of speaking, he was a pack brother at that time. Broke his nose when he didn't let me in her room," Randall mumbled as he licked his thumb and used it to wipe under my eye. "You should wear waterproof mascara. We both know you cry over the silliest things. It's okay... I'll make sure to clean you up. We can't have people thinking I've upset you when we leave."

"Leave?" I croaked, panic screaming at me to get as far away from this man as possible.

"Of course, I can't let you stay around here when those men are going to steal you from me. Your family was no help either. No matter what I tell them, they disagree that you're mine," Randall explained absently, using his shirt sleeve to clean up another spot on my other cheek. "There, now we're good to go. All I have to do is inject you with this sedative so you don't get too excited with all the travel. Can't risk you hurting your heart until we get you looked at by your new doctor. I made sure to research the best of the best in all of Trastle."

Trastle! That wasn't just leaving town, it was fleeing to another fucking country.

"Randall, please don't use that on me," I begged as he started to drag me toward the front of the building. "A sedative could kill me."

He just clicked his tongue at me. "Nonsense, I made sure with the doctor it wouldn't cause any trouble. Why would I dare risk doing something that could kill you? You're mine."

No matter how I dug in my heels and tried to pull out of his grasp, it didn't even slow him down. As he dragged me past the tool chest with all the oil paint tools, I darted to the side, making him stumble with the sudden change. Yanking open a drawer, I found a metal palette and palette blades.

"Bailey-Rose, what the hell are you doing?" Randall demanded, yanking me back and spilling all the tools to the floor. "Now is not the time... we need to go. I'll make sure you have anything you need to be happy, so leave it."

"Wait, please. I left something important... just stop for

one second," I pleaded, gripping the palette as tightly as I could.

He snarled as he turned to face me. "What? What could you possibly need that I can't give you?"

"Happiness," I answered, and using all the strength in my body, I slammed the palette against the side of his face.

"You fucking bitch," Randall screamed, shoving me away from him so hard I crashed to the floor, slamming my hip and wrist against the concrete. "Why would you do something like that, Bumblebee? I've been nothing but good to you and bent over backward to deal with all the problems you have."

He started to advance on me, anger flashing in his eyes. Something in me knew if he got ahold of me, I wouldn't survive. Spotting the palette knives scattered on the floor, I started to crawl backward but cried out when my left wrist gave out, shooting pain up my arm.

"Don't you get it? There's only me, Bailey-Rose," Randall taunted. "I'm the only one who sees any value in a pathetic fucking Omega who's one goddamn hard fuck away from dying. I'm willing to put up with all of that as long as you do as you're fucking told."

Trying not to let the terror of this situation cause me to freeze, I retreated as best I could, but it seemed Randall was done watching me struggle. He loomed over me, making me scramble back, blocking out the pain of my wrist as I flipped over.

"Where are you going, Bumblebee? The door is the other way," Randall informed me as he grabbed my ankles.

In a desperate move, I kicked out, catching him in the chin, which loosened his hold enough for me to grasp a palette knife before he dragged me back to him. He flipped me once more onto my back, gazing up at his crazed eyes.

My heart thundered as my breath came in quick gasps, and the tell-tale buzzing started on my wrist. Hope surged through me. All I needed was to raise my heart rate high enough to get help.

"Are you done with this little outburst, Bumblebee?" Randall asked in a cool tone.

Gathering up what spit I could, fear making my mouth bone dry, I spat that wad right into his face. "I'm not fucking going anywhere with you, asshole."

Rage unlike anything I've seen in the face of another human took over Randall's expression. The next thing I knew, his hands were wrapped around my neck, squeezing so tight I couldn't breathe.

"If you won't come with me, what makes you think I'll let them have you?" He sneered. "All you have to do to end this is blink twice, accepting the fact you're mine, Bailey-Rose."

There's no fucking way I'd ever accept that, you bastard.

A shrill alarm started blaring from my wrist, drawing Randall's attention, his hand loosening enough for me to suck in a little air. Gripping the handle of the palette knife tightly, I stabbed it into his shoulder. I tried to pull it back out to keep my weapon, but it was stuck, and Randall jerked away from me, leaving me there coughing and spluttering, trying to catch my breath.

The sound of sirens in the distance had Randall panicking, and he decided it was best to leave me here on the floor, gasping for air. Clutching his shoulder, he gave me one last glance. "If you live through this, just know I never give up on what's mine. I won't let anyone have what I've claimed." With that promise, he bolted.

I don't know how long I laid there unable to catch my breath, my vision blurry, and my heart struggling to keep me alive. The blurry outline of a person hovered over me, asking me questions I couldn't answer. I could only think to hold my wrist up, but that turned out to be more like a half-hearted slide.

"Found her," a man yelled as he grabbed my wrist. "Oh fuck, I need oxygen now."

More people gathered around, but I couldn't understand what they were saying. Every ounce of my concentration was on ensuring my heart kept moving, beating, and feeding my body blood. Vaguely, I registered that they'd lifted me and assumed put me in the ambulance. I drifted in and out as sirens blared, the ground swayed, and I kept pleading for my heart to hold on a little longer. We couldn't die, not when we'd just started to live.

"I'm Dr. Arbour... this is my patient. We need to get her up to surgery this instant. I don't want you even to move her from this gurney. There is no time if we want a shot at saving her life," Dr. Arbour ordered. "Bailey-Rose, I can see you're fighting. I need you to give it all you've got for me, darling. Trust me, I'll get you through this, and you'll be able to spend a long, happy life with your Alphas."

I whined at the mention of them, tears slipping out of the corners of my eyes.

"Shh, they will be here soon, but I can't wait. I wish with all my heart I could do that for you, but I choose to give you forever with them instead of a moment. I hope after this is all over, you all will forgive me," Dr. Arbour said hurriedly as I was being rolled to surgery.

More people shouted, and bright lights had me cringing, then a hand slipped under mine. "This is it, Bailey-Rose," Dr. Arbour stated. "We are about to begin the hardest fight you'll ever have to face. Give my hand a squeeze and let me know you're in this with me."

Images and memories of the past week with Ulysses, Warrick, Gareth, Vili, and Yun-Sun appeared before me.

Damn right, I was all in for this fight.

I had five men I needed to get back to.

Five men I loved and wanted to spend the rest of my life having adventures with.

Squeezing Dr. Arbour's hand with all the strength I had, I needed him to understand that I wasn't going anywhere.

Hang on, my loves. You might not be here when I close my eyes, but I know you'll be the first thing I see when I open them.

To be concluded in *Petals & Promises: Part 2*

About the Author

Elizabeth is originally from Illinois but is now living in sunny Phoenix, Arizona. Though she is newer to publishing, Elizabeth has been writing for nine years. She started in YA Fiction but recently found herself loving the Reverse Harem genre. Like her favorite books, Elizabeth loves to write about strong women of all varieties. Not all strength is flashy or apparent at first glance—some lie just under the surface.

Don't Miss Out!

Be the first to know what is coming next by following Elizabeth's social media! You never know when or what will be coming next!

Website: ElizabethKnightBooks.com
Facebook: Elizabeth Knight's Unicorn Queens
Instagram: elizabethknightauthor
Newsletter: sign up here

Also by Elizabeth Knight

<u>Sunshine & Rainbows Omegaverse</u>

Bailey-Rose Duet - Clouds & Daydreams & Petals & Promises

Lyra & Eli Duet - Knot Now Knot Ever & Yes Now Yes Forever

<u>Knot All Omegaverse</u>

Knot All Is Lost: Part 1 & Part 2 (Complete)

Knot All Is Ruined: Part 1 & Part 2 (Complete)

<u>Omega Assassin - Complete series</u>

Book 1 - Dual Nature

Book 2 - Hidden Nature

Book 3 - Perfect Nature

<u>Caprioni Queen - Complete Series</u>

Book 1 – Glitter & Guns

Book 2 – Blood & Heartache

Book 3 – Revenge & Truth

Book 4 – Love & Power

<u>Gun Runner Princess (Caprioni Queen spinoff)</u>

One for the Money

Two for the Show

<u>Standalone Books</u>

Nicolette: Ladies of the MC

Lying Lainey

<u>Hidden Empire Series – Complete series</u>

Book 1 - Two Tricks

Book 2 - Three Tricks

Book 3 - Four Tricks

Book 4 - More Tricks

Book 5 - Our Tricks

<u>Hidden Empire Novel</u>

(Suggested to read after Four Tricks)

Harper's Renegades